THE UNDEAD. DAY TWELVE

SEASON TWO

RR HAYWOOD

Copyright © 2024 by RR Haywood

All rights reserved.

No part of this book may be reproduced in any form or by any electronic or mechanical means, including information storage and retrieval systems, without written permission from the author, except for the use of brief quotations in a book review.

THE UNDEAD
Season Two
Day Twelve

CHAPTER ONE

Day Twelve
Tuesday

My eyes snap open. I'm sitting up, breathing heavily, with sweat pouring down my face. I must have been dreaming, but already the images have drained from my mind, just leaving the aftereffects. It feels early, that essence of the day when you can just tell it's still morning.

Lani's bed looks unused. We cradled on my mattress last night, crying into each other's arms until we fell asleep. The memory of what happened hits me like a sledgehammer. My head sinks as I groan.

Easing myself to the side of the mattress, I look for my trousers, then remember I washed them late last night and left them outside to dry with my boots. I rub my face trying to get my thoughts in order. Opening my eyes, I see my trousers are folded up next to the door, my boots on top of them. Someone must have put them in while I slept.

Quietly, and with a heavy heart, I push my legs through the dry and stiff material of the trousers–at least they're clean now. Clean socks and then my boots. Walking out, I see the others in the main room. No one is talking. The loss weighs heavy on all of us. The success of getting the dog and then that happens.

'Coffee,' Lani walks over, holding a cup out towards me. I take it gratefully and sip at the warm, bitter liquid.

'Thanks,' my voice is hoarse and rough. The dog gets up from lying in the corner and walks towards me, wagging her tail and panting lightly.

'Amy's been in and checked the wounds. She's fine,' Lani says quietly.

'Who's Amy?'

'The vet, we met her last night when we got back …' her voice trails off, the memory still clear in her mind.

'Is that her name? I didn't know.'

'She seems nice,' Lani says distantly.

'Yeah …' I sigh and sip at the coffee again.

'You okay, Howie?' she asks with a sudden and intense glare, her eyes locked on mine. I nod back.

'It wasn't your fault,' she says quietly but with force. My hand drops down to rub the top of the dog's head. Her ears twitch as she pushes against my hand, enjoying the fuss. Looking down at her brown eyes, the long pink tongue hanging out, her soft fur under my fingers. She doesn't realise the sacrifice we made for her. The cost to all of us. What we did, what we had to do.

'Hello?' A young lad appears at the door, leaning in and looking at everyone in awe, his eyes lingering on the weapons scattered about, axes, knives, assault rifles, and kit bags.

'What's up?' I ask him.

'Sergeant Hopewell said the meeting is about to start. She asked me to come and tell you,' he explains, obviously nervous at being sent to speak to us.

'Okay, I'll be down in a minute,' I reply.

'She said to tell you they need to get on with it,' he says.

'Mr Howie said he'd be there in a minute,' Dave cuts in with a hard glare at the poor lad who nods and runs off. I feel sorry for the kid, but I can't muster the energy to say anything to Dave.

I sigh again before draining my coffee and rubbing the sleep from my eyes. 'I'll go down.'

'I'll come.' Dave stands up.

'Is that his kit?' I look at the pile in the corner, the assault rifle and kit bag set apart from everyone else's like a symbolic gesture.

'Yes,' Dave replies in his flat tone.

'You coming?' I ask Clarence. He nods silently, stands up, and heads out the door. I follow behind him with a last look at the rifle and kit bag.

We walk down in silence. The heat is already high with the promise of another sweltering day. The fort looks busy despite the early hour, the signs of last night still clearly visible. The atmosphere is muted, just low murmurs of voices drift over to us. The smell of cooking hangs in the still air, wood smoke and the distinct scent of fish. They must have started fishing from the back door.

The whole fort stops and watches us walking down, silence descends as they stare. What we did, what we had to do may be too much for these people. It feels like the hostility is coming off them in droves.

Reaching the police offices, we walk straight in. I was expecting a full house, and I was right–everyone seems to be in here. The noise drops off as they see us walking through, the dog sniffing at the ground but otherwise staying close.

I keep my head down, avoiding eye contact as we move into the middle. Dave stares back as normal, but I notice Clarence also keeps his gaze down. Sergeant Hopewell stands at the end with Ted, Chris, Sarah, Terri, and a few others. Doc Roberts is already present, so is Kelly and Amy, the vet.

Chris nods at me with a brief smile. Sarah and some of the others smile too, but I notice a few keep very straight faces as they avoid eye contact. The atmosphere is charged, the tension palpable.

'Everyone here?' Sergeant Hopewell calls out, glancing round. 'Good, then we can make a start. What the hell happened last night?' She snaps at me, getting straight to the point.

'Debbie, take it easy,' Chris says.

'It's okay, Chris,' I say. My voice trails off as I think to the events, of what we did, what I did and in front of so many people too.

'Well?' Sergeant Hopewell demands.

'Chris said Paco Maguire was there?' Sarah asks softly.

'We've heard that bit from Chris,' Sergeant Hopewell snaps. 'I think we need to hear the rest now ...' Glancing up, I can see the anger set into her face, pursed mouth and scowling.

'I want to hear it all,' Doc Roberts cuts in with surprising patience. 'It might be relevant to all of us.'

'We know they got the dog, we know about the big fight, we know about Paco Maguire. There's no need to go back over that ...' she speaks slowly through gritted teeth, the hostility pouring off her.

'Okay, let me explain.' I interrupt.

'I think you bloody should explain,' she shouts. The patronising tone sets me off, the anger coursing instantly through my system. I glare back at her, unblinking with a fixed gaze. Feet shuffle in the uncomfortable silence. I can feel the energy pouring off Dave and Clarence next to me. The tension reaches the dog who gives a low growl.

'Keep hold of that bloody dog,' someone shouts. Dave's hand drops down to grip the makeshift collar on her neck. Just a leather trouser belt cut to size.

I take a deep breath, lower my eyes, and get control of myself. They have a right to know.

With a stilting voice, I start to explain.

CHAPTER TWO

'Is she okay?'

'She seems fine,' Lani calls back.

'Is the blood coming through her bandages?' Clarence asks, twisting round in his seat to look down the dark interior of the Saxon.

'No,' Dave answers.

'See if she wants some more water,' Blowers urges.

'She's got water,' Dave replies.

'Maybe she's hungry,' Cookey cuts in as he rustles in his bag. 'Here, try this.'

'You can't give chocolate to a dog. It's bad for them,' Blowers says.

'Is it?' Cookey asks.

'Have you got chocolate?' Nick asks. 'I'm fucking starving, and you've got chocolate in your bag.'

'You're always starving, Nick,' Cookey replies, passing the bar to Nick.

'Ha! Cheers, mate,' Nick says, ripping the wrapper off and taking a big bite.

'Yeah, share it round then, Nick,' Lani adds in a sarcastic tone.

'Sorry, you want some?' Nick says with a mouthful.

'Yeah, all of it,' Lani lunges for the bar quickly pulled back with a yelp by Nick.

'Piss off,' Nick laughs.

'Almost had it,' Lani laughs.

'So are all Alsatians immune then or just this one?' Cookey asks.

'German Shepherd,' Dave says.

'Don't know, mate,' I call back, 'I haven't seen any others.'

'So what happens now?' Cookey continues. 'Do they like take her blood and put it in us or something?'

'You fucking twat,' Blowers laughs.

'What?' Cookey replies innocently.

'Yeah, they just inject her blood into your arm, and it makes you immune,' Blowers keeps on.

'That's what they do in the movies,' Cookey huffs.

'Unbelievable,' Blowers chuckles.

'Yeah, so what do they do then?' Cookey asks in a challenging tone.

'Well, they got to, you know, do tests and stuff,' Blowers answers with a faltering tone.

'Yeah, you know, tests and stuff,' Cookey says, imitating Blowers voice and getting laughs from everyone else. 'What tests then, Einstein?'

'Well, I don't fucking know, but I know they don't just inject her blood in you. Might as well just bite her leg if that was the case.'

'I'd like to see that,' Tom says.

'Piss off, the size of her! I'm not biting her leg,' Cookey replies. 'Mr Howie!' he yells.

'I don't know either before you ask,' I reply.

'But you know everything.'

'Probably something to do with antibodies. The dog must have antibodies that kill the virus, so they'll need to work out how she does it and then create a safe vaccine using a dose of the virus already made inert by her defences,' I reply, thinking out loud.

'So you did know,' Clarence mutters.

'Just guessing ... Isn't that what they do with the flu vaccine?'

'Something like that, I think,' he replies.

'So, they take a sample from her cells or her body, or whatever, and they make a vaccine from it. Then that vaccine gets given to everyone else. Is that right?' Cookey asks slowly, in a loud voice.

'Probably something like that. I don't know.'

'Ha, in your fucking face, Blowers. So they do give the dog's blood to everyone.'

'Oh, my god,' Blowers sighs as Lani, Tom, and Nick start cracking up.

'If all Alsatians are immune, does that mean we've got to go and find more of them?' Nick asks.

'German Shepherds,' Dave adds.

'I don't know,' I reply again.

'What happens to the dog now?' Cookey persists.

'I don't bloody know, mate,' I reply with a groan.

'No, I mean where does she live? Like with us or somewhere else?'

'I don't– Actually, that's a good question.'

'She should stay with us,' Lani calls out. 'She'll be safer.'

'Why us?' Tom asks.

'We've got Dave and Clarence,' she replies matter of fact.

'Oh ... fair one,' Tom replies.

'That's a good point,' I say to Clarence.

'But the medics will want her for tests and stuff,' Clarence replies.

'Only to take samples, other than that, she should stay with us.'

'That would mean we stay in the fort, then. We can't afford to take her outside with us.'

'Then we'll have to stay in the fort. Someone else can go out for supplies,' I reply.

'Not in our Saxon, though,' Blowers cuts in.

'This is our vehicle,' Nick adds.

'Er ... who is on the GPMG?' I call back.

'I said to stay inside the vehicle for the trip back, Mr Howie,' Dave replies.

'I think the Saxon should stay with the dog, with someone on the GPMG all the time. We take turns and keep a guard on her,' I say.

'They've got another heavy machine gun now. They could use that,' Clarence says.

'What, for protecting the dog or going out for supplies?'

'Either,' he shrugs. 'The engineers should be able to rig a frame for it on something, a pickup maybe.'

'I think we should stay with the dog. We've got this far together.'

'It should go on the wall facing out to the estate,' Dave says.

'Eh? What should?' I ask him, confused.

'The other GPMG. It should be set on the wall in case they come again. When they come again.'

'You think they'll come again, Dave?' Blowers asks.

'What was the population of this country?' Dave asks.

'About fifty million. Something like that,' Clarence replies.

'Fifty million people. Where are they all? We saw how many were in that town. We might have killed a lot but compared to the population ...'

'They're not all zombies, though,' Nick cuts in. 'Plenty of survivors, and loads must have been killed too.'

'True, but that still leaves many,' Dave replies.

'And if they continue to mutate, what's to stop them all becoming like Smithy or that Marcy woman?' Blowers says.

'We'd be fucked,' Nick sighs deeply.

'Fuck 'em, we'll win! We've got Missy Elliot on loudspeaker. No one can defeat us now,' Cookey says, adding an evil laugh at the end.

'We still going for a swim when we get back?' Lani asks.

'Oh, yes,' I call out, 'once we've got the dog sorted ...'

'Weapons and kit first,' Dave intones to a few jokey groans.

'This heat has wiped me out,' Blowers moans quietly. 'I feel fucked.'

'Can we get those girls if we go for a swim?' Cookey asks.

'Yeah, right,' Nick laughs, 'we'll go tent to tent until we find them. Nothing odd with asking two strange girls to come for a swim in the middle of the night.'

'I bet that Julie would look fit in a bikini,' Cookey says.

'Hey, she might go topless,' Lani joins in, goading Cookey.

'Really? Wow, yeah, they might not have packed their bikinis and will be like "oh, Cookey, but we don't have our swimsuits" and I'll be like "hey, just go topless", and they'll be like "oh, great idea, Cookey, but only if you promise to keep that pervert Blowers away from us", and I'll be like "hey, ladies, don't worry, Blowers doesn't like girls–he'll be looking at my arse, not yours".

'Fucking hell,' Blowers groans. Tears of laughter spill from my eyes as Cookey keeps on with the self-narration, talking himself into believing all the girls of the fort will be running out to jump around topless in the sea with him.

'Blowers, you okay?' Nick asks with a concerned tone.

'Fine, mate, just fucked from all this running about in this heat. Has anyone got an energy drink?'

'Here,' Lani passes one from her bag.

'I feel ropey too,' Tom says with a groan.

'What, like shaky and a bit weak?' Blowers asks. 'Me too,' he adds at Tom nodding.

'Heat exhaustion,' Clarence says. 'Get some fluids down. You need glucose. How do you put the air con on in these things?' He examines the switches and finds the right one, turning it on high.

'Oh, that's nice,' Lani calls out at the cool air filling the vehicle.

'Alex, how do you feel?' Dave asks.

'Fine, Dave, I feel fine. Tired but okay other than that,' Cookey answers in a serious tone, not daring to be flippant.

'Nick?' Dave asks.

'Fine, Dave. Hungry and tired, but okay.'

'Lani?'

'I'm okay, Dave. Same as the others, just hot and tired.'

'Mr Howie?' he calls out.

'Fine, mate,' I reply.

'Me too,' Clarence adds.

'Just you two losers, then,' Cookey jokes and gets promptly told to piss off by both Tom and Blowers.

'Almost there,' I call out as we pass through the estate. We enter the flatlands, with Cookey giving us another running commentary on how he's going to woo the two pretty girls he saw at the cash-and-carry.

'*Chris to the fort,*' the radio crackles to life.

'Fort to Chris, go ahead. Is that you coming down the road?'

'Chris to fort. Yes, two vehicles coming in. We've got the dog. Inform Doc Roberts we've had heavy contact, so we'll need the examination tents up and running. Get some cold water at the gates for us too.'

'Fort to Chris. Roger that.'

'He thinks of everything,' I say to Clarence. We pull up a few metres back from the gates and ease ourselves out of the vehicle, into the stifling heat of the night air. The contrast from the air-conditioned vehicle hits all of us with audible groans.

The dog bounds out from the back, running about to sniff the ground before she drops her back end down and takes a long piss.

'At least she didn't go in the vehicle,' I remark, watching the puddle pooling out from under her back feet. She finishes and twists round to sniff at her urine for a few seconds; then, seemingly satisfied, she continues her general sniff about as the outer gate opens.

'Is that her?' Doctor Roberts' voice booms out as he strides towards us with Sergeant Hopewell and a few others. Sarah runs past him, heading towards us and coming to a sudden stop as the dog spins round to fix them with a hard stare.

'Is she okay?' Sarah asks in a concerned voice.

'Get her on a lead. She could run off,' Doctor Roberts walks straight past Sarah, towards the dog. She stands her ground, watching him intently as he walks close, stops, and stares down at her.

'Why does she have bandages on her stomach?' he asks accusingly.

'She got bit a few times. We cleaned the wounds and put the dressings on,' Chris replies, walking over from his vehicle.

'Bit?' The Doctor enquires.

'Yeah, bit … with teeth …' Chris replies too quickly, getting a fierce glare from the doctor in response.

'How long ago?'

'Maybe just over an hour or so,' I reply with a shrug.

'And she hasn't turned,' he nods, crouching down and letting the dog come to him. He stays still as the dog sniffs his legs and hands, all the time staring at her eyes. Eventually, he slides a small torch from the top pocket of his white lab coat and shines it on the dog's face, in her eyes, ears, and down her sides.

'Right, we need to check her over. Where's the vet?' He stands up.

'Here, and I'm not a vet. I wasn't qualified.' A young woman with pulled-back, blonde hair steps forward.

'You are now,' the Doctor answers curtly. 'You! Give me your belt,' he turns on one of his medical staff stood nearby.

'Eh? What?' the poor man stammers.

'Your belt, give me your belt,' the Doctor shouts. The man fumbles his fingers, undoing the clasp before sliding it out of his belt loops. The Doctor snatches the item away and fashions it into a collar for the dog.

'Knife,' he barks, holding a hand out. Dave steps forward at hearing his favourite word and cuts the belt in the place indicated by the Doctor.

'Good. Now, you give me your belt,' he turns on another member of his staff.

'I'm not wearing one,' the man replies.

'Then go and bloody get one,' he shouts, tutting as the man runs off towards the gate.

'You had contact, then?' Sergeant Hopewell asks.

'Yeah, heavy too. They were charged up like crazy,' I reply.

'Everyone okay?' Sarah asks.

'I'm sure we can hold this mothers' meeting later. It's the middle of the night and some of us like to sleep during the hours of darkness,' Doctor Roberts cuts in. 'If no one has been hurt, then we'll get the examinations done.' He takes the belt offered to him by the flustered-looking medic and fastens it to the make-shift collar. The dog pants away while he does it until he steps back holding the lead and clicking his tongue, leading the dog towards the fort.

'I thought the dog was staying with us all the time,' Clarence says quietly.

'Do you want to tell him that?' I reply.

'No, thanks.'

'Do you want me to get her?' Dave offers to quick glances from Clarence and me.

'No, mate, she'll be okay for a minute,' I say as an image of Dave and Doctor Roberts facing up to each other fills my mind.

'Come through to the middle. We'll get you checked over,' Sergeant Hopewell calls out as she heads back through the gate.

We traipse through with heavy legs, the tiredness really plucking at us now. I go first, entering a tent with two medics ready to check me over. We go through the procedure quite quickly, stripping off while they shine torches onto my skin, into my ears, up my nose and backside. On leaving, I see Lani has already gone into another examination tent. Dave goes after me as someone comes out to say they've got another one rigged up.

We stand about, drinking water and chatting quietly. Nick hands smokes around. Blowers and Tom both sit down on the floor, clearly struggling after the hectic day we've had.

'Who's left to go?' Clarence asks as he comes out.

'Blowers and Tom,' I reply.

'I'm going back to the vehicle. It's cooler in there,' he mutters. The rest follow him out, leaving the three of us.

'Tom, you go next, mate,' Blowers says.

'Do you want me to stay?' Dave asks.

'No, you carry on, Dave, start getting the kit done so they can chill out quicker.'

'Okay, Mr Howie.' He strolls out after the others.

'You alright, mate?' I ask as Tom gets unsteadily to his feet, swaying a little.

'Whoa,' he grins sheepishly. 'Sorry, I felt a bit dizzy.'

'Is he okay?' One of the medics rushes over to support Tom.

'Heat exhaustion. They both said they felt rough on the way back, weak and shaking a bit.'

'You should have said something. We would have got them in first,' the medic chastises me. He leads Tom away and calls out to his mate inside to assist Blowers into the next tent.

'I'm fine,' Blowers says, getting to his feet and marching towards the other tent, leaving me smiling at his stubbornness.

I stand alone for the first time in ages, enjoying the peace and quiet, the low murmur of voices in the background, the stars in the sky, smoking a cigarette and feeling pleasantly tired at getting the dog safely back to the fort.

Something decent and promising now awaits us. We just need fuel for the generators and then wait while they do tests, and it gives us a reason to stay in the fort for a day or so. The lads need to relax and unwind a bit. I smile to myself at the thought of the lads hanging round whatever tent those two girls are in.

A strangled yell comes from one of the examination tents at the same time as I hear Meredith starting to bark. I ditch the smoke and move towards it just as two figures fall out of the entrance flap. They roll across the ground, fighting, as I realise one of the medics is attacking Tom. I rush in and drag the man off, beating him with my fists as Tom squirms and breaks free. I catch a quick glance through the tent flap at the other medic lying on the floor, clutching a large bite wound to his neck.

'Not me …' the medic I'm holding gasps. I spin round to see Tom turning to run towards the inner gate. A quick flash of his face illuminated by the generator lights–blood round his mouth, dripping down his chest.

'TOM,' I bellow as the sudden realisation hits me. He doesn't flinch but keeps running, slamming into the unlocked gate. I run after him, drawing my pistol and firing two quick shots. The rounds strike the wooden frame as he disappears into the fort.

'DAVE,' screaming at the top of my voice, I reach the gate and plough through to see people running towards the gates and Tom sprinting towards the lines of tents being used as homes. Within a split second, the knowledge of what he could do if he reaches the masses hits me. With no other choice, I raise my pistol and fire at his back while running after him. The rounds miss Tom, whizzing into the densely packed living area of the tents.

He powers into the tents, lunging at a man stood there watching with a look of horror. He takes the man down quickly as my pistol clicks empty. Cursing, I eject the magazine and slam a new one home. Tom is up, running off. The man he bit lies squirming on the ground. I pause long enough to shoot the man through the skull before taking off after Tom. More bodies lie bleeding from being hit by my missed shots. Tom turns quickly into a lane running between the tents. I'm screaming for everyone to run while trying to get a shot at him. He roars and lunges into a large open-ended tent. His movements are quick and deadly, taking bites out of necks, faces, shoulders, anything he can get his mouth onto. Several have been bitten by him. His actions driving him on to get as many bites as he can. I keep after him, pausing to fire into the heads of the victims with bite wounds. Men, woman, and children are bitten and then shot by me, screaming as loud as I can for someone to stop him.

Two men run out from the side, powering into Tom. Having to stop and shoot the bite victims has made the distance between us greater. The two men take Tom to the ground, landing in a heap of writhing bodies.

Tom lashes out, gouging, biting, and fighting desperately. He bites into both of them as they squirm on the ground. I fire into the mass, the rounds striking all three bodies. The pistol clicks empty as I get to them. I go for Tom first, slamming the pistol butt down into his face over and again. He fights like a demon, ignoring the blows and scrabbling to get up from under the bodies of the men. I jump up and use my feet to stamp down on his head, kicking him as hard as I can.

'GIVE ME THAT KNIFE,' I scream at a man stood there holding a long-bladed butcher's knife. He jolts forward, giving Tom enough time to surge up and away from the bodies.

Snatching the knife, I take after him. His injuries slowing him down enough for me to drive my shoulders into the back of his legs with a rugby tackle, bringing him down to the ground. He twists as he falls, landing on his back. I get one hand under his chin and push his head away from me. His lips are pulled back, baring his gnashing teeth. Blood and spittle flies from his mouth. I twist my own head away, avoiding the bodily fluids. I stab down again and again, the blade slamming into his chest. He ignores the blows. His arms lashing and beating at my sides. I drive the point of the knife through his throat, hacking and sawing away, ripping his jugular out. He goes limp, and I'm up, running back to the two men groaning on the ground.

'GET BACK! MOVE BACK NOW,' I scream as people rush in to help them. Some of them respond. One woman doesn't and gets punched hard to the face, sending her reeling away. I kick out at others, forcing them away from the downed bodies. Confusion erupts as people try to pull me off. I lash out, punching and hitting them away from me, desperate to get to the two men before they turn.

'MR HOWIE,' Dave roars as he sprints through the tents, followed by the others.

'TOM TURNED. HE BIT PEOPLE. FIND THEM,' I scream back. Blowers and Cookey run to me, both of them holding their pistols at the ready.

'Those two ... on the ground ... They've been bitten,' I yell while fighting off the people who are trying to restrain me.

The lads run in, firing their pistols into the heads of the bodies. Blowers runs to the body of Tom, firing point-blank into his skull.

'GET BACK NOW. MOVE BACK,' Cookey shouts, waving his pistol at the people crowding round me. The gunshots do the trick as they wilt back from me. I change my magazine quickly as Blowers comes back and checks the bodies again.

'Was anyone else bitten?' I ask the people near me. They look at each other, some screaming in grief at the men, others slack-jawed and not responding. I shine my torch from body to body, checking for blood and bite wounds. One woman is stood staring at her bloodied hands, her face frozen in shock. I check her hands, yelling at other people to get water and clean the blood off quickly.

A few spring to action, grabbing the woman and pouring water bottles over her hands. She starts screaming and fighting against them. They pin her down to complete the task.

More single shots ring out as the others work the route of devastation we just went through.

A guard arrives, holding a shotgun, his breathing laboured from sprinting across the fort.

'These three bodies are infected. Don't let anyone touch them,' I shout at him, making sure he understands before moving off with Blowers and Cookey, working back along the trail Tom took.

An adult woman screams hysterically, clutching a young girl with a bite wound to her cheek. She sits rocking back and forth, holding the child in her arms. I run towards them, seeing the girl is unconscious or dead. Either way, she could turn any second. The woman sees me coming and holds the child tighter, screaming at me as I try to pull the child away from her.

Others try to help, prising the woman's grip from the child, begging her to let go. She fights back, staggering to her feet and spinning round. The child comes back, twitching, convulsing. She opens her red, bloodshot eyes and sinks her small teeth into the woman's shoulder. She screams, dropping down as I shoot the child first and the woman second.

Glancing round, I see Blowers punching someone in the face, beating them back while Cookey shoots a body on the ground.

We work quickly, screams and utter panic ripping through the fort. 'MOVE BACK, GO TO THE BACK!' Chris bellows. Others take the order up. Dave, Clarence, and the guards all shouting for everyone to move away. I don't like the idea as it means anyone with a bite will be amongst the masses being moved away, but within seconds, they're running away from the area, flooding to the rear and spreading the panic throughout the whole fort.

What's done is brutal and violent. I shoot several still living people in the head as they scream and beg, others fighting their families to stay back. Corpses are shot, anyone with a bite wound is shot. It's utterly brutal and the most horrific, awful thing I have ever known, but it is done from necessity.

'Clear,' Dave shouts to me. 'They're all shot.' We start to gather together at the entrance to the lane Tom ran down. Shotgun blasts sound from the rear. More screams erupt, accompanied by loud shouts.

'HOWIE, THE DOG ...' Doctor Roberts shouts from somewhere near the front. I turn to see Meredith bounding through the tents, the white of her bandages reflecting the low lights. For a second my heart stops with the thought that she's turned. She appears, panting, her hackles up and teeth showing, but otherwise normal. She fixes her gaze towards the rear, growling low, which rises to a deep bass sound. She starts barking, sprinting alongside us as we run towards the rear.

A whole mass of people, hundreds, maybe thousands all running into one area. Tents get ripped up, people trip over ropes and lines, cooking fires get knocked over, bedlam everywhere. Shots ring out, but we've no idea of who is shooting who.

'Dave, shout for a ceasefire,' I call out to him.

'CEASEFIRE, CEASEFIRE!' his enormous voice carries clearly across the fort.

'Blowers and Cookey, get the Saxon in here. Clarence, you stay with that dog. Dave, I want you to call for everyone to get down onto the ground. Do it now!'

'DOWN ON THE GROUND, GET DOWN, GET DOWN NOW!' he continues bellowing into the crowd. The effect is slow at first as the nearest start dropping down. The ones behind them realise what's going on and start going down too. Dave keeps going, roaring the order out. Clarence joins him, their two voices driving the order into the crowd.

They sink down slowly, people dropping down to lie with their arms covering their heads. Adults drag screaming children to the floor, holding them close. Families group together, strangers cling to each other through sheer terror.

Slowly, bit by bit, they drop down. Dave and Clarence continue to scream the order out. Within a few seconds, we can see a small group over to the side, writhing in a melee. We head that way, with Dave and Clarence still repeating the order. Pistols aimed and ready, Meredith bounds forward with incredible speed. She launches into the bodies, taking out an infected by the throat and dragging the body away from the crowd to rip its throat out. We get in, trying to pick our shots. In the end, the whole lot of them are cut down by pistol shots. We have no choice but to fire into them all. The dog launches again, taking another one down.

Within a few seconds, there are just the guards, Chris, the police, and us still standing. Everyone else is down on the ground.

'Everyone, stay down. You're going to be okay. If you see anyone with a bite mark, then shout out clearly but please stay down.' I move amongst them shouting out. Chris and the others join me. We walk steadily, with pistols drawn and shining our torches down into the terrified faces.

The Saxon's deep engine rumbles closer as it drives along the side of the crowd, coming to a stop near the rear.

'Nick, on the GPMG. Blowers and Cookey, hand out the rifles,' I shout, glancing at Nick running towards the vehicle. Our assault rifles get handed round, Chris taking one and walking over towards me.

'What now?' I shout at him.

'Howie, Chris,' Doctor Roberts strides towards us, still wearing his white lab coat, 'we need to check everyone. We'll set up an examination point by the vehicle.'

I head over to the Saxon and grab the handheld microphone to use the loudspeaker system, cursing loudly as I flick the switch, and Missy Elliot booms out. It takes a couple of seconds for Nick to drop down and do something with the wires before handing me the microphone with an apology.

'Everyone, listen up. We're going to get everyone checked. We need you to stay down until we come and get you. Women and children will be first. Stay calm but please stay down on the floor,' I relay the instruction a few times. Doctor Roberts gets his staff up to the rear, setting lights and tables up next to the vehicle. Sergeant Hopewell finally arrives with Terri and Jane, demanding to know what happened. Chris takes her aside, explaining what took place. She stares at me throughout his talking, Terri and Jane both bursting into tears at the news of Tom.

There isn't time to dwell. Doctor Roberts works quickly, organising his staff. The grumpy character replaced by a very calm manner full of authority. Kelly and the pharmacist are amongst them, getting instruction from the Doctor as he tells them what to check for.

A couple of minutes later, and we're starting to send the closest ones over. The checks are done quickly, lights shined into eyes and mouths, looking for wounds and any tears in clothes.

Hearing whimpers, I turn to see the dog moving amongst the people. Her nose down and sniffing as though she's searching for the infected. Dave goes over to her and grips her collar. He says something quietly, and she sits, staring out and staying by his side.

The adrenalin starts to wear off, leaving a gaping hole in my conscious. I can't seem to process the order of events. One minute, I was stood there, looking at the stars and thinking ahead to a swim and then being alone with Lani. The next thing, and I'm shooting people in the face, living people with such small wounds that would've seen them waiting for hours in any hospital emergency department.

Shaking my head, I switch on and focus on the task in hand. The survivors get taken down, families going together under the close watch of the guards and my lads. Lani stays near the medics. Cookey and Blowers walk through the crowds, reassuring everyone that they'll be okay. Clarence walks between them and the guards, accompanied by Sarah now holding a pistol. I didn't even know she could use one. Everyone seems to be armed now with pistols or shotguns.

The checks are done surprisingly fast. As more of the crowd are cleared, so more of the people are recognised to be decent, trusted workers who, in turn, start helping out with the checks.

Kelly organises the removal of the bodies to be taken outside and stacked away from the fort. Eventually, I can see my lot are swaying on their feet. Nick fighting heavy eyes on the GPMG.

I speak to Chris and organise my lot standing down and heading back to our rooms where Tom's absence becomes even more noticeable.

'Weapons and kit,' Dave says as we file in.

'Tomorrow,' I reply dully. 'Get some sleep.'

'But we–'

'Tomorrow,' I cut him off. He nods back. Everyone heads off to their rooms. Poor Nick having to suffer the loss of not having Tom in his room.

In my room, I kick my boots and filthy trousers off, shoving another pair on before heading back outside to hose and scrub my trousers down. The others have all crashed out, which is what I should be doing, but my mind won't switch off. I scrub at the trousers with all my might, removing the traces of blood and gore.

A gentle hand touches my shoulder. I look up to see Lani stood there, with a soft look in her eyes. She takes the trousers from me and wrings them out before draping them on the back of a chair. Once done, she takes my hand and leads me into our room. I follow her like a sheep, the shock of it all hitting me hard. She eases me down onto the mattress and pulls my clothes off. No words are spoken. I lie back, staring at her. Nothing needs to be said.

She strips down to her underwear and eases herself down onto my mattress. The image of that woman holding her child sticks in my head, the people I shot before they'd turned. I killed living people as they begged for their lives.

A sudden choke sputters from my throat. Lani pulls me close, turning me onto my side as the tears come. She wraps her arms round me, drawing me in. My body wracks with sobs, silent crying, with hot tears spilling down my cheeks, onto her chest. She rubs my back gently, the heat from our bodies making us sweat. I feel her own tears falling onto my cheek. Her body heaves with sobs as we cling to each other.

We stay like that for eternity. Two people lost in a world of devastation, having done things that no person should ever have to do. We cry together until we sleep.

CHAPTER THREE

'Let me get this right,' Sergeant Hopewell says with forced patience as I finish speaking, 'Tom, who was one of my officers was turned at some point during the fight. You then brought him back and allowed him into the fort.'

'We didn't know he was turned.'

'You then chase after him, discharging your weapon into a densely populated area and shooting innocent people.'

'But–'

'Then you kill Tom with a knife while your ... *team* ...' she says the word with venom, '... run in, shooting everyone that had blood on them. You caused panic and a virtual stampede of frightened survivors. You then held them on the ground until the medical people could check everyone. Is that right?'

'It wasn't just Howie. Some of those decisions were mine,' Chris cuts in.

'Nevertheless,' she doesn't take her gaze off me, 'it was Howie's team that brought Tom back into the fort. It was Howie himself that fired his weapon into the living area, and it was Howie and his team that then shot innocent people.'

'We didn't have time …' I start to explain. Voices murmur around me. The way she says it, her tone and clear voice, the choice of words, it makes it sound so bad.

'I don't like the tone of this,' Clarence says.

'Debbie, you can't speak to them like this,' Sarah cuts in. 'They did what they had to do …'

'I will speak how I feel is appropriate in the circumstances. Are you saying that no one can ask Howie to account for the events of last night?'

'No, I didn't mean that, but the way you're doing it–' Sarah says.

'Forgive me for feeling tired, grieving for the loss of another one of my officers and having to deal with this bloody mess. Tom was a fine officer, so was Steven. They volunteered to go with Howie's team and look what's happened to them. Both of them killed within days of each other …'

'What?' I ask with incredulity.

'That's out of order,' Sarah shouts.

'None of his team have been killed, have they? Both Steven and Tom were killed by Howie himself. Steven shot, and Tom stabbed to death.'

'They were fucking zombies,' Clarence shouts.

'Were they? How do we know this? Steven had been allegedly bitten. Tom was running through the tents.'

'He was fucking biting people,' I join in with the shouting.

'You saw him fighting with a medic. There was one dead medic already inside the tent, but you assumed that Tom was the guilty party causing those injuries. He could have been simply running away.'

'What? He had blood on his mouth, the medic had been bitten, and Tom had fucking blood on his mouth. I shouted at him to stop. The other medic told me it was Tom.'

'Did he?' Sergeant Hopewell asks pointedly.

'Ask him. You must have got his account by now.'

'We would, but he was shot by a member of your team,' she replies.

'What?'

'I shot him. He was bitten,' Dave says.

'Oh ...'

'Exactly, so we've only got your word that he said Tom had turned.'

'I saw him. I saw the blood on his mouth. I saw the way he ran ...'

'Running away from you.'

'Yes! Running away from me.'

'Running away from a man firing a gun at him.'

'What? No. I shouted at him to stop. I kept on shouting. Debbie, he was attacking people and biting them.'

'Was he? It was dark and very confusing, with many people running around. Your team had been out all day in this extreme heat. They were tired and confused, probably suffering from heat exhaustion. You saw Tom running and decided to run after him, firing a gun into a densely packed–'

'Too bloody right I did,' I shout back. 'Tom had turned. He was one of them. He was running for the tents and biting people. They take two minutes at the most to turn, and the infection is mutating all the time, so it could be less now.'

'How do you know Tom was biting people?'

'Because I bloody saw him.'

'You saw a running man actually biting people? After

long days spent running around, fighting with insufficient food and rest? You actually saw Tom opening his mouth and biting into people.'

'Yes! I saw Tom biting people. He was lunging at them, his head was sinking down, and then he let go and ran on. Doing it again and again.'

'How far back were you?'

'Maybe twenty, thirty metres. I'm not sure.'

'That's quite a distance in the dark. People running everywhere, confusion all around ... I grant you that somebody was biting. We've seen the bodies and the bite marks, but what concerns me is that you automatically assumed it was Tom. Not only that, but you took it upon yourself to shoot everyone that had anything that resembled a bite mark or had blood on them. Do you know how many people you killed last night? I'll tell you. Over forty people were shot last night. Forty people! You killed forty people within the safety of the fort.'

'They'd been fucking bitten,' I snarl. 'Those forty ... No, just one turned in that lot could infect the whole fort.'

'Yet you assumed it was Tom.'

'Debbie, Tom was one of my team. He was one of us. He was a great lad, brave and courageous. Losing him like that is awful, but he turned, and he put everyone at risk.'

'Yes, someone was turned, but my point is that you assumed it was Tom and charged after him like a maniac, shooting everyone that got in your way. Some of those forty people didn't have bite marks! Some of them hadn't been bitten. You shot innocent people,' she yells with fury. Her words slam into my mind.

'It was dark ...' I start to explain. The lack of sleep, the heat, the shock all making my mind fuddled and my words stilted.

'Yes, it was dark. Yes, it was confusing. Yes, you had to act quickly, but the way you did it? Firing into crowds of people, shooting survivors just because they had blood on them? You broke a woman's nose just for trying to help her husband. One of your team broke a man's jaw punching him away from his daughter ... as she was executed by another member of your team.'

'If she'd been bitten then—'

'If? If she'd been bitten, so even you're not sure, are you? It was dark and confusing. She could have just had blood on her face, yet she was shot dead in front of her family, and her father suffered serious injury for simply trying to protect his family.'

'This is wrong,' Clarence says, but even his voice is low and unsteady.

'Damn right it is,' Sergeant Hopewell storms. 'Two more men who helped you subdue Tom, risking their lives after seeing the hero Howie chasing someone, they stepped in and got him down, and then you attacked him and stabbed him to death. You almost cut his head off,' she screams. 'Then the two men were shot dead.'

'They'd been bitten.'

'Had they? Where Howie? Where were the bite marks?'

'They were covered in blood. One of them was clutching his neck, with blood coming out.'

'And that was a bite, was it? It couldn't have been caused by something sharp cutting him when they took Tom to the ground? The blood might have been Tom's or someone else's, but you didn't wait, did you? You ordered your team to execute them without question.'

'Please just—'

'What? Just what? Let you explain? I don't think we

need to. We've got several thousand people out there who want to string you up.'

'What?' I look up to see many of the faces averting their eyes from me.

'That's not true,' Chris sighs. He looks exhausted, completely drained.

'Not everyone blames Howie,' Sarah says.

'True,' Sergeant Hopewell concedes. 'Howie still has his supporters, but the majority are clearly deciding they hold him and his team to blame. Without question,' she locks eyes on me again. 'Your actions led to the death of many innocent people. You didn't wait for help. You didn't assess the facts ...'

'There wasn't time,' I reply.

'A trained person would have assessed the situation, but that's where the problem starts. You are not trained, are you, Howie? You were a manager at a supermarket less than two weeks ago, yet here we are, putting all our faith and trust in a supermarket manager, leading a bunch of unemployed kids on a rampage round the country. Only two of you have training. Dave, who clearly suffers from learning difficulties, and Clarence, who seems to hang on every word you say ...'

'What?' I snarl, the anger surging through me. 'My team have saved every one of you time and time again. We put ourselves at risk and did what had to be done. We went after Darren. We found him and led him away from you so those women and children would have a chance of surviving. We've been out day after day, getting supplies, fighting those things ...'

'And we thank you for it, but that initial start is over now, that blind panic of getting everything done instantly is over, we have a community with rules...'

'Where the fuck were you when the fighting was going

on? Where were you last night, Debbie, when the bullets were flying? You didn't turn up until the end. Where the fuck were you on the Isle of Wight when we had to fight Darren?'

'You didn't let us fight,' Terri cuts in. 'We bloody asked you. We begged you to let us fight, but you said no. You said you worked better just with your team …'

'Howie, there is no doubt that you have sacrificed an enormous amount for us. You have lost the same as the rest of us, but we're getting back on our feet now. We've got trained and experienced people here who know what they're doing. We've got ex-soldiers and trained military people here. We've got engineers and doctors. This is a society now, and one that is taking the first tentative steps towards recovery.'

'I've heard enough,' Chris snaps, stepping forward to stand with his arms folded and a look of determination on his face. 'I have no doubt that the actions Howie took last night were the right actions. If anything, he prevented the spread of the infection to everyone in the fort. Forty people died, but this isn't normal times. Millions have died already, and many more will die, but he did what he had to do under the circumstances. We all did,' he sighs. 'I have every faith in Howie and his team, and I will not stand by and listen to this … this character assassination …'

'Chris, I–' Sergeant Hopewell snaps.

'No! I said I've heard enough. You've said too much already. I've seen how Tom was accepted into their team. I fought alongside him last night, alongside all of them. Anyone of them would have given their life to save that dog, and unlike everyone else who ran away and hid last night, they ran in and did what had to be done, without question, without hesitation. Those are the people we need to protect us.'

'Now listen,' she rages, trying to shout him down.

'I said NO!' Chris bellows, spittle flying from his mouth. 'Tom turned. It could happen to anyone that goes outside and does the things they do every day. Do you understand that? They take that risk every time they leave this fort, but they do it willingly for the good of everyone. You were more than happy for them to go out and find supplies while the rest of us were safe behind the walls … Tom turned. It could have been from a scratch, a bite, a bit of blood getting in his mouth. He turned, and it was our fault he got into the fort.'

'Our fault?' she flares in anger.

'Where were the bloody gate guards? Why was the inner gate unlocked? How did Tom get in?'

'I accept there were failings in other areas–' she starts to reply.

'Failings in other areas? This isn't a review or an investigation. This is survival. Don't be fooled for one second that because we've got these walls, we're safe and everything will go back to how it was. What happened happened. That's it. We learn from it quickly and make sure the guards stay on their bloody posts in the future. We set those procedures up for a reason, and if we need to make changes, then so be it.'

'I don't think you understand the intensity of the feelings out there,' she seethes quietly.

'Don't I? Where have I been all night, then? Have I not been up all night with you, trying to get this sorted out? Don't talk down to me, Debbie. I don't appreciate it, nor do I appreciate the manner in which you have vilified Howie and his team.' Watching Chris now makes me understand why

Clarence said he was such a good diplomat. 'And as for stating Dave has learning difficulties ... That man served with the most elite military unit in the world, and saying Clarence follows Howie like a sheep is absurd. Clarence has been with me in every warzone this country has been involved with in the last twenty years. He is a professional soldier, and by taking leadership from Howie, he shows the rest of us that Howie has an instinct for the role he does ...' My admiration for the man has just increased tenfold. I couldn't understand why he stood back, letting Debbie attack us that way, and for a few minutes, I honestly thought he agreed with her. But by hanging back and letting her speak, then stepping forward, and asserting control by the use of speech, he shows how skilled he is.

'The people within the fort have lost faith in Howie and his ability to protect us,' she states, clearly showing the argument isn't over.

'Firstly, we do not entrust the safety of this fort to him. Not to any one person. This is a concerted and combined effort by many. Every person plays an equal part as regards the safety of the fort. Some people hold guns, others stand on the walls with bows and arrows. We've even got people trained to use the cannon we've got left. Doctor Roberts ensures our safety by vetting everyone that comes in. Terri and Jane do their part by speaking with everyone outside the gates before they enter. The cooks do their part by making sure all of those people are fed and watered.' He draws breath, letting his words sink in. 'Secondly, if it wasn't for Howie and his team as you call them, we wouldn't have this fort. Darren would have gone through this place like a hot knife through butter. He would have decimated this place and everything in it. Howie led the battle and those of us that were on that field know what happened ...'

'Why did Darren come here in the first place?' Sergeant Hopewell interjects.

'He came after us,' I give the reply.

'So if you hadn't of come here, then neither would he. Then we would never have had that battle in which so many innocent lives were lost. We would never have had to go to the Isle of Wight …'

'You're being serious, aren't you?' Chris cuts her off in a disbelieving tone. 'You really believe that? If it hadn't been Darren, it would have been someone else, and we took out thousands of them, and as for the continued use of the *innocent lives* phrase, that will not work. We're all innocent of this. Every person that has suffered from this event was innocent, so don't for one second try to make out those people out there play no part in it.'

'I didn't mean–' she starts to explain but gets cut off by Chris in full flow now.

'Thirdly, Howie's team have brought us weapons and ammunition when we were down to shotguns. He brought the stock back from the cash-and-carry and the pharmacies, plus the hospital equipment, and despite the long, awful day they had yesterday, which you were so quick to point out, they volunteered to go back out and search for that dog, not only finding it but running miles through streets in this awful heat, and then fighting a running battle. Any one of you could have volunteered to go out and search for the dog,' Chris scans the room, his eyes lingering on faces that suddenly find the floor very interesting. 'Nothing was said by anyone about limiting the number of people to go and search. I never said anything like that. We've got vehicles and weapons, so why didn't you join in? I'll tell you why. Because it's bloody nasty out there.'

'How dare you,' Sergeant Hopewell's face goes bright red, her mouth pursed with rage.

'I've heard enough,' I say loudly, surprised at the volume in my own voice. 'This is bullshit. I'm sorry so many got killed last night, sorry that Tom turned, sorry that Steven died. I'm sorry all of this happened, but if you think for one second you will stick all the blame on us, you can fuck off.' She blanches at the force in which I spit the words out. 'You heard me.' I glance round, staring at the many faces. Some look back at me, but most cast their eyes away. 'You can all fuck off. I don't give a shit what you think about me. I don't care. Blame us for what happened last night, go on, blame us. We'll take it, and when you're done patting each other on the back and saying how nasty those brutes are, we'll still be out there, killing 'em. We don't have the time to stand here, whining. We need fuel for the generators so the Doctor can start doing whatever tests he needs ...'

'I haven't finished,' Sergeant Hopewell shouts over me. Something in my manner, the glare in my eyes that fixes on her cuts her off. The utter fury I can feel bubbling away that seems to radiate from every pore in my body.

'Yes, you have,' the words come out in a low growl, far harsher than I intended. 'Ted, you make sure those gates are kept locked and secure with armed guards on both sides. Kelly, I want you to rig an alarm up. Anything will do. Something that can be heard throughout the fort, and I want everyone drilled in case that happens again. What we did last night, by getting them onto the floor seemed to work ... unless anyone has any other sensible suggestions that don't involve forming a bloody committee and sitting round with bean bags and flip charts, then I suggest we do that again.'

'You want everyone–?'

'Yes,' I cut her words off with a glare, 'if they'd done that last night, we would have stood a chance of getting him quicker. Get everyone drilled once Kelly has an alarm rigged up. Doctor, let me know if you need anything other than fuel. We'll get some rest for now and go back out later.'

'Fuel is the priority,' he says with a quick nod, and I swear a small wry smile twitches on his lips.

'These are decisions and actions that need to be discussed by trained and experienced people,' Sergeant Hopewell continues doggedly. 'You cannot just assume command just because you don't like something that was said, snatch off a few angry words, and stride out, thinking everything is alright because it bloody isn't alright.'

'The gates need to be kept locked and secure with armed guards on both sides. I think that much is clear from what happened last night. We don't need a discussion on it. We just need someone to do it.'

'My point,' she ploughs straight on, 'which you just happen to keep missing, is regardless of whether or not that decision is a good one, it isn't yours to make.'

'We're going round in circles here,' Chris interrupts, 'Howie, I see what Debbie is trying to say. I don't agree with it, but I understand it.'

'Thank you,' she exclaims, clearly claiming it as a victory. 'My recommendation, after serving over twenty years in the police, is that we form a council, one that is made up of all the main personnel and that we discuss and agree any actions as part of that council.'

I groan and rub my face. 'A bloody committee ... I knew this would end up with committees being formed. Will that get us the fuel we need for the machines? Will it get the machine gun mounted on the wall? What about the alarm? Will the committee get that done too?'

'Yes,' she replies, 'if the committee, which will be made up of representatives of a wide cross section of our society, so decides that those measures need to be put in place, then they will be allocated and actioned.'

Chris steps forward holding a hand up towards me. 'Howie, I agree with Debbie. Otherwise, we'll be here all day. Right, listen in!' Chris speaks to the room, his voice carrying clearly. 'Everyone, please leave, and we'll sort out who is on the initial council. Those that are asked will meet back here in one hour, understood?'

That's it. The meeting breaks up. Chris makes a point of striding out the door so he can't be dragged back into any further discussion. Sergeant Hopewell is immediately surrounded by people talking at her, Terri and Jane animatedly joining in the conversation. The three of us head outside wordlessly, Dave leading the dog at his side.

Once out in the sun, we fall into step, slowly heading back to our rooms.

'You alright, Boss?' Clarence asks. I can see he is fuming, and how he has the presence of mind to ask me if I'm alright is beyond me.

'Confused, mate,' I reply. 'Seems simple to me–lock the bloody gates and put guards on, stick the GPMG on the wall, and get an alarm rigged up.'

'She looked possessed in there,' he says quietly, 'really gunning for us. I bet she's been out all night, whipping everyone up.'

'This'll go down well, explaining it to the lads.'

'No, it won't,' Dave says, clearly missing the sarcasm.

Like a single seed within a field, Marcy sent those few out with strict instruction to only cause enough injury to turn the survivor and limit the damage to the host body. Their hunger for flesh was only held in check by the awe they held for Marcy. Desperate to please their leader, they went off, turning small groups and leading them back to Marcy.

As the numbers grew, so did her need for greater communication. More were enabled to speak and communicate. Each one becoming submissive to her status of unquestionable supremacy. As Maddox denoted powers to the crew chiefs, Marcy created generals within her army. Sending the communicators out with small groups into predefined areas.

The results were staggering. Communicators were given streets, going from house to house and turning every survivor they found. A wave swept through that town, a devastating tsunami that grew in power, volume, and strength with every passing hour.

As the freshly turned hosts were led back to Marcy, so more communicators were sent out. The massed infected stayed with Marcy, following her every movement from a respectable distance. Within a few hours of the tenth day, Marcy had hundreds of pairs of eyes staring at her with unbridled loyalty.

That town was turned. The whole of the place was exhausted. The battle with Howie had already caused the losses of many, but now, with the communicators working every street, it wasn't long before they were ready to move on.

At the end of the tenth day, Marcy led that horde along the main road and into the next village. Using a simple street map book, she sent groups out ahead and to the sides.

They knew what to do–find and turn the survivors and rejoin the main group.

Marcy kept her pace slow. Throughout the night, she kept them working, holding herself at the head of the ever-growing horde. Communicators returned to the line, getting their hosts into the main body before heading to the front and relaying the results to Marcy.

Now, early morning on the eleventh day, Marcy marches down the wide road, with the long horde stretched out behind her, heading towards the central main town. The communicators constantly moving to the front and reporting the results.

Some were good, some were outstanding, and those were given high praise. The losses were also reported, and this was done as an act of Marcy making the communicators feel responsible and suffer the shame of having to say those losses in front of the others.

The communicators felt an allegiance to each other, showing respect and sympathy in equal measure.

'How many now?' Marcy asks a bespectacled infected male walking just behind her.

'One thousand, two hundred and thirty-nine taken with sixty-three losses during the night,' he replies instantly.

'Good. Very good.' Marcy flicks an arm at a row of stone-built cottages set back from the main road. 'Barry, take them,' she calls out. Barry reacts instantly, dropping back to gather a small group before peeling off, towards the access lane.

She presses on, leading the infected army down the hot road. Sweat forms on her brow as she feels the pull of the hunger. Being in the central command position meant she had not taken any survivors herself, but she also knew that no matter how many she took, the hunger would be there relentless and sustained. The main town ahead contained the commercial and industrial centres of the island and a densely packed residential area. Marcy knew the yield would be high, but only if it was done right.

'Take the school,' she sent another one scurrying to the rear to select a small horde before moving off towards the square brick buildings set further back from the road. The chances of anyone being in the school were remote, but it was worth a go.

The road wound through the fields and hedgerows, passing cottages, farms, and dwellings. Each time a communicator was dispatched to search them. The infected moved with purpose, expending vital energy during the hours of daylight, but the results were worth it.

Marcy smiled to herself, the satisfaction from doing something right. The power was incredible but not corrupting. She sensed how easy it would be to slip and foolishly think this was all hers–her army for her purpose, to do with as she pleased. But it wasn't. It was for the survival of the species. She thought back to Darren, how she had made him wear the jeans tucked into the boots, how she confused the old world with the new. Clinging to old fancies that simply didn't translate into this new existence.

Darren hadn't been sent to find her; this wasn't an act of planning by some forward-thinking ideal. It was simply fate that brought Darren to the hotel she was hiding in, and to think otherwise would allow that corruption to take root.

She stared ahead, her eyes scanning the route as the road opened out at the mouth of the large roundabout. Coming to a stop, she took the sight in, processing the information as the plans formed in her mind.

To the left of the roundabout was a large leisure centre with a cinema; to the right was a wide road leading away from the town. Ahead was the town centre. The junction of the High Street presented to the edge of the roundabout. She stared at the junction, a small wry smile twitching on her perfect lips at the sight of the barricade stretched across it.

The survivors had thought ahead and taken the commercial heart of the area. The shops within that zone would contain everything they needed to keep going–supermarkets, convenience stores, chemists, medical centre. The old mediaeval town had narrow streets leading in, perfectly suited to be blocked and sealed.

The wide junction here at the High Street was filled with trucks, vans, cars, wooden pallets, and all manner of objects stacked high.

'Interesting,' she muses with one raised eyebrow and a slight pout. 'Now, what would Darren do?'

'I never met him,' the bespectacled male answers, 'but I would imagine he would have a full-frontal attack that would incur heavy losses.'

Marcy smiles at the answer, showing her even, white teeth. Her skin retained the natural tone, the infection having drawn back as much as possible and allowing her own body to function in much the normal way. 'I would say that is right. He would spout a load of vile abuse, then charge wildly while laughing like a maniac.' The High Street is long and mostly straight, with smaller roads feeding into it. That meant more barricades which would be manned and controlled.

'April, take them round the back of the cinema building, find a fire exit, and get them inside, out of the sun. Find water and make sure they drink. They'll hate it, but they need fluids to sustain energy.'

'Yes, Marcy,' April replies. Turning round, she marches

quickly back to the horde. The will of Marcy is pressed upon them without conscious thought. They simply comply with what is required. To follow April where she leads them and do as told until otherwise informed.

The horde would follow the instruction without April leading them, but they wouldn't be able to communicate any dangers and would be at risk of acting without guidance. By using April, Marcy is assuring the horde will be not only led safely but directed in the event of something happening, which can then be reported back to Marcy in a logical manner. Simple but effective.

The horde moves off, leaving Marcy with her communicators. They stand patiently as their leader examines the barricade ahead.

'Spread out and work your way to the junctions, do it discretely, do not engage with any survivors unless you're cornered or trapped. Wait at the junctions. If you do get trapped, do not let them hear you speak,' Marcy relays the instruction, watching as the infected move off in different directions. She knows they'll melt into the background and slowly make their way into the town centre.

'And me?' the bespectacled male asks.

She stares at the man, looking at his straight-cut, brown hair and his long-sleeved, white, button-up shirt still tucked tidily into his trousers. 'You, Reginald,' she muses, 'you come with me.'

They skirt round the edge of the roundabout, going behind the cinema building still being accessed by April leading the horde to shade, across a car park, and onto a town access road with junctions leading into the sealed off area.

They keep low, moving carefully from building to building, using abandoned vehicles for cover, and stopping every few metres to check for movement. Reaching the next junction, Marcy looks down the road, noting that the survivors have used the natural building line to form the barricade. After watching for a while, she decides this barricade doesn't allow access or egress and is just a solid wall across the road.

Working further down the road, they find the next junction and the next barricade. The same format applied here, with the building line used to create a sheer wall. The doors and windows of the buildings attached to the sealed-off area have been carefully boarded up, with thick sheets of freshly cut plyboard securely fastened in place. Doors screwed and bolted closed.

There are definitely survivors inside, the smell of them permeates the air. The stench of many humans living in one area–cooking, eating, shitting, pissing, fucking. Their tempting scent is everywhere, wafting on the warm currents of air sent up from the heat they generate.

'The fear isn't that strong,' she whispers to Reginald.

'No, Marcy.'

'Eleven days in relative safety has lulled them into a false sense of security. They must have strong men inside, probably armed and ready to defend their territory. Food, clothing, and shelter. There must be organisation too, a hierarchy within. Otherwise, they'd be petrified ...' her voice trails off as her monologue reverts to an internal discussion. Organisation meant there would be guards on every point of access, armed guards that were vigilant and ready. No, an all-out attack would never win this. Well, maybe they would win, but the cost would be great, so why suffer high losses if there was another way?

'How are they getting in and out? There must be a point

of access … and where are all the zombies? Oh, don't flinch, Reggie.'

'I don't like that word,' he replies haughtily.

'It's what we are my dear.'

'I prefer the term living challenged.'

'Living challenged?'

'Yes, Marcy, living challenged. We are not zombies. Zombies cannot speak or organise. They simply want to devour brains, and we are more than that.'

'Are we?' she asks with a wry smile.

'Far more.'

'So you don't want to eat any brains, then?'

'On the contrary, I do want to eat brains. I want to eat brains as much as the next one, but that is not all I desire.'

'What else do you desire, Reggie?'

'I desire to be called by my full and proper name for a start, which is Reginald, not Reggie. I am not a London gangster, nor am I your local refuse collector, happily whistling away while I collect your bins, to wit I do not like my name to be abbreviated to Reggie or Reg, but simply Reginald.'

'Anything else?'

'Of course, I have a whole host of desires. I desire many things, some of which I shall never be able to achieve.'

'Such as?' she asks, unable to refrain herself from prying further.

He stood upright, straightening his sleeves and smoothing his shirt front down. 'I desire immortality, but that can never be achieved. I long desired to be *desirable* to members of the opposite gender, but again, that was never achieved …'

'Oh, a life lived in regret then, Reggie? I mean Reginald.'

'Thank you. Quite the opposite, I would say. I devoted my, albeit short, life to study and the advancement of my mind, which I found to be most satisfying.'

'So you didn't get any?'

He pretends to ignore the point. 'Any what?'

'Did you die a virgin?'

'Marcy, there are two points to that question. Firstly, I believe that when you die, you are dead. We are not dead; we're walking, talking, and breathing, so I would question the validity of saying we are dead. Secondly ... yes, I am still a virgin, but be that neither here nor there. I had plenty of opportunities, but it was through choice that I retained that title that so many of this generation find a thing of distaste.'

'We've got a whole horde now, Reginald. Any one of them would drop their knickers for you,' she smiles evilly, laughing softly at the soft blush rising in his cheeks.

'I ... well, in order to respond, I would first have to ...'

'Oh, Reggie, I'm only playing, dear.' She pats him affectionately on the arm.

'Reginald,' he says slowly.

'Sorry, Reginald,' she corrects herself.

'Do you have a plan?' he asks.

She stares back at him for long seconds, taking in his red, bloodshot eyes but his otherwise immaculate appearance. 'I do,' she nods.

'I see, and are you sharing this stratagem?'

'I am,' she replies with a smile. 'How do I look?' she asks, catching him off guard and waiting patiently for a second while he blusters and composes himself.

'You ... er ... well, that is to say you look ... well, you look like you normally do.'

'Reginald, I'm not asking you for a compliment. I'm asking if you can see that I'm a zombie? Oh, for god's sake, don't look at me like that. Okay, do I look like a living challenged person?'

'Thank you, and no, you don't,' he nods graciously.

'I look normal, then?'

'Yes, Marcy, you look entirely normal,' he replies, a slow look of confusion spreading across his face as she stares back at him for longer than is comfortable.

'That's why you never lost your cherry. Come on, oh, Giver of Compliments,' she strides off, a slightly perplexed Reginald hurrying after her. 'The plan is to get them to take me inside willingly.'

'And exactly how do you propose to do that? Your eyes still retain the reddening of the living challenged.'

'Ah, the wonders of make-up, but first, we need to find the access point. Keep 'em peeled, Reggie.'

'Reginald.'

'Whatever.'

The High Street is in two sections–lower and upper. The two halves separated by a crossroads bordered by the town square, complete with large statues of long-dead war heroes. Marcy leads the increasingly alarmed Reginald towards the centre, taking refuge by clambering through the hole in the smashed window of a shop. Crouched down amongst the debris of the store, they stare down the street, towards the town square, looking at the stacked-up bodies of their dead brethren, cut down in droves over the last eleven days and left to rot in the sweltering sun.

Marcy scans the barricade made up of more trucks and vans, some of them piled on top of one another. The barricade wall stands high, almost reaching the first-floor windows of the neighbouring stores. The crossroads has been cut off, maintaining the integrity of the High Street as a sealed environment. But the bodies of the infected mean the survivors have been out to not only kill them but stack them too.

'Could you not find another shop?' Reginald whispers.

'Why? What's wrong with this one?' Marcy replies, keeping her eyes locked on the barricade as she probes for an access point.

'It is somewhat distasteful for a man of my education and bearing to be within such a premises, and I would be grateful if we could move on forthwith.'

'What are you going on about?' she asks, glancing at the very concerned expression on his face.

'Good god, have you seen the size of these ... monstrosities?' he asks in horror, holding a long, thick, pink-coloured dildo up. Marcy's mouth drops open at the sight of the sex toy. She glances round at the dildo and vibrator littered floor, eyes sweeping across the hanging displays of sexy nurses outfits, crotch-less knickers, and lacy negligées. She presses her hand against her mouth, stifling the snigger coming from it. Reginald holds the pink dildo as though captivated, staring at the absurd size of the object.

'You're blushing Reggie.'

In shock, Reginald misses the incorrect moniker and continues to stare at the thing held in his hand, wobbling it side to side and watching the rubberized sway. 'Do women actually use these things? I mean the size of it. Doesn't it cause horrendous injury? Have you ...?' his voice drops off as a look of realisation steals across his face, a sudden awareness of the question he was about to ask.

'Reginald! Were you about to ask me if I ever used a giant dildo?'

The blush spreading deeper across his face answers the question, instantly dropping the thing. It lands with a thump and rolls across the floor to knock into Marcy's knee.

She stares down at it, then up at him, shaking her head as he flinches and goes to move it, then changes his mind, and instead looks at his nails.

'No, I didn't,' she answers before looking back outside.

'I did not need to know that information,' he replies meekly.

'You asked.'

'I did not!' he exclaims.

'You were about to.'

'Yes, well, that was shock. Honestly, I do not know where to put my eyes.'

'Try putting them on that bloody barricade and finding us a way in.'

'I'd be glad to. Anything would be better than looking at these ... things. Er, did you just say us?'

'Yes, I did.'

'Us? As in you and me?'

'Yes, Reginald, me and you need to find a way in.'

'Right, I thought that's what you said. Now, forgive my question, but what exactly do you mean by us, more to the point, what exactly am I supposed to do when we find said way in?'

'What do you think?'

'That is precisely what I am concerned about. Are you suggesting we go in there and take on the surviving members of the human race held behind that barricade?'

'Yes, Reginald, that is precisely what I am suggesting.'

'Marcy, I do not think the terms of our relationship are entirely clear. I am more than willing to attend your every whim and fancy. I am the right living challenged person to assist you with the organisation of this excursion, but to suggest that I actually take part in attacking is really something I am not altogether happy about.'

'What?' She turns slowly to stare at him. 'Did you just say you're scared to go and attack people?'

'Not scared. I never said scared; unsuited to the task is the best way of describing it.'

'Are you a zombie or not?'

'No, I am a living challenged person.'

'Right, which means a zombie, which means we eat brains, which means you have the hunger and should be happy to attack at any given second.'

'I have the hunger; of that I can assure you. But I have always found violence to be abhorrent. I do not wish to partake in savagery of any kind.'

'You're helping me plan a way in, so I, or we, can slaughter and turn every living person in there. Wouldn't you say that was partaking in savagery?'

'Well, yes, but not the actual savaging bit.'

'You don't want to bite anyone?'

'No.'

'Right, I see. So I'll go in there and do it, shall I?'

'Well, yes. I thought that was the plan.'

'And you don't feel bad about that?'

'About what precisely?'

'Letting me go in alone.'

'God, no! Why on earth would I feel bad about that? You carry on and have some fun, but please don't feel obliged that I need to actually bite anyone and have a share in it. Oh, the thought of it turns my stomach.'

Sighing, she turns back to face the barricade, noticing an end panel on the far left, the ground in front of it being clear of any debris or litter, whereas everywhere else was covered in stuff.

'There's a door over there. See that patch of clear ground? That must be one of the access points.'

'I see it, yes. So how are you going to get inside exactly?'

She frowns with thought, the smooth skin of her forehead creasing with the action. Looking down at herself, she stares at her cleavage, placing her hands under her own breasts and pushing them up and together, forming a higher, deeper cleft.

'What are you doing?' Reginald asks, unable to tear his eyes away from the bulging boobs.

'Thinking,' she replies quietly, still pushing her boobs together.

'Do you always do that when you think?'

She looks up at him, smiling at the sight of his eyes locked on her bosom. 'Wait there,' she whispers before crabbing deeper into the store.

'What? Where are you going?' Reginald turns to watch her move along the display stands, working her way down to the bra section. She pulls several of the stands, staring at the sizes before selecting a heavily padded, black one. Nodding to herself, she stands straight and pulls her top over her head, exposing the bra she's already wearing and causing Reginald to splutter in panic.

'Marcy! What on earth?'

'I'm changing my bra. Now, you can watch if you want; it really doesn't bother me, or you can turn away and keep an eye on the front.'

'Is this really the right time to be making underwear selections?' he stammers, rotating his head to stare out the window. He listens intently to the strange noises of elastic pinging and stretching and Marcy grunting with effort as she grapples with the straps.

'Ready. What do you think?' she calls out, crabbing back towards him.

He turns slowly, looking first at her face before dropping his gaze down to the now super enhanced cleavage threatening to topple from the edge of her top. 'Oh my,' he says in awe, 'oh my.'

Perfect, she thinks to herself. The perfect reaction. All she's got to do is hope and pray there is a horny man on the other side of that gate and not some big mamma.

'Won't they fall out like that?'

'No, Reginald, they will not fall out.'

'They look like they're going to fall out.'

'They are attached to my body; they cannot fall anywhere.'

'Yes, indeed.' He forces his gaze away from her chest and back up to her eyes, swallowing hard and hoping to hell he's not required to stand up straight for next few minutes.

'I'm going in, then,' she whispers.

'Okay,' he whispers back, relieved at being able to stay in a crouched position, although it was starting to hurt a little.

'On my own ... going in ... to attack the giant masses of survivors behind the barricade ... on my own.'

'Yes, I heard you the first time. Good luck.'

'Thanks, Reginald,' she says caustically before easing herself back out the window and into the street. She pauses and clambers back in. Reginald rapidly withdrawing his hand from his groin area in a quick attempt at rearranging the cramped quarters.

'Almost forgot,' she whispers. Pulling a long mascara stem from her pocket, she works quickly, applying the make-up liberally to her eyes, coating her already thick lashes with the black liquid. Reginald watches entranced as she puts more and more on and staring in wonder as she pushes the mascara into her back pocket and pulls out another alien implement. This one she uses to apply dark colours above and below her eyes. When finished, she tussles her hair, pulling the long strands down to frame her face.

The effect was dramatic. With the strands of dark hair, the dark eye shadow, the mascara, and the heaving cleavage, the last thing you would actually look at were her eyes. It wouldn't withstand careful scrutiny, but it would get her damn close.

'I'm off again.'

'Okay,' he yelped, causing her to look sharply at him.

'You alright, Reginald?'

'Cramp, just cramp …'

'Oh, well, you have a nice rest and stretch it out while I go and kill everyone,' she tuts, moving out of the shop again to stand in the street. Reginald stares as she thrusts her chest out and starts tottering towards the barricade, tussling her hair so it falls across her face some more.

'Thank god for that.' Reginald thought as he eased the cramping tent peg within his trousers. 'For one awful second, I thought she was going to hint at me going with her.'

CHAPTER FIVE

Day Ten

The men sit round the commissary table. Hard men with scowling eyes. Tattoos of the old style, green ink faded and blurred with time, black tribal markings mixed with multi-coloured images of skulls, pin-up girls, and hearts etched with "MUM".

One of the oldest Victorian prisons in the country, HMP Parkhurst over time had housed the most dangerous offenders known to society.

The fall of society had little impact on the prison life for the first few hours. The outbreak started late at night, during lockdown. The prisoners were contained within their cells, and the officers on duty were busy doing patrols and visual checks. It was only during the early hours that the officers became aware of anything happening.

During tea break, they listened to a hasty news report transmitted on the staff room radio, giving details of every town and city in the country exploding in unprecedented violence. The officers listened with growing horror as the news bulletin rushed through hasty reports of the initial stages.

By Saturday morning, the prison was devoid of staff–all of them had left to be with their families. The night staff had waited with growing concern. Some of them had simply left their posts and gone home immediately. Others had waited, hoping beyond hope that the situation would change. When it did change, it became worse. The televisions stopped working, the radio stations ceased their broadcasts, and everyone fled.

There was no plan for this, no manual that stated what to do in the event of the apocalypse. The last two officers simply detached the outside door keys from the large keyrings and left the keys on the desk, knowing they would be found. They then activated the electronic door opening procedure. As one, over five hundred doors clicked audibly as they unlocked.

The officers knew the prisoners would be aware of the early opening within seconds, and they didn't hang around. Minutes later, they were gone. The outer doors were locked, the inside of the prison wasn't. The prisoners could move freely about the wings.

Within one short hour of the doors opening, there was utter carnage. Stabbings happened quickly, grudges held in check for fear of the consequences were dealt with, debts recovered. Rapes took place, riots broke out, the offices and staff sections were ripped apart. Anarchy reigned supreme as the men held contained for so long were able to explode and do as they wished.

Many lives were lost. The meek fled to the strong. The strong flourished as they grew in number and formed gangs. Black versus white, religion against religion, creed against colour. The alliances changed hourly as allegiances were made. Gang joined gang to fight a common enemy, then turned on each other.

Word spread of the devastation in the outside world. None knew where the information came from, but it was common practise for prisoners to hold mobile phones, smuggled in by corrupt officers for a hefty price. Some only thought of escape and quickly set about planning on ways to break out. Others became fixated with the gangs and alliances, consumed with a need for violence and revenge for any perceived slight.

Contained within the prison with all exterior doors locked, the prisoners were truly captive. The windows were barred and thick. The floor was several feet of solid concrete. The doors were thick, metal structures, designed to withstand massed violent upheaval. The word prisoner was never truer than now.

Over the next week, several leaders emerged. Strong men not just physicality but with strength of mind and traits of leadership. Quick-witted enough to let the violence play out and thereby reduce the numbers contained within the walls. The battles for the food held in the kitchens saw the most violence. Gangs defended the fridges, stores, and tuck-shops with their lives. Staff offices became headquarters. Those unwilling to fight were killed, leaving no choice but to pick a side.

The leaders slowly took control. Establishing themselves at the top of the pecking order. As the days slowly went by, each wing became the ground of a gang. Five wings meant ultimately five gangs, each controlled by one man. Five leaders. Three white and two black.

On the tenth day, after constant careful negotiations, the leaders all agreed to meet within the central canteen area. The terms were agreed in advance. No other men would be allowed access, no weapons would be taken in.

Jonas, the leader of A wing and holder of the coveted tuck-shop stares round at the faces sitting at the circular, plastic, moulded table. Deep suspicion on all their faces. Silence held them in check, none of them wanting to be the first to speak. Jonas knew he would have to take the lead. It was almost expected. He was the leader of A wing, the top wing, the number one wing. Alpha.

'We all got something the others want,' he began, choosing his words carefully. 'I got the tuck-shop, B wing holds the staff offices with the phones, radio, and guard room, C wing has the library which contains information we all need to survive and the porn magazines,' Jonas looks to each man as he speaks, inclining his head respectfully and watching as they acknowledge his reference to them, 'D wing has the showers and ablutions, the fresh running water, and I don't know about you, but I don't like drinking water from a toilet bowl.' The joke fell flat, all the men remaining poker faced. Moving on swiftly, he continues, 'And E wing has the gym.' Jonas pauses as he looks at the leader of E wing. The most feared man within the prison and one of the largest men Jonas had ever seen. Randall was a huge brute of a man, an American power lifter attending a competition in the UK. His unbroken bench press record was smashed by a young northern English lad. Randall could just about hold his legendary temper in check at losing the record, but when the young lad disrespected him, Randall snapped. A Los Angeles gang affiliated man, and respect was everything, in the street, in the gym, in the penitentiary. Respect had to be given. For the loss of respect Randall beat the lad to death with a dumbbell. It took twelve police officers with Tasers to subdue him when he was arrested. That was ten years ago.

Randall remains expressionless for long seconds, his fierce eyes staring hard at Jonas. He leans forward, resting his overly muscled arms on the table. Veins bulging along his forearms and looking to burst from his biceps. Black-skinned, with a bald head and short, black beard, he was a fearsome sight, and he knew it.

'Randall?' Jonas prompts the man, expecting him to say something.

'What, motherfucker?' Randall sneers, his voice deep and aggressive.

'You agree? We all got something the others want.'

'Fuck you. Fuck your mother fucking showers and fuck your library.'

'You need to eat Randall. I got the food,' Jonas replies, keeping his tone neutral and not reacting at the language of the other man.

Randall looks away dismissively. He knew he needed the food, and he too didn't like having to take water from the toilet bowls each cell had, he also craved to have access to the library. Despite his formidable appearance, Randall knew the brain was a muscle that also needed regular exercise, but damn if he was going to beg anyone for them.

'I agree,' the leader of B wing says. 'We need to work together and resolve this fucking mess. We got dead bodies stacked up that fucking stink ...'

'I want out,' D wing leans forward, his angry eyes staring at the others. 'My wing is in the middle. We're fucking trapped, and I want out. You can have the fucking showers, just give me an outside wall to start working on.'

'It's been tried,' Jonas replies. 'They're too thick.'

'Ain't fucking trying hard enough,' Randall growls.

Jonas leans forward, drawing a packet of cigarettes from his pocket. All other eyes fall on the sealed box, watching as Jonas casually strips the plastic film off, removes the foil inlay, and taps a tailor-made cigarette out.

'You're a cunt, Jonas, fucking doing that in front of us. I ain't had a smoke for a week now,' B wing moans, with his eyes fixed on the packet.

'Don't …' Jonas replies, his temper evidently bubbling away, '… call me a cunt! Here, help yourself.' He pushes the pack into the middle of the table. Watching with satisfaction as the other men all reached out to grab it, all apart from Randall who looks at them with clear disgust.

'Any of you motherfuckers blow smoke my way, and I'll beat on your ass,' he says quietly.

'Easy, Randall,' Jonas cuts in. 'So what we gonna do?'

'Do? Do, motherfucker? I'll kill all you sons of bitches and shit on your motherfucking rotting corpses.'

'I fucking knew he'd be like this,' the leader of C wing sits back, blowing a plume of smoke into the air.

'Randall, you agreed to this meeting along with the rest of us. We need a plan, a way of cohabiting or of getting out of here.'

'Who said anything about getting out? You heard what's going on out there. Fuck that. I'm staying here until it's over,' B wing cuts in.

D wing leans in, tapping his fingers on the table, 'And when will we know when that is, eh? We fucking won't, will we? It could be over now for all we know.'

'You dumb motherfucker, you want to stay in here? Man, you stupid. Jonas is the only motherfucker with an outside wall. That's where we need to be.'

'You got an outside wall, Randall,' D wing replies.

Shaking his head, Randall pauses before answering,

'The gym wall leads into the yard, you stupid motherfucker. There's two more walls before you even get near the perimeter.'

'I think,' Jonas clears his throat, 'we need to come up with a solution so we share what we've got and work out a way of getting out.'

'You got the outside wall and the fucking tuck-shop, Jonas. Why ain't you getting that wall down, eh?' D wing asks.

'Because we don't have the tools. We've got plastic chairs and nothing else. We can't take a fucking wall down with our bare hands.'

'What you gonna use, then?'

'The showers in your wing have iron pipes. We can use them and the barbells and equipment from the gym. It'll be done in no time.'

'So you want the pipes from my showers and the stuff from Randall's gym, eh? What do we get in return? And why the fuck is the librarian here? What's he gonna do? Throw books at the walls?'

'Fuck you! B wing has the offices, what the fuck can they do with offices?' C wing, the holder of the library, protests.

'They got the phones and the radio,' Jonas replies, speaking louder to drown the arguments out. 'We all got something the others need. I got the wall, but I need tools and men to use them.'

'So what you suggesting then, eh? That we call a truce or something?' D wing asks.

'Pretty much, yes,' Jonas nods. 'That's about all we can do ... or we keep going as we are until the food runs out, and we all die.'

'I'm in,' B wing says. 'We got no food left. We're fucking starving to death already.'

'Me too,' C wing adds.

'Randall?' Jonas and the others look to the man sat flexing his arms, making the veins bulge out even more.

'We do this and work together, then we want an equal share of the food and water from the showers. I want access to the library and the offices too.'

'We all want access to everything. My guys are busting a gut to get back in the gym,' Jonas replies.

'How can they go to the gym if we're using the stuff to get out?' B wing asks with a confused look.

'We don't need to use everything; the weights machines won't be used, just some of the barbells and maybe some dumbbells,' Jonas says.

'So, gentlemen, are we in agreement? From this point on, all feuds are forgotten. No fighting, no attacks, no shanks. Everyone goes where they want, and we get the fuck out of dodge.'

'Jonas, I like you, but if you cross me, you motherfucker, I will kill you, bring you back to life, and kill you again,' Randall glares.

'We're all criminals here. We'll cross each other for a fucking glass of juice, given the chance,' B wing adds.

'But we're all working towards a common aim,' Jonas says. 'No crossing, send someone from each wing to stay in the stores with my man. That way there can be no funny business.'

'Shake on it?' C wing offers, standing to extend his hand.

'Stupid motherfuckers, I don't need no fucking handshake with you dumb fuckers.' Randall stands up, stretching to his full height and pushing his massive chest forward.

'Later, losers,' he adds before walking off. Jonas swaps handshakes with the others, quietly breathing a sigh of relief at finally making some headway.

The wing leaders stride out, heading back to their wings to relay the news. The prisoners of each wing receive the update with grim faces at the prospect of more fighting and battles erupting. The prisoners are hungry and feeling more cooped up than ever before in their sentences. No daylight or yard time, no exercise, and surrounded by dead bodies. Even the bodies removed to the end cells are now stinking the wings out.

Slowly they emerge from their wings, the central canteen being the first place they start to mingle. Groups stay together, wings massing as they watch and stare at one another. The wing leaders moving amongst them with a watchful eye.

An hour later, and the tension has eased. The gym stripped of the long, solid metal bars to be used to start attacking the thick outer wall on A wing. Iron bars from the showers are removed, along with men rushing into the ablutions to have their first proper wash in days. Some scuffles break out, which are quickly dealt with by others desperate to keep the peace and get out.

A reluctant peace descends as they set to work. The constant hammering of metal against stone echoing through the wings as the men set to work with fierce determination.

CHAPTER SIX

Marcy reaches the far end of the barricade unhindered. 'Hello?' she calls out gently, making her voice quaver with fear. She taps on the metal shutter, noting that it doesn't rattle or vibrate, securely fixed in.

'Who's that?' a male voice calls out. She smiles, hearing the young tone.

'Hi, my name is Marcy. I just got here. I was hoping to find other survivors.'

'Hang on,' the male voice calls out. She listens to the sound of metal against metal. A thin sliver of a gap forms in the panel as a lookout slot is opened, a pair of brown eyes stare out. Marcy drops her head, stepping closer, just enough to show her body and her cleavage on display. The trick works. The young man barely glances at her face before gawping at her low-cut top.

'Hi, er ... are you alone?'

'Yes,' she nods, exaggerating the movement to appear frightened and vulnerable. She turns her head, nervously looking about the area as though worried at being attacked.

'There's lots of bodies out here,' she adds in the same quavering tone.

'Yeah,' the man replies, his eyes still fixed on her chest.

'Did you kill all these?' she asks.

'Not all of them, but well, yeah ... I got quite a lot, though.'

'Wow, you must be so brave. I've been so frightened travelling on my own. They kept chasing me, but I got away and hid, and that noise they make at night ...' She shudders, lowering her head to cover her eyes, giving a heave as though crying.

'Have you been bitten or anything?' the man asks.

'No,' she shakes her head. 'I guess you'll need to check me all over ... I don't mind doing that. I know you have to be very careful.'

'Oh, yes, we've got really strict rules here. No one gets in without being checked, like you know, all over and everything.'

'I understand, you have to be very thorough, do you want me to take my clothes off now?'

'Yes! Oh, no! I mean ... well, not there, in the street.'

'I'm so frightened. What if those things come here ...' she crosses her arms across under her bosoms, knowing she'll be pushing them higher.

'Don't worry. We'll get you inside. I just need to get another woman to—'

'Please don't leave me out here. I don't mind if you check me over. Really, I don't mind. You must be like the leader or something if they put you on the gate, so I know I'll be safe with you.'

'Well, I'm not the leader, but yeah, you know, I'm quite high up.'

'I bet you are. Please let me come in. You can check me

all over. I'll do whatever you say,' she purrs, dropping a shoulder slightly so the strap, which she adjusted for this very purpose, falls down slightly. She can hear his breathing increase, the lust in his eyes clearly evident.

'Okay, but you'll have to be checked really thoroughly.'

'Of course, will it just be you and me? Alone?' she asks, drawing the last word out. Bolts and scrapes sound out from the other side as the man works quickly to open the panel.

'Er, yeah, you know, respect for privacy and all that,' he grunts with exertion as he moves something heavy.

'Oh, I am glad. You've got such nice, safe eyes. My mother always said you can tell a man is kind from his eyes. What's your name?'

'Robert. Er, well, everyone calls me Robbie.'

'Oh my god, Robbie, you have no idea how happy I am to find this place. Are there many people inside?'

'About four hundred, I think, something like that. Hang on. Right, that's it, stand back a bit so I can push the gate open.'

She does as told, standing back with her feet together and her hands clasped in front, head hanging low, the true pose of the demure woman being rescued by the brave knight.

'Quick, get in,' he urges, and she notes the huskier tone of his voice caused by getting a full look at her.

She steps inside, moving deftly past him and taking in the private alcove. A high stack of sandbags forms a wall, with a narrow gap leading into the High Street beyond.

'At least it's nice and private in here, Robbie,' she says softly. 'Do you want me to get undressed now?'

'Er, hang on. I got to put all this back yet,' he grunts, quickly shoving heavy bags of concrete against the door.

'Wow, you're so strong,' she smiles, watching the thin-built youth struggling with the heavy bags. 'How old are you, Robbie?'

'Nineteen, but I'll be twenty in a few weeks,' he adds. 'There, all done,' he turns round, his eyes sweeping over her body. Swallowing nervously, he suddenly seems unsure of what to do.

'So, Robbie, do you want to check me now?' she whispers. She watches with amusement as he swallows again. His mouth trying to work, but no words coming out. 'You'll have to tell me what to do, Robbie.' Still he doesn't speak but just stands staring at her boobs. *My god, another virgin,* she thinks to herself. She pulls her top off, exposing her push-up bra and almost laughing at the young lad blushing furiously. 'Can you help me, Robbie? I can never get these things undone easily.' She turns her back, presenting the clasp of her bra to him. *Bless him, must be the first pair of boobs he's ever seen in real life. Mind you, it'll be the last ones too.* She rolls her eyes as his shaking fingers fumble at the clasp, pushing and tugging away, and getting nowhere.

'Sorry, I'm, er ... not used to these particular bras. The others have always been, you know ... different.'

'Oh, I know, Robbie. They're so complicated,' she smiles with delight, almost feeling sorry for the young lad.

'Got it!' he exclaims as the elastic pings open. She turns slowly, holding her bra over her boobs and watching his face go slack. Slowly, she starts to lower the bra, inch by inch, taking great delight at the expression on his face. At the point of full exposure, the blood drains from his face, causing him to sway.

'Hey, Robbie, are you okay?' She holds a hand out to steady him.

'Yeah, wow ... sorry ... must be the heat,' he stutters, unable to take his eyes away from the now naked breasts.

'Robbie, look at me,' she steps in close, her face just inches from his. 'Robbie ... hey, look at me,' she urges softly. He responds slowly, his face tilting up as he focusses on her face, lost in love, the poor sod. He smiles meekly, still not noticing the red eyes.

'Have you ever kissed a girl before, Robbie?' she asks softly. He shakes his head dumbly, too love-struck to even consider lying. 'Kiss me then, Robbie, kiss me now,' she leans in, feeling increasingly sorry that he'll never get to sleep with a woman. Their lips meet. She goes gently at first, smiling softly at feeling the hand gently squeezing at her left breast. The kiss of death carries on as her saliva drips into his mouth. Soaking into the soft tissue of his tongue. A much slower way to infect but still effective.

She remembers where she is, realising someone could come and check on young Robbie. She nips gently at his lip. Just enough to draw blood. He winces but is too far gone to notice the blood drawn. She kisses him again, ensuring her saliva enters his bloodstream. She puts one hand over his, holding it tight against her boob.

'I'm sorry, Robbie,' she whispers.

'Me too,' he replies without any idea of what he's saying sorry for. The infection courses through his system, cells turning as it takes hold in every organ. He turns his head, feeling a woozy sense flooding over him. His legs start to shake, his hands dropping to his sides.

'Easy, Robbie,' she takes his weight, lowering him down to the ground. His breathing becomes harder as he fights to keep his life so quickly ebbing away from him. Vision blurring, senses cutting out. She strokes his head, murmuring softly into his ear. He slips under, his heart gradually ceasing.

Marcy smiles sadly, feeling better for at least letting him

have a kiss and a grope before he died. She dresses quickly, doing the bra up and pulling her top over her head.

Dropping down to his side, she watches patiently for the first twitch, cocking her head to one side as the convulsions run through him. His eyes snap open, staring up full of blood.

'Welcome back, Robbie,' she smiles. 'How do you feel?'

'I feel great,' he whispers, his voice dull and flat.

'Good. Now, get up and move those heavy bags for me.' She steps away, keeping watch out the gap in the sandbags as Robbie removes the heavy bags and pushes the panel open.

Staring out, she takes in the scene. The long High Street looks relatively normal. Some of the shop windows have been smashed in but are now covered with boards. The ground is free from litter, and no vehicles parked up. People walk through the street, some alone, others in couples or small groups. They look healthy and well-fed, clean, and remarkably unconcerned.

Soon change that, she muses.

'Marcy?' a voice whispers from outside the barricade. She turns quickly, leaning out the open panel to see one of the communicators stood there.

'Just you?' she asks.

'More over there,' he points back to the junction.

'Get them here, move quietly,' she watches as the male runs off towards the junction. 'You okay, Robbie?'

'I'm fine, Marcy,' he replies flatly.

'Hungry?'

'Yes.'

'Not long to wait. Here they are ... Come on, quick, stay inside the sandbags,' she ushers them inside, turning to see them standing cramped inside the alcove. 'Split up, give it about five minutes so we're all up and down the street, then go for it. Got it?' They nod back, the look of awe oozing from their faces. 'Go on then! Off you go.' She watches as they filter out into the street, quickly walking away from the alcove in different directions. All of them doing varying actions to hide their eyes, holding their hands over their heads, lowering heads, wearing sunglasses.

Marcy walks out last with Robbie, knowing he'll be recognised by the people within the compound. They stroll away from the gate, heading down the High Street.

'Lower your head, Robbie.'

'Sorry, Marcy,' he responds, dropping his head to stare at the ground.

'Alright, Robbie! Your shift finished already, has it?' someone calls out from a shop doorway.

'Just going for a piss, Mr Thomas,' Robbie replies, his voice still flat and getting a strange look from Mr Thomas but fortunately nothing more than.

'Well done,' Marcy whispers.

'Thank you,' he replies, feeling a deep sense of pride at getting a compliment from his beloved leader.

They reach nearly to the end of the High Street. The high barricade at the roundabout now very close. The first scream rips through the air, carrying easily through the quiet street, funnelled by the high buildings, and with no vehicles or traffic, the noise travels to every corner. More screams joined the first. Marcy smiled with satisfaction, copying everyone else by turning to stare at the other end of the street. She watches as one of her communicators runs from a doorway, lunging at the back of a man stood staring into the distance. He bites quickly, ripping a chunk of flesh away from the back of his neck and already moving off to take another as the man spins round, clutching his bleeding skin.

Several are bitten before anyone has any real sense of what's happening. Marcy watches as the scene explodes in front of her. People screaming in blind panic, running in all directions. Men run into the street, holding shotguns, but clearly with no idea who to shoot. People shout instructions, drowning each other out. Confusion abounds. Marcy nods at Robbie, giving him the go-ahead to have some fun. He runs off, attacking a group of people bent over trying to stop a victim from convulsing.

'This couldn't have been easier,' she mutters.

A body falls close, the blood oozing from a bite wound to the neck. A hand claws at her leg, desperate, pleading, begging for help.

The agony they suffer is a rite of passage, for only by suffering that agony can they be reborn into the perfect state of being.

More than anything, Marcy wants to reach out to all of the humans to show them they can lay quietly hand in hand with their loved ones, close their eyes, and wait for the glory to work through them. If only she could do this, could reach out and ease that pain.

A single tear rolls down her cheek as she remembers the fear she felt when she was infected. The act of dying alone in a dirty street while being held by a monster with red eyes. The words he gave were soft and comforting. She, like these humans now, fought against the final act, as if that struggle would somehow prevent her from dying.

The screams gently cease as the last are taken. Single voices now cry out as the last are hunted. She watches the road, seeing as the bodies twitch and convulse. All around her new life is beginning. Like roses blossoming under the beautiful summer sun, she watches the bodies jerk as they enter into the new world. Every one of them now feeling at peace, no longer suffering or feeling the indignity of life. They stand slowly, their movements unsteady. She stands with them, a small smile forming on her lips.

The suffering has passed for now. Many more will have to pay that price, but it is a small cost for what they now have. Men, women, and children all move silently towards her. Their feet ungainly at first as the infection quickly masters the thousands of nuances it takes to control each separate host.

'Welcome,' her voice carries clearly in the now silent street. 'I am sorry for the pain you had to endure, but it's over now. We are one, and we are together.' They stare back, eyes full of wonder and awe.

A bespectacled man appears at the far end of the street. Marcy watches him weave down the road, moving between the hosts as he nods and greets them politely. 'Welcome, hello, nice to meet you. Good gracious, this is a quite a few more. Yes, hello,' he repeats the salutation over and over, finally reaching the end and spotting Marcy standing there.

'Reggie, my love, you made it then,' she says warmly.

'Reginald, please. Yes, I made it, although I did not appreciate being left in that store on my own. Do you know some of those items of undergarments were incomplete.'

'Incomplete?' she asks.

'Yes, Marcy, incomplete. I really don't know how the retailer allowed them to be placed on display. I thought initially that it was just one item like it, but on closer inspection, I realised the manufacturer must have mass produced from a flawed schematic. I mean who on earth would fail to see that the knickers they were selling did not have sufficient material in the crotch? Honestly! That is why the retail industry was struggling …'

'Yes, Reginald, very true,' she smiles inwardly, feeling somewhat touched at his naivety and innocence. 'Get a headcount for me, please,' she requests, pulling the map book from the back of her waistband, and moves to the shade, deciding to simply work out from the centre. She waits until Reginald returns with the numbers. 'Four hundred and twenty-seven gained. I think we lost two,' he explains, 'and one is in a wheelchair, and I am not entirely sure of your policy with regard to living challenged persons who suffer from a physical disability or impediment.'

'They can come with us. Someone can push them along,' she answers.

'I will see to that. Is that to be the case with all living challenged persons suffering from a physical disability or would you rather assess each one on their individual circumstances?'

'I don't want any left behind unless they are so disabled as to cause delay or undue hardship.'

'I understand entirely, Marcy.'

'And get someone to the cinema building and ask April to bring our group here. There's plenty of shade for them to rest in.'

'Yes, Marcy, and if I may add,' he clears his throat, straightening his sleeves out before continuing, 'I would like to say that I think you have done a remarkable job so far, and the taking of this compound was perfectly executed.'

'Of course it was. I'm a genius,' ahe adds with a movie-star smile and a wink as he runs the errands set for him.

She busies herself dispatching communicators away with small groups, allocating them streets to check and clear. Robbie stands nearby, watching his leader closely as she steadily works through the area.

Marcy pauses her work as April returns with a long and steady flow of hosts pouring through the access gate. Reginald directs them into shaded areas, busily arranging sections and sending April down to Marcy.

'Any trouble?' Marcy asks as the woman approaches.

'No, Marcy. How many did we gain from here?'

'Over four hundred with only two losses.'

'That's great,' April smiles with genuine pleasure. 'Where do you want me?'

Marcy continues, giving street names to small groups and watching them nod in understanding as they file away. 'Robbie, can you arrange for some water to be brought out, please.'

'Water?' Robbie asks in the same dull tone.

'They hate it, but it's very hot, and we need to keep them as refreshed as possible. In fact, that will be your responsibility from now on, keeping them watered as much as possible.'

'Thank you, Marcy,' Robbie swells with pride, moving off quickly to fulfil the request. She smiles again, shaking her head as she returns to the map book, her finger tracing the roads out of town. Another couple of hours will see this town done. The amount of hosts she had turned to communicators allowed the progression to be done that much faster.

CHAPTER SEVEN

'Get your mother-fucking backs into that mother-fucking wall. You are weak, weak as a little baby in a crib, crying for its momma. My mother-fucking grandmother is stronger than you motherfuckers. Gimme that mother-fucking bar.' Randall strides forward, snatching the seven-foot barbell from the inmate. 'Get the fuck outa my mother-fucking way,' he snarls, eyes wide with fury. The inmates step away, giving the large, angry man some space. Randall grasps the bar two-handed. Standing side on to the wall, he drives the end into the hard surface, forcing a chunk of plaster to fall away. He strikes again harder, the dull thud resounding through the wall. Plaster fractures and falls, exposing the hard blocks underneath.

Each strike gets harder as he powers more strength into it, twisting his upper body round and driving the bar in, using his back, shoulders, and arms. His face becoming demonic as his energy increases with each strike. Those that know him recognise the look from the intensity of his workouts. Lifting phenomenal weight seemingly just from the strength of his mind.

'You,' Randall pauses to stare at a large-built man stood watching with his arms folded, 'get in here with me. Stand opposite me, you motherfucker, hold that bar hard, boy. You hold it hard and move with me, like this ...' Randall swings back gently, slowly driving the end into the wall. The man stands opposite, so close he can smell the musty body odour from Randall. They go easy, pulling the bar back to drive it in slowly. They master the motion, going harder with each strike, Randall keeps the motion steady, working up to a rhythm. 'Now, motherfucker, command that wall to break, say it with me, you motherfucker, say it with me.' The man mutters the words softly, feeling self-conscious at the overt character of the American.

'What the fuck is wrong with you? Say it like a mother-fucking man. I command you to break! I mother-fucking command you to break!' The man repeats it louder, the knuckles of his hands going white from gripping the bar. 'Man, you need to take that energy and channel it. You gotta channel that mother-fucking rage inside you. How long since you had a woman? How long since you had a drink like a man? When was the last time you saw some mother-fucking titties? You wanna see some mother-fucking titties?' Randall stares at the man, both of them gripping the bar, drawing it back to slam it forward into the wall, each strike building power. The man's face flushes from the relentless words Randall shouts at him. 'You want some mother-fucking titties? You want to smell that fresh air? You gotta get mad, get mad with me, come on. I command you to break!'

'I command you to break,' the man sputters with growing anger. They pull the bar back, driving it with increasing power.

'Come on, get mad, you motherfucker. You a married,

man? I'm gonna find your wife and fuck her. I'm gonna find your mother-fucking wife and fuck her good. That make you mad?' The man gives a gargled yell. His face now a deep shade of red, eyes ablaze. 'Get in here, you dumb motherfuckers. Two more!' Randall glares at two inmates stood watching. They dart forward, too fearful to do anything other than ordered. They take position either side of the bar, standing shoulder to shoulder with Randall and the other man.

'I'm gonna fuck all your wives and get me some big old titties. I command you to break. I command you to break.' The chant gets taken up, repeated with every strike. The power builds as the men drop into the rhythm. The blocks start chipping, fracturing, with chunks breaking away. Mortar breaks up from the constant pounding. Another barbell is taken up alongside them. Men grasping the metal tube and dropping into the rhythm dictated by Randall. They focus on the section below the heavily barred windows, hoping the wall will be weaker. Inmates keep glancing up at the glass, seeing the width of the wall extend beyond the line of the window, judging how much further they will have to go.

Randall drops back, bellowing at the other inmates to rotate round and keep the strength and energy high. The noise flows through the prison. Inmates flood to the area. Iron bars from the showers are ripped out and carried to the outer wall. A long line of prisoners attacks the wall, driving the metal pipes into the solid structure. A cacophony of sound accompanied by the chant urged on by Randall cajoling, threatening, and goading them.

The inner part of the wall starts to degrade. The men work harder, battering the concrete blocks away. A small hole forms, causing a loud groan to be taken up at the sight of the next layer of undamaged blocks.

'What you whining for, you motherfuckers? You think this is over? This ain't over. There could be fifty walls here, and we will mother-fucking destroy them all.'

Jonas stands back, watching, organising water to be brought in for the men working. He stares at the blue sky outside the window, both longing to be outside and away from this violent environment but also extremely concerned at what lies out there. No word from the outside world since it began. The many mobiles within the prison had been tried until the batteries ran out. Some were charged up until the electricity failed. The landlines in the office were tried repeatedly until they too failed.

The radio from the staff room was continually retuned across all frequencies, constantly scanning for any broadcasts. For all they knew the world had entirely ended. No vehicles could be seen on the road, no people walking across the fields. The cattle were still at graze in the meadows. Some elements of conflict waged within Jonas, a feeling that breaching the security of the walls was somehow a mistake. But to stay in here would mean certain death, either from the violence constantly erupting between the inmates or simply starving to death.

Jonas knew that it wouldn't be long before these men turned to cannibalism. As far-fetched as that may seem, he understood better than anyone that while these men were the very dregs of society, they were also born survivors and would do anything to stay alive.

No, getting out was the best option for staying alive. He'd already identified a small group to move with, knowing that large numbers would just cause further problems. A large gang might make them harder to attack, but finding food would be difficult and keeping a large gang in check would also be hard. Keep a small group of carefully selected men with him and move as far away from the prison as possible. Head north and find the coast, get a boat and back to the mainland.

Randall was a concern. The man possessed an awe-inspiring energy and simply didn't conform to any basic, fundamental rules. He owed no allegiance to any man and had the ability, both mentally and physically, to take what he wanted.

'You worried, Jonas?' One of his close associates saw Jonas watching Randall closely, understanding the look of concern on the leaders face.

Jonas breathes out a deep sigh as he watches the hard American bully the inmates into working harder. He dominated the room. The black tattoos etched onto his arms, shoulders, and neck, the thick, black beard, and huge, defined muscles. By mere presence alone, he could dominate any environment, but now, bellowing with an unsurpassed energy, he looked unstoppable, like something from a comic book. 'He's dangerous,' Jonas mutters quietly.

'We're all dangerous, Jonas. That's why we're here.'

'He poses a danger to all of us. The second we're out, he'll try and take control. Look at him. They're all frightened. I've never seen anyone have that effect before.'

'What's the plan, then? Take him out once we get outside?'

Jonas pauses before answering. His face passive, but his mind working quickly. 'Yeah,' he nods gently, 'get some weapons ready. We'll need to work quickly. Tell the lads to go for his neck and cut deep, sever an artery, stab his eyes out, but it will have to be quick. You understand me?'

'Yeah, I got it. Leave it with me.' The man slips away, walking slowly through the wing to spread the word.

CHAPTER EIGHT

'Another fifty-two just arrived,' Reginald reports to Marcy.

'Good, what are we up to now?'

'Just under two thousand,' he replies.

'Reginald, that's not very precise for you.'

'On the contrary. I am aware of another group heading in, and I have anticipated their numbers in advance, adding them to the sum total thus achieved and calculating there will be just under two thousand, but without the precise number of the approaching group, I am unable to give an exact amount. However, if you wish the figure as it stands at this time within the boundary of the barricade, then–'

'Reggie! It's fine,' she laughs at his serious manner.

'Reginald,' he says automatically.

'We're doing well, very well. Another couple of hours, and we can move on.'

'Marcy, I have a question if I may?' he asks politely.

'Is it about dildos or crotchless knickers?'

'No! Please, Marcy, I have no desire to discuss such topics. The very thought of those ... things is simply disgusting.'

'Okay, calm down, dear Reggie. Now, what was it?'

'Reginald,' he says on autopilot. 'My question concerns the structure and manner within which you are able to choose the roles of the living challenged people that currently encompass the mass of our group.'

'Pardon?' She blinks at him, confused as to whether he made a statement or asked a question.

'Putting it simply, how do you decide who is able to speak and who is unable to speak? Is it a decision based on intellect of the person or is there some other criteria used for your decision-making process. I only ask as it appears that, for the most part, the vast majority of the living challenged are unable to speak or communicate and are simply driven by their need to feast.'

'In short, I don't know,' she replies seriously. Scanning the area, she takes in the various groups of infected. As Reginald said, the vast majority are inert and possess no faculties greater than the average sheep. The communicators move amongst them. They speak to the masses and to each other. Their manner is robotic and dull, just as Robbie is. No varying tone of voice, no inflection within the volume other than to express shame at a perceived failure or pleasure from a compliment given by Marcy. 'It just seems to happen. If I need them to speak and communicate, then they do. If not, then they don't.'

'If you needed them all to speak, would they do so?' Reginald probes.

'I'm not sure,' she shakes her head slowly. 'Darren ... I told you about him before.'

'Yes, I recall,' Reginald nods.

'He could see everything they saw, had access to their collective conscious, and could drive them by mere will, but the power corrupted him. He assumed he was the chosen one, and they were there to serve him alone.'

'But they … we do as you bid. It would appear we all have a connection to you.'

'True, I can exert my will upon them …' They both watch as every host body within sight turns to stare at Marcy. The masses and the communicators all ceasing their activity to stand silently. Without a word spoken, they all take a step to the left. A brief pause, then a step to the right. 'I can do that by mere will. I think it, will it to happen, and they do it, but then it relies on my ability the whole time. I then have to think for everyone and understand every movement they make. It feels simpler to have some that can speak and communicate. Somehow they have greater intelligence while still retaining a submissive manner. To be honest Reginald,' she smiles at him, the sound suddenly coming back as the compound once more goes back to what they were doing, 'I don't fully understand it, not on an intellectual level, but maybe on an instinctual level.'

'I see,' he replies, 'but I didn't comply with the request you just made. I did not turn to face you, nor did I take the step.'

'That's because I didn't want you to,' she smiles. 'I can though if you want me to.'

'No, thank you,' he replies stiffly.

'Are you sure, Reggie?' She smiles as he suddenly starts walking forward. His face looking down in horror at the movement his body is taking.

'Marcy! What are you doing to me?' he calls out in alarm.

'Who me?' she answers innocently.

'Marcy … please stop this …' he begs as she pushes him towards a female infected. The female steps out from the crowd, walking towards Reginald. 'Marcy,' he calls with increasing concern, 'what are you doing to me?'

'Oh, Reggie, you should see your face,' she laughs.

'It's Reginald,' he shouts, staring in horror at the woman coming to stop in front of him.

'Is it?' she laughs. Reginald's hands lift up from his body, his palms facing the woman as his hands lift towards her chest area.

'Marcy ... no!' he begs, unable to stop himself from hovering his hands inches away from her breasts.

'Can I call you Reggie?' she laughs harder.

'No, my name is Reginald. No ... Marcy ... this is improper,' he wails as his hands draw closer to the slack-jawed zombie stood staring into the distance.

'Oh, Reggie,' she laughs, tears rolling down her cheeks as she clutches her stomach.

'It's Reginald,' he shouts. 'Now, please desist from this activity. It is neither funny, nor is it productive.'

'Productive,' she bursts out laughing harder, bending over from the spasms heaving through her body. 'It's not productive,' she mimics him.

'Oh, my word, my hands are touching her bosoms ... Marcy, I can feel her breasts, and I am sure this woman does not appreciate being touched in this manner.' Marcy doesn't reply. The sight is too much for her. She breaks the connection, watching through misted eyes as Reginald steps away, apologising profusely to the female infected, begging her forgiveness for the inappropriate action.

'Oh, Reggie,' she sighs, slowly recovering her senses and wiping her cheeks as the soft chuckles keep coming.

'Reginald,' he replies sulkily. 'Please do not do that again. If you must exert your control over me, please direct me to a chess board or even a Sudoku puzzle in future.'

'Will do,' she says.

'But what I still am unable to fathom is why I have retained such a grasp of faculties, whereas the other communicators are more like automatons. Here I am, a living challenged person, asking questions and having the same mental capacity as before when I was human.' The control exerted over his body does little to dampen his curiosity as he continues, 'Are you able to explain that?'

'Maybe you are what was needed at that time, Reginald. Someone who could think, count, and take care of the hundreds of little things I don't have time to think about.'

'I see. So perhaps I am the brain to your brawn,' he says, staring into the sky.

'Brawn? I am not brawny …'

'Ah, yes, perhaps brawn was the wrong word. Maybe I am the brains to your beauty then or your cunning wiles.'

'So basically, Reginald,' she asks pointedly, 'I am either brawny or just a beauty with no intelligence.'

'Ah,' he says, realising the offence he may have caused.

'Ah, indeed!' She stands up, walking towards him. 'Do you want to have another grope?' she asks.

'God no, thanks, and while we're on the subject, is this not maybe the right time to put your … well, those things away?' He motions his head at her chest and the cleavage still threatening to spill out.

'For calling me brawny, I will be leaving them like that all day … just for you,' she smiles sweetly, almost laughing as he tuts and turns away.

Marcy stares at his back while he walks off. The little man with the sensible haircut plucking at his sleeves to straighten them out and pushing his glasses up his nose. Despite his almost insolent manner, she feels nothing but warm regard for the way he speaks to her, like having a prudish uncle around, constantly berating her for showing too much skin.

The High Street fills as groups are led back by the communicators, hundreds of hosts turned with *the* minimum of injuries inflicted. She watches their steady shuffle as they follow each other into the area, being directed into the various shops and stores to keep them out of the glaring sun.

For the most part, they look fresh. The days of getting by on limited food had reduced some body fat, causing some of them to become weak and looking emaciated. Some faring better than others, with a motley collection of clean, dressed ex-survivors and bedraggled specimens that didn't look too far from natural death.

It was surprising to Marcy just how many had survived the outbreak. Hiding in their homes and praying to go unnoticed until the nightmare ends.

The advancement of the intelligence the infection allowed the host to retain was further assisting the cause. Those freshly turned were able to lead the others to those they knew were also hiding, and so it was that the main town was steadily purged of all human forms with very few losses.

CHAPTER NINE

'How we doing?' Jonas asks, walking back into the room. The men had worked all through the night, taking it in turns to hammer at the solid wall with whatever makeshift tools they could find. The shower pipes were soon discarded, the metal too soft and pliable to sustain the constant battering.

'Three walls of concrete fucking blocks. The stupid fucking cunts built this fucking prison to last,' someone says, spitting dust and filth from their mouth.

'It was used to house terrorists back in the day,' Jonas shrugs. 'It had to be secure.'

'What like fucking al-Qaeda?'

'No, you twat, this was well before them. Irish terrorism was the flavour back then.'

'Careful what you say now, fellas,' a tall man stands up straight, his strong Irish accent carrying clearly down the room.

'I don't give a mother-fucking shit about your fucking terrorists. You having a fucking political chat about the formation of this institution or are we about to perpetrate the greatest mother-fucking prison break-out this country has ever seen?' Randall strides about the room, glaring at the sweat- and grime-encrusted men taking a break. 'Get your mother-fucking backs into it,' he rages, eyes wide and bulging out nearly as much as the veins on his arms.

'We'll be putting something in his back soon enough,' someone whispers quietly to Jonas.

'Ssshh now! He's doing a good job,' Jonas replies. 'Looks like they're on the last wall now.'

'Yeah, but Jonas, they've only made a small hole—no one can fit through that.'

'True enough, but once they see the light on the other side, they'll work faster and tear those walls down with their bare hands. Jonas watches carefully as the men work at the deep hole. Two layers of concrete block already hacked through to reveal the third and final layer. Some of the gym machines had been ripped apart, any length of metal being brought to the outer wall. Many of them, like the iron pipes, had proved completely insufficient, but for the first time since the outbreak began, every man within the five wings worked together.

One more glaring thing stood out, and that was the way every man revered Randall. Even the truly psychotic killers found it difficult to oppose his explosive character. The force of the man was staggering, and it worried Jonas. Made him concerned that when the time came, they would find greater opposition than initially planned for.

Pursing his lips with concentration, Jonas thought through the anticipated action. Maybe it would be better to do it now, lure Randall away somewhere, and have him done in, but no, that would raise immediate questions and cause more violence. At the point of getting out, but that would see all the men in one place, and an act like that just couldn't be done unnoticed.

Maybe it didn't need to be done. They could simply part company and move away quickly. But leaving Randall on the loose would not only be a danger to them but to mankind in general. Jonas was a killer and had taken many lives despite only being convicted for the one murder. But the killings he carried out were on people who knew the business they were in. It was bad play to kill someone unconnected, not simply for the bad press it drew, but it was just morally wrong.

Same as having Randall on the loose would be morally wrong. He'd find the nearest town and decimate it. Tear the place apart and have every woman turned into his sex slave within hours. Shit, most of the men would do that given the chance, but Randall ... well, he was something else. Jonas just knew that to leave Randall alive would only invite trouble.

'We almost, there you nasty sons of bitches. Get your mother-fucking hands on that bar and drive it in. Come on, man, drive that bar in. Command that wall to break. We so close now I can just see them mother-fucking titties on the other side of that wall. A big-ass pair of juicy titties all ready to suck on. They waiting for you. Get that wall down,' Randall urges the men to work harder, the exhaustion clear on their faces. Days of hardly eating, sleepless nights, and constant fighting had weakened them. Still, they grinned like fools at the idiotic chanting the man threw at them. His enthusiasm was infectious, that hard-edged American voice speaking like a full-on gangster from the movies.

'Oh, there it is, the last bit of mother-fucking wall. I told you we would break this wall. I told you dumb asses this mother-fucking wall could not withstand us. Hit it! Hit it harder, drive that bar in. Come on. One, two, three, strike! One, two, three, strike! Put some mother-fucking energy into it! Come on now! One, two, three, strike that wall! Oh, baby, there it is. The outside is there ... look at the world beyond your wall, you crazy motherfuckers.' The bar drops with a clang as an almighty cheer erupts. Men flooding into the room, desperate to peer through the tiny hole in the wall and the clear sky beyond it. Handshakes took place, men patted each other's shoulders. Randall stands back with his arms crossed, feet planted wide apart, and grinning like a maniac.

'Come on now, you bitches. This ain't over. This ain't no mother-fucking time to be stroking each other, Get that bar up and smash that hole like it's some mother-fucking pussy.'

'Told you,' Jonas sighs, watching the men grab the bars with renewed energy, buzzing with adrenalin. They throw themselves into the effort, slamming the bars into the gap, sending chunks of masonry and concrete flipping into the room. The hole widened; bit by painstaking bit, it got bigger. What first could fit a pencil through was soon large enough for a fist. Aggressive shouts scream out. Hands bleed onto the bar as the blisters formed on the sweaty palms rip open.

'Now hold on, you motherfuckers,' Randall bellows. The men pause, breathing hard from the exertion. He moves to the wall, leaning through the now formidable dent and pushing his bald head through the hole. 'I see something,' he yells. Drawing back in, he stares at the men watching him expectantly, 'I see big, juicy titties out there,' he grins, an explosion of laughter bursting in the room. Jonas looks sharply at the man stood next to him grinning like a fool. 'Sorry, Jonas,' the man stifles his smile, looking awkwardly at the floor.

'Not long now. Is everyone ready?' Jonas asks after a weighted pause.

'Yeah, tooled up and ready,' the man nods respectfully. 'So where we going when we get out, like?'

'Mainland. We'll go for a city, get some supplies, and work it out from there once we see just how bad it is.'

'Never thought I'd see the outside,' the man says quietly. A double life sentence for multiple murders meant he'd be in his eighties before he could even be considered for release, and he also knew that many inmates simply didn't reach that age.

'Same for most of us,' Jonas replies. 'Not exactly the freedom we had in mind but …'

'Fucking hell, Jonas, anything's better than this shithole. Listen, are we doing him as soon as we get outside? Only I was thinking that we still got the outer wall to go yet, and that fucker's covered in bastard razor wire.'

'I want him done as soon as we get through this wall,' Jonas says.

'I get what you're saying, Jonas, but think about it. That fucker gets 'em going good. We should let him get that outer wall down before we do him.'

'That outer wall,' Jonas stares hard at the man, 'is reinforced concrete. You know what that means? Means it's got solid steel running through it. There ain't no way anyone is getting that wall down unless we find a fucking bulldozer.'

'What you motherfuckers talking about?' Randall marches at them, glaring suspiciously.

'The outer wall. Jonas says it's reinforced concrete,' the man says smoothly, 'got steel wire running through it …'

'I know what reinforced means, you dumb motherfucker,' Randall shakes his head at the audacity of it.

'A barbell ain't gonna get that wall down, Randall,' Jonas says.

'You got a plan, then?' Randall asks, his voice transforming to a quiet, respectful tone.

'Yep,' Jonas nods, locking eyes with the American.

'And you ain't gonna share it with no dangerous motherfucker like me, are you, Jonas? No, sir, you gonna keep that plan tucked up tight in that brain.'

'You got it,' Jonas smiles without a trace of humour in his eyes.

'I'd do the same,' Randall shrugs, holding eye contact with Jonas. 'Just don't be thinking of double crossing me, Jonas. I got mother-fucking eyes in the back of my mother-fucking head.'

'Sure you have, Randall,' Jonas nods.

'We should team up once we get out. Me and you, Jonas, we can rule the mother-fucking roost. Ain't no motherfucker can stop us if we work together.'

'I was thinking of that myself,' Jonas smiles, nodding with enthusiasm. 'It'd be good to have someone watching my back.'

'I don't like any other motherfucker in this pen, Jonas. What's the plan for the outside? You got any ideas?'

'Yeah, course, we stay local, go into the towns and have some fun, get our shit together, and find some ground.'

'Motherfucker,' Randall exclaims with a broad grin, 'that's a good-ass plan, Jonas. We find us some pussy, get some liquor, and live like kings.'

Jonas matches the broad grin, giving a laugh as Randall walks off laughing.

'Dumb fucking cunt,' the man shakes his head, still smiling.

'Yep,' Jonas replies.

'What the fuck was all that about, Randy?' A muscular inmate sidles up to the big American, speaking quietly.

'They got something cooking,' Randall lowers his head, keeping his voice low. 'Once we get out, they'll go for me. Jonas probably got them shanked up and ready.'

'Cunts,' the man growls.

'Get our boys ready. Soon as we all get out, we take Jonas and his fuck ass gang,' Randall moves away before the quiet conversation can be noticed. The man stays still for a few seconds, watching the inmates work at the wall. He kicks some rubble at his feet, waiting for a minute before he seemingly thinks of something else he needs to do and turns to walk out the room, heading to the central canteen to spread the word.

'Quiet, there's one of Randall's blokes now,' the leader of C wing says. The two men stand quietly, waiting for the pensive-looking inmate to walk through.

'He's gone,' the B wing leader whispers. 'What were you saying?'

'I said them two fuckers will stitch us up. Fucking guarantee it,' C wing says.

'What Jonas and Randall?' B wing leans in, frowning at the suggestion.

'Fuck yeah, thick as thieves them two. I bet they jacked up that fucking meeting between them.'

'Why would they stitch us up?' B wing asks.

'Fucking hell, mate, 'ave I gotta spell it out for ya? There's what, like five hundred blokes here that all want to shag something, get pissed, and eat tons of food. If this thing is as bad as everyone is sayin', then how the fuck are five hundred blokes all gonna find something to fuck and eat?'

'I get it,' B wing nods, 'they'll cut the numbers down, then?'

'Fuck yeah, they will,' C wing urges. 'They'll want the

spoils for themselves, won't they? Two big fuckers like that, they don't want us about being a thorn in the ointment.'

'Thorn in the side or a fly in the ointment,' B wing says.

'Whatever ... My point is they'll fuckin' 'ave us soon as we get out. We gotta get in there first. You saw those looks between 'em at the meeting, like fucking funny signals and shit.'

'Yeah, yeah, course I did,' B wing nods.

'And did you hear Jonas? "So, Randall, what do you think of this plan?" They was in it together.'

'Yeah,' B wing continues to nod. 'What d'you reckon, then? We team up or something like that?'

'Fuck yeah,' C wing looks round before continuing with the conspiring. 'We gotta do this, mate. We'll be fucking killed if we don't. This is like life and death right here.'

'Alright, get our boys tooled up, then. When you wanna do it?'

'Wait for them to make the move,' C wing says, 'but for fucks sake, keep it quiet.'

In the day room of A wing, the men continue to attack the wall, increasing the size of the hole and working at the several layers of concrete blocks. With the light pouring through the hole, the energy levels remain high as men whisper, passing information discretely. The hushed conversations are noted by everyone else as they too have their own scheming chats.

The inmates, desperate to show that nothing is going on, act overly friendly towards each other, laughing at crap jokes, patting each other on the back with forced humour.

'Jonas,' the leader of D wing nods in greeting, standing back from taking his turn on the barbell and patting the dust from his blue prison trousers.

'One of my boys just said B and C were having a nice

chat,' D wing remarks casually, rubbing his hands and sending a shower of dust particles falling to the ground.

Jonas lifts his eyebrows and turns the edges of his mouth down, tilting his head at the same time with a look of mild interest.

'Proper little chat too. Lots of looking about and funny winks going on,' D wing continues. He smears the sweat from his face, grimacing at the greasy film now coating his hands.

'Were they now?' Jonas says quietly.

'Aye, reckon they'll be planning something nice for the rest of us.'

'Don't seem right that–two against everyone else,' Jonas lets the words hang in the air.

D wing nods, staying quiet and unsure how to proceed.

Bloody hell, how the fuck did he get in charge, Jonas thinks. Still, he could be useful. 'They ain't the only ones that can team up, are they?'

D wing nods slowly, nervously glancing about and acting overly casual. 'Me and you then, Jonas?'

'I think we might have to. We don't want to be left out in the cold now, do we?'

'No, no way,' D wing shakes his head, eyes narrowing.

'Just keep watch then. Anything happens, then we work together, and watch that fucker Randall. I don't trust him one little bit. I reckon he'll go for you quickly.'

'Me?' D wing looks surprised, taking a step closer to Jonas. 'Why me?'

'You're the one he fears the most. Didn't you see the way he was looking at you in that meeting? Couldn't take his eyes off you.'

'Shit,' D wing exhales, an angry expression blossoming across his face, 'that dirty cunt.'

Jonas nods, looking at the man directly. 'He is a dirty cunt, and he'll come after you. You get him first, and my boys will watch your back.'

'Thanks, Jonas, cheers for the heads up. We always got on well, me and you, Jonas.'

'Old school. We gotta stick together.'

'You're a canny bastard, Jonas. I'll give you that,' Jonas's man says quietly as the D wing leader strolls away to get the message to his men.

'Survival,' Jonas replies. 'We ain't no different to any other fucking species.'

CHAPTER TEN

'Reggie, what are these three unmarked buildings on this map?' Marcy hands him the book, watching as the small man peers closely at the point her finger indicates.

'It is Reginald, and those are prisons. Three of them,' he replies.

'Prisons? Of course ... They might still be alive. How many inmates do they hold?'

'One of them closed just a little while ago, so that only leaves two. This one is the sex offenders' unit, and the other is Parkhurst, a category B prison that mostly contained offenders serving long sentences with a small section on remand. The sex offender unit only has about two hundred or so, but the other one has approximately six hundred, but that fluctuates as the prison service has been closing many institutions lately, so some of the others were doubling up ...'

'How do you know all this?' she asks, mildly surprised at his depth of knowledge.

'How do you *not* know this?' he replies. 'You lived on this island too. It's common knowledge if you read the local papers and attend the local meetings.'

'Yeah, I wasn't big on doing that kind of thing. We're going for the prisons next. Should be an easy acquisition.'

'Did you just say acquisition?' Reginald asks.

'Yes, why?'

'Oh, no reason,' he looks away. 'It's a good word,' he shrugs. 'That's all.'

'I'm not just a pretty face and big boobs, you know.'

'Clearly not. I think we're almost done here. There are some smaller streets that can be checked on the way if you wanted to move out now, or we can wait for the last few to come back?'

'Time is of the essence, my dear. We are moving out now,' Marcy steps away, staring down the street at the barricade. Her face barley flickers with concentration as the horde suddenly animate and start heading down the road, towards the high make-shift wall. The first ones to reach it start work immediately, clambering to the top to start throwing items down. As the huge numbers join in, the area becomes a hive of activity, thousands of pairs of hands all working together and in silence, taking the wall apart.

As the barricade gets smaller, it reveals the vehicles used as the base, cars and vans parked end on end. The hosts make light work of pushing them aside, the sheer press of bodies sliding even the heaviest of vehicles away. A gap forms, large enough for several people to walk through side by side.

Marcy strides down the street, watching as the horde all cease their work and stand back to the sides, quietly watching her walk past with Reginald; the communicators behind them. The horde filter through, hundreds and hundreds of infected bodies shuffling through the gap in the barricade to follow their leader to the next target.

It felt good to be moving again, the action of progression. Marcy smiles at the thought, liking the phrase. Progression. That's what they were doing, progressing. Building a firm base for their species to live and function. Her mind flowed to the end plan, the fort she had heard so much about. Howie's fort. Darren had explained how it remained defended, how none of them had breached the walls, having been stopped in their tracks on the ground around it. He also said it contained thousands of people, and she imagined that word would spread amongst the humans and many more would go there.

This wasn't personal vendetta against Howie, nor any of them. But if that fort did have so many people, then she needed to take it. Not in a full-on attack like Darren did. No, something else, something subtle. The cities would still have many left in them, more barricaded areas like this one. They could be taken one by one, but that fort was something she could work from. A safe place where thousands of hosts could stay in safety.

The plan was there–gather as many hosts as possible and lead them to the mainland. But the next step was the prisons. Her face flinched at the idea of turning sex offenders. There was enough of the human traits left in her to feel the repulsion towards the nefarious predators that had inflicted so much pain on their own kind.

She would take them; the end result would be the same. She knew that. But how they were taken would be different. The regret she felt at the suffering the humans went through on passing wouldn't be there this time. These men could suffer slowly and die painful deaths. She might even take a few herself, just for the pleasure of seeing that suffering.

'April,' she calls out, her mind working ahead as she forms the next plans.

April jogs forward, falling into step beside Marcy. 'Yes, Marcy.'

'Find me the prettiest girls we've got, make sure none of them have visible injuries, and none of them smell, then get them ready at the front.'

'Yes, Marcy,' April replies, starting to drop back.

'Oh, and April, make sure they look good, use sunglasses or hair to cover their eyes. I want to see some legs too.'

'Okay, Marcy.'

'One more thing, April. You're very pretty, so you'll be with them. Make sure you've got some sunglasses or something for yourself.'

'Thanks, Marcy,' April beams with pleasure, the other communicators hearing the compliment smile appreciatively at April, feeling genuine delight at the praise she received.

'I am assuming, from that conversation, that you are intending to use the same method of entry again but on a larger scale. It would seem that you are going to take advantage of the men within the prison being sex offenders and also the fact they've been incarcerated for long periods to tempt them with our most aesthetically pleasing living challenged persons.'

'Reginald, why didn't you just ask if I was planning the same trick again?'

'I did,' he frowns in confusion. 'May I ask, are you planning on leading this venture yourself? Only that it does somewhat expose you to risk, and I fear that we would be left without a leader should anything untoward take place.'

'Untoward? In a prison full of sex offenders? Perish the thought.'

'Marcy, it sometimes feels that you are mocking me,' he says, with his nose in the air.

'Oh, Reggie, my dear, if I do, then it's with love, not malice.'

'It's Reginald,' the instant reply comes quickly from his lips. 'I should advise that this plan is fraught with danger and urge you to find someone else to lead.'

'Are you volunteering? You'd look good in a frock. I can get some of the girls to give you a make-over on the way if that helps.'

'Good heavens, I shall do no such thing,' he exclaims, completely missing the sarcasm. 'No, I was rather thinking of April. She seems a steady enough girl, with a good head on her shoulders.'

'I'll give it some thought, Reggie, but don't be disappointed if I do choose to go in.'

'By the way, I have meaning to ask you ...'

'You are just full of questions, aren't you, Reggie?'

'My name is Reginald, and yes, I am full of questions as I find it the most satisfactory way in which to gain information and thereby increase my knowledge. How did you turn the guard when you went in? There isn't a mark on him.'

'Robbie?' Marcy laughs. 'Bless him, he was rather captivated by my boobs, so I gave him a kiss. Couldn't have him leaving humanity with having never kissed a girl or felt a–'

'Yes, thank you! I get the picture, Marcy,' Reginald huffs, looking away with a dour expression.

'Has that offended you?' Marcy smiles.

'And why would it do that?' Reginald asks. 'You foresaw the easiest and most logical method of gaining entry and in doing so reduced the risk to yourself. No, I am not offended.'

'You speak like that pointy-eared bloke from Star Trek.'

'Doctor Spock? I have had similar comparisons in the past, and although I am a committed fan of both the series and the old movies, although I hasten to add not the newer movies, I would not compare myself to Doctor Spock.'

'Not offended then, maybe just a little jealous instead.'

She watches his face bluster at the implication, delighting in the easy way he reacts to the gentle teasing. 'I was not jealous! I merely asked on the method you used to gain entry.'

'Oh, my mistake. You just looked a little jealous.'

'I can assure you I *was not* and *am not* jealous.'

'Okay, you can have a kiss too if you want.'

'I do not want a kiss. Thank you for the offer.'

'Sure? Oh, come here, my little Reggie, give Marcy a kiss.' She steps closer to him, laughing as he blanches away with a look of horror. 'I know you want a kiss.' She pouts her lips, pushing them out as far as possible.

'I do not want a kiss,' he protests.

'I can do that controlling thing you like so much, Reggie. I can make you kiss me!' She laughs as he scampers away, yelping with fright.

'Marcy, are these okay so far?' April calls out, leading a small group of infected women from the bulk of the horde.

'Wow,' Marcy smiles at the sight of the gorgeous girls. All of them with long hair pulled down to hide any bite marks on their necks. Slim figured, fuller bodied, blonds through to raven-haired, and all of them with stunning looks. 'Very good, very, very good,' Marcy grins at April. She nods back, glowing from the praise.

'Reggie, what do you think?' Marcy calls out to the man now walking several metres away and pretending not to notice the girls.

'Reginald,' he says. 'Oh ... I see ... yes, I think they are, er

... very, er ... suitable for the task you have in mind,' he stammers.

'But are they kissable?' Marcy asks, with an edge to her voice.

'Marcy ... don't you dare,' Reginald warns, his voice rising in panic.

'Girls, I think Reggie needs a kiss,' she bursts out laughing as the gorgeous group led by April move towards Reginald, all of them smiling and showing him their charm.

'Marcy, you're stopping me from running away. This is not fair! Let me run away. Oh my, yes, thank you. Hello, very nice to meet you. Shall we just shake hands instead? No? Oh right. Oh, another one ... Yes, well, this is very pleasant, and yes, hello to you too. Oh, another kiss ... Marcy! This is intolerable! Yes, my dear, I am very pleased to meet you. Really, there is no need to keep kissing me ...'

'Okay, girls, I think Reginald has had enough for now. We don't want him getting ideas now, do we?' Marcy watches as the girls remove themselves from being draped over the small man, forming back into their group. Reginald walks slowly onwards, readjusting his skewed glasses, smoothing his hair down, and plucking at his shirt sleeves, the whole action being done with a faraway look in his eye.

'So, what's your verdict now, Reggie?' Marcy calls out, exchanging a grin with April.

'Reginald,' he says quietly. 'I think they'll do fine,' he mutters.

'Hear that, April? Reginald gives his seal of approval.'

'Oh, I am very glad,' April replies with absolute sincerity.

Marcy stares ahead, watching the heat shimmer on the road, and just as with the humans, she feels the oppression of the heat bearing down. *Those inmates won't know what's hit them,* she smiles gently.

CHAPTER ELEVEN

'There it is, you motherfuckers, there is the promised gate to the outside world. I said I would get you out, and I mother fucking done it,' Randall stands next to the man-size hole in the wall. His strong hands rip the last section down, creating a gap big enough for the largest man to get through.

Men stand with hands on knees, panting and dripping sweat onto the rubble-strewn floor, chests heaving from the final, frantic exertion. Nerves already frayed from the incessant scheming and whispered conversation, long looks and quick, furtive glances, nods passed, hands pressing against each other as weapons are passed from man to man. Razor blades pilfered from the tuck-shop, iron bars put ready in reach, dumbbells strategically placed. Every man within the prison knew something was going to happen. It was just a matter of when and who would make the first move.

'Jonas, you crazy motherfucker,' Randall singled the man out with a huge, white toothed grin, 'you had this idea, so you should go first, man. Take the position of honour and slip your ass through that wall.'

'Careful, don't put your back to him,' an inmate stood

behind Jonas covers his mouth and whispers. Jonas nods back, signalling that he heard.

'That would be my pleasure, Randall,' Jonas grins warmly, making sure he looks directly at the American for fear one of the other idiots would give a not so discrete nod and spark the fight here and now. Jonas walks through the men, shifting his gaze from Randall to the hole. His instincts scream inside to scan everyone and watch for movements, but the tension has increased so much in the last few minutes that the mere act of looking could spark it. Enough safety measures have been put in place; every wing has men strategically placed to attack. Faces smile, heads nod with pleasure while hands grip weapons tightly. 'Well, gentlemen, I would like to say that serving with you in this fine establishment has been a pleasure ...' he pauses for effect. '... But it fucking hasn't,' he adds to a ripple of laughter. 'Here's to pastures new.'

Jonas grips the edges of the hole, willing himself to turn round and go out backwards but refusing to show a weakness now. Presenting his back, he grimaces, waiting for a blade to plunge in or a bar to ram into his skull. Keeping his movements purposefully slow, he scrabbles through the hole, bunching his big shoulders together.

The intense heat hits him like a hammer, the concrete paving beneath the hole reflecting the intense rays back into his eyes, causing him to squint. Sweat drips down his face, his hands feel slippery as they grip the rough edges. He pauses on the final step, just a few feet down, and he'll be out. He lowers down onto his backside, ungainly and vulnerable. His feet push out until they dangle over the lip. Carefully, he lowers himself down, eyes clenching shut as he waits for the blow to the back of his head.

Opening his eyes, he realises he's stood on the ground,

the final drop not registering within his mind–so convinced was he of the impending attack. A slow grin forms on his face. He lifts his head to the sun, feeling the warmth of the rays. Breathing deeply, and for the first time in days, his nose doesn't fill with the stench of decaying bodies, shit, and stale sweat.

Turning round, he grins up at the hole, at the face of Randall staring out at him.

'Come on, mate, it's fucking lovely out here,' Jonas motions with his head for the man to come out.

'I don't need no mother-fucking invitation. Hey ...' Randall turns back to the room behind him, 'fuck y'all!' He grins and jumps out, athletically landing on the ground. A loud cheer erupts from inside, the sudden noise causing both Jonas and Randall to tense and make ready. They glare at each other, hearts racing, fists clenched. Slowly, they both relax; wry smiles form as they nod with respect and turn back to the hole.

'What you fucking waiting for?' Jonas bellows. Men start dropping through, and each man pauses at the sight of the outside world. The beautiful sun high in the sky, deep blue sky, and glorious fresh air. Jonas and Randall stand under the hole, helping each man out. Something changes, an act unspoken as the impact of getting out takes over from any other intended plan.

The men clap each other on the back, some move to stand on their own, staring up at the sky. Others get carried away, cheering and whooping noisily. The sound is infectious and carries to inside the room, creating a sense of urgency to be out of the place, as if the hole will close up if the exodus isn't completed instantly.

The leaders of B and C wing, hanging back and waiting

to see who makes the first move, cast nervous glances at each other; minute shrugs as they show their confusion. They too get caught up in the fever of escape and quickly join the line ready to drop down.

The last man stands in the hole, a few feet higher than everyone else and cheering with one arm raised in the air. The men respond, whistling and screaming jubilantly as he drops down. They stand there, looking round, the familiar coupled with the unfamiliar. The familiar from the general presentation of the prison, the same hues of grey and brown mixed with harsh concrete. The unfamiliar from not having been to this side of the building before, this not being part of the exercise area and only used for vehicle transport and officers.

The cheering and jubilation ebb away, voices slowly dropping in volume as the initial excitement wears off. Inmates become aware of who they're stood near, where their wing mates are. The smiles fade as the tension soars, faces become grim. Most of them, in their haste at getting out, had dropped or simply not picked up the weapons they had been eyeing earlier.

Movement starts very casually as men start shuffling, creating space between each other. Eyes warily scanning other faces, heads turning to take in all sides. Feet scuff the ground; hands disappear inside pockets to hold the smaller weapons some of them had secreted. Wings began to form as the natural inclination to be part of a pack takes over their instincts. Jonas stepped carefully, his hands loose down at his sides, head slightly lowered to increase his peripheral vision.

Around five hundred men merge, move, sidle, and shuffle into five distinct gangs–each one headed with their leader front and central. Still nothing was said, just long, hard looks. Fists balled, arms tensed, and feet planted wide apart. The conspiring they had all taken part in causing the delay as they each wait for the other to start.

Jonas watches Randall closely. D wing looks to Jonas, B and C look to each other, the leaders keep their expressions plain, revealing nothing.

D wing switches his gaze to Randall, remembering the words Jonas had told him and watching for any movement from the American. Seconds tick away, minutes form and drift as the silent stand-off continues. The unused adrenalin starts to fade away, causing legs and hands to tremble slightly, and the men tense their limbs to hide the shakes for fear of being seen to be scared.

'We gonna stand here all day?' Jonas's deep voice penetrates the silence. All eyes flit to him standing there with arms crossed. He looks round at the assembled men. 'I guess this is the point where we all start taking chunks out of each other,' he adds.

'Why don't we each take a direction? Like one goes north, the other south ... that kind of thing,' D wing says.

'Great idea, you fucking dumb-ass. Only there are five mother fucking wings and only four mother-fucking points of the compass.' Men snigger at the quick-witted reply from Randall. D wing blushes with both anger and embarrassment.

'Two wings could go together,' B wing adds with a quick nod towards C wing who nods back.

'I go where the fuck I please,' Randall shouts, his eyes wide and fierce.

'Which direction do you want, then? You choose what you want,' Jonas offers.

'I don't mother-fucking know. I'm not from this fuck-ass place. How the shit should I know where the fucking towns are.'

'The biggest town is about three miles that way, which is south,' Jonas says.

'You think I'm gonna trust you?'

'You'll fit in well, then,' someone shouts from the back of one of the groups.

'Who the fuck said that? Step up, motherfucker. Step up and say that shit again. I dare you! I fucking double dare you with a mother-fucking cherry on the top.'

Jonas winces as Randall steps forward glaring angrily around, demanding to know what *pussy-assed motherfucker* said that.

'Step back, Randall,' D wing says.

'The fuck did you say?' Randall turns to the man.

'I said,' D wing repeats slowly, 'step back so we can sort this out.'

'Who the fuck are you to tell me to step back? What are you? The mother-fucking playground monitor?'

'You know what,' D wing steps forward, 'I've put up with your fucking voice for years. That fucking noise is like a gnat buzzing away.'

'What the fuck is a gnat? Speak English, you fucking dumbass.'

'Yeah, I am English,' D wing snaps, his arms dropping from being crossed. He strides at Randall. The restraint now gone, out in the open with no guards, no weapons, just man on man, and D wing was serving a life sentence for dealing with pricks like this. Randall stands stock still, his arms loose at his sides as he lets the other man come on.

Jonas flicks his gaze between them, waiting for the

perfect moment to join in. D wing bulls into Randall, arms flailing as he loses control, going into a psychotic rage. Randall stays calm and steps quickly back, using the leader of D wing's momentum against him. D wing stumbles from expecting to find resistance and finding nothing but air. Randall is on him instantly, pulling the man's head down and holding it in place as he repeatedly brings his right knee up into his face. The crack of the nose bone smashing carries above the dull thud of the impact. Jonas hesitates, realising just how hard and skilled the American is. If he rushes in now, he could end up being alone, fighting against a much stronger opponent.

D wing pulls free, staggering away and holding his hands to his face, blood pouring between his fingers. 'Jonas, you fucking cunt,' D wing's voice is muffled but still carries. The implication is clear. Randall snaps his head to glare at Jonas.

'Fuck it. NOW!' Jonas screams. Men from all sides join the roar as they surge in. Randall dances back, punching out at anyone within range. Carnage ensues as violent men explode with fury, full of fear, nerves, excitement, and they drive in. All of them in the blue and grey colours of the prison clothing. None of them able to distinguish who is from which wing. All-out battle takes places. Men punch friends, head-butt associates, kick at cell mates. Razor blades held between fingers slice into faces; sharpened toothbrushes stab and snap into necks. Socks filled with rubble get swung round, smashing cheek bones and fracturing skulls.

Randall fights like a demon, his sheer brutal strength demolishing every opponent that comes at him. His men gather round him, desperate to prove their worth and show their loyalty. The other wings disintegrate as every man fights for his own survival. Jonas and his close associates stick together, forming a tight circle as they batter at anything within reach.

Men, who minutes before clapped and cheered each other for the freedom they had gained, kill and die without discrimination. Bleeding out on the sun-scorched concrete, slipping into unconsciousness never to awaken. Feet stamp down on the fallen, the fighting is dirty, eyes gouged out, ears bitten off. Anything goes. These men were held away from society for a reason, and they show it now. Weak men become warriors as they launch from foe to foe. Strong men become overwhelmed at the numbers around them, becoming confused who to attack and where to go.

Minutes go by as the killing continues. The exhaustion starts to show as the men stagger away to bend over, breathing hard and fighting for breath. Men lean against other, trading feeble blows. Some find inner strength and lash out with a final ferocity, ending their opponent's life and staggering away to drop down.

Jonas and his group stand their ground, chests heaving, knuckles and hands bloodied, feet sore from stamping and kicking. Cuts and bruises on all their faces.

'Jonas, you motherfucker,' Randall screams. 'Me and you, right now, we end this.'

'Don't do it, Jonas. We stick together,' one of his men mutters between gritted teeth.

Randall starts moving his group towards Jonas, their faces set and determined. Everyone else pauses, watching the action play out. The two titans of the prison about to go head-to-head.

Jonas stares at the oncoming group, his face bitter with anger and regret. This didn't play out the way he intended. Now there's too many of them. He glances round. Nowhere to go, no place to run and hide. There is only two ways out of this, and one of them involves dying.

'What's up, motherfucker?' Randall taunts him with an easy grin. 'You wishing you spent more time in the gym now or what? Sat in your cell, being all lord of the manner, and now look at you, you sweating like a rapist, Jonas. Your face is all red and shit, out of shape, Jonas,' he laughs, a grim disturbing sound. 'Hell, I'm not even warmed up yet, motherfucker.'

Jonas pauses, the future mapped out. Not just the immediate future which, he knows, involves his life ceasing to be within the next few minutes but the future for mankind. Men like Randall will rule from now on, their strength and character will give them power over everyone else. Jonas suddenly feels very sorry. Sorry for every bad thing he ever did, sorry that men like him and Randall walk this earth. He stands up straight, letting his arms drop and walking quickly towards Randall. His men call him back, too fearful to break their rank and go after him.

'I'm done, Randall. I'm too old for this shit. Leave my men out of this. They just did what your blokes did and followed their leader. They'll follow you from now on.'

Randall drops the act, standing with a serious look on his face. He nods at Jonas. 'You got my word on that,' he says softly.

'Do it then,' Jonas growls.

'Oh, I will, Jonas,' Randall launches in, grabbing Jonas by the throat with one massive hand. His fingers dig into the sides of his windpipe, squeezing hard and compressing the small, fragile trachea. Jonas gargles at the suffocation, dropping to his knees as Randall increases the pressure of his grip. Eyes wide, his mouth smiling demonically. Jonas stares up, his eyes bulging and filling with blood. His hands flail weakly at Randall's arm, his vision blurs, sound gone, only his conscious remains. That inner part that makes him human. Silently he gives thanks that he won't be a part of the suffering he knows men like Randall will give out. His body shuts down. The brain, starved of oxygen, begins diverting the remaining blood to the vital organs. Jonas slips first into unconsciousness, then dies. A nasty, brutal death delivered one-handed by a man of almighty strength.

Randall stands back, releasing the body and watching as it falls to the side. He stares down, amazed at watching the very second the life went away. Silence everywhere. Jonas's men stand ready as Randall slowly lifts his gaze up to them.

'Prisoners don't make promises,' he says softly. His men surge in, led by Randall as he attacks the remaining men. They're ripped apart, destroyed, and killed within seconds. Every other man just stands watching with a sense of sickening unease growing in their stomachs.

As the last one of Jonas's men falls, Randall spins round, glaring at the fifty or so men that remain standing, albeit covered in blood, cuts, and bruises.

'You men,' Randall booms, 'have proven yourselves worthy of life. You are mother-fucking warriors born to survive. Well, here we are, the last men standing. Crazy, dumb-ass motherfuckers too stupid to die, I want you with me. I want strong men with me. Fuck your wings, fuck what happened inside that place. This is a new life we got. We stick together, and we'll survive. Hell, not just survive, but we'll live like mother-fucking kings surrounded by big-ass titties.'

Some of the men nod quickly, stepping forward to show their allegiance. The few that move quickly prompt the others. The sense of power shifting instantly as all eyes take in the new leader. Not one man stands back. Every one of them knows the outcome if they decide anything different.

Randall grins at them, nodding back as they slowly converge.

'Now, how the fuck do we get out of this shit hole?' he asks with a smile.

CHAPTER TWELVE

Half a mile down the road, a world away from the violence erupting behind the walls of Parkhurst, Marcy stands in front of a vast horde of infected.

'Well, the main gate is open, so I think we should just send them in and wait here,' Reginald says. 'There really is no need for you to go in. April is more than capable of leading this venture.'

'Okay, okay, Reginald. You've made your point. In fact, you've made it many times in the last hour. I'll go part of the way and make sure they can get in, but I won't enter the area where the inmates are. Are you happy with that?'

'I would agree to those terms,' Reginald sniffs, 'but I don't believe for one second you will be able to resist going all the way in.'

'April, you are going to lead the girls in, and I will stay outside ... unless ...' Marcy adds quickly, 'something develops which requires me to go in.'

'That is not fair. The something could be anything, which only you would know and then tell me about later.'

'Well, if you're so sure I'll be telling you about it later, then why are you so worried about me going in?'

'In case there isn't a later for you to tell me about?'

'Wait, I'm lost … Oh, forget it. Look, I'm going in to make sure they can actually get in. Wait here,' she tuts, shaking her head and moving off. April and the girls walking just behind her.

The solid, metal vehicle access gate was slightly ajar, allowing enough room for the women to walk through, entering an area used for searching vehicles as they entered and exited the prison.

Marcy looks with interest, seeing another high wall beyond the search area topped with coils of razor wire and a spike-topped metal gate set in the middle.

She frowns at noticing this gate is also ajar. Looking at the inner gate, then back to the outer gate, she guessed the hasty exit the guards would have made as they came to realise the world around them was falling. Marcy leads them through the inner gate, into the prison grounds proper.

Everything spick and span, the concrete road leads curved to the solid, squat buildings ahead. Windows narrow and high, firmly set in place and never opened. The grounds looked sculpted and manicured, more like the grounds of an historic house than a prison. Lawns cut short but showing signs of unimpeded growth. Edges neatly trimmed, flower beds laid out in exact patterns and free from any signs of weeds.

Pristine benches dot the area, each one clean and looking well maintained. It was amazing that a place like this, used to keep the sickest people safely away from society, could have such an elegant and beautiful setting. Most public parks were covered in graffiti, littered with waste, with foul-mouthed youths swigging from bottles of cider, used syringes by the bushes, and dog shit everywhere. Something about the sight made her feel disgusted, that the evil men within could be allowed to live in such surroundings. She figures it would be the inmates themselves who kept the grounds so pristine, but even that thought disgusted her. That they could work in the open, creating something so nice while everyone else suffered the daily toil of working dead-end jobs, struggling to make ends meet while meeting the expectations of the communities within which they lived.

There should be piles of concrete delivered every day and a big stack of sledgehammers for them to smash it up.

This isn't right. Something about this plan makes her feel uncomfortable. She looks at the grounds, then at the girls who seem so perfectly suited to the exquisite surroundings.

'April, run back and bring me men. I want the biggest, ugliest, and nastiest-looking men we've got.'

'Yes, Marcy,' April jogs off quickly, leaving Marcy staring with determination at the building ahead. Giving these girls over will be rewarding the men inside, giving them a final act of pleasure before they're turned.

They pause at the front of the building, staring at the thick metal door propped open to reveal a reception area within. April returns, jogging ahead of a collection of big infected males. Marcy nods with satisfaction at the sight of them. Turning, she walks through the door, entering the reception area.

A high, wooden desk fixed to the end of the wall. Everything looks clean, but the smell inside is strong. The scent of humans, male humans. Marcy walks to the far door, a thick, metal, cell-like door firmly closed and locked. The other standard interior doors within the area lead to offices, meeting rooms, and cupboards.

'Here,' April says from behind the desk, holding up a large bunch of keys, 'there's a note too.'

'Read it,' Marcy says.

'It says …

The cells have been opened. The cell blocks are not sealed. Be warned-the inmates within the main block are loose. We waited for change over, but no one came. We tried calling the governor and senior staff, but the phones were down. Harry Holbrook went into the estate to the governor's house, but he never came back. We waited until Saturday, but we have families too. The senior officer on duty made the decision. The inmates know something is happening from the radio broadcasts they heard.'

A dull thud rings out from the other side of the metal cell door, a muffled voice calling out. Marcy presses her finger to lips, indicating to the others to remain silent. A needless act as they never speak unless required. She moves closer to the door, pressing her ear against the cool metal.

'I heard voices. I'm telling ya, someone is out there,' a male voice speaks on the other side. More thuds bang against the door, firm hammering that vibrates the door within the frame.

'HEY, ANYONE THERE?' the same voice calls out. Marcy turns back to her horde. As one and in perfect synchronisation, the men move to the side of the door, pressing themselves against the wall. The girls stand just a few feet back, staring at her. Marcy looks at the door, then at her girls and moves them back, creating a greater distance.

'Hello?' she calls out.

'Shit, I bloody told you. Hey, yeah, we're in here. Who is that?'

'Marcy, I work in the admin building. Are you all still in there?'

'Oh, thank god. Yes! We're all still in here. We been left here for days now. What's going on? We've heard nothing.'

'There was an outbreak of a disease. They're getting it under control now, but it's taking time.'

'Yeah, we heard on the radio, but that was like over a week ago. There's been nothing since then.'

'Everything went down, the masts, the satellites. It's been awful,' Marcy replies.

'Where are the officers? Are they coming back?'

'They lost loads from the disease. The ones left have been sent to the young offenders' prisons. They're using the army on the streets, soldiers everywhere. They asked me to come and find out if you were still here. No one knew.'

'Yes, we're still bloody here. The foods almost run out and our bedding is filthy. I can't believe we've been left like this. There's been fights and everything. This isn't on. We cannot be treated like this. We've got rights, you know.'

'Why didn't you break out?' Marcy asks.

'How? We're well inside the block, we got no way of doing anything, and we didn't know what was going on. It could have been more dangerous out there …'

'Okay, how many of you are there?'

'You should know that if you work in the admin block.'

'I do the finances for the officers' expenditure, and I only started a month ago,' Marcy replies.

'Look, love, this is an outrageous way to treat human beings. Some of us need medications that ran out bloody ages ago. We've had no counselling sessions, no treatments. Just left alone to rot. We're going to start a civil action as soon as we can. You know that, don't you?'

'Oh, right, no. Well, I guess you can do that.'

'Course we can. We're not having this! We got rights. There's laws and rules that say about how we should be treated, dignity and respect, and all that ... Heads are going to roll for this.'

'How many prisoners are there?'

'Prisoners! We're not prisoners. We're patients undergoing treatment. That is unacceptable terminology to use.'

'But you are convicted inmates, though, aren't you?'

'Yes, but we're not called prisoners. We're patients ... We've got illnesses and psychological problems.'

'The army asked me to find out how many were inside?'

'Why aren't the bloody army here doing it themselves?'

'They're busy. They've got loads to do, and I think they're stretched as it is.'

'Stretched? You hear that? Stretched ... That is disgusting, leaving us here while they sort everyone else out first.'

'How many?' Marcy asks again, keeping her voice light but with an increasing look of hostility on her face.

'One hundred and twenty-two.'

'Is that all? I thought there were hundreds of you.'

'Christ, don't you know anything? This is going down on the list, you know, sending us a bloody trainee to ask stupid question. Should be an accredited officer, you know. We've got rights.'

'Why so few of you?' Marcy presses.

'Because, my love,' the man says in a distinctly patronising tone, 'we are a high dependency unit that requires intensive therapy with a higher-than-normal staff to patient ratio.'

'Why?' Marcy asks.

'Why? Why do you bloody think? This place is full of rapists and child molesters. That's why.'

'Oh, I see, so you're all serious offenders, then?'

'What is this? What the hell has that got to do with us getting food and clean sheets? This is a clear breach of our human rights, you know. It infringes on our civil liberties and causes undue distress.'

Marcy grips the keys, sorting through them to match the right one to the lock. 'Hang on. I'll open the door. There's some food coming in a minute.'

'You're opening the door?' the man asks in a shocked tone.

'You said you needed food and sheets. There's some coming. I've got some of the admin girls here to help get you sorted out. There's no danger to us is there, after what you just said ...?'

'We're not bloody animals, you know. Get this door open, and maybe you'll avoid being listed on our civil action.'

'I'm just looking for the right key,' Marcy replies.

'Just hurry up,' the man snaps. 'Go and tell the others they're opening the door for fresh food and bedding,' the man's voice muffles slightly as he turns to speak to someone else. 'Okay, I'll ask ... What about meds? We need meds in here too.'

'Meds? I don't know anything about medication,' Marcy replies, still sorting through the many keys.

'Well, I suggest you get someone who does, get an army

doctor up here so we can speak to them. This isn't right ... I haven't had my sleeping pills for over a week.'

'I see,' Marcy says thoughtfully. 'But well, there are people dying out here. The disease has crippled everything ... I don't think sleeping pills will be at the top of their agenda.'

'I don't care,' the man shouts. 'I don't care what the hell is going on out there. We're patients undergoing treatment, and we've got rights!'

'There we go! I've got the right key,' Marcy says, applying tension to the key and feeling the first bite of the lock retracting. 'Now listen, you're not to step over the threshold. There's only me and a few girls here, so we're putting ourselves at risk here for you, and the soldiers are all down in the town ...'

The response comes slowly, 'Okay ...' A drawn-out sound that speaks volumes of the sudden intent forming.

Marcy turns the key, disengaging the lock and pulling the door open. She keeps her head low as though watching the swing of the door. Glancing up, she takes in the men all stood there watching her. Jaws going slack at the sight of her cleavage hanging out from the low-cut top, her tanned skin, and tussled hair. She draws the door open, revealing the *admin* girls stood looking down.

More men arrive to stand beyond the threshold, their animated faces becoming dazed at the sight of the women.

'Hi,' Marcy smiles quickly, dropping her head and making a meal of pulling the key from the lock. 'Now, you promised not to cross the threshold. There's only us here ... all vulnerable and alone.'

'Fuck that,' the man at the front says. Marcy recognises his voice as the man speaking to her through the door. He looks slimy, with a permanent sneer etched onto his stubbled face. His eyes lingering with undisguised hunger on her figure. He steps forward, a slow movement, eyes fixed on Marcy.

'Hey now,' Marcy steps back, 'you said you wouldn't cross the threshold.'

The men start pushing through the doorway, following the spokesperson as he steps to the edge of the open door, his eyes fixed on the gorgeous girls.

'Yeah ... look at you ... opening the door to a load of sexual deviants and dressed like a dirty slut. You're just asking for it, begging for it ...' His hand goes to his groin as he starts rubbing himself, clearly not bothered about doing it in front of so many people. Marcy notices several of them are doing the same thing, touching themselves in full view of everyone else.

'Oh,' Marcy says, making her voice sound full of fear. She backs away, stepping into the group of girls.

'All alone, eh? No soldiers here, you said ...' The man advances beyond the edge of the door, his breathing becoming hard and rapid, with the hungry, lustful look clear in his eyes.

'Not quite alone,' Marcy smiles, a brilliant grin full of white teeth. 'We brought our brothers with us.'

'Ha! Where are they, then?'

'Behind you,' Marcy whispers, watching with delight as the inmates turn to see the huge monsters standing with their backs pressed against the wall behind the door. Big men, dripping with aggression, wide shoulders, thick limbs, faces showing a myriad of busted noses, scars. and deformed ears. Rugby players, nightclub bouncers, builders, weightlifters, and every one of them staring with wide, bloodshot eyes.

The colour drains from the man's already pale face. His

legs visibly shake as he goes to step back, his movement impeded by the line of inmates behind him.

'Look at you, all dressed like that … You're just asking for it …' Marcy says softly. 'Begging for it …' she pauses, feeling an intense pleasure at the fear pouring of them in buckets. She nods for effect. Her infected men step forward. The inmates try to turn, barging into each other and screaming in panic.

A melee starts instantly as the ones at the back still try to push towards the open door, sensing freedom and catching glimpses of the beautiful women. The ones at the front scrabbling to get back inside.

The infected pile in, moving quickly as they pluck the inmates out one by one. Strong hands grabbing heads; mouths biting into the exposed flesh of their necks. The infected take their time, biting slowly and savouring the taste of the flesh, and enjoying the fear of the inmates.

Marcy takes the spokesperson, dragging him away. He fights frantically, lashing out and squealing in fright. She grips his face, leaning in and biting into his cheek. He screams, flailing at her with his hands. An infected male steps behind him, pinning his arms to his side, protecting the leader. Marcy steps back, aware of the all-out slaughter taking place but content to stay with this one man for a couple of minutes.

'I'm infected with a deadly disease. All of us are … That disease just entered your bloodstream. Right now it's infecting every cell in your body … It's going to kill you slowly with untold agony, and then you'll turn and come back, and I will be your leader … and you will suffer again,' she speaks softly to him, watching as the fear grows in his eyes. Tears start spilling down his cheeks; his legs shake and give out. The infected male holds him upright, keeping him standing so Marcy can watch him.

'Can you feel it? Does it hurt?'

'Yes,' he gasps, feeling a sudden pain in his stomach. The feeling intensifies, spreading out to his whole body.

'I want you to turn slowly … really slowly,' Marcy says. She doesn't know if she can have any control over the speed of the infection, but right now, she wishes she could.

The infected man drops him, letting him sprawl onto the floor. His breathing becomes laboured and slow. His life slowly leaving him as his body shuts down. Marcy watches, willing the agony to continue. He dies within the same time as everyone else; a sense of mild disappointment passes through her.

She stands there, waiting until he starts twitching. Glancing up, she notices the room is now mostly empty apart from the corpses on the floor starting to convulse. Her infected have ran into the prison, playing the best game of hide and seek ever.

The spokesperson comes back. His twitches end as he sits up and opens his eyes, revealing the true look of the infected. He cranes his head, staring up at Marcy. She looks down at him, willing him to be able to speak, to have normal intelligence and awareness so she can kill him again. The hatred she felt for him still drives her action, her desire to make him suffer. She stares down, teeth gritted as she wills him to be like he was, show that trait he had so she can enjoy it. His red eyes look back at her with devotion, complete love. She could do anything to him right now, and he would take it without reacting. That very thought repulses her. If she hurt him now, she would be the same as him, the same as he was. Making an innocent suffer for her own sadistic pleasure. Whatever he was is gone now–the turn has changed him and taken away all the bad.

She stands back, realising that the urge to make him suffer is a human urge, a desire bred from years of living in a society that nurtured hatred and vengeance. Stepping forward, she holds her hand out to him, helping him up onto his feet.

'Welcome,' she smiles. 'What you were is gone; now you're one of us.' The other inmates start to rise from the floor, standing unsteady for a few seconds as they adjust to the new way of being.

Marcy wills them to head into the prison and use their knowledge to find the others. They respond immediately, staggering through the cell door and into the block. She leans against the desk, lost in thought. The human psyche is driven by chemicals. These monsters had urges to hurt others and were considered to be so sick. They were a risk to society, so they were kept away. But now they're not a risk. If the infection can control those urges they felt when the whole of medicine and science had failed to do so, then what else could it do?

Could they all be allowed to speak? Is there a future where all the infected hosts carried on life as normal, breeding and communicating, only taking what is needed to survive. No greed or jealousy, no will to control others. Like a nest of ants all striving towards a common aim.

Marcy knew she was different to Darren; she didn't have his sick perversion, but more than that, the difference between them proved there was scope to change quickly. The evolution just between them two was staggering, and the fact that she could make others communicate. Was this her doing it, or the infection inside her? Both, it must be both. The infection must understand that in order to continue to survive now that the element of surprise has gone, it must change and adapt.

That must be it, the infection is giving her a chance to use her own abilities to protect the species. Even Marcy, a former hotel waitress, knows the power of the brain was far greater than most people used. Some people could do highly complex calculations, others had perfect memory recall, remembering everything they had ever read. She remembers seeing a programme about autistic children that could see a building once, then draw it perfectly from memory. Children that could compose perfect musical arrangements. Every one of those people had the same grey matter contained in their skulls. It was just that some had different neural connections which gave them greater skills.

Marcy senses the possibility, and it makes her heart quicken. Like a fantasy that could never be achieved now being a realistic and tangible thing.

A thought strikes her, an incredible, powerful thought that makes her reel, holding her hand out to grasp the desk. Shaking her head, she thinks it couldn't be possible. It just couldn't ... Could it?

'Marcy, are you okay?' April walks in from the main block, wiping a smear of blood from her chin and looking at her leader with concern.

'Stay here and wait for the others, bring them out when they're all taken,' Marcy says, not looking at April but thinking frantically, her face staring down at the ground.

'Okay,' April replies as Marcy runs out the door. She jogs down the road, the need to find out now burning away in her soul. It couldn't happen like that. It just wouldn't be possible. But Darren said he had tens of thousands of infected with him. The odds must mean some of them ...

She speeds up, racing through the gates, turning

towards the massed horde and Reginald stood there patiently.

'Marcy? Whatever is wrong? Do you need more in there?' Reginald asks at seeing the state of her.

'No, Reginald, have you ever been sick?'

'Pardon? Have I ever been sick?'

'Yes, have you ever been really sick or suffered from a disease?'

'Marcy, I think I have something of that nature within me right now ... We all do,' he says slowly.

'No, I mean...' she forces herself to be calm, breathing deeply and fighting to control the rush of excitement. Her will. She must use her will. But it doesn't work like that. She can get them to do things but not answer questions ... Would it work?

'Listen, I want all the communicators over here with me now,' Marcy calls out. She watches as the chosen ones file towards her. Reginald in the lead and watching with worry etched onto his face.

Test questions. She needs to be sure they will answer. Ask test questions.

'Er, did any of you live in a house?' she asks. Reginald stares at her perplexed, some of the hosts reply with one word 'yes'.

'Use your hands. Put your hand up if you lived in a flat.' She watches hands lift, the faces all staring at her. 'Okay, put your hand up if you had a driving license.' Again, she watches as some hands drop and others lift up. 'Right ... hold your hand up if you worked in a skilled job, something that required training and qualifications,' she pauses, holding her breath at the more complicated question. A few hands go up; the majority stay down.

'You,' she points at one woman with her hand up, 'what did you do?'

'Legal advisor for a pharmaceutical company,' the woman answers in a flat tone.

This is it–she can ask the question. She pauses again, suddenly realising what it will mean if they answer.

'Have any of you,' she asks slowly, 'no ... do any of you suffer from, er, an illness like ... diabetes! Yes, do any of you have diabetes?' She watches as one hand lifts into the air. 'You have diabetes?' she asks.

'Yes,' the man replies.

'Did you need medication for it? Tell me ...'

'I was insulin dependent. I had to inject every day and carried it with me all the time.'

'Was?' Marcy breathes out. 'How did you cope when the outbreak started?'

'I had insulin, and I was careful,' the man gives the answer instantly, his tone as dull and lifeless as Robbie's was.

'What about now?'

'I don't need it now.'

'Why not?'

'I am not diabetic now.'

The answer hangs in the air as Marcy looks to the only other being that could understand the implication of what was just said. Reginald stands there, his mouth hanging open.

CHAPTER THIRTEEN

'I call this meeting to order, this being the first council meeting of the community known collectively as Fort Spitbank, but referred to simply as the fort,' Sergeant Hopewell stands at the head of the hastily arranged tables. Looking round at the people chosen to make the first council up. Chris, Sarah, Ted, Kelly, the bloke who said he was a pharmacist, and that annoying idiot that was going on about making a shrine or a multi-faith place of worship.

'Terri Trixey, who is the officer sat behind me, will be keeping a record of the meeting unless anyone opposes that?' She looks up, staring round to see if anyone does oppose it. Nobody does, of course. They all just nod back at he., 'It is important to keep structure, and I am aware that not everyone here will know everyone else, so first of all, we need to introduce ourselves. My name is Debbie Hopewell. I am a sergeant with the police, and I have vast experience in organisation and establishing working practises to suit the task at hand. Chris?' She sits down, clearly expecting Chris to stand up and showing a look of irritation when he simply leans forward and rests his elbows on the table.

'You all know who I am,' he smiles, 'so I won't bore you.' He looks to his left at Kelly.

'My name is Kelly. I was chief engineer for many years ...' And so it goes on. Everyone introducing themselves and giving a brief rundown of their working lives.

Of course, I was invited to the council, but I was the only one from my team, and I insisted that Clarence come with me. That caused another disagreement, which Chris smoothed over with some soft words.

Thankfully, the pharmacist is very brief, giving just his name and saying what his job was, which is enough. Unfortunately, the preacher man isn't so brief, going into great detail about all the studies he's done of the many religions, how he's worked with drug users, and helped with youth counselling services. I feel myself starting to fidget, getting annoyed at the idiot for hogging the limelight and talking so much. We need fuel for the machines, we need to get Meredith tested ... Why can't these people see that?

'Mate,' the words come out of my mouth before I realise what I'm doing, 'no offence, but we need to move on.' That earns me a sharp look from Sergeant Hopewell and a few others while Chris nods and Clarence smiles into his coffee mug. That shows how much I've changed. I would never have dreamt of saying something like that a couple of weeks ago.

'Oh right, yes, of course. I do apologise. I have a tendency to go on a bit. It's just that I find all of these things so very interesting, the social formations we structure around the faiths, and of course, the way that having faith, in whatever God or deity you choose, does help enormously and–'

'You're doing it again,' I cut across him.

I earn an even sharper look from Sergeant Hopewell

and a mutter from Clarence before he introduces himself, 'Making friends already there, Boss. I'm Clarence. I worked with Chris in the Parachute Regiment. I'm part of Mr Howie's team now.' He looks at me expectantly.

'My name is Howie. I was named after my father Howard, but it was too confusing to have two Howards, so I became Howie. I am twenty-seven years old, and I worked as a supermarket manager before the outbreak.' I have no idea why I said all that. I guess the tiredness and fatigue is making me reckless. I feel like I just don't give a shit what these people think of me.

'Thank you,' Sergeant Hopewell says, giving me a strange look. 'So we all know who we are. The first thing we need to do is set an agenda of items for discussion. We go back round the table, and everyone has an opportunity to put forward what they wish to discuss.'

'Where is Doctor Roberts?' I ask, interrupting her.

'He has too much work to do; he couldn't make it,' she replies without looking at me. 'So if we start–'

'Who represents the medical side of things, then?'

'If you were listening, Howie, you would have heard James saying he was here on behalf of the medical team.'

'Oh, sorry, James,' I smile at the man who nervously smiles back, 'I wasn't listening.' Glancing round, I see Sarah staring daggers at me, Chris examining something on the table, and Ted staring at the ceiling.

'As I was saying,' Debbie continues. 'Anyone who wants to put an item forward can do so.'

'Are you a doctor, then?' I ask James sitting opposite me.

'Er, yes. Well, I'm a junior doctor actually, but yes, I am a doctor,' he replies with another nervous glance, this time at Sergeant Hopewell.

'Moving on,' she says through gritted teeth. 'I'll go first'

'Why you?' I ask immediately. My voice casual, but my intent to be as annoying as possible is quite clear.

'Because I am the chair,' she replies, 'so I chair the meeting, and in order to give everyone an idea of the kinds of things we need to discuss, I thought I would go first.'

'Why are you the chair?' I ask with a neutral expression. 'Did I miss a vote or something?'

Her face goes red with anger as she fights to control her temper.

'Good point,' Clarence rumbles. 'Why *are* you chairing? Why not Chris or Mr Howie?'

'Or Ted for that matter. Surely, it's up for everyone to decide who the chair is. I mean if we're going to have a committee ...'

'A council,' she corrects me.

'A council,' I concede with a nod, 'then it must be done fairly.' I smile round the room, seeing Sarah shaking her head at me and rolling her eyes, 'I propose we vote on who the chair should be. Who wishes to be considered for the position of the chair?'

'It's not *the* chair. It's just chair,' Clarence corrects me politely.

'Oh, I do apologise. Who wishes to be considered for the position of chair?' I stare round the table with a look of pure innocence. 'Chris?'

'I'm happy to do it,' he replies, rubbing his beard.

'What about you Mr Howie?' Clarence asks me with a light tone.

'Me? I'd love the chance to be a chair.'

'It's not *a* chair. It's just chair,' he says.

'I did it again, sorry.'

'Are you going to do this the whole way through?' Sergeant Hopewell asks with forced patience.

'Do what?' I ask.

'Disrupt the proceedings?' she replies.

'I'm not disrupting the proceedings. I merely questioned why you get to put the first idea forward and why you are the chair, sorry … why you are chair… This has to be a fair system. We are not some autocratic society here, Debbie, that does what you tell them to do.' We lock eyes. I've just made myself an enemy, that much is clear. The hatred pouring from her is palpable.

'Fine, so who wants to be the chair?' she asks.

'Chair, not *the* chair,' Clarence says.

She takes a deep breath and looks down for a few seconds. 'Who wants to be chair?'

'I do,' I reply.

'You want to be chair?' she asks.

'Yes, please.'

'I second that,' Clarence adds.

'Okay, all those who want Howie to be the … to be chair, please raise your hand.' To my surprise, several of them lift their hands up. James being one. Sarah does and both Chris and Clarence. Even Kelly raises her arm.

'Is that over half? It looks like over half. Does that mean I can be the chair?'

'Chair,' Clarence says.

'Yes, it would appear that is the case,' Sergeant Hopewell smiles. 'Please carry on, then,' she nods to me and sits down.

'Er … right, and what does a chair do? Other than for sitting on, obviously.'

'This is bloody farcical,' she explodes, slamming her hands down on the table.

'Please do not disrupt the proceedings,' I say calmly. 'Now about this idea thing that was mentioned ... Who has ideas they want to discuss? Only serious ones will be considered ... and definitely nothing about religion or places of worship.'

'You can't do that,' the preacher man says.

'Why not? I thought I was the chair?'

'Chair,' Clarence says.

'Howie,' Sarah says, 'you have to allow everyone a chance to put their ideas forward.'

'Do I? Okay then, sorry,' I nod at the preacher man who smiles back at me, all trace of humour gone from his eyes.

'Well, ladies first, I guess. Oh, hang on,' I correct myself, 'that is both sexist and discriminatory, and I apologise to the members of the council. We could go with the oldest first, but that would be ageist ... so er ... anyone?' I ask, catching a wry smile on Kelly's face.

'Yes, I would like to discuss the placing of a multi-faith area within the fort. I think this would be of great benefit to the community for a variety of different reasons ...'

'I'll stop you there,' I cut him off before he has a chance to get going. 'This is the bit where you put your suggestion for discussion, not the actual discussion.'

'Oh, yes, of course. Sorry, chair,' he glances at Sergeant Hopewell, flusters, then corrects himself, looking at me. 'I mean chair,' he nods.

'Anyway, that idea is dismissed,' I say. 'Next?'

'You can't do that!' the preacher says, shocked.

'Can and I just did. Next?'

'I would like to discuss keeping the gates locked with armed guards on both sides, also placing the heavy machine gun on the top of the wall ...' Clarence says.

'Got it, two items there for discussion. Great ideas too, I might add. Anyone else?'

'I would like to discuss getting an alarm system set up,' Kelly says, clearly getting into the swing of things.

'Another great idea. That's three. Anyone else?'

'We need fuel for the generators. We can't do any tests on Meredith until we get some,' James says.

'That makes four. Anything else?'

'But hang on,' the preacher leans forward, 'you can't just choose what items to discuss.'

'Okay, quick vote. All those who do *not* want to discuss religious stuff, please raise your hand.' The same people all vote again, clearly over half the room. 'Vote counted, and it goes against you. Sorry but we are not discussing it.'

'But …' he stammers.

'Democracy,' I cut him off again, 'can't argue with it, I'm afraid. The people have spoken.'

'Howie this is outrageous,' Sergeant Hopewell shouts.

'Why?' Kelly leans forward, her voice clear and steady. 'Why is it outrageous? This was your idea to have a council. Mr Howie asked the members to vote, and they did.'

'But he's doing it on bloody purpose.'

'Doing what, Debbie? What is he doing?' Kelly asks.

'Being immature and infantile, blundering on and using his popularity to make this awkward.'

'It has been done fairly, as you decreed it should be done,' James says with a very cultured voice that I didn't pick up on earlier.

'But he's a bloody supermarket manager,' she shouts. 'He's running rings round you, manipulating everyone.'

'Last night …' I say with my voice dropping to a growl. 'I stabbed one of my own team through the fucking neck.

Which was right before I shot a baby as it bit into its mother's neck; then, I shot the mother … Those things had to be done, and this,' I cast my arm round the table, 'is a stupid waste of time. This is something that is done in a few months when we're on our feet. It hasn't even been two weeks yet, and we're sat round a fucking table, taking fucking votes. *This* is the ridiculous thing and if you …' I point directly at Sergeant Hopewell, 'cannot keep up, then I suggest you fuck off and let those that can get on with it. We have a dog out there that is immune to the virus, we have machines that can test that dog and find out why it's different to everything else, but instead of getting fuel, we're sat here talking about fucking religion. We need people going out to scavenge and find food. We need ammunition and weapons, better security, more lights, and above all else we need fuel.'

The preacher drops his eyes, uncomfortably fidgeting in his seat. Sarah stares at me with a strange look. I look across the table to Sergeant Hopewell. It looks like the fight has gone out of her. She goes to say something, then stops. Her mouth open but without any words coming out.

'Terri, start a list of actions, please. James?' I look to the doctor sat opposite me, 'other than fuel, is there anything you're desperate for?'

'Antibiotics, penicillin, blood, and anaesthetic,' he replies.

'Terri, add it to the list, please. Kelly, what do you need to get an alarm rigged up?'

Roger Hastings, the old fort curator, leans forward, clearing his throat and speaking for the first time, 'There was an old loudspeaker system here. The wiring is old, but it might be salvageable.'

'Show Kelly where it is, and Kelly will let the police office know if we need anything else.'

'I'll need to assess it first, but we'll get something rigged up, even if it's a line of people stood with megaphones,' Kelly adds.

'Ted, the guards …'

'I'm on it,' he replies. 'That won't happen again. Guards will be on both sides of the gates.'

'And they'll be kept locked,' Chris says.

'Yes, Chris, they should have been last night, but I think a combination of the heat, exhaustion, then Howie getting back with the dog … Things just slipped. Inexcusable, but it happened.'

'We're not blaming you, Ted,' Chris says. 'We're all at fault. Have you got enough guards?'

'No. We need more. We're already using everyone that's had experience of weapons.'

'We'll get more trained,' Chris replies. 'Terri, put that on the list as a priority action. We need volunteers for weapon training and guard duties. Next?'

'The second GPMG we brought back from the navy ship … Dave suggested we get it rigged up on the wall facing out onto the flatlands,' I say.

'Should be doable,' Chris nods, looking at Kelly.

'I've no experience of mounting weapons,' she says, 'but we can have a look. Shouldn't be too difficult.'

'Wouldn't it be better to put it on the ground outside the main gates behind a wall of sandbags. It'll cover the immediate ground area then and give a visible deterrent,' Ted asks.

Chris rubs his beard, nodding while thinking. 'Good point, Ted. Yeah, we could do that, I suppose.'

'A visible deterrent is also a visible target,' Clarence

says. 'That would mean keeping guards outside the gates all night. All it would take is for someone to nod off and get taken, and we've lost our best weapon.'

'Good thinking,' Ted nods. 'I take it back. Best to leave it inside the perimeter, then.'

'Agreed?' I ask, looking at the three men with the greatest experience. They nod back. 'Terri?'

'Got it,' she says.

'Next?'

'Sanitation.' James says. 'I took a walk round yesterday and saw people eating food with their hands. Dysentery is one of the biggest concerns in refugee camps like this.'

'What do you propose?' I ask.

'The toilets in the visitor centre are barely coping too. They keep getting blocked up and we're using so much water,' Terri jumps in, giving a quick nervous glance to Sergeant Hopewell glaring into the room with a foul look on her face.

'Knives and forks,' James shrugs, 'and clean hands. We can use antibacterial gels and cleaners, but we need to stress the importance of basic hygiene and keeping the eating utensils clean too.'

'What are we doing now? With the eating arrangements.'

Everyone looks at Sergeant Hopewell who shrugs and looks away.

'Er ... the stores are giving out the rations of food and people are cooking within the living areas,' Terri explain.

'Is there anything else we can do? How about we serve everyone from one point. They take it in turns, section by section or something like that.'

'We could, but that would take some doing,' Sarah cuts in. 'There's already a lot of people here.'

'Okay, Sarah and Terri, I want you both to look into it and liaise with Doctor James to establish a better practise. Kelly, can you get someone to look at the toilets?'

'Already done. We keep on looking at them. People have got to stop shoving so much toilet paper down them.'

'Okay, get signs up. Toilet paper goes into bins which can be taken and burnt, not down the toilets. Sarah and Terri, are you happy with looking at the food arrangements? I didn't want you to think I was asking you, seeing as you're both women,' I say with a smile.

Sarah smiles back, shaking her head at me. 'No, it's fine,' she replies. 'We'll sort something out.'

'Speaking of burning,' Kelly says. 'The bodies still haven't been done yet.'

'Fuel,' Chris replies, 'all comes down to fuel ... That is the top priority.'

Sighing, I rub my face, turning to Clarence. 'We'll have to go back out.'

'Okay, Boss,' he nods.

'You say it like it's a bad thing. Something wrong?' Sarah asks.

'Nah, nothing,' I shake my head. 'We've been pushing the lads non-stop, and I promised them some downtime, but this comes first ... What we doing with the dog in the meantime?'

'What about her?' Ted asks.

'Well, she's with us inside the fort, but if we're going out ...'

'We cannot risk anything happening to that dog. Doctor Roberts is adamant about that,' Doctor James says. 'The dog must stay here.'

'Then it must stay with Chris, by his side,' Clarence replies. 'No offence but ...'

'You don't need to say anything else,' Ted holds his hand up. 'Everyone knows to protect that dog above everything.'

'Right, good … Anything else? Only it seems to me that's enough for now.'

'No, nothing from me,' Doctor James says. Kelly shakes her head. A quick scan round the room shows everyone else nodding in agreement.

'Good. Right. One more thing,' I say before they all head off. 'I think Chris should continue with the day to day running of the fort and be in overall command. Does anyone oppose that?'

'Why Chris?' Sergeant Hopewell snaps, her eyes filled with malice.

'Because he's being doing it already pretty much. Makes sense to me,' I reply.

'Debbie and I have both been doing it,' Chris says. 'That would make the most sense … if we both keep doing it.' He offers her the olive branch. His tone neutral but clearly wanting her to agree.

'Go to hell,' she looks away. Olive branch rejected, snapped, burnt, and thrown away. An awkward silence descends. No one quite knowing what to say or do.

'Fair enough,' Chris keeps his tone soft.

'We'll get going for the fuel. Any suggestions where we try?'

'Dockyards,' Ted suggests with a pained look at Sergeant Hopewell. 'Always loads of diesel for the ships.'

'Okay, dockyards it is.'

Outside Clarence and I walk slowly back to our rooms, chatting quietly, when Terri runs up calling my name. I turn round to see her looking pensive.

'What's up?'

'Listen, Debbie has taken it really hard losing Steven and Tom. She blames herself for letting them go with you …'

'Seems like she blames us not herself,' I reply.

'Yeah, well maybe, but … just give her a bit of time.'

'Time? There isn't time, Terri, If she's struggling, she can withdraw and be quiet somewhere, do mundane stuff or whatever. No one will think any worse for it, but saying the things she said and getting everyone whipped up is dangerous.'

'I know. I was angry at you too. We all were but, I … I don't know,' she trails off, with a look of deep sadness in her eyes.

'It looks to me like she's losing it.'

She flashes a look of anger at me. 'She's not losing it,' she snaps.

'What was that then? Perfectly rational behaviour?'

'Howie, this has been hard on all of us. You're not the only one having a hard time, you know.'

'Really? Well, fuck me, I didn't notice,' my tone is harsher than I intended. She blanches at me. Her face a mixture of hurt then anger. She doesn't reply, just shakes her head, and walks off.

'Come on,' I snap at Clarence. He gives me a pointed look, shrugs, and starts walking.

'Bit harsh, Boss,' he mutters. 'I think she was only trying to sort things out.'

'Probably, but I've had it with pussyfooting around them. These are hard times, and they've got to face up to it.'

'True enough.'

'Dave, get everyone ready. We're moving out as soon as possible,' I call out as we enter our rooms.

'Fresh coffee on the table,' Blowers says, nodding at the steaming mugs.

'Cheers, mate.'

'How did it go?' Lani asks, walking into the main room as she ties her hair back into a ponytail.

'Okay, I guess.'

'The boss snapped and shouted at everyone, but it looked like most of 'em were on our side anyway, so we got away with it,' Clarence explains.

'Bloody hell, wish I could have seen that,' Cookey says,

'And he told Sergeant Hopewell to fuck off again.'

'Yeah, maybe that was a bit strong,' I groan.

'No, it was needed. It got the right things done. Did you see the way Ted was joining in the conversation after you went off on one?'

'Most of them were, actually,' I reply.

'So, what's the plan? We going for fuel?' Cookey asks.

'Yep, situation is desperate. They can't run the machines or burn the bodies without it.'

'What about the dog?' Blowers asks.

'She stays here,' I reply. 'But she'll be with Chris,' I add at the worried looks they exchange.

We drink the coffee and make ready for another trip out. Tom's absence feels profound. He was only with us for a few days, but the sight of his kit in the corner, alone and away from everything else is chilling, a stark reminder of what we have to do.

Looking at Cookey, Blowers, Nick, and even Lani, I question if this is too much for them, if I'm asking too much. Debbie's words keep spinning through my mind, *a supermarket manager rampaging round the country with a bunch of delinquent kids.* They didn't ask for any of this. Fate brought us together, but something else keeps us together.

Any one of them could stand down and say they've had enough. Especially the three lads. They've been non-stop since this began. Not a day has gone by without them putting themselves at risk for something I want them to do. The closeness between them is striking. I know they didn't know each other before they arrived at Salisbury, but to look at the way they interact, you'd think they were lifelong mates. Lani gels with them brilliantly. A wise head on young shoulders but with a cracking sense of humour, bouncing of them with ease.

Staring at Tom's kit bag, I feel a deep sense of wanting to give up, to stay here, and not do it anymore. Let them find someone else to be put at risk.

With the skills we've learnt, we could just go, get in the Saxon and drive off, find somewhere safe away from everyone else, and have some peace. But then what kind of life would that be? How long before we got bored and fed up with each other's company? When the banter grows stale and the grief and shock sets in from everything we've faced. I should be on the floor, crying about Tom, weeping for the ones we've lost, having nightmares about Tucker and shooting Steven and holding McKinney in my arms as he died, watching Dave shed a tear over Jamie.

Even last night, fighting alongside Paco Maguire and watching a hero die in battle, fighting to protect a dog. Even that should have tipped me over the edge, but I don't feel the grief. Instead, there's an icy fist clenched inside my stomach, something that wants me to destroy every infected I can find. Rip them apart and reap vengeance for every misery they've caused.

'You okay, Mr Howie?' Dave's voice penetrates my dark thoughts. I turn to face him. Just the two of us alone in the room; everyone else outside getting ready to go.

'Just thinking about Tom.'
'Okay.'

'Dave,' I ask as he goes to turn away. 'I don't feel ... I ...' he stares back at me, his face devoid of expression. 'I ... just don't feel ... Nothing, I don't feel anything.'

He shrugs, his eyes fixed on mine. 'You will. Just not the time for it now. You've got work to do, Mr Howie,' and with that he walks off, leaving me alone and wondering why he has to be so bloody strange.

CHAPTER FOURTEEN

'Will you look at that,' Randall exclaims. The inmates gather to the sides and behind him, staring at the open gates and the service road beyond. Randall turns to look at the building just a few metres away. Just round that corner, they broke out and died, not knowing the open gates were right here.

'Dumb-ass motherfuckers,' Randall sighs, shaking his head. Still, it meant more for him. Five hundred men running about would soon cause problems, but fifty was a far more manageable number. Enough to cause carnage and take what they needed, but not so many that couldn't be controlled.

Some of the inmates stand with eyes closed, reeling at what could have been. Knowing their mates died just yards away from freedom. The violence they brought on themselves doesn't factor into the thinking of the many, just a few realise the irony of it.

Randall strides forward, a huge grin spreading across his face as he crosses the threshold of the gate. Two weeks ago, he would never have thought this possible. With no chance of appeal, the murder he committed being witnessed by many other powerlifters, judges, and officials, he knew he would see his days out in prison. Early parole for good behaviour just wasn't possible for someone like Randall. His character and personality meant he would always be seeking confrontation. But this, walking out of a prison on a beautiful summer day with an army of tough mother-fucking inmates at his back was an indescribable feeling.

'Which one of you crazy-ass bitches knows the way to the closest town? I need to get laid,' he looks at the grinning men, noticing how exhausted they all look.

'That way,' one man steps forward, pointing down the access road. 'That goes t' main road which leads t' town,' he adds in a strong northern accent.

'What the fuck did he say?'

'He said that road leads into the town,' another inmate translates.

'How you know that?' Randall demands.

'I kept having t' go court, local like, and that's t' way we went.'

Randall glares at the man, trying to comprehend the accent.

'He said they kept taking him back to court, and that's the way they went,' the same inmate translates again.

'Bitches, you hear that? This man knows the way to the mother-fucking town. He is my new best friend, even if I can't understand a mother-fucking word he says,' Randall laughs, draping a muscular arm over the man's shoulders and pulling him in tight. 'Lead the way, friend, lead the way.'

'Okay,' the man grins, embarrassed at the attention. They start walking down the road, a narrow double carriageway running between the two high walls of the prisons.

'You think them nonces have got out yet, Randall?' one of the inmates calls out.

'Nonces? You keep on saying that word, and I don't get it. You mean the mother-fucking rapists and such like? I hope for their sake they still inside jerking each other off cos I know what I'm gonna do if we meet them.' His response gets more laughs. Despite the common sexual practises within the prison, the utter hatred that mainstream inmates felt towards sex offenders was legendary, especially the hardened inmates serving life sentences who had nothing to lose and everything to gain from the prestige of killing a molester.

'Hell, if I wasn't so busting to get me some pussy, I might go in there and fuck 'em up,' he adds to more laughing.

They laugh and joke while rubbing sore knuckles and limping on feet still painful from stomping on faces and joints. All of them staring ahead at the end of the walls to where the ground opens out and the main road in the distance. The walls either side still give the effect of being enclosed, of being contained. They talk of the women they'll fuck, the booze they'll drink, the drugs they'll take, and the food they'll eat. The reality of the apocalypse yet to hit them.

Reaching the end of walls, they walk out into the open, headed by Randall holding his arms wide as a gesture of freedom.

'Get back quick,' someone mutters. The inmates come to a sudden stop, crouching down.

'Get back, go back to the wall,' Randall urges the men, pushing the ones closest to him. The men stagger back behind the line of the wall, pressing against it and staying quiet.

'Who the fuck are they?' someone asks.

'How the mother-fucking shit should I know,' Randall snaps. 'Shut the fuck up and let me look.' He drops down and crabs forward, inching out from the wall and staring across the ground. The wide grass area dotted with trees and shrubs obscures his view, but the size of the crowd is still clear. Thousands of people stood in front of the main gates of the sex offenders' prison, eerily all still and silent. No movement apart from two stood just in front of them, a man and a woman.

Cursing under his breath at being so close, he watches them intently, wondering what the hell such a large number of people are doing outside a prison when society was meant to have fallen.

'What they doing?' an inmate whispers hoarsely.

'Just mother-fucking stood there,' Randall whispers back. 'Fucking freaky motherfuckers,' he adds more to himself.

He watches as a small group break away from the crowd and stand closer to the man and woman. The distance being far, Randall can't see the detail, but just from the body language, he can tell they're talking, discussing something, all of them looking at the woman. He continues to stare, puzzled as some of them start raising and dropping their arms.

'What they doing now?' the inmate asks.

'Man, shut the fuck up and let me watch,' Randall snaps. The inmate starts crabbing forward, dropping down at Randall's side to watch next to him. 'Just what the fuck are you doing?'

'Watching with you,' the inmate replies.

'Did I say you could watch with me? No, I did not say you could watch with me. You are taking a mother-fucking liberty.'

'Sorry, Randy, you want me to go back?'

'If I wanted you to go back, I would mother-fucking say to go back, but I distinctly fucking remember not telling you to go back.'

'Erm ... what you want me to do then?' the inmate asks, confused.

'Dumb motherfucker, have I got to think for you? Stay the fuck here.'

'I'm Colin.'

'Why the fuck are you telling me your name? Are we on a date? Are we holding hands and eating mother-fucking popcorn?'

'Sorry, Randy.'

'Just shut the fuck up.'

'Okay.'

'I said shut the fuck up.'

'Okay.'

'Say okay one more time and see what happens. Go on, motherfucker, say it! Say okay again ...' Colin stares at the wild, bulging eyes locked on his face, feeling the word forming in his mouth and fighting with every ounce of his being not to say the word. 'Your lips are moving. I will beat you to death right here, you motherfucker.'

Colin nods, clamping his lips shut and willing himself not to speak. Looking away, he feels Randall's insane gaze boring into him. Shifting uncomfortably, he spots the crowd starting to move towards them. He looks back at Randall, desperate to tell him but too fearful of the consequences. He makes eyes, widening his lids and pointing to the left, back at Randall, then rotating his eyes again.

'What the fuck is wrong with your eyes? Why you doing that? Quit doing that.' Colin grimaces, still too afraid to speak. Nodding his head, he starts motioning across the grass, the movements increasing with range each time.

'Crazy motherfucker is having a fit,' Randall mutters with a look of disgust. He glances across the ground, noticing the crowd walking towards them, the male and female clearly in the lead. 'Shit, they're moving. Why didn't you say something, fuck-ass? Come on, move.' They scurry back to the wall, keeping low until they reach the edge. Randall takes one last look, noticing the still crowd not making any noise, all of them walking in the same manner, a steady shuffling gait with stiff legs.

'What the fuck,' he mutters. He pushes Colin back from trying to edge forward again, giving him a glare in the process. Turning back, he picks up on something not being right–the dynamics of the crowd just isn't right. Something about them ... too quiet ... too still, all heads facing forward.

'Get moving,' he urges the inmates after moving back behind the safety of the wall. They start running back up the access road.

'Not there, you dumb fucks. Go up the road,' Randall calls out, his voice muted but still conveying a level of aggression. The inmates veer away from the gate they were heading towards, Randall shaking his head that they'd go back to the same place for somewhere to hide.

The days of fighting, getting very little food, being up all night working on the wall, and then fighting like crazy have left them exhausted. Within a minute, they're struggling for breath and jogging along with heavy legs and sweating faces.

Glancing back, they keep going, aiming for the curvature of the road as it turns at the end of the wall. Randall drops back, physically shoving and threatening the stragglers, not caring if they get hurt.

They get round the corner, moving a few metres down before stopping to rest their backs against the wall, coughing and spluttering, bent over, and breathing hard. Randall creeps back, looking for any sign that they saw them. None of them break away or start running; instead, they keep the same steady movement, with the male and female at the front. Without the trees and shrubs and being on an open road contained between two high walls means the view is sharper and unobstructed. The man and woman are talking, nodding their heads as they speak. None of the others are joining in, just walking at exactly the same pace and looking forward.

The sight unnerves him, the sheer volume of people walking so quietly without any motion other than the steps they take.

'What they doing?' Colin whispers in his ear, causing the big American to flinch at the warm breath on his skin.

'Take your fucking mouth away from my ear.'

'Sorry, Randy ... What they doing?'

'Walking towards the gate.'

'Walking towards the gate?'

'Yeah, that's what I said ... walking towards the motherfucking gate.'

'Okay ... What they doing now, Randy?'

'They still walking towards the gate. Man, you are annoying. Did anyone ever tell you that?'

'Ha,' Colin chuckles, 'you're funny.'

Randall turns his head slowly, not quite believing anyone could be this dumb. Colin stares back, grinning stupidly. His face bruised and a cut above his right eye. He glances down, looking at his large hands and the bruises on his knuckles.

'What they doing now, Randy?' he asks again, still grinning like it's a game. Randall feels his neck tensing. A deep longing to hit the man grows in his stomach. Gritting his teeth, he turns back to the road, watching as the crowd get closer to the gate.

'Still walking,' Randall whispers.

'They're going slow then, aren't they Randy? You think they'll see the bodies?'

'You mean the two hundred dead bodies we left next to the building with the big fucking hole in the wall?'

'Yeah, them.'

'Yes, they'll see the bodies, you dumb-ass fucking motherfucker. Man, how the hell did you survive every day? Did someone get you dressed in the mornings?'

'Huh, don't be silly, Randy. I can dress myself,' he nudges the big American jovially.

'Touch me again, and I'll kill you.'

'Okay, sorry, Randy.'

'Some are going in the gate; the rest are waiting on the road. Who the fuck are these people? Where the fuck they come from?'

'You want me to go and ask them, Randy?'

'Yeah, great fucking idea.'

'Okay.'

'Get your dumb ass back here, you crazy motherfucker.'

'Sorry, Randy, I thought you said …'

'Shut the fuck up.'

'Okay.'

'They're just standing there, doing jack fuck all. Ain't no talking, ain't none of them moving either … This is fucked up. Holy shit, they're all looking this way ... Motherfucker, that is the creepiest thing I ever saw,' he jerks back behind the wall, turning to face Colin. 'They all just turned and looked up the road. Together ... all of them at the same time.'

'What does that mean, Randy?'

'How the fuck would I know that? Quit asking dumb questions.'

'What they doing now?' Colin grins.

'And quit grinning ... Fuck, they're all turned this way now, just fucking standing there ...'

'Can I see?'

'No, and get your fucking hand off my shoulder. I told you I'd kill you if you touch me again.'

'Sorry, Randy, I forgot.'

'Some are coming this way. One of them just ran inside the gate.'

'We better go,' another inmate says from a few feet away.

'They going slow. We got time,' Randall says, his eyes fixed on the small group shuffling away from the main crowd and heading their way. 'The one just ran back from the gate ... Looks like she saying something to the group coming our way. They're going back ... Holy fuck!'

'What? What is it?' Colin asks excitedly, desperate to peer round the wall and look.

'They got chicks coming our way ... hot-ass chicks.'

'Fuck off!' the inmate from earlier says disbelieving.

'Man, I am not joking ... There are several hot-ass bitches heading our way.'

'You're having a laugh, mate.'

'Look for yourself, just stay low.'

'Can I see, Randy?' Colin pleads.

'No, sit your dumb ass down and let the man get

through. Stay low and look, tell me my mother-fucking eyes ain't broken.' The man drops down, inching forward until his head reaches the end of the wall. He peers down the road, shaking his head in wonder.

'He ain't joking, lads. One, two, three ...' he counts silently, eyes flicking from woman to woman, '... eight women coming this way. Look at them legs. Fucking hell, they go all the way up.'

'I fucking told you,' Randall whispers.

'What's going on? Why they coming this way?' the man asks, unable to drag his eyes from the women.

'Hell, I don't know, but we're leaving right fucking now.'

'Leaving? You're having a laugh, aren't you? Have you seen them women?'

'Man, this ain't right. We're getting the fuck out of here.'

'Randy, you're on your own, mate, I'm staying right here.'

'I said we're going, motherfucker,' Randall snarls.

'Who put you in charge? Get fucked. I'm staying right here.'

'Man, I will beat you the fuck to death ...'

'Yeah, will ya now? And I'll shout my fucking head off and get all them people running this way ... Fuck off if you want, but I'm staying here.'

'This ain't right. This ain't mother-fucking right, something ... Fuck, this is fucked up. I'm going ... Who coming with me?'

The inmates stare at each other, several having whispered conversation. Colin steps close to Randall, showing his loyalty. Some others walk towards him, nodding and agreeing to come with him.

'Yeah, fuck off,' the man on the ground chuckles quietly,

'leave more for the rest of us. But I reckon if you're going, you do it now cos they're getting closer.'

'You dumb-asses, fucking crazy dumb-asses,' Randall growls.

'Yeah, you dumb–arses,' Colin says. Fifteen men join Randall as he marches off, building up to a light jog as he moves away from the corner. The rest of them stay behind the wall, licking their lips as the man on the ground whispers about the girls' long legs and tits bouncing about. The fifteen sense Randall's concern, the hardest man in the prison being spooked is enough for them to follow his lead. They run away, moving down the road, alongside the wall. A high fence on the other side keeps them funnelled. Randall leads them to the end of the fence, hastening them over a gate and into the undergrowth. They filter into the bushes and trees, moving stealthily back along the fence line to watch the remaining men hiding behind the wall.

The inmate left at the wall on his belly greedily watches the women walking towards him. The lust for sex growing inside. He goes quiet, ceasing the narration as his mouth dries up at the sight of the beautiful women. Long legs, full figures, perfect arses, and breasts straining against flimsy tops. Long hair cascading down elegant necks and slim shoulders, tanned skin, alabaster tones, and all of them looking even more alluring with sunglasses on.

Must be models. You'd never see women like this normally. Even the average Saturday night in the town centre wouldn't see such a group of stunning women all together. The inmate fixes his gaze on the woman in the centre and a step or two ahead of the others. Long, curly, blond hair that weaves and bobs as she walks, fine legs dressed in tight jeans, and a vest top. He finally looks past the girls, spotting the crowd disappearing from view into the prison gates. Shaking his head at the good fortune, not considering why the rest would be going into the prison, but locking his eyes back on the blond at the front.

Urgent whispers call out from behind him, inmates demanding to know what he can see. He doesn't reply, his tongue glued to the roof of his dry mouth. Swallowing nervously, he mutters something unintelligible. The men, impatient for an update, creep up behind him, stepping out to take a peek and standing still at the sight walking towards them. One by one, they move out, all of them struck dumb. Hands quickly smooth hair down, wipe blood away, and try to fix their filthy clothes straight.

'Dumb motherfuckers,' Randall mutters to himself from the safety of the undergrowth, lying low and staring through the chain link fence at the inmates as they put themselves on full view. Even now he realises something isn't right. The girls didn't flinch at the sight of the men stepping out from the side of the wall. A bunch of desperate men, covered in cuts and bruises, dressed in filthy prison clothes, and they didn't flinch, didn't look at each other, didn't break stride. Nothing.

April watches with interest as the men step out from behind the wall. Their foul stench of shit, piss, sweat, and blood had indicated the route they took, and now here they were. Big, hardened men all stepping out to stare at her and the infected women.

'Hi there,' she smiles, showing white, even teeth. The women all smile, all of them showing what appears to be genuine pleasure at finding the men there. This was a perfectly normal thing to happen, a good thing, a nice thing which gave them pleasure.

'Hi,' the inmate, who had been lying on his belly watching them, replies, his voice low and hoarse.

April smiles at them, looking from man to man as she silently counts. Thirty men and eight women. It will please Marcy greatly if she can turn these men without losses. They look tough, fresh cuts and bruises from fighting. A straightforward attack will incur losses; she must use their desire and lust against them.

'What's going on? I mean … what's happening?' the inmate asks. 'We heard something bad had happened.'

'It has,' April says sadly. 'A disease has wiped out millions of people.' She walks forward, smiling at the man, the expression on her face conflicting with the words she speaks. 'Millions have perished, societies have fallen, everyone is suffering. There's not enough food to go round, and dangerous people are forming tribes to take what they can.' She weaves between the men, smiling as they take in her form, eyeing her legs and arse. 'We need protection,' she continues. 'Those people down there are scared and afraid. We decided to come to the prisons and find some tough men to protect us.' She turns round, watching as the women copy her actions, all of them moving between the men, smiling at them coyly.

'Protection?' the man laughs at the thought of Randall running off.

'Yes,' April continues, her voice still flat but going unnoticed, 'and in exchange, you can have what you want.'

'What we want?' the inmate repeats.

'Yes,' she smiles at him. 'What you want … what you need … what you've missed …' her voice trails off. The man breathes deeply, his eyes misting over.

'Who … who is attacking you?' he asks slowly.

'Local men, gangs, but nothing like you, not as big and tough as you.'

'You've got nice tits,' an inmate sighs at the chest of a

woman straining against her top. She smiles at him, pushing her chest out as his mouth drops open.

'So, they sent you to ask us?' the first inmate asks.

'No,' April smiles, 'we volunteered.'

'Volunteered?' he asks, swallowing noisily.

'Yes, there's plenty more women in our group, but we said we'd come and ask you, maybe see if you needed convincing.'

'You must be desperate, then.'

'Very, very desperate,' she steps in close to him, her face inches from his. He stares at his own reflection in the sunglasses.

'I have an eye infection,' April says. 'They're very sore, but we can't get the medication as one of the gangs took it all ...' she slides her glasses off, showing the man her red, bloodshot eyes. He flinches from the sight, taking a quick intake of breath.

'Christ, love,' he says.

'I know ... I need the medicines, but no one will get it for me ... Will you get it for me?'

'Fucking right, we will,' he replies firmly.

'I can pay you in advance if you like.'

'Pay?'

'Yes, we can show our appreciation for your help ... show how grateful we are. You must all be very ...' she pauses for effect, '... frustrated after being in prison for so long.' She leans forward, gently pressing her lips against his. The surreal shock roots him to the spot. Surviving the carnage of the fight, breaking free, and now this ... The kiss sends shockwaves through his body, every other inmate staring with surprise at the gorgeous woman kissing the inmate on the lips.

They watch with open mouths as her hand drops to the

front of his trousers, kneading away while she presses her lips harder against his. Some of the quicker thinking men look at the other girls. They step closer to the men, leaning in to press their lips against the inmates.

The sexual tension ramps up as greedy hands start fumbling at the girls' breasts. The thirty men all standing round the girls, groping and squeezing as the girls move their mouths from man to man. Kissing hard, pushing saliva into their mouths. The groping means nothing to them. There is no feeling of disgust or repulsion. The foul taste and smell of the inmates' breath doesn't revolt the women. Instead, they fight their urge to bite, doing as willed and making sure they pushed their spit and drool into the men's mouths.

One of the inmates unzips himself, taking his penis out to start stroking it one-handed while pulling a girls top down to reveal her naked breast. More follow suit, taking their cocks in hand as they groped at the women. Some of them taking the girls hands to place on their stiffened members.

April, sensing the urgency of the man she was kissing, does what Marcy advised and gently bites into his lip. He jerks back with a glare in his eye, not as passive as Robbie. Wiping the blood from his mouth, he grabs her round the waist, pulling her in close to rub himself against her. She goes with it, content to wait for the effect to take hold.

'Bitch bit me,' another inmate snaps, slapping one of the girls across the face as he steps back.

'Fucking pussy,' another inmate laughs, helping the girl to her feet and taking over the kissing as he pushes her hand onto him. 'Come on, give me a stroke, darlin'. Yeah … that's it.'

The girls stay pliable, doing as bid, getting groped and

squeezed as the actions of the men got rougher. Their lust growing as they push against each other, pulling the girls' hands away from other men.

Randall watches. Getting sexually aroused at the sight while also being very worried. This shouldn't happen. Things like this don't happen.

The first inmate, the one bitten by April, lurches back. His hands clutching at the piercing pain shooting through his stomach.

'What's wrong?' April asks, watching as he staggers back, falling to the floor and writhing. The men look over with concern as another one drops down holding his midsection.

'What have you done?' April asks, staring at the men like they've done something wrong. They look at each other, some of them dropping down to help the injured inmates. Others take advantage of the distraction to get the girls' sole attention.

The inmates writhe on the ground, agonising pain ripping through their bodies. Another one drops, then another one. Randall stares with wide eyes, watching as the men drop to the ground. A few men still pay no attention and carry on groping at the girls, too heated and turned on to realise what's going on around them.

One by one, they drop. The first inmate breathes slower, his body fighting for life and giving up. He dies quietly, the pain preventing him from calling out. More die, the infection coursing through their systems. The women stand back, watching with plain faces as the men writhe and die.

Randall stares with morbid interest, watching as the first inmate to die starts twitching, like an electric current is being passed through him. He sits up, making Randall think he's alright. The man stands; his movements slow and awkward. The distance too great for Randall to see the eyes, but the motion of the man is stark. Clumsy and stumbling, like drunk or something.

Others start to twitch, doing the same as the first man. They too start sitting up, all of them copying the actions as they clamber to their feet. None of them speak, none of the girls say a word. They just stand and watch. As the last stands up, they all turn and walk off. No order or command given. Just an instant thing of them all turning to walk away. The inmates all walking with that slow, awkward shuffling motion.

Randall watches them walk away, knowing what he just saw but refusing to believe it.

CHAPTER FIFTEEN

'Do you understand what this means?' Marcy demands, staring hard at Reginald.

'Yes, of course,' he nods, his face looking shocked.

'We're not the disease. We're the cure.'

Her own words send her reeling. She looks at the vast crowd, the thousands of people stood watching her. Silent and dignified.

'Marcy, that is just one illness. It may not mean that all illnesses are … cured,' he suggests.

'Of course. But … I'm … okay. I mean. Did anyone else here require medication for anything?' Several hands lift up, still abiding by her instruction to use hands instead of voices.

'You, what did you have?'

'Asthma,' the woman replies.

'And you had medication for it?'

'Yes, Marcy.'

'Everyday?'

'Yes, Marcy.'

'What about now?'

'I don't know, Marcy. I was turned last night.'

'Too soon,' Reginald says.

'Okay, you what did you have?'

'Schizophrenia,' the man replies in the same flat tone.

'And you had medication for that?'

'Yes, Marcy.'

'How long have you been turned?'

'I was turned yesterday morning.'

'What happened if you didn't take the medication?'

'Nothing at first. The effects would take a few days to show.'

'Again, too soon,' Reginald repeats.

'Can you tell if there's any difference?' she asks the man.

'I feel fine, Marcy.'

'Different to before?'

'Marcy, that is not a fair question,' Reginald says. 'We all feel different now.'

'Okay. You, what did you have?' she asks the last man stood with his arm up.

'Antidepressants.'

'Discounted, that is a behavioural issue that takes time to manifest,' Reginald says. 'There are too many variables here. We could all carry a different strain of it. Darren could have had something different to what you have. You could be different to me. Hmmm. But that said. We do have the same infection giving us the urge to infect more hosts. So, perhaps yes, the infection could mutate in some way with each individual it passes through, but ultimately, it would be the same infection, although, I hasten to add, this is pure conjecture.'

'But he said he doesn't have diabetes anymore.'

'He may well have said that, but only time will tell if indeed he does not suffer from a diabetic attack.'

'Darren had a large group with him; none of them dropped from anything other than the injuries that were inflicted.'

'Be that as it may, we cannot form a judgement based on what *we think* we know.'

'And I suppose we're still in the early days. All of these have only been turned since yesterday,' Marcy adds.

'Exactly, I am sure that what you are saying is correct, that the infection somehow cures other diseases, but we cannot prove it, nor can we say for certain that is the case.'

'That gate's open too,' Marcy says, peering up the road to the entrance to the mainstream prison. 'Can you smell that?'

'I can indeed smell that, Marcy,' Reginald replies. The scent of blood hangs in the air, fresh blood and from somewhere close by, a strong smell mixed with the stench of the living. Reaching the open gate, they pause as Marcy examines the area.

'It's coming from that way too,' she says, indicating up the road. She leads a small group inside the gates, following the smell round the corner of the building to the concrete area where the bodies of the recently fallen inmates lay.

'Fresh,' Marcy looks down at a corpse. The blood still wet on the body, and sticky pools on the ground.

'Very,' Reginald nods. 'It would appear they have broken out of their confinement using that hole in the wall, had a fight, following which the victors have gone up the road.'

'You should have been a detective,' Marcy says drily. 'How on earth did you deduce that.'

'From the hole in the wall and the bodies on the ground and–'

'I was being sarcastic, Reggie.'

'Reginald, and I noted your sarcasm and chose to ignore it.'

'April, the inmates must be close. Take the girls and find them.'

'Yes, Marcy.'

Marcy moves from body to body, examining the wounds on each one. Her head shaking at the violence they have wrought on each other.

'And they think we're the violent ones, the bad species that needs wiping out,' she says out loud. 'I would bet my life that not one zombie has –'

'Ahem,' Reginald coughs. 'They're not zombies. They're not dead.'

'Yes, okay, not one living challenged has turned on another like this.'

'This one is alive,' one of the male communicators states. Marcy heads over, stepping round and over the bodies. She looks down at the body, a large built male that had been bleeding heavily from a stomach wound. She drops down, probing at the stomach of the unconscious male.

'Stabbed.' She grips a small plastic handle and pulls quickly. The object sucks noisily as it retracts from the skin. Holding it up, she looks at the item. A standard toothbrush, with the handle filed to a sharp point.

Standing up, she watches the body for several seconds, looking at the shallow rise and fall of the man's chest. His face looks beaten and bloodied, nose broken, swollen eye and mouth. She pushes her foot into his side, nudging the body.

'What are you doing?' Reginald asks. She ignores him and nudges harder, driving her foot into his ribs which causes no reaction. Dropping down again, she opens his eyes, peering at his pupils. She leans back and lightly presses her finger into the stomach wound.

'He couldn't fake that,' she says as he shows no reaction.

'Fake what exactly?' Reginald asks.

'Fake being unconscious. My finger is inside his wound now.'

'And precisely why would he fake being unconscious?'

'No reason. I just wanted to be sure … So you agree, this man is definitely unconscious.'

'Yes, it would appear that he is, although again, I am, and neither are you, a medically trained professional.'

She leans over his stomach, pulling his shirt back to reveal the pasty, hairy skin of his torso. Hovering over the puckered wound, she draws a mouthful of saliva and lets it fall in, holding her hair back with one hand to prevent it getting covered in his blood.

Standing back, she watches with interest. The man stays the same as before, with no discernible change. After a minute, his breathing becomes laboured, slowing until his chest ceases to rise.

They watch patiently, eyes fixed on the corpse. Marcy giving a big grin when it starts twitching, and a few seconds later, the infected sits up and opens his eyes.

'Can you speak?' Marcy asks as the infected stares at her without the gleam of intelligence in his eyes. 'I'll take that as a no, then.'

'Marcy, I hate to be the bearer of bad news, but that experiment did not prove anything other than you were able to turn an unconscious man. He may well have regained consciousness on his own.'

'But it does show an element of recovery. His brain had shut down from his injuries … Isn't that what happens when you become unconscious? The brain shuts down?'

'I can only answer that I think that to be the case, but again, I am unable to answer confidently.'

'But the infection brought him out of it.'

'After killing him first and then restarting him.'

'He's not a car, Reggie,' Marcy sighs.

'I agree the infection is a wonderful thing. My intrinsic desire is to love the infection and you along with it, but the intellectual part of me knows that I am now programmed to believe that … as are all of them.' He casts his arm at the infected gathered nearby and the rest shuffling in through the gates.

Marcy falls quiet, absorbing his words. Reginald was right. She wanted to believe in the possibility that the infection cured everything, but she knew caution was necessary. The infection was powerful enough to mask pain. The simple overriding command was to take more hosts, at any cost. But therein lies the problem. What happens when the last human is taken? What then? The infection could keep the bodies going for some time, maybe weeks, months, or even a year or two, but without food and water, the body will perish.

Other species could be taken. They could start on the animal kingdom, but they too would turn on each other until they are as exhausted and depleted as the human race.

The infection is finite. In the current state, it can never achieve the ultimate objective of survival simply because it will eventually exhaust all other hosts. And when the last living creature is turned, be that a cat, dog, fish, or any creature, then it reaches extinction.

Doomed from the outset. Never destined to succeed.

With that in mind, the thought of the effort to keep going and turn more hosts seems futile. What's the point? We're all fucked anyway.

No, there has to be another way. There has to be a reason for this and a solution.

'Marcy, April has returned with the inmates,' Reginald says softly, not wishing to interrupt her meditations.

She nods, still staring into the distance. Existence is suffering, the futility of it now seems absurd. To keep going, to take the humans, and turn them just so they can die. That isn't right. But her instinct is screaming inside that there is another way. She is the key, and any others like her, Reginald for instance or Darren, they all show there can be another way. The infection has allowed her to keep her own personality and thought processes. Reginald too. There must be others like her around the country and across the world. The infection must be advancing others to the same level she is. If the infection can do this, can evolve to the extent that the host retains normalcy, and in doing so, it can put the body into a perfect state of being, killing off any other infections, diseases or viruses, then why shouldn't the hosts evolve further? Become more human, eat, drink, procreate, and continue life as before. But without the suffering. Without the disease. Without the violence, jealousy, and hatred.

'We're going,' she says out loud. Striding towards the gate, she notices the freshly taken inmates and the sorry state they're in. Glancing back at the bodies on the ground, she shakes her head with disgust. 'Animals ...' she mutters as she walks past. The inmates sense her displeasure, dropping their heads as a feeling of shame blooms inside them. Reginald stalks behind Marcy, shaking his head and tutting at them. The communicators follow, also casting looks of dissatisfaction. The prisoners file in behind them, merging with the general crowd as Marcy turns to head up the road, away from the main road.

'Where are we going? The main road is the other direction,' Reginald asks.

'The prison estates are this way.'

'I understand,' Reginald nods, sensing she has more to say.

'Reggie,' she starts, her voice slow as she thinks her words out loud, 'we've controlled the urges to, you know, attack and be all frenzied. I mean. You and I and the others I control. They're only doing what's needed to pass the infection now and not tearing people apart. And my skin feels healthy. I mean. I just feel *healthy*. What I mean. God. I don't even know what I mean. But it's like the infection has withdrawn to a background thing maybe. Does that make sense? What if we find a way of doing that to all of the hosts? So we can, you know, like harness the healing power and whatever but not the bad things.'

'Like eating people?'

'Yes, that for a start,' she smiles at his quip. 'How would we do that?'

'How? Well. To be blunt, Marcy. We can't do anything like it. We'd need scientists and facilities, which would mean making contact with humans and allowing tests to be conducted ...'

'But all the scientists and doctors are either dead or already turned. Unless ...'

'Unless what?' Reginald asks.

'Howie said something to me. It's stuck in my mind.'

'You met him?'

'No, just a snatched conversation while Darren was trying to kill him. Anyway, he said they had doctors and equipment and that seeing as I could talk, they might be able to find a cure. He offered to take me in.'

'Was it perhaps a trick so you would present yourselves in order to be killed?'

'No,' she shakes her head. 'He meant it. If I had walked up those steps and surrendered, he would have taken me in. Darren kept saying Howie was so good and, like, self-righteous that it made him want to puke. But honestly. Even then, in that stairwell when we were throwing everything at him, he spoke with kindness and humility, and his lads were doing everything they could to wind Darren up,' she smiles with the memory. 'I shouldn't laugh, but looking back, it was rather comical.'

They turn the corner, Reginald stopping to stare down at the ground. 'Excuse me, Marcy,' he apologises. 'Who left their knickers here?' He turns to the horde behind him, looking at April stood in front of her girls.

One of them steps forward, a gorgeous brunette wearing a knee-length summer dress.

'Put them back on, please,' Reginald sniffs. 'We may be the scourge of mankind, but we shall not wonder about without our underwear on. That is not proper. Yes, well done, pick them and– Oh, my word, young lady, I did not mean you to hitch your skirt up and put them on now.' Reginald turns away, blushing from the woman pulling her dress up. 'Good grief. Now, what were you saying? Although, I fear I have somewhat guessed where this is leading.'

'I just told you. Howie told me they have doctors and equipment inside the fort ...'

'This being the same fort with the big walls, where Darren led tens of thousands of living challenged and got them all killed? The same fort with the thousands of people living inside it, with weapons and guns ...?'

'Yes, Reginald, that same fort.'

'Marcy, are you suggesting we take our thousands of infected hosts to this fort? They'll kill us on sight.'

'If we turn up on mass, they'll slaughter us, but not all of us need to go. Both you and I are able to communicate fully ...'

'We might not feel pain, Marcy but we can still die, and they'll kill us on sight,' he repeats.

'Not if we do it the right way. We're going to Fort Spitbank, Reggie. That is final.'

CHAPTER SIXTEEN

Across the road, on the other side of the high chain-link fence and deep within the undergrowth, several men lay covered from view, watching and listening.

They had discussed what they had seen, with the girls seemingly making all the inmates fall to the floor, then get back up, and follow them.

Heated, whispered conversations took place with theories being put forward, ideas banded about, and their fear evident. Randall let them speak for a while, thinking furiously and trying to make sense of what he'd seen.

They were still in situ when the large crowd came out of the prison gates and walked briskly up the road, towards them. Spreading out and dropping low, they once again lay silently as the crowd reached the corner. Randall straining his ears as their conversation drifted into hearing range– someone called Darren and Howie, a big fort with thousands of people living in it, doctors, and equipment. These people were infected with a virus. That must have been what made the inmates fall down and then get back up like robots.

Randall focussed sharper as he heard mentions of weapons and guns. A fort with thousands of people, doctors and weapons, and guns. Someplace that had already killed tens of thousands of the infected people.

He listened carefully, trying to understand where this fort was, imagining a stockade with chopped trees forming a perimeter, men on horsebacks like something from a western movie.

The name came through clearly, Fort Spitbank. Then they moved off, the whole of them walking quickly away down the road, towards the prison estates.

Randall keeps his men still for long minutes, waving his hand at them and glaring until sure the people were well gone. Only then did he move out, creeping slowly from the bushes to work his way along the fence and over the gate.

Motioning his men, he takes them in the opposite direction, pressing his finger against his lips with a threatening look, leaving them in no doubt that he expects them to be silent.

He leads them back down the road, jogging past the prison, over the main road, and into the gardens of a house opposite. Still pressing them to stay quiet, they make their way from garden to garden, moving away from the prison. Spying an open back door, he sends two in to check the house, waiting quietly until they return, announcing its empty.

Inside, the fifteen men go straight for the sinks in the kitchen, toilet, and bathroom, using cups, glasses, and hands to drink cool water. Taking turns to wash the worse of the blood and filth off. Cupboards are rooted through. Whatever food was left is devoured by the starving inmates. The meagre supplies in the house only serve to whet their appetites.

'What was all that about?' an inmate asks the men stood crowded in the kitchen and hallway.

'You heard that woman. She said they were zomb–' someone starts to reply.

'Fuck off! Don't be so fucking stupid.'

'You saw what they did to the blokes having a go on them girls.'

'That woman said it. She said they're infected or diseased, or whatever ...'

'Zombies don't fucking speak, you cunt.'

'How the fuck do you know what they can do? This ain't the fucking movies.'

'They had the inmates in the crowd. I fucking saw 'em stood there looking as dumb as cunts.'

'Who the fuck is Darren and this cunt Howie? What the fuck is going on?'

'Shut the fuck up and let me think, you motherfuckers,' Randall snaps harshly. His voice cutting through the multitude of voices as the discussion builds.

'Yeah, shut the fuck up and let Randy think,' Colin adds, glaring at the others.

'That means you too, dumbass.'

'Yeah, that means you too– Oh, you mean me? Sorry, Randy.'

'You heard that, bitch,' Randall growls. 'You motherfucking saw what they did to the prisoners ...'

'Yeah, but Randy ... This is fucking nuts,' an inmate replies, his voice rising with panic.

'Get a grip, motherfucker, that bitch said they infected. She said they zombies ... All them mother-fucking people stood there quietly and shit, not moving, not speaking, no weapons, no guns, no knives, or shit ... and talking about a mother-fucking fort.'

'That explains where the officers all went, the phones not working, computers offline ...' another inmate says.

'Is it just here, on the island?' another asks.

'Can't be,' someone answers. 'They would have sent someone over by now.'

'Fort Spitbank is on the mainland,' an older inmate says.

'You know this place?' Randall turns to the man, a grizzled, big man with a long, grey beard and old, faded tattoos over his hands and arms.

'Yeah,' he nods, voice deep and slow, 'on the coast, few miles from Portsmouth.'

'What is it?'

'Some old fort,' the man replies, 'used to fight the French or Spanish years ago.'

'How long ago?' Randall asks.

'Hundred and fifty years or somethin'.'

'Shit, motherfucker, you been there?'

'Years back,' the ex-biker nods.

'This ain't no interrogation, motherfucker. Quit giving short answers.'

'What?' the bearded man shrugs.

'Holy fucking shit, you must be the dumbest motherfucker I ever met. What's your name?'

'Harry.'

'Harry, you look more like grizzly mother-fucking Adams. What's this fort like?'

'Big.'

'Quit doing that, motherfucker! I swear I'll kill you. You hear me? I will fucking kill you ...'

'It's big, got big walls, sea on one side ... old buildings inside.'

'Do the military use it?'

'No.'

'Harry, I swear to almighty I will ...'

'Open to the public, visitors go there, old cannons ...'

'Well, thank mother-fucking you,' Randall glares, 'if this shit is on the mainland, then this shit is everywhere. That bitch Marcy said this motherfucker Howie killed tens of thousands. We go to this fort ...'

'They ain't gonna let a bunch of inmates in, Randy.'

'We ain't gonna be inmates. We gonna be normal Joes, coming to warn them about this bitch Marcy planning to attack them ... We mention Howie and Darren, and they let us right in.'

'But that Marcy said she weren't gonna attack 'em. She said she wanted to talk to 'em.'

'They don't know that, motherfucker. All we gotta do is get in; then, we see what the fuck is going down ...'

'There'll be loads of pussy in there and booze ... but armed men too.'

Randall stares at the men throwing comments at him, a desperate bunch that look like exactly what they are–hardened criminals. 'Fuck that. Them motherfuckers don't know who the fuck we are. They think they're tough motherfuckers? Try spending ten fucking years in that fucking place and then say you're a tough motherfucker. We get inside and see how the mother-fucking ground lies. How the fuck do we get there, Harry?'

He shrugs, huge shoulders lifting up a few inches to drop back down. 'Don't know.'

'Dumb motherfucker,' Randall sighs. 'Which one of you bitches knows how to get there?'

Another inmate steps forward, lifting his hand as though in a classroom. 'North, Randy, we go north and get boats across to the mainland.'

'Come on then, motherfuckers. We going north ...' He

threatens the men to stay quiet, leading them out the back door and across the gardens, moving steadily away from the prisons. With the new plan in place, Randall keeps them away from the town, skirting the edge and keeping to the side streets. The short journey into the urbanisation brings home the devastation they had suspected. Bodies litter the streets, decomposing corpses left in the scorching sun and crawling with flies and maggots. Dark, scabbed, dried pools of blood smeared across the pavement and road, cars abandoned with doors open, windows of houses smashed in, and doors hanging off.

At the roundabout, they pause, looking over the flat ground to the end of the barricade at the base of the High Street and the wide gap smashed through it. Not a sign of a living person, no vehicles moving about, no army or soldiers. The quietness both oppresses and provides some comfort. The comfort from the knowledge that they've done something very bad. Broken out of a prison and killed other men in doing so, but no one is chasing them, no helicopters or police with dogs.

Randall pushes them on, determined to be away from the centre and the huge crowd of people following Marcy and that little guy with the glasses. He keeps replaying the conversation he heard, the words they used–infected, zombies, not feeling pain, battle, fights, cures, forts.

Now, street by street, and seeing the reality of it for himself makes him understand this is happening, this is real. A sense of excitement grows in his stomach, a sense that suddenly the power has shifted. Dangerous men that can fight and kill were locked away. Now though, they'll be a valued resource, warriors that can protect the rich. People will be vulnerable and frightened. This is a situation they can use to their advantage. Only fifteen men, but these fifteen are worth fifty normal pussies and had already proved they're willing to kill to survive.

The heat becomes almost unbearable. The men strip their upper clothing off–defined black bodies, pale, muscular torsos, tattoos everywhere. Randall realises the sight of them would scare anyone, the prison blues too distinctive, the dried blood and dirt still clinging to their skin.

In a quiet street, he stops the men, sending them into the houses, two by two, to find clothes and get washed up. Staring with a huge grin as they come back out, skin scrubbed and raw, hair wetted down and dressed in a variety of clothing. After seeing them all in prison clothing for so long, not one of them looks comfortable wearing normal garments.

Jeans, trousers, vests, t-shirts, shirts, shoes, trainers, sandals. They all look and feel self-conscious. Harry wearing a pair of baggy shorts with a Hawaiian tropical-coloured, short-sleeved shirt contrasting against his long, grey beard and tied back, greying hair.

Randall, along with some of the other bigger men, has to search several houses to find suitable clothes that fit them, unwilling to settle for the shorts and tropical clothing of Harry.

Prison clothes ditched, skin washed, the smell of stale sweat now gone, bellies filled with food from cupboards, and thirst quenched from cold water taps, and each of them with a sharp kitchen knife stuffed into their waistbands, they move on. Street by street, they see the signs of devastation, not realising they're tracking the reverse route of Marcy and seeing the signs of her passage everywhere.

After an hour of trudging, the tiredness starts to take effect. The new clothes now sodden with sweat and clinging to skin. Randall again calls them to a stop. Spying vehicles parked on driveways, he sends the men into the houses to find keys. It takes several houses, but three cars are found and started. Fifteen men cramming into them, with Randall in the lead vehicle sat in the leather passenger seat of a new Mercedes; the air-con on full blast. Harry crammed in the back with another two inmates, shoulders digging into each other but feeling the relief of the icy cool air.

'Which way is it?' Colin asks, seeing two main roads branching off from the roundabout a few miles out of the main town.

'Any of you fuckers know?' Randall twists round, looking at Harry and the other two shaking their heads. 'Dumb motherfuckers,' he mutters, 'they both go north. Choose one, and for your sake, you better pray it's the right one.'

'Okay, Randy,' Colin grins, navigating the roundabout and taking the left road. The other vehicles follow behind them; the speed recklessly high as the sense of freedom permeates into the men from the years of containment.

The vehicle immediately behind the Mercedes pulls out to the left, accelerating harshly as it prepares for the overtake; the inmate driver grinning like crazy behind the wheel.

'Don't let that motherfucker own you,' Randall shouts, 'put your foot down.' The third car comes into the play, pushing the two in front faster through the wide road, curving gently through the fields and meadows. The roar of the engines splitting the peace apart as the three cars power along. The Mercedes holding lead, drifting into the middle of the road, jigging the wheel left and right to block the path of the two behind.

The men scream in competition, sticking fingers up at each other, and opening windows to shout abuse. Randall bellows at Colin, shouting threats of instant death if he lets either of the other two cars get past them. The speed increases as the driving becomes erratic, the pressure to win builds with each passing second. None of them knowing where they're going but lost in the moment of watching the bushes and trees fly past the windows.

The fields end abruptly as they race into tree-lined streets, with wide pavements and big Victorian houses set back behind large front gardens.

'Hey, hold up. What the fuck is that place?' Randall shouts as they negotiate a long corner, flashing past a set of high metal gates. Colin slams the brakes on, the car fishtailing down the road, the men in the back slamming into the seats as the momentum propels them forward. The following vehicles narrowly avoid collision as they anchor on the brakes, swerving round the Mercedes. All three vehicles come to rest, engines ticking over noisily as they look back at the long, black skid marks scored onto the surface of the road.

'Turn round and go back,' Randall orders. Colin complies, slowly turning in a wide arc to start going back up the road. The other two vehicles move in, forming a lane between them. The Mercedes slows to a stop, the cars drawing level.

'What are those big fucking gates for?' Randall shouts to the other vehicles. They shake heads, answering they didn't even see the gates. He tells them to follow as Colin pulls away, taking it easy and giving them time to catch up.

Back up the road, they head towards the long corner. The gates coming into view ahead of them. Huge wrought iron things, well over ten feet high and painted high gloss black and gold, with a strange motif across the front. A solid, high wooden fence runs off both sides of the gate, bordering grounds seen through the gate bars.

Randall gets out the vehicle which stops just a few yards in front of the gates, sauntering over to look through. Wide grounds with big, manicured lawns, square cut hedges, flowers beds, and orchards.

'What the fuck is this place?' he asks the men gathering behind him.

'Osborne House,' one of them reads from a sign set into the fence further along.

'Queen Victoria's old house,' another says from memory.

'The Queen lived here?' Randall asks in surprise. 'I thought she was in Buckingham Palace.'

'Old queen,' Harry explains bluntly. 'Years ago.'

'Who lives here now?' he asks.

'Says here English Heritage own it,' an inmate reads from the sign. 'Says it's open to the public.'

'Public? Hell, we're the mother-fucking public now, my bitches,' Randall grins. 'They gonna have some fine food in a queen's house, some fine mother-fucking food.'

'Closed,' Harry says, staring at the high gates.

'Fuck that shit,' Randall walks to the gates, examining the thick chain and padlock. 'Any of you motherfuckers done a ram-raid before?' He gets grinning nods from several men, one of them running back to get behind the wheel of the Mercedes, backing it up while motioning the others to move out the way.

They scatter quickly, jogging from the gates as the Mercedes roars to life. The powerful engine screaming as the driver surges towards the gates.

'Holy shit,' Randall laughs as the vehicle rams into the

solid metal gates. An ear-splitting boom, coupled with a mighty wrenching sound, fills the air as the gates burst open. The front of the Mercedes crumples, airbags deploy, whacking the driver in the face. He loses control, his foot still pressed down on the accelerator as the car propels down the driveway, slamming into a wooden guard building next to a single-arm barrier. The ages old guard hut bursts apart, wooden timbers flying in all directions. The uneven ground causes the Mercedes to flip onto one side, still ploughing forward onto the lawn, gouging the perfect turf with deep trenches.

'Holy motherfucker,' Randall laughs maniacally as the men pour through the now open gates and see the Mercedes coming to rest on one side. They jog forward, laughing and smiling as the sound of screaming reaches them.

Getting to the car, they look through the smashed windows at the driver slumped over to the passenger side, a long-bladed knife blade buried deep into his stomach, blood pumping out. His nose freshly broken from the airbag and streaming blood down his face.

They push the car over, bouncing it down onto all four wheels. The man inside screaming louder from the movement. Rough hands open doors and drag the man out. His hands clutching the knife buried in his gut.

'You stupid motherfucker,' Randall shakes his head with disgust at the man. 'Any fool knows you put your seatbelt on, dumbass.'

'Argh, fuck, it hurts ...' the man gasps, his breath coming hard and fast.

'You are fucked, man. You gonna die now from your own dumb-ass stupidity,' Randall says.

'No ... no, just get me some help ...'

'Help? What fucking help? Ain't no fucking doctors now, you dumb-ass ... You are fucked up.'

'We can't just leave him,' one of the inmates says.

'Fuck that,' Randall drops down. Taking a grip of the knife handle, he wrenches it out of the wound. The man screams in agony as fresh blood spurts out. Randall pushes him down, holding him in place with one strong foot. He stabs down, driving the point of the knife deep into the man's throat, slicing, and hacking the windpipe apart. The man thrashes violently which just worsens the action of the knife in his neck. Gargling, sputtering, he dies slowly, eyes staring as his hands grab out at the inmates who jump back out of reach.

'Dumb motherfucker,' Randall steps back, throwing the knife down as he looks down at the fresh corpse.

'We leaving him?' someone asks.

'Go ahead and bury him ... I don't give a fuck,' Randall replies, turning towards the lane and walking off. The men shrug at each other and fall into step behind the American.

The death is quickly forgotten as the big house comes into view. Low whistles and exclamations sound out at the sight of the palatial building. Huge and sprawling, surrounded by perfectly cut lawns with laser-straight lines. Old-style gothic fountains dot the grounds. Built into the surroundings so well, they seem part of the natural gardens, organic almost.

The now fourteen men spread out into a long line, all of them taking care not to step in front of the alpha male Randall. They stare at the high windows, the arched doorways, the turreted architecture, but the splendour of the view is only marginal in comparison to the expectation they have of what's inside.

'Spotted,' Harry mutters. Randall follows his

outstretched hand pointing at the ground floor patio-style doors leading out onto the gardens. Curtains moving, silhouettes of people inside, faces appearing to stare out.

The inmates cut across the lawn, walking a straight line towards the main house and ignoring the many low-rise outbuildings dotting the grounds. Crossing the tarmacked road, they enter into a gravelled area with a large, circular sculpted marble central section and the main house recessed back from the large wings.

Their feet crunch the gravel, the combined steps forming a cascading noise that bounces round the enclosure from the high sides of the buildings.

The main doors ahead of them open to reveal an older man dressed in a checked shirt, the sleeves rolled up above the elbow, green corduroy trousers, and a ruddy, balding head. A long-barrelled shotgun rests across the crook of his arm. He stands still, watching the men. The doors close behind him.

Randall keeps his eyes locked on the sentry. His body language and posture portraying his intentions perfectly, stoic and solid. As they get closer, Randall watches his eyes cast along the line, taking in the sight of the hard men walking towards him. Only fourteen of them, but their size and appearance give the effect of there being many more.

'Help you?' the man calls out. He closes the shotgun. Not an aggressive act, just a subtle motion that resonates with a clear click as the barrels slot into place. Randall comes to a stop. Keeping his face plain, he stares back at the man, sizing him up.

'We need food,' Randall replies.

'Where have you come from?'

'Old man, you asked a question, and I answered you, but do not mother-fucking think for one second I am your bitch to stand here in this mother-fucking heat and be fucking interrogated,' Randall's voice grows in volume and aggression as he speaks. 'Now, do you have food?'

The man blanches at the unsuppressed aggression of the huge black man stood in front of him, his arms bulging with muscle, thick veins standing proud on the skin. The other men looking every inch as frightening, with swollen mouths, bruised eyes. The white men amongst them look oddly pale, like they've been away from the summer sun. Exposed arms and necks reveal a plethora of tattoos.

Other than the infected, every survivor's worst nightmare just arrived. The old man knows which way this will go. One shotgun with two shots. The intent on them is clear, the sick grins and knowing smiles.

'We got food. If we give it to you, will you go?' he replies in a shaky voice, wishing now he'd let one of the younger men come out who might have portrayed less fear than him.

'We'll go when we're mother-fucking ready to go. Stand out the way, old man, before someone hurts you.' Randall strides at him with not a flinch as the shotgun lifts. The inmates follow suit, walking straight at the door. The old man's hands sway as he tracks the men. Not one of them flickers. The power is with them. He couldn't pull the trigger if he tried, and they know it.

His shoulders slump; the shotgun lowers to the ground. Breathing a sad sigh, he steps to the side, watching as the grinning black man with the black beard walks past him and opens the door. The inmates file past him, each one of them glaring with violence at the old man. The last one to pass makes a quick lunging motion, laughing as the old man wilts back with a start.

'Look at this,' Randall stands in the central hall with hands on hips, wearing black jeans with a tight, black t-shirt.

He casts his gaze at the opulence of the interior. 'Now this mother-fucking beats the place we had.' The men burst out laughing, sniggering as they too look in wonder at the furnishings.

'Who are you?' An old woman steps out from a doorway, followed by more scared faces. Young and old, all of them looking pale and drawn. A couple of them still wearing English Heritage uniform from working the night duty the day the world fell.

'We,' he stares at the elegant, old lady, fixing her with a grin, 'are convicts just escaped from the local prison. We're hungry, and we're horny,' he replies. Something about the grace of the old woman, her grey hair swept up into a tight bun, firm mouth, and intelligent eyes, stops him from cussing.

'We can feed you, but as for the other ...'

'For the other ma'am,' the American drops back into old habits of addressing an older woman, 'we'll take what we're not given.'

'I see,' she drops her gaze to the floor; a sadness comes over her. 'I would offer myself, but I rather think I am not what you desire.'

'You'll do for me, love,' one of the inmates says, getting a few cheap laughs.

'Shut your mother-fucking mouth,' Randall explodes, everyone within the hallway jumping at the sound of his voice. 'If I hear one of you motherfuckers cussing in front of this woman, I will fucking slit your fucking throat and drink your fucking blood.' He turns back to the woman, fighting to bring his temper back under control. 'I apologise for my associates, ma'am.'

'I implore you, a man of clear morals,' she pleads with

hands clasped together as though in prayer, 'to take what food you need and leave us.'

'Oh ,we'll take the food ... and anything else we want, and then maybe ... if you're lucky ... we'll leave. You boy, come here,' Randall looks directly at a thin-built teenage boy, standing in the doorway of a room, watching with wide eyes full of fear. 'I said come here, boy,' Randall growls. 'Come here, or I will come and mother-fucking get you,' he screams when the boy doesn't budge.

'Leave him alone,' the old woman pleads.

'Grandma, my decency towards you has a limit. I may choose not to cuss at you, but I will stick this knife in your face.'

'Why do you want the boy?' A woman steps into view, stepping quickly to shield the boy behind her.

'Who the fuck are you? His mamma?' Randall takes in her shapely figure. An older woman but well maintained. He nods in approval, the leer evident on his face.

'Aunt ...I'm his aunt. His mother didn't make it.'

'She dead? Hell, bitch, just say it ... Ain't no good hiding it from the boy. Hey, boy ... your mamma is dead, you hear that? Get tough and deal with it or curl up and fuck yourself.' He laughs at himself, a big, hearty sound that fills the echoing chamber. Inmates behind him grin sickeningly. 'How she die?'

The aunt stiffens, holding herself straight with dignity. 'The things took her.'

'The mother-fucking *things* took her. You hear that, boys? The mother-fucking *things* took his mamma, and now his sexy-ass aunt is taking care of him. Man, I wish I had an aunt like you when I was a boy.'

'Just leave the boy alone, please. He's suffered enough ... We all have,' the aunt says softly.

'Suffered? You wanna hear what suffering is? Suffering is being cooped up in a mother-fucking English prison with people talking in accents I don't even know what they are. Ain't no one gonna touch a hair on your boy's head. I give you my word on that, lady, but you ... well, you gotta make sure my boys are kept busy.'

'I've heard enough. Get out. All of you, get out now,' the old man barks, holding the shotgun pointing at Randall. Silence slams in the elegant hallway as everyone turns to look at him. The inmates bursting out laughing at the sight of the old codger trembling with anger.

'You gonna shoot me, old man?' Randall asks with a grin. 'Go ahead, shoot me,' he adds, spreading his arms out wide, 'come on now, you motherfucker, fire that piece.'

'I'm not joshing now, young man. Come on, all of you, just get out.'

'Arthur,' the old woman says in a warning tone.

'No, Mildred, I won't stand by and listen to this ... These men are leaving right now.'

'Arthur,' Randall seizes on the name, 'you gonna shoot that thing or what, homeboy? Cos you know, don't you ... that you holding a shotgun filled with pellets that will spread and just about put holes in every mother-fucking thing stood here ... But you know that, don't you, Arthur? Hell, even Mildred here can see that, you dumb-ass mother-fucking dumbass.'

'Well, I can just as easy shoot one of them,' Arthur says, swivelling his aim to the inmates stood watching him.

'Them? Go ahead. I don't give a fuck about them,' Randall laughs. 'Hell, you got two shots, old man, and there's over a dozen of us. We'll kill every one of you, dumb sons o' bitches.'

Arthur freezes, panic setting in again. He wants to do

something; he should do something. This shouldn't be happening. Men always panic and do what the man holding the gun says, but these men aren't doing that. They're mocking him. His finger twitches, an involuntary action caused by fear clenching his muscles, contracting the digit of the finger extended over the trigger. The shotgun booms with a deafening roar. One of the inmates, taken off his feet and slammed into the staircase, loses most of his upper body from the force of the pellets. Women scream, the inmates starburst, diving all directions. Randall stands with a shocked expression, not quite believing what he just saw.

Arthur, panicking at what he just did, drops the shotgun to the floor. It lands with a thud, the vibration triggering the second barrel which fires at the front door, bursting a big hole through the antique door.

Harry is there within two strides, one big hand gripping Arthur by the throat and pushing him back against the now ruined door. Arthur is lifted up, his feet dangling helplessly a few inches of the floor. Harry grips his knife, stares into the old man's eyes, and sticks the blade deep through his stomach. The action is quick, a deep thrust that buries the blade up to the hilt.

Mildred screams, the shock causing her to feint and fall to the floor. Harry twists the knife, jerking the handle to one side. A spume of blood pumps out, coating the thick hair on Harry's hand and wrist. A reedy gurgle comes from Arthur, his windpipe compressed so much that barely any air escapes.

Harry jerks the knife back and drops Arthur to the floor. Inmates surge in, lashing at the poor man with feet. Kicking and stamping as he wails and cries on the floor, desperately trying to curl into the foetal position. The aunt grabs the boy, pushing him away and telling him to run. Everyone else, the scared survivors of the apocalypse who've safely hidden in this luxurious setting, start running.

The inmates beat Arthur to death, his face and body pulverised by their heavy feet. Randall twists round and sees the aunt ushering the boy away. He lunges and grabs the back of her hair, wrenching with a violent twist that sends her hurtling to the floor.

'Run,' she screams at the boy. He hesitates and starts back, screaming at Randall to leave his aunt alone. Randall lashes out, a back hand that slams into the boy's face, breaking his nose. The boy flies back, smashing his head into the wall. He slumps down unconscious as blood pours from his nose.

The aunt screams, fighting valiantly to her feet and lashing out at Randall. He laughs demonically, enjoying the thrill of the violence and not paying any attention as the inmates scatter off chasing the survivors, whooping and crying out with joy as they chase their prey down.

The aunt flails her arms at Randall, smacking him in the chest and head. Her blows go unnoticed as Randall grips the front of her shirt and pulls it down. She backs away from him, her hands desperately trying to push her shirt back up and cover her modesty. He stalks her, an evil grin spreading across his face at the sight of the flesh on display.

She backs into a wall, her eyes flicking to the boy who looks like he's coming round, a low moaning escaping from his lips, and his head slowly lifting.

'Okay ... okay,' she gasps as Randall turns to look at the lad, 'okay, whatever you want, but please not here ...'

He looks back at her. The grin still wide, showing his, big white teeth. She staggers a couple of steps to the side, her hands groping the wall to feel for an open door.

'In here ... please,' she begs. He stays still, staring at her, not speaking. His eyes casually drift back to the boy as he lifts the knife up.

Crying out, she lifts her hands away, letting the ripped shirt fall open. 'Here, in here … please,' she begs. Tears stream down her face as her trembling hands scrabble at her bra, pulling it down to reveal a naked breast. 'Look … take what you want … in here …'

Randall's eyes fix greedily on the breast, the pale skin and light freckles stark against the pink of the nipple. Without a word, he walks at her, pushing her roughly into the room and slamming the door closed behind him.

CHAPTER SEVENTEEN

'You off?' Chris asks, striding towards us, Meredith trotting happily at his side on a lead.

'Yes, mate,' I reply as the others load into the back of the Saxon which had been prepped and made ready while Clarence and I were in the meeting.

'She went off on one when you left.'

'Who? Debbie?'

'Yep, went fucking nuts,' he nods grimly, 'said the council was wrong and the meeting was void, that you were twisting everything to suit you, and shouldn't be trusted anymore.'

'Fucking hell,' I sigh with a feeling of anger building up. 'What does she want?'

'Another meeting, but this one chaired *properly*' he says, making finger quote marks with one hand.

'Fuck me, Chris, I've had about as much of this as I can take ...'

'I know. They're still arguing about it now.'

'Still? What the fuck, Chris! We haven't got time to deal

with that kind of thing. This place needs shit loads doing to it, and she's just causing delay after fucking delay now.'

'We'll get it sorted,' he says, but the tone doesn't match the confidence of the words.

'Chris you gotta get that gun rigged up the top, get the guards on the gates, and the alarm ...' Clarence urges.

'I'm trying,' he says through gritted teeth.

'Try harder,' Clarence snaps.

'Tell you what Clarence, you stay here and sort this fucking mess out, and I'll go out with Howie, yeah?'

'Fine by me,' Clarence retorts. 'I'll fucking sort her out.'

'And how you gonna that?' Chris demands, glaring at Clarence.

'I'll fucking lock her up if she causes anymore trouble, for a start.'

'Yeah, that'll go down well. What kind of message will that send out to everyone?'

'Message? Who gives a fuck about what message we send out? They're alive, aren't they? They've got food, don't they?'

'Yeah, thanks for the input,' Chris snaps. 'Have a great fucking day.' His face goes bright red with anger. He turns, marching back towards the police offices, with the dog at his side.

'My turn,' I say to Clarence. 'That was a bit harsh.'

'Like you said, Boss, I'm getting pissed off at pussy-footing around. He better get a grip of that woman.'

We climb into the Saxon, slamming the doors closed and pausing for a second before I fire the massive engines up. The vehicle vibrates to life, the dull roar giving us all a sense of comfort.

'Soooo,' Cookey says, 'bad day to ask for a raise, then?'

'Yep,' I reply, easing the vehicle forward. We go at a

crawling pace for fear of causing any more damage or annoying anyone. Which is a mistake as it gives Sergeant Hopewell plenty of time to see us coming and march out of the office to stand in front of the vehicle.

'What now?' I gasp with exasperation.

'Boss, why don't you stay here ... I'll go see what she wants,' Blowers offers.

'No, it's okay,' I reply with a sigh, opening the door to drop down.

'I'm staying here. I can't handle her anymore,' Clarence says firmly.

'Fair enough. Debbie ... what's up?'

'What's up? You know perfectly well what's up after that little performance in there,' she snarls at me.

'Debbie, it was done fairly. Yeah, I might have taken the piss a bit, but everyone voted, and we agreed it. Sorry if you don't like it but–'

'Damn right, I don't like it. I'm going to speak to everyone here and see what they think.'

'What, all these people?' I ask, motioning towards the vast array of tents.

'Bloody right. Let's see what they think. If you want a democracy, Howie, then you'll get a proper one.'

'Fine, that's fine, but don't you think they've suffered enough without you canvassing them for support like some fucking politician. Debbie, this is going too far. You're out of control ... Get a grip.'

'Don't patronise me. How dare you say I'm out of control ... Forty people, Howie ... Who killed the forty people last night?'

'They were infected,' I sigh. This is futile, completely pointless. 'Look, we're going for fuel. Do what you want, okay, ask everyone, go and speak to every last person here if it makes you happy.'

'Oh, I bloody will,' she shouts, her voice carrying easily to the people nearest in the tent area. They turn to look, listening intently. 'Go on, Howie, go and kill another forty innocent people, go and shoot some more babies while you're out there ... Murder obviously means nothing to you.'

Her words stop me in my tracks. A terrible feeling flushes through me, a deep fury that threatens to burst me apart. The rear doors slam open as the lads burst out, all of them charging towards Sergeant Hopewell still screaming at the top of her voice.

Dave runs after them, shouting loudly for them to stand down and get back inside. Blowers looks furious, his face contorted with rage. 'We ain't murderers,' he shouts as Lani and Nick start dragging him back.

'Delinquent murderers,' Sergeant Hopewell screams. Clarence drops down, grabbing hold of Cookey as he runs past, lifting him off the ground to move him back.

'They were infected, infected .... They were infected,' Cookey wails.

'You killed children. You're murderers,' Sergeant Hopewell screeches. Terri runs at her, grabbing at her arm and getting pushed back.

'Debbie,' Ted walks forward, trying to call her back.

'Tom wasn't infected. You murdered him. You murdered all of them.'

Terri shouts for her to stop. Ted tries pulling her gently away. Sarah steps in, trying to help Ted. They all get screamed at as Debbie continues to rage at us, hundreds of people moving closer to listen and watch. I glance round, seeing their hostile faces watching us.

'Get inside the Saxon now,' I bark. Dave grabs Blowers,

pulling him harshly back. Clarence carries Cookey bodily, launching him into the back, but I can see even his face is filled with fury. Lani and Nick pause for a second, both of them staring at Sergeant Hopewell with dark faces.

'Delinquent murderers! Baby killers!' she screeches, her voice cracking with the strain. She gets flooded by bodies all dragging her away, but the damage is done. By the time we're in the vehicle, with Clarence stood at the back doors, preventing the lads from getting back out, the whole camp is there, faces watching us as we drive through. No smiles this time, no friendly nods or waves. Just plain hostility. We're the bad guys, the monsters that killed their families and children.

'Fuck this place. I don't ever want to come back here,' Blowers rages. 'We fucking killed for them ... We lost our mates for them ...'

'Simon, sit down,' Dave orders him. He complies. Anyone would, with Dave shouting at them, but he does it reluctantly.

'They were infected,' Cookey says softly. 'They were ... I saw the bite marks ...'

'Alex, stop it,' Dave snaps. 'They were infected, and they would have killed everyone. You all did the right thing. Listen to me!' his voice grows larger, the tone impossible to ignore. 'Have you ever seen me doing anything wrong? Have you?' he demands.

'No, Dave,' Cookey answers.

'I killed more of them than you. I killed far more than any of you. They were all infected. They were bitten and would have killed everyone. You did the right thing.'

'You did,' Clarence adds. 'There was no doubt.'

'Why she saying that, then?' Cookey asks, his voice breaking with emotion. 'We didn't kill no babies ...'

'I did. I shot a baby and its mother,' I shout back as I navigate the vehicle through the gates.

Silence returns my words. Nothing said for a few seconds. 'The baby was bitten. The mother was clinging onto it. She wouldn't let go ... The baby bit her neck. I shot both of them.'

'Shit ... But if they were turned, then why she saying all that?' Cookey asks. I glance round to see tears falling down his face.

'Cookey, she's upset ... She's having an emotional breakdown. She's done well to do everything she's done, but losing Tom and Steven has tipped her over the edge,' Lani speaks softly, her voice so soothing to hear.

'Yeah, but ... calling us murderers ... and everyone looking at us like that,' Cookey replies.

'Come here,' Lani moves to sit next to him, he bursts into tears, sobbing as she holds him close. Nick stares down at the floor. Tears of his own falling onto his boots.

'Come on, son, you've done nothing wrong.' Clarence drops into the seat the other side of Cookey, placing a giant hand on the lad's shoulder.

My own eyes sting with hot tears as I listen to Cookey sob. Blowers and Nick both stay silent as Clarence rumbles away in his deep voice.

'Lads, I'm proud of you. I've served all over the world. Dave too ... And I've never been prouder than I am to serve with you. These things happen, okay? People lose it, and sometimes the wrong people get blamed, but Chris is back there. Sarah too ... and they'll put everyone straight.'

'Yeah, but ...' Cookey starts.

'No buts, son,' Clarence cuts him off gently. 'Chris is brilliant at this kind of thing. He always was ... You heard us arguing back there, but we've known each other for over twenty years. Like you three always taking the piss, that's me and Chris, but I trust that man with my life, and he'll get this sorted. And Mr Howie is the best boss I've ever worked for. There's no one better to follow with all this going on ...'

'You're only saying that cos you fancy my sister,' I reply quickly to a snort of laughter from someone.

'Was it that obvious?' he replies with a chuckle.

'Glaringly,' I call back. 'Someone want to grab the map and tell me where I'm going?'

'I'll do it,' Nick replies.

'You can't read,' Cookey quips with a sniff.

'Words, not maps, you dickhead,' Nick replies.

'What about the words on the maps?' Blowers asks.

'Fuck it. I'll just make it up,' Nick says.

'Fuck that. We'll end up in Scotland,' Blowers says.

'Or he'll set something on fire again,' Cookey adds.

'Piss off ... That was an accident. Do you wanna do it, then?'

'Nah, I get sick if I read in a car.'

'Me too,' Cookey says.

Nick grabs the map, opening the pages and staring at them for a few seconds. 'What does that word say?' he asks.

'That says map,' Blowers answers.

'What about this one?'

'That says atlas,' he replies.

'Fuck, this is going well,' Cookey says.

'I'm joking,' Nick smiles. 'Where did you say we're going?'

'Ted said to try the docklands. They should have fuel for the ships,' I call back.

'Docklands ...' Nick repeats, leafing through the pages. 'Er ... how do you spell docklands?'

CHAPTER EIGHTEEN

'Are you sure this is what you want to do?'

'Quite sure,' she pauses, staring at the clear, blue sky, feeling the sultry heat of the air against her skin. 'Yes, quite sure.'

'This is not the only option open to you, Marcy. There is the option of staying here and continuing with the highly successful method we have thus far established.'

'And then what?'

'And then, well, we continue to gather more.'

'So we exhaust the island, turn every human, and then once complete, we leave and start on a different shore, moving from village to town, to city.'

'That is an option.'

'And then what, Reginald? Once we've turned thousands or millions, what then?'

'I ... we ...' he drops into silence. The only urge he has is to keep going, turn more, get more, take more, the all-consuming hunger driving his thought process. 'I see,' he says at length. 'Yes, I see ... Once we have turned everyone, we have no further … er … well, that is to say we cannot continue, well. I …'

'Reginald, the infection has programmed us to desire gathering more hosts, but eventually, there will be no more hosts, or the few survivors left will organise and co-operate into fighting back on such scale that we all suffer.'

'The futility of mankind,' Reginald sighs.

'The futility of existence without progression. The futility of just being without advancement.'

'There were tribes in the Amazon rain forests that had lived unchanged for thousands of years. While all around empires rose and fell, they continued in near state of stasis,' Reginald says.

'Yes, and they were content until someone showed them what they *could* have. Once that rot set in, they were doomed. I saw the documentaries too, Reggie. I saw the people sat by the side of the river, talking about how they long to be left alone to continue their existence in the way they had done, but I also saw they were wearing jeans and t-shirts, baseball caps and using boats with outboard engines.'

'So if we continue, we become that tribe, content to do what we've always done.'

'Always,' Marcy scoffs. 'This just happened, like less than two weeks ago. Look at the world now in those few days. It's near collapse … but if we do the right thing now, we can turn this devastation into the most wonderful event that mankind has ever known. This is the future, Reginald. The planes are sat on the tarmac waiting to be used, the hospitals are still there, the fire engines are still in place, the whole infrastructure is ready to be taken back up but by a species that appreciates it …'

'Us,' Reginald says matter of fact.

'Yes, us, we're that species …'

'So you're convinced this is the correct course of action?'

'Unequivocally.'

'Good word,' he remarks. 'I would say you are unerring in your beliefs.'

'My mind is unencumbered.'

'Many would find your position unenviable, Marcy.'

'On the contrary, Reginald. I find my position unequalled.'

'I would go so far as to say your view is understandable and that your methods have become quite understated. While some might argue that I have become your understudy, I would suggest that I have been unfailing in my loyalty to you. I am unexpurgated in my regard for you. Which has grown from seeing you become unflinching and unflappable. However, I have great concerns that the humans at the fort will find you unfathomable, but I would expect you will be unfazed in your response to their unfavourable treatment towards you. I shall watch these events unfold, for they are unforeseen and truly unforgettable. Indeed, the humans will consider our actions so far as unforgivable, which is unfortunate, and if they only take the time to understand you, they will see their fear is unfounded, that we are not an ungodly species who are unhinged and ungovernable. If they allow you to explain uninterrupted and unfurl your plan, they will see their ungainly actions have been unnecessary for we only seek to unify our species in a unique union which is uninhibited and unlimited in its desire to become a unity …'

'Reginald,' she snaps him back to the present.

'Sorry,' he shakes his head. 'I used to do that a lot in my former life. It really was quite unfortunate for those around me. So we are going to the fort, then?' he asks cheerfully.

'Yes, Reggie.'

'Can we not arrange transport? We are in the middle of the island, and it is rather a long way to the north coast. Plus, we've already walked this way once, you know.'

'And how do you propose we do that? Getting a couple of thousand zombies into cars, or shall we use the bus?'

'Not the Z word, please. Can you not get them to drive?'

'No, Reggie, willing hundreds of them to drive would make my head explode probably ... It doesn't work like that.'

'On foot then,' he sighs. 'I always did hate walking, was never my thing, you know ...'

'Never mind, Reggie. The fresh air will do you good, get some colour to your cheeks.'

They walk on. Marcy and Reginald, side by side, leading a long, drawn-out line of infected headed by the ever-watchful communicators. The conversation between them continues, with opinion, counter opinion, argument, counter argument, discussion, and counter discussion. Reginald probing continually but with respect and patience. Doing as told by Marcy by taking the opposing view to make her think of all the options and avenues of thought.

The intense heat saps at the horde. They should be shuffling slowly and conserving energy for the coming night. Instead, Marcy keeps them at a solid pace, intent on getting back to the north side before nightfall.

They discuss the future, of how the species could enable mankind to progress far more than ever before. On the main road, they follow the route of Randall until they reach the roundabout, the midway point between the centre and the north.

'We should take the left road,' Reginald says as they approach the junction.

'Why the left road? The road we came in on leads us to

the north shore. We need the north shore to get across to Portsmouth.'

'And how do you propose we do that? Where will we find boats for our few thousand living challenged? The left road does take us to the north shore, albeit further from the proposed destination, but it is also the port of the vehicular ferry which is of a size capable of transporting our group.'

'You want to use the car ferry?'

'Yes.'

'Why didn't you just say that?'

'I did, and further it will enable us to increase the size of our retinue.'

'We just discussed the futility of increasing our group until we have a future. That drive you feel is the infection within you.'

'But if we are passing through the town, then we might as well gather a few more,' he pleads, unable to contain the urge.

'For a start, it won't be *we*. You haven't turned anyone yet, and why cause more misery and suffering if we're unsure of how our future lies?'

'But what if they're already suffering, Marcy? They could be dying from illness and disease right now? The infection can save them ... You said that yourself.'

'Cheap shot, Reggie,' she laughs.

'But a valid point nonetheless.'

'Okay, yes, a valid point. We'll go your way if it makes my little Reggie happy.'

'Reginald.'

Taking the new route, they lead the horde down the wide tarmac. The ever-present heat shimmer taunting them mercilessly as it hovers over the blacktop. The route is easy enough, a wide road that meanders through fields and meadows. Sun-dappled shade offers a brief respite from the sun from tall trees bordering the road.

They lapse into a comfortable silence. Marcy lost in thoughts and recent memories of Darren, his wild reckless nature leading so many to their needless deaths. Imagining if she'd been in charge, she could have discussed things with Howie, maybe reached a mutual conclusion that satisfied them both. But no, that was then, and she was just as bloodthirsty as Darren. She felt the power he had and wanted it. It was only by his failure that she understood this better way.

She would have failed too. Darren had to die the way he did for all of this to happen. Many events happening in a set order led her to this time. Take any one of the events away, and maybe she would never have reached this conclusion.

'I thought I could smell something,' Marcy says a couple of hours later as they reach the bend in the junction and look through the broken gates to the carnage caused by the Mercedes obliterating the guard hut. 'Looks fresh too,' she adds, spying the blood-soaked body lying on the grass.

'Are we going in?' Reginald prompts, seeing the urge crossing her face.

'Yes, I think we shall,' she replies quietly, eyes fixed on the corpse. They enter the grounds, Marcy and Reginald heading across the lane to step through the wreckage and examine the body.

'He's still warm,' Marcy says, holding her hand to the body's face.

'Is he dead?'

'Quite dead,' she nods. 'Shame. What's up there?'

'Osborne House. You must have been here before,' Reginald replies.

'No, I heard about it. Queen Victoria's house, wasn't it?'

'You've never been here?'

'No.'

'Are you from the island?'

'Yes, Reginald, and no, I've never been here ... This is for tourists, and I couldn't afford the entrance fee either.'

'Well. We're here now. You really should see the main house. The architecture is sublime. You know, Prince Albert designed it himself. It was said he missed the view of Naples in Italy, which is why they decided on this location. Has a view of the bay, you know ... and he designed it in the style of an Italian Renaissance Palazzo ...' He walks off in full flow. Marcy walking to catch up, with the vast crowd walking slowly behind them.

'The grounds are incredible and were also designed by Prince Albert. He truly was a very remarkable man in many respects, and Victoria was devoted to him ...'

Marcy listens patiently as Reginald plunders on, giving a full history of the house, the grounds, the history, and how a Swiss cottage was brought over from Switzerland.

'There you see,' Reginald beams as the main residence comes into view. Marcy makes polite, appreciative noises, nodding in the right places as he carries on with his flow of information.

'Oh ...' his voice drops off as they enter the courtyard. Coming to a halt at the sight of the hole in the main door, bits of wood strewn across the gravel driveway, and the body of an old man lying a few feet out.

'I take it this isn't normal, then?' Marcy asks.

'No, not at all,' Reginald replies seriously. 'That's two bodies now.'

'Well, let's go find out what we've got, shall we?' Marcy starts walking, pausing as Reginald holds back.

'Er ... maybe someone should stay with the group?' he asks nervously.

She smiles, seeing the trepidation on his face. 'Good idea, Reggie. You stay here and keep an eye out. April, you bring a few with me.'

'Yes, Marcy,' April nods at a few of the communicators, leading them after Marcy towards the door.

Marcy stops at the body of the old man, looking down at his blood-soaked clothing. Both bodies stabbed through the stomach, and both of them fresh.

Her head snaps at the sound of wailing coming from inside, a long drawn-out cry filled with pain and misery. She tussles her hair, pulling the strands over her face to disguise her eyes and steps through the door.

A scene of horror greets her. A man shot to pieces slumped at the foot of a grand staircase. People stood about, looking down at the body of a teenage boy being cradled by a woman. As her eyes adjust to the gloom, she casts her gaze at the women stood in the hallway. All of them with bruised faces, clothes torn and ripped off. The few men stand, looking helpless. The smell of blood is strong. Blood, fear, and sex all mixed together.

She looks round, spotting another body of a woman lying with a knife buried to the hilt in her chest, a crimson bloom across her naked torso, the still wet blood pooling at her sides.

'Who are you?' someone asks weakly. A few faces turn to stare, all of them looking pale and shocked.

'Just walking past ... saw the car in the grounds and came up ... Didn't you see us?'

'No,' the woman replies. Her skirt is hanging in shreds, showing her blood-spattered thighs.

'What happened?' Marcy asks. The humans are terrified, truly terrified but not scared of her. They haven't seen the huge horde outside and have no idea of who she is. Something else has done this.

'Men came,' another woman sobs, 'from the prison …'

'The prison?' Marcy asks.

'Said they just broke out,' the woman starts sobbing, her chest heaving as she smudges the wet blood dripping from her nose.

'How many were there?' Marcy asks.

'I'm surprised you didn't see them,' a dignified, old woman walks out of a room. Red, tear-stained eyes, but the only female without ripped clothing or visible injuries.

'We didn't see anyone.'

'They left not half an hour ago,' the old woman replies, her voice strained. She looks round at the survivors, stretching a quavering hand out to a young woman stood nearby. The young woman flinches, cowering away with her arms wrapped round herself.

'They did this?' Marcy asks. None of them need to confirm what she means by *this*. The bodies, the raped women, the injuries.

'Yes,' the old woman replies, 'killed Arthur first … Poor Arthur, the silly, old fool was just trying to protect us.'

'Have you been here since this began?' Marcy asks. The question goes unanswered. The grief and immediate after-effects too strong for anyone to focus.

'Jerry,' the woman cradling the teenage boy wails, 'oh, Jerry …' She rocks back and forth with the body, clutching it close. A man drops down, pressing his fingers into the boy's neck. He closes his eyes as he focuses on what he can feel.

'Keep him still,' he says quietly to the woman rocking him. The old woman moves over and rests her hands on the woman holding the boy, steadying her.

'He's alive, but the pulse is very weak.'

'Are you a doctor?' Marcy asks.

'No, just first aid,' the man replies sadly. His hand drops away from the youth. Marcy steps closer, seeing the thin trails of blood coming from the boy's ears.

'What's wrong with your eyes?' a woman asks, her voice low and flat as she stares vacantly. The reaction is instant, heads snapping round to stare at Marcy. Gasps of shock as people flinch and move away. One of the women cries out, a low heart-rending wail. Faces go pale as the shock hits home. Eyes flick between Marcy and the silent group stood behind her, all of them with red, bloodshot eyes.

'Them,' the old woman gasps.

Marcy nods, standing still while holding her head high to stare back at the people watching her.

'But … how did you … what …' a man stutters, his mind failing to form the words as he struggles to compute what's happening.

'I can speak,' Marcy says flatly. 'So can they,' she indicates the group behind her.

'They don't speak,' another man spits. 'Who are you? What do you want? Can't you see we've suffered enough.'

'Everyone has suffered,' Marcy says softly. 'We are those things but not the same. We're …' she pauses, unsure of what to say, '… different.'

'Different?' the man shouts, the fear clear in his face.

'Different,' she nods. 'We don't want to hurt you.'

'Shit, there's fucking thousands of 'em outside,' someone shouts from a room nearby.

The old woman steps forward, putting herself between the survivors and Marcy. She stares into the red, bloodshot eyes, seemingly examining Marcy's skin. 'You don't look like them. The eyes do but …'

'Trust me, we are those things, all of us ...'

'What happened to you, my dear?' the old woman asks softly.

Marcy shrugs, thinking of how to explain, 'I don't know ...'

'But those things just attack and attack. They don't stop. I've seen 'em killing ... We all 'ave,' the same man says.

'And it's daytime. They just shuffle ...' someone else adds.

'We are those things,' Marcy presses. 'We attack and take people. Where do you think all that lot came from?'

The man shouting at them slumps down, his back pressed to the wall as he sobs into his hands. Others just stare dumbly, shell-shocked and rooted to the spot.

'The men raped his wife, then killed her,' the old woman explains.

'Her?' Marcy indicates the woman's body lying in the hallway.

'No,' the old woman shakes her head, 'another one.'

'They were laughing ... fucking laughing,' the man shouts, slamming his fists against his head. 'Just fucking laughing ... They forced me to watch!' he screams.

Marcy drops her head, feeling a deep sense of shame. 'We thought they would just take what they wanted and go, but they didn't,' the old woman looks down sadly. 'They got worse, goading each other and laughing.'

'Marcy, is everything okay? I heard you talking,' Reginald pushes his way through the group, his movements slowing down as he takes the scene in, staring at the bodies and the injured women.

'Inmates from the prison. They must have got out before we got there,' Marcy says.

'But we took the inmates. April did it.'

'Must be others,' Marcy replies.

'Are they still here?' Reginald asks.

'No, we just missed them.'

'Oh ... oh dear ...'

'You're not zombies ... You can't be ... This is some kind of ...' another man shakes his head, his voice dropping off.

'We are,' Marcy repeats. 'What's wrong with that boy?'

'He got knocked out. One of the men hit him,' the old woman half turns, looking down at the boy still being cradled.

'He's dying,' the woman sobs, holding him tight. She looks terrible, with vivid welts across her face, her lips swollen and covered in dried blood. Clothing ripped and torn.

'You can't know that. He might just be unconscious,' the old woman says in a gentle tone.

'His pulse is getting weaker,' the man who checked his pulse says.

'We can save him,' Reginald says. Faces turn to him. 'We can,' he adds.

'How?' the old woman asks.

'We can turn him,' Reginald says bluntly.

'What?' a man shouts, a cacophony of voices burst out. Loud, angry tones shouting in confusion.

'But ... what do you mean?' the old woman asks with a puzzled expression.

'We're those things. We can turn the boy and save him. He'll be one of us, but he'll be alive.'

The old woman shakes her head slowly, desperately trying to understand. 'Will he speak? Will he know who he is ... or was?'

'I don't know if he'll speak,' Marcy replies. 'Some do.

Most don't ... but he won't feel a thing, no pain, no suffering ...'

'No,' the same man shouts angrily.

'Can you do them?' the old woman asks, nodding at the bodies in the hall.

'No, they're dead. Doesn't work like that.'

'I can assure you the boy will feel no pain. It takes just moments, and he'll be one of us, safe and protected,' Reginald walks forward slowly.

'We don't have to bite him. I told you we're different,' Marcy adds.

'Bite him? Oh, my god,' the man shouts. He steps forward, then back again, his hands wringing in front of him. 'Oh my god, oh my god ...'

'Calm down,' the old woman snaps. 'What if we say no? What then?' she asks, turning back to Marcy.

'We'll leave you in peace. We won't attack any of you.'

'Marcy, I think ...' Reginald starts.

'I said we won't attack anyone,' Marcy cuts him off firmly.

'Okay, as you wish,' Reginald replies.

'You'll leave if we ask?' the old woman asks.

'Yes, I promise you. You've suffered enough, and we're not going to add to that, but you must understand that others won't be the same as us. They could come tonight, and they'll be the same as before ...'

'Why can't you stop them?' the man shouts. 'You can speak! You got thousands!'

'If we see any, they'll come with us, but I cannot promise that we'll get all of them. We're only passing through here, and I also promise that we'll deal with the men if we find them,' she adds.

'The prisoners?' the old woman asks.

Marcy nods firmly before looking down at the boy. 'We can save him,' she says.

The man who checked his pulse drops down again, pressing his fingers back into the boy's neck. He shakes his head sadly. 'Weaker, much weaker.'

The woman holds him tight, rocking back and forth. Tears spill down her cheeks, wetting the boy's face.

'Is he your son?' Marcy asks.

'Nephew,' the old woman says. 'The boy's mother was taken when it first happened.'

'His father?' Marcy looks at the gathered men.

'Didn't have one. Single parent,' the old woman says.

'Let him go in peace,' the shouting man blurts out. 'It's unnatural.'

'How will you do it?' the woman holding the boy asks suddenly, her face turned up to stare as Marcy.

'My saliva. I can put my saliva into his wound.'

'He doesn't have one,' the aunt replies.

'In his mouth then. Takes slightly longer, but the result is the same.'

'Result is the same … This is sick!' the man bellows angrily. 'Get out! All of you, just get out and leave us alone.' He takes a step towards Marcy, his face contorted with rage. The infected all take a step forward. Reginald takes a step back.

'Wait,' Marcy turns to hold them. 'We'll go if you want. It's your decision,' she says to the aunt.

'No pain?' the aunt asks.

'No pain.'

'He won't feel anything?'

'Not a thing. No pain and no suffering. I promise you,' Marcy implores.

'Don't do it,' the man shouts. 'I won't let you.'

Marcy ignores him, watching the aunt instead as she struggles to cope with the decision. The aunt stares up at the old woman, fresh tears pouring down her cheeks, a look of pleading.

'This is wrong ... Let the boy die in peace,' the man shouts again.

'What would you do?' the aunt asks the old woman.

'I ...' the old woman looks away, 'I don't know ... I ... the boy won't suffer?' She turns on Marcy. Marcy pauses, staring back at the old woman. She turns slowly, walking over to the woman's body on the floor. She puts her back to the group and pulls the knife from the chest with a wet, sucking sound. She wipes the blade on the woman's ruined skirt before walking back to the group.

'Here,' she offers the handle to the aunt, 'if he suffers, then you can kill me. I won't stop you, and none of them will either,' she glances back at her horde. April nods in understanding.

'Marcy,' Reginald says in a warning tone.

'Take it,' Marcy urges. The aunt reaches up with a trembling hand, grasping the knife. She takes it gently, looking at the blade, then back up at Marcy. She nods once, firmly.

'Sure?' Marcy asks. The aunt nods again, still holding the knife out in front of her.

'Sick ... this is fucking sick ....' the man screams.

'Stand back,' the aunt shouts, gripping the knife and pointing it at the man.

'This is wrong,' he says but doesn't come closer.

The aunt grips the knife, her eyes ablaze with anger. 'Take him,' she says to Marcy.

'Hold him for me,' Marcy says softly.

The aunt drops her gaze to the boy cradled in her arms. She bends slowly, kissing his head and wiping her wet tears from his cheeks. 'Jerry ... if you can hear me, I'm so sorry ...'

Marcy crouches down, leaning forward until she hovers over the boy's face. With her head turned down, she bites into the inside of her cheek, drawing blood into her mouth. Her fingers move to the boy's mouth, gently opening the lips. She leans forward, dropping her mouth down until she connects mouth to mouth. The aunt sobs, Marcy feeling the woman's movement through the boy. She lets the blood and saliva pool into the boy's mouth, holding still for a second before pulling back. She wipes her mouth, then presses her hand gently over the boy's mouth.

'Is that it?' the aunt whispers.

Marcy nods, moving back, 'Takes a couple of minutes. He'll start twitching, but that's normal ... He will not be in pain.'

'How do you know?' the man demands.

'Because it was done to me,' Marcy replies.

'And me,' Reginald adds. 'He won't feel a thing.'

Silence falls. The quietness only broken by the gentle sobs as the survivors watch the boy with morbid fascination.

The aunt examines his face closely, smoothing his hair back and stroking his cheek. The knife on the floor at her side. She murmurs softly. Kind words of love.

'Nothing's happening,' someone says. The voice cuts off as the boy twitches, his arms jolting at his sides. Gasps sound out; the aunt holds him closer.

'Oh, Jerry,' she cries. He twitches harder, the electric shock effect passing through his body, 'What's happening?' the aunt asks with worry.

'It's okay,' Marcy reassures her. 'Just let it happen ... Not long now.'

They watch fascinated as the boy convulses, his body

going rigid, then relaxing. Spasms shooting through his limbs. He stops suddenly, his body instantly relaxed.

'His eyes will be like mine,' Marcy explains. The aunt looks at her, staring into Marcy's eyes and nodding.

The boy sits up; a sudden, smooth motion. The aunt goes with him, almost helping him. He opens his eyes to more gasps and sharp intakes of breath. The red, bloodshot eyes stare out, unfocussed and glazed. He blinks and turns to look up at Marcy.

'Welcome,' Marcy says with a gentle smile. 'Can you speak?' She wills him to speak. Sending all her energy into the boy, demanding him to speak, commanding him to speak. Seconds go by, long seconds as he stares unflinching at Marcy, the love and devotion clear in his eyes.

'Jerry?' the aunt asks softly, a begging tone in her voice.

'Don't be alarmed,' Reginald says. 'Most don't speak ... Only few have the ability.'

'Will he ... bite?' the old woman asks.

'He'll want to, but he won't,' Marcy replies. She stares at the boy, her eyes locked on his.

'Jerry ... oh, Jerry,' the aunt strokes his cheek, smoothing his hair away from his pale, young face. 'I'm so sorry, Jerry ... I'm so sorry.'

The boy turns his face slowly, looking at his aunt. 'Don't be,' he says.

CHAPTER NINETEEN

The men stagger out from the gates, laughing and pushing each other. Every one of them grinning stupidly, bragging about the women they took. Moaning about having to go second and third as there weren't enough women to go round.

The hatred they feel for sexual offenders and the actions they just took don't correspond in their minds. The two are different, not the same. These are new times where the powerful and strong can take what they want, and anyway ... those bitches enjoyed it. You could tell they enjoyed it. Screaming for more they were.

Long years spent cooped up within the prison walls. There was pornography, but it was the same stuff that got passed around again and again. Most men used their hands for relief. Some used other men. But the sexual release they feel now sends them bouncing along, without a care in the world.

'We took their food and fucked their women ... What a perfect day,' Colin grins. 'Eh, Randy, what a perfect day.'

'Shut the fuck up, you dumbass,' Randall snaps but with

a massive grin. He glances at Harry, the ex-biker, the only one not laughing. Randall saw him stab the woman through the chest, and he did it while inside her. They all did sick things. Randall knows that, but that took the biscuit, and he realises Harry is one to watch.

'Where we going now, Randy?' Colin asks.

'The fort, you dumb motherfucker. How the fuck can you forget that? Your brains must have come out the end of your mother-fucking cock.'

'Night soon,' Harry says.

'What the fuck difference does that make?'

'Can't go at night, Randy,' Colin cuts in.

'Why the fuck not?'

'Dangerous,' Harry replies.

'You are fucking joking, right? This coming from the mother-fucking Hells Angel that just stabbed a mother-fucking girl to death while fucking her.'

He shrugs and keeps walking. Not a flicker of emotion on his face.

'He's right. We can't go at night ... We could end up anywhere,' another inmate says.

'Let's find some more mother-fucking bitches,' Colin shouts with glee.

'Don't fucking copy me,' Randall snaps, 'and where the fuck we gonna find pussy in this shit town?'

'PUSSY!? WHERE ARE YOU?' Colin shouts. Randall grimaces at the sudden sound before bursting out laughing along with the other men.

'We'll find somewhere to hole up,' Randall chuckles. 'You crazy motherfuckers are sick, man, fucking sick.'

'That bitch was sick,' an inmate adds. 'Well, she will be in about nine months anyway.'

'Yeah, that'll be an interesting call to the CSA. *Someone from Parkhurst got me pregnant.*'

'Fucking slag. She was fucking begging for it. Did you see her? Couldn't get enough ...'

'I bet her husband had a go after we left. You see him watching?'

'What that fucker crying? Fucking pussy, should be happy we gave his missus a good time.'

'Good time? What all thirty seconds of it?'

'Fuck off, I been locked up for twelve years, you cunt. What you expect?'

'You reckon they got women in that fort, Randy?'

'Dumb fucking question. Of course, they got women ... They got hot-ass bitches just itching for some penitentiary cock.'

'Look at that fucker. What's he doing?' One of the inmates points down the road to a man walking slowly towards them.

'He's going fucking slow enough,' someone remarks.

'Motherfucker looks drunk ...' Randall says. They walk down, staring hard at the man shuffling slowly up the centre of the road. His head lolling from side to side, arms dangling limply as he walks stiff-legged.

'What is wrong with that motherfucker?'

'I don't know, Randy ...' Colin replies.

'It was a mother-fucking rhetorical question, you dumbass.'

'Ere, look at his eyes. They all fucked up,' Colin says as they get closer. The infected watches them, his head rolling about as he shuffles towards the food source.

'Now, that is one fucked up motherfucker ...' Randall says as the men gather in a rough semi-circle round the man and stare at his red eyes and thin lips pulled back to show yellow, rotting teeth while maggots writhe in an open wound on his neck.

'He must be one of them things, eh, Randy?' Colin says.

'You fucking think?' Randall retorts.

'Look at him shuffle. He's all fucked up ... Ere, mate, I said you was all fucked up,' Colin shouts at the shuffler.

'What the fuck are you doing?'

'I'm talking to him, Randy ... Those others could talk, didn't they?'

'Man, he drooling like a rabid mother-fucking dog,' Randall looks in disgust, stepping back as the infected turns to shuffle towards him.

'He likes you, Randy,' Colin laughs.

'More,' Harry mutters. The men turn to see infected shuffling from a house a few doors up; slow, ungainly movements, stiff-legged as they totter towards the gate, slowly spilling out onto the road.

'These are some ugly fuckers,' Randall says.

'These like the ones from the movies,' Colin says, 'all slow and shuffling ... Why they different to them other ones, eh, Randy?'

'How the fuck would I know the answer to that? I ain't the mother-fucking zombie expert.'

'They've all stopped. What they doin' now, Randy?'

'They wondering why you keep asking dumb-ass questions, is what they're doing.' The inmates stare, transfixed as the infected all stop and slowly turn their heads to the now dark sky. As the sun drops below the horizon, the howling begins.

The inmates flinch in surprise. Having been safely away from the infected since the event happened, they watch with fascination as the gathered infected howl and roar into the night. The sounds coming from all directions.

Colin throws his head back and howls. The others start laughing, then joining in. Long, whooping noises of wolves or dogs. They keep going, mocking the infected and laughing as they get louder. Several group together, doing a wolf harmony.

The sound of the infected ceases abruptly. It just ends, leaving the inmates mid song and trailing off to look about them bemused.

The infected change; the heads become fixed instead of lolling. The eyes fix on the inmates, the movements suddenly not so slow and ungainly.

The closest infected lunges at Randall with frightening speed. Randall lashes out, smashing the thing in the head with a hard fist, sending it reeling off to the side.

The other infected burst into action, charging at the inmates. Instead of running, the inmates stand ready, clenching fists and shouting with aggression.

The infected are taken down, just a few of them against the many strong inmates. The fight is over within seconds. The prisoners stamping and kicking at the things, killing them easily.

'What the fuck was that?' Randall shouts.

'More,' Harry says. The others turn, seeing the drawn-out line of infected staggering round the corner and running at them.

'Fuck this,' Randall mutters. They start running. Jogging away from the infected and heading further into the small town.

'Why ain't we getting the fit birds?' Colin wails. 'Ain't bloody fair.'

'Shut your mother-fucking mouth and keep running.'

'Fight,' Harry says, his breath coming hard from having

to run. Randall looks across at the man, seeing his red, flushed face as he struggles to keep up.

'You wanna fight them things?' Randall asks, his own breathing coming easy enough.

'Can't run.'

'You fight them if you want. I'm fucking running.'

Harry looks back, the long beard brushing against his chest as he cranes his neck round. His breathing getting harder and harder, heart hammering in his chest. A big man like Randall but just bulk and a lifetime of hard living now taking its toll.

'There,' one of the inmates shouts, pointing ahead. They peer down the long road to the small collection of shops forming the tiny town centre. A supermarket on the corner of a paltry town square; the doors smashed in, offering a tempting hole to run through.

The men keep going, the slight descent of the road aiding their motion. Harry breathes harder and harder, struggling with pain shooting through his chest.

'Move your fat ass,' Randall shouts, shoving the man ahead. He stumbles, feet pounding the road surface.

The group reach the supermarket, forcing their way through the busted doors to stand bending over with hands on knees, gasping for breath.

Randall moves quickly, scanning the looted interior. Surging forward, he grabs the end of a shelving unit and starts trying to drag it. 'Get the end,' he shouts. Inmates grab at the unit, dragging the heavy, long shelves across the tiled floor, shoving them against the gap of the front doors.

The unit is pushed in place as the infected reach the doors; growls sound from the outside as they slam into the shelves. The men brace themselves against it, digging their feet in and pushing backs to hold it against the doors.

'More,' Harry shouts, his face an unhealthy, crimson colour.

'Stay the fuck there,' Randall shouts at the men holding the unit. He takes the others and grabs more shelves, dragging them over to stack in the doorway. They work quickly, glancing at the large plate glass windows as more infected stagger past, to the front doors.

'Top,' Harry shouts. The busted-in doors prevent the shelving units from being flush against the opening, leaving a gap large enough for the infected to squeeze through and climb over. The first face appears, wild with fury; spittle hanging from the pulled back lips. Eyes wild and red as the clawed hands scrabble to gain purchase. The thing drives forward, ignoring the glass shards slicing at its skin and the sharp metal edges gouging into its legs.

Harry pulls his knife, steps back and stabs up, jamming the point into the thing's face. It slices deep through the cheek but causes no reaction other than blood spurting out. The thing, seeing its prey so close, scrabbles harder, heaving its body higher onto the units. Harry stabs up again; more knives join in, thrusting the points deep into the creature's face, cutting the skin to hanging, bloody rags.

'Move,' Randall shouts. The men step aside as he swings a heavy fire extinguisher at the head, slamming the end of the tube into the thing's head. It snaps back, the force propelling it backwards to drop out of sight.

More clamber up, following the actions of the first one and using its downed body to step on. The men stab the cheeks and faces of the infected. They ignore the blows and keep going. Blood pissing from many wounds, pouring onto the top of the units and dripping down the front. The inmates tilt their heads back in an effort to avoid the dripping blood.

The upwards motion causes the blood to spurt onto their blades and drip over the handles onto wrists and down forearms.

Shoulders start to burn from the exertion of the constant thrusting up. The men shout and growl, muttering oaths as they fend the things off.

An infected pushes through, the body slithering across the blood-slick top of the units. It drops down into the store, landing heavily at the inmates' feet. They stamp down, ending the thing under a reign of blows.

A loud thudding, cracking noise snaps their heads round to the wall-sized plate glass window at the front of the shop. Infected on the outside, slamming their bodies into the glass. Long spiderweb cracks form as the glass starts to fracture.

'Move back,' Randall shouts. The men dart away from the shelves. The sudden removal of their weight causes the shelves to topple forward from the press of bodies clambering against the reverse side.

It crashes down with infected landing amongst the debris. The window smashes: a deep cracking sound as the glass shatters and more infected bodies fall through, getting cut to ribbons by the long shards.

The men back away quickly, moving deeper into the store. Randall leads the way, heading towards the heavy plastic curtain at the back separating the store from the rear storerooms. He pushes through, shouting in anger at the infected coming at him.

He stabs out, plunging the blade of his knife deep into the chest. The thing ignores the blow, pushing forward. Randall braces and explodes out, forcing the thing off its feet to fall back onto the floor. Randall pulls the knife and stabs down into the neck. A spray of hot blood arcs out as the main artery is severed.

The delay is enough to allow the infected coming through the store to catch up. Fierce fighting breaks out at the heavy plastic curtain. Men shouting as they lash out, stabbing at the heads and necks of the infected fighting to get at them.

The dozen or so men fight furiously, using skills honed over years of violence and living in the confines of a hardened prison. Harry, now the running is over, comes into his own, lashing out with enormous power as he uses his bulk and size to drive them back.

More infected stagger into the rear storeroom. Randall and a couple of others fight forward, cutting them down as they beat a path to the rear doors.

The first inmate goes down, slipping on blood and dropping to the floor. Infected lunge down instantly, digging teeth into any exposed flesh. The man screams, thrashing out violently. The other inmates ignore him as they back away, leaving him to become engulfed.

Randall gets to the rear doors, bursting through into the open air. Just a few infected stagger towards them, wild with fury as they surge at the fresh prey. The men get through the door. No order or control, just every man fighting for himself. They push and shove against each other, swearing to move out the way.

In the back street, they still can't turn and run. The constant press of infected coming at them through the store keeps them focussed, knowing if they try and turn, they'll be taken down.

They move quicker, fighting backwards across the road. Randall and a few others attacking from the sides. Slashing and hacking at the monsters, cutting into necks, and stabbing deep into the sides. Puncturing with rapid movements. They wrap strong arms round the infected necks as they drive the knife points in again and again. Blades sawing at jugulars. Fists lash out, hammering into faces. Feet kick out, driving the things back.

Another one drops, tripping on the kerb and losing his balance enough for an infected to dive in and drive him off his feet. Again, the men ignore his pleas for help, constantly moving back as the man is taken. Bites covering his arms and legs, teeth gripping and tearing into his neck.

Through the midst of the battle, Randall notices the inmate taken down in the store staggering from the back doors. For a second, he thinks the man has fought free; then, he sees the staggering motion that matches the other things perfectly.

'Motherfucker,' he mutters through hard breathing as the infected inmate surges into the fray.

The sound of fighting rolls down the quiet streets, alerting infected who start staggering towards the noise, drawn by the promise of a feast.

The inmates battle on, unable to flee and having to fight their ground as yet more of the things appear through the store and at the ends of the street, staggering and running as fast as possible.

The situation becomes impossible. The inmates, as strong, violent, and tough as they are, soon become heavily outnumbered.

Taken one by one, the numbers start to dwindle, cut down as the last few days of physical exertion takes its toll– arms getting slower and slower, the power of their stabs dwindling. The cheap knife blades becoming blunt; handles too slick to keep hold of fall from hands.

Randall loses his own knife, driving it deep into the

chest of an infected who falls to the ground, pulling the knife down with him.

'Motherfucker,' Randall rages at the injustice of it. Breaking free from prison just for this to happen in some shitty, little street. The small group form into a tight circle. Colin, despite his stupidity, fights like a demon. A pure vicious streak gives him constant pleasure from the wounds and injuries he can inflict. The danger of the situation doesn't register as he revels in the gore, screaming with delight every time he stabs at one of the things.

Another goes down, infected surging in to push him bodily to the floor. The inmates close ranks, leaving him to die noisily.

Randall fights with bare hands, his knuckles bruising from the constant punches he lands. Busting infected noses and jaws, fracturing skulls as he stamps down.

He punches straight, his fist impacting the mouth of an infected. The dirty, yellow teeth split the skin on Randall's knuckles, slicing the flesh open. The wound is tiny and unnoticed with the adrenalin of the fight. The saliva from the infected thing's mouth coats the knuckles, soaking into the wound.

The infection surges through this powerful physique, the awesome strength of the man doing nothing to stop the spread as the virus drives through the organs, turning every cell. Within seconds Randall becomes aware of pain in his stomach.

Grimacing, he fights on, ignoring the growing pain. The agony grips him. Still, he fights on, refusing to succumb to the pain. Years spent powerlifting and used to the burning feeling of lactic acid in his muscles. His mindset allows him to keep going. Focus and keep going, ignore the pain, and do what you set out to do.

He roars deeply. Eyes wide and bulging. The infection takes over his body. The infected suddenly move away from him. Somehow recognising he is now taken. They switch to the others, leaving Randall unchallenged. The confusion hits him as hard as the pain. No longer able to ignore it, he clutches his stomach, staggering away from his group which spells their end. The infected swarm them through the gap he creates.

The inmates are taken down, overwhelmed by a pressed attack. Teeth dig into fingers, hands, legs, ankles, necks. Anything that can be bitten is bit.

Randall staggers away, refusing to give in. The pain increases as he fights it. Roaring with sheer stubbornness. His vision becomes blurred as hot tears sting his eyes. He drops down to his knees, still refusing to let the pain defeat him.

His impossible refusal does nothing to stop the inevitable. The infection takes him, driving him to the ground as it starts to shut his body down. He sinks to the floor, lying on his back. Veins bulging from his muscles as he tenses against the agony.

Rage burns through him, pure fury as he keeps fighting to the very end. He dies noisily, screaming, shouting, and swearing, which slowly drops down to growling mutters. Gritting his teeth, he fixes his eyes on the bright moon. Breathing coming harder, heart slowing, the infection takes him. Kills him.

Randall dies.

CHAPTER TWENTY

She looks up at me, craning her head to stare through tear-misted eyes, but all I can see is the exposed neck. Smooth skin just waiting to be bitten. My mouth fills with saliva as the image grows in my mind. I swallow it down, breathing deeply to gain control.

The boy stares at his aunt. I can tell he wants to bite. The urge in him must be so strong. My will stops him. There was a connection, a different feeling as he came back. I was willing him to be able to speak. Focussing all my energy into that one thought. Was it me that gave him the ability or the infection simply allowing him to speak and retain intelligence?

The humans smell so good. So very good. The fear coming from them is like the scent of freshly baked bread early in the morning. The horde want them so much. So do I. But this isn't the way. If we take these people now, we prove we are the monsters. They think we are, and there will never be change.

The infection urges me to do it. It tells me this group won't matter. They're isolated and alone. No one would know. Easy targets that can be turned easily. They've suffered greatly, and I know within a few minutes they could be at peace with us and that pain would be gone. They haven't even run away; they're so full of fear and shock from what just happened with the prisoners that escaped.

The stench of sex is strong too. Male sweat, lust, and semen mixed with blood. All of those smells draw me to take them. Tempting, taunting, goading, provoking.

But I won't. If there is to be change, then it has to start here. The boy was taken with consent, albeit not his but still with consent.

He turns to look up at me. Every face in the big entrance hall is fixed on him. The man that was shouting stands quietly with a look of absolute shock.

The aunt looks back at him, frozen to the spot. Barely believing what she's seeing.

'Jerry?' she says quietly.

'Yes,' he turns back to her, smiling.

'Does it hurt …? Are you in pain?'

'No,' he shakes his head as I watch intently to see if he will be flat and monotone like Robbie and April or have a greater recall like Reginald and me. 'I feel fine … I feel great,' he keeps smiling. His voice is young, unbroken yet.

'Jerry, do you feel any pain at all?' I ask him. I don't need to ask. I know the answer, but I do it for the effect.

'None,' he shakes his head again. 'I feel … amazing,' he adds after a slight pause.

The shock in the room is palpable, an extreme reaction manifesting in everyone staying rooted to the spot, unable to draw their eyes away from the boy.

Jerry stands, a smooth movement using the power of his legs to simply drive upright. Colour slowly returns to his previously deathly white face. He looks round to the assembled survivors, smiling with kindness. This kid should get an award. I know he wants to take them. The urge in him is as great as the rest of us, but my will holds him back. Instead, he displays kindness and grace, showing them he's in no pain.

'Take me,' a woman steps forward, her face fixed on mine.

'Sally, what're you doing?' the same man shouts in horror. He reaches out to grab her arm, but she jerks free, stepping away from him and closer to me.

'Four men pinned me to the floor and raped me. They laughed while they took me,' her voice is hoarse and low, full of misery. 'It hurts more than anything I have ever known ... It hurts ... Take that away, please ... please.'

'Sally, don't do this,' the man sobs.

'You watched,' she screams at him with sudden fury. 'You watched them.'

'I couldn't do anything,' he cries.

'You should've done something. You should have fought.'

'Sal, they had a knife to my throat ... I couldn't do ...' his voice snaps off with a sob.

'Take me, please,' she begs me.

'Okay,' my answer is blunt. It's her choice, and she's right. The pain will go. The physical pain of being taken like that and the hurt inside too. All of it will be gone.

'Jerry was unconscious. You're not, so there might be some pain. Not much, and it doesn't last long.'

'Just take me,' she begs, 'do it ... Please just do it.'

I step close to her, my mouth flooding with saliva again as my body prepares for the bite. This close I can smell the semen and blood on her. She's bleeding between the legs and from her backside too. The poor woman. She must be in agony, absolute agony, and it defeats me how she's still on her feet.

Her eyes stay locked on mine as I move in close; our faces just inches apart. My hand touches the side of her face, tender and soft. She closes her eyes; her swollen lips part as I lean in. My hand snakes gently to the back of her head, holding her in place.

Our lips touch. I push harder, sealing our mouths in place as I push my saliva in. My tongue darts forward, to ensure the saliva is pushed in. It feels like a kiss, but there is nothing erotic, just a tender moment of one woman saving another. I hold her close for several seconds, silence all around us. My eyes stay open, watching her face. This close, and I can't see the bruises. She looks serene.

The pain and humiliation she endured was awful. The degradation of mankind is too much to bear. This is why we have to change. We're nothing more than those prisoners otherwise. Intent on causing misery to every living thing that crosses our path.

The seal is broken as I step away. She stays still for a few seconds. Her eyes closed. Too late now; nothing will change the outcome.

'Sal,' the man cries. She turns round to face him. They come together, crying and holding each other close.

'Sal,' he breathes.

'It's okay. It's going to be okay,' she says softly, stroking the back of his head. 'I'm sorry for what I said. You couldn't have done anything. They would have killed both of us. Know that I love you. I love you so much.'

'Sal,' his voice breaks, holding her tightly; arms wrapped round her back. She grimaces as the first of the pain starts. I can see it in her face.

'Sal?' he asks with alarm.

'It's okay,' she smiles bravely. She clutches her stomach, bending double and dropping to the floor.

'What have you done?' he shouts at me.

'It'll be over soon,' I reply. He bends over her, murmuring and stroking her face. The pain takes her under, her already damaged body simply unable to take any more. She slips away as he kisses her cheeks and forehead, begging her to wake up.

The twitches come quickly. She convulses, and again, the others stare at her form. The man stays with her, holding her head.

As with the many before her, she sits up and opens her eyes. Again, I will her to speak, sending all of my energy into that one desire. I don't know if it works, but I focus everything into that one thought. She looks straight at me, the same as Jerry did. Her red, bloodshot eyes locked on mine. Speak. I command you to speak. I demand you to speak. I want you to speak. Please. Please speak.

'Can you?' I ask after seconds pass, and she doesn't look away.

'Sal,' the man says to her, 'look at me, Sal.' He turns her head gently round to face him, staring into her red eyes. 'Sal? Can you hear me?'

He leans forward, getting closer and closer to her face. He kisses her forehead, stroking the hair away. Pulls away and implores her again.

'Not all can speak,' Reginald says.

'Sal? Please?' he begs and leans closer again, his mouth heading towards hers.

'Don't kiss her,' I call out. 'You'll turn.'

'Kiss me,' she says to gasps from everyone else.

He lunges in clumsily, forcing her head back. I exert my

will so she doesn't bite, unsure if she'll be able to resist with him clamping his mouth on hers. He kisses her greedily, almost distasteful in manner. Pushing harder as he clamps the back of her head. She remains passive, letting him do what he wants, but I know her mouth will be full.

Glancing over, I see a wry smile on Reggie's face. We're turning people through their own choice now. No force needed.

The same thing happens again. He pulls away, staring into the distance as though waiting. The pain comes. He clutches his stomach and rolls to the floor, groaning. He dies. He twitches. He comes back.

I don't will him to speak. Something about the man annoyed me. Maybe he was right not to fight back if his life and hers was at risk, but something about him grated on me. He isn't that man now. He's one of us, but still ... Old habits die hard, and the grudge carries over as he comes into the new order.

I turn round to see another of the women stood with lips locked to April. The same tender action taking place as April holds the woman's head. I wasn't expecting that and have to blink the surprise away.

Another girl approaches Reggie, who blanches in fright.

'Not me,' he says. 'Ask one of them.' He waves to the horde. She looks round in confusion.

'Come here,' I cut in softly. 'Reggie isn't comfortable with kissing. Are you sure this is what you want?'

She nods back, looking scared and vulnerable. Her hands wringing in front of her, trembling with fear.

'You don't have to if you don't want to. You can stay here ...'

She shakes her head, still not speaking. Her eyes implore me, beg me to turn her, or is that the infection interpreting her fear into a message I want to see? Either way, she's coming closer, seemingly determined.

She seems unsure, as though the final act of stepping in to kiss me is too much. I move closer to her, and she doesn't back away. She closes her eyes.

'Sure?'

She nods again. I go through the process of pressing my mouth to hers. She opens her lips willingly, letting it happen without hesitation. I push my tongue forward, forcing the saliva into her mouth. Her own tongue darts into my mouth, and I have to fight not to bite down. I break away, the temptation almost too great. She looks at me in alarm, like she's done something wrong.

'It's okay ... You'll understand in a minute,' I say with a low voice. I will my horde to move in amongst the room, but to do it slowly without threat.

They respond immediately. Gently walking forward with respectful looks. None of them look threatening, and for a minute, I give thanks none of the inmates we turned are amongst them.

The frightened girl clutches her stomach. The old woman moves to her side, helping her to the floor. She lowers the girl down and stays with her, smoothing her face and muttering soft words. The girl doesn't say a word, not the whole time, but goes under quickly, almost willingly.

Is that something new? If the host is willing, does it take less time to turn? Sally went quickly, so did her husband.

Some of the survivors back away from my group who tactfully move away; others make a decision and step forward. I can't believe this is happening, that they're giving themselves willingly.

Their willingness prompts their husbands and partners to go with them. The bond of love binding them together.

Every one of the communicators asks them if they're sure before they do it. That isn't my will; that's them learning from what I did and copying me.

'Are you okay?' the old woman asks the girl as she sits up to open her eyes. The girl, the same as with all of them, looks at me first as if seeking me out to pour her love and devotion towards me.

'I'm fine,' the girl smiles at the old woman. I didn't will her to speak. I didn't will anything. It was done without me.

The husband of Sally is the only one that doesn't have the ability to speak. Of all the survivors who give themselves willingly, they all talk, apart from him. Maybe he can speak but chooses not to, sensing my dislike for him.

Several survivors remain human. The old woman being one of them. She stares round at the abused women who stand with almost serene smiles.

I stay quiet. Content to watch the interactions. The survivors asking the new hosts if they hurt, what it felt like. The new hosts all answer the same–there is no pain, even the agony inside is gone now. Just a nice, warm feeling. None of them mention the hunger which is a deceit but an important one. Try telling them we're all fine and don't feel pain, but we've got this urge to rip your face off and eat your brains.

'Mildred? Are you coming with us?' Sally asks the old woman.

'No, dear,' Mildred answers, 'it isn't for me. I'm too old to change now.'

'No, Mildred, your age doesn't matter. This fixes everything. You won't feel the pain from your arthritis.'

'I may not feel it, but it will still be there,' Mildred replies. 'Will it not?' she turns to ask me.

'I don't know,' I reply with a glance to Reginald.

'We have a chap who suffered from diabetes. He says he doesn't have diabetes now, but we simply don't know how it works yet,' Reginald explains.

'I see,' Mildred says. She seems to think for a minute as her eyes become distant. 'No ... no, this isn't for me,' she snaps back to the present.

'Are you going to stay here? This place isn't safe now,' I say.

'I, er ... well, I don't know,' she looks about. 'We may have to find somewhere else.'

'Remember what I said, others won't be the same as us. They might still come for you if they see you or smell you.'

'Or hear you,' Reginald says. 'You'll be safer with us ... far safer.'

Another couple, listening to the conversation, change their minds and step towards April. A low conversation takes place. They both nod resolutely; minds made up.

Mildred watches the kiss taking place. April and another both pressing lips to the couple, who then step away and hold each other tight. They go to the floor, entwined as the pain takes them. Again, the turn is much quicker as they seem to submit without struggling.

'I'll go with you ...' Mildred says quietly, still watching the couple on the floor. 'But I'm not kissing you, my dear,' she adds with a sad smile. 'Some things are just not done. Is there another way?'

'If you have an open wound,' I reply, 'or if you don't wish me to do it, then Reginald will oblige with respect and dignity.'

'Me?' Reginald says in surprise.

'I'm sure you're a charming man, but no ... I would rather not kiss anyone. Would a prick in my finger suffice?'

'Yes,' I nod. She draws a safety pin from a pocket.

Holding one finger out, she pricks the end. A tiny bubble of blood comes from the hole, making my mouth fill with drool.

'Here you are,' she offers politely.

'Are you sure?'

'Quite sure,' she nods firmly.

I take her pin and prick my own finger. Blood comes out, and I quickly press my finger against hers. She watches with interest as I hold them in place, gently moving the wound round to ensure the blood gets mixed.

'Oh,' she looks down, feeling the first sensation.

'Let me help you,' I guide her down to the floor so she's resting her back against the wall. 'Go with it, and it's much easier. Breathe deeply and relax.'

'Okay, dear,' she closes her eyes, taking a deep breathe in to slowly exhale. She goes very quickly. One minute she is breathing calmly; then, she isn't. The infection kills her easily and brings her back just as quickly.

Within two minutes, she is standing up again; her eyes red and bloodshot. She smiles at me and flexes her wrists. Tentatively at first, then harder, rotating the joints. She lifts one foot off the ground, moving her foot round in small circles.

'No pain,' she marvels.

The last four or five refuse to offer themselves. The urge to just *take them* is so strong, so very strong. But I gave my word, and I must honour it. This is the point where I prove we are different and not the same monsters that hunt them in the hours of darkness.

I draw the others away, sending them out into the hot evening air to gather outside. The last few say farewells to their associates they'd been hiding with. The hosts try one last time, urging them to turn. They refuse; the fear in them too great to submit.

Outside the vast crowd accepts the new hosts with barely a flicker. The communicators being the only ones to express anything akin to emotion.

As the sun starts to drop, we move off, traipsing through the once perfectly manicured lawns to head into the town and the vehicle ferry port.

I know Reginald wants to turn more, or rather, he wants me to turn more while he watches from a safe distance. But that is no longer the way. I'll defend myself and my group, and I'll take those that are offered, but I won't take anymore by force.

Unless I find those prisoners.

CHAPTER TWENTY-ONE

'I don't want to go through the city. Try and find a route round if you can.'

'We'll have to go through it at some point unless we find something else on the way,' Clarence replies, having taken the map from Nick due to the lads pissing about too much.

'But I fucking hate Portsmouth. The place is a shithole ... It was bad enough when me and Dave went through it days ago. God knows what it'll be like now.'

'Give me a minute,' he mutters, examining the map. 'How we gonna get the fuel back?' he asks suddenly.

'Oh, shit, didn't think of that. I guess we can drive a tanker back if we find one. You drove the last one, didn't you?'

'Yeah, but that was lucky. I doubt we'll find another one.'

'The docks must have shit loads of ships going in and out. They need fuel, so there must be tankers.'

'I think a lot of it is piped. Plus, you're thinking of Southampton. That's the commercial docks. Portsmouth is a naval docks.'

'Okay, we'll try Portsmouth first, and if that doesn't …'

'What about the refinery?' Lani cuts in.

'Refinery?' I ask.

'Fawley, the big refinery in Southampton. It's huge, like the biggest in the country or something … We studied it in school for environmental studies.'

'Why did you do a refinery for environmental studies?' Nick asks.

'Impact on the surrounding land. They got a marsh thing next to it. You know, one of those places that birds use, salt marsh! That's it, a salt marsh.'

'Dave? You've got experience of refineries. What do you think?'

'How does Dave know about refineries?' Lani asks.

'He blew one up once,' I reply.

Clarence starts chuckling, shaking his head. 'It was seen by the astronauts on the space station,' he says.

'No fucking way,' Cookey exclaims. 'Shit … That's fucking awesome.'

'Are they still up there?' Blowers asks. 'The astronauts, I mean?'

'Oh, shit, yeah,' Nick says. 'They must be. Poor fuckers …'

'They must be able to get back down, like with a one of them pod things,' Cookey says.

'Nah, it's all controlled by Nasa. They have to work out the re-entry approach and the time, all that kind of stuff; otherwise, they burn up or land in the middle of the ocean,' Nick explains.

'Imagine that! Poor bastards get through and land in the Pacific. They'd be fucked,' Cookey shakes his head at the thought.

'Refinery,' Dave says, bringing the conversation back to where it should be.

'Yeah, the refinery ... Worth a go? Got to be, I reckon ...?'

'Try the docks first. If they're negative, then we go for that instead,' Clarence suggests.

'Hmmm, I'm in a mind to go straight there. We might be able to bring shit loads back before anything happens to it,' I reply.

'Like what?' he asks me.

'Like some crazy bastard like Dave blowing it up. I'm joking,' I add quickly as he starts to protest.

'Shouldn't they have people there all the time to shut things down and stuff,' Nick says. 'It might go up on its own if they don't switch stuff off.'

'Well, it hasn't yet,' Blowers replies.

'How do you know?' Cookey asks.

'It's a fucking refinery. We'd bloody see it ... and feel it ... and hear it. Fuck me, Cookey, if they saw one from space, then I'd think we'd know about it from like twenty miles away.'

'Fair one. You're still a twat, though.'

'We can take the motorway around Portsmouth and go straight there,' Clarence says, looking at the map. 'It's an easy enough route, and we can avoid the city centres.'

'That's got to be better then. Right, we'll go for the refinery. Everyone happy?'

'The longer we're away from the fucking fort, the better,' Blowers mutters.

'Fact,' Cookey adds.

Clarence guides me to the motorway as the lads settle down to their banter, but it feels different, almost forced. The shock from last night and then this morning has hit them hard, harder than anything yet. Losing Tom was bad enough, and then being called baby killers was the final touch.

The heat is intense again. Incredibly, it feels hotter than yesterday. A humid heat that saps energy and drains patience. Heat hazes hang above the road surface, creating shimmering patterns. Already the world is starting to feel alien and different.

I lean forward, trying to expel the heat building up between my back and the seat. My hands feel sweaty and greasy. We gain the motorway, building the speed up as we fly past signs for towns and villages, historical places of interest. In the distance are buildings, commercial properties with long, flat roofs, and small clusters of houses.

As the road lifts higher, we catch glimpses of the sea, vast and blue. Glittering from the sun reflecting off the still surface. We pass junctions for towns that will simply fall to ruin after being looted and emptied of anything of use. If we do ever defeat the infected or create a vaccine or cure, then it will take years to rebuild what we had. The over-reliance on mass production, mass farming, mass everything has left us de-skilled for survival.

I think of my own life before this happened. I could use a computer easy enough, navigate the operating systems for work and leisure, and like everyone, I spent hours online, surfing the internet but not learning anything of use. I think back now to the time I spent watching video clips, reading random forums when I could have been learning about survival techniques, how to grow crops, make weapons, engine maintenance. But then, like everyone, I was wrapped up in a comfortable, little bubble of existence. Thinking everything was safe. There were wars and international difficulties but never close to home, and the doomsday prophets were all labelled as freaks.

We all thought it would be oil that caused an eventual collapse. It would run dry, and everything would break apart, but not in our lifetime. We were safe, content. Go to work, come home, eat food, see friends, go to work, come home, watch shit videos online, get drunk, go to work. Whole lives spent in state of being blinkered.

Now it's all gone. The whole thing is fucked beyond repair. So many things I wished I did. Travelled and seen the world, broadened my horizons or whatever they call it. Spent more time with my family. That's the biggest one. Of all the things, that is the one that hurts the most. Still not knowing what happened to my mum and dad. They left their house to look for me, and that's it. Wiped out or turned into one of those evil, rancid fucking things. Those things took everything we had, took all the good, and made it shit, and caused the suffering, the death and pain for so many millions. More than that. It must be billions by now. Every person on the planet must have been affected by this.

The fear my parents must have felt at realising what was happening and still being brave enough to go out into the collapsing world to try and find their son. Risking and ultimately losing their own lives in the process. They could have been killed by me or Dave. They could have been in the flatlands with Darren, cut down by the GPMG or sniped by Jamie. Stabbed or hacked apart as they fought to take our flesh.

The thoughts spin through my mind. Some of the survivors in that fort would have had people they know on the flatlands. Their own children or parents, siblings even. Last night that mother held her child close, refusing to accept what was happening. No one could ever blame her. She was fighting for the life of her child and too frantic to know what was happening. The memory of the child's head blowing apart from the bullet flashes through my mind. A split-second action done amongst many others, but that image is burnt in forever. The mother screaming as I shot the girl, her face as I pointed the gun at her and pulled the trigger. Her face already coated with blood from the first shot.

The faces that went white with fear as I pointed the pistol at them; the wide-eyed looks of disbelief, shock, and terror. The anguish of last night is etched into my soul. We've seen worse; we all have. We've all killed infected children before without a flicker of emotion, but the fort was meant to be our safe place. It wasn't our job to keep it secure. They had guards with guns that should have been there, ready to deal with anything at the gate. They fucked up. They caused this, and we had to respond to deal with their mistake, and then ... then we get hung out to dry for it.

'Boss,' Clarence's deep voice penetrates my thoughts. I snap back and realise my hands are gripping the wheel, knuckles white from the pressure, and my right foot pressing harder to the floor. The massive engine screaming as the speed builds faster and faster.

I ease up, gently lifting my foot and letting the vehicle slow to a steady pace. Looking over, I see Clarence staring at me; a concerned look on his face.

'Sorry, mate,' I mutter. He nods before turning his head to look down at the map stretched out on his lap.

I feel angry at the injustice of it, that we're being blamed for something they should have prevented. Anger at having to be at those meetings, justifying our actions, when we should be pushing forward and getting things done.

Fucked up. This is all fucked up. How much worse can it get?

CHAPTER TWENTY-TWO

They say that childhood shapes who you are and who you become. They say those years are the most important for development of the mind. The people around you should nurture you and guide you to become a good person. I was fucked from the start.

My daddy was a mean son of a bitch. Drinking, whoring, gambling, fighting. He did it all. He did it all, and he did it hard. He whupped my ass every week. Sometimes the bruises were so bad I couldn't sit down for days in a row. No one cared. No one gave a shit. That was life, and you got on with it.

South Central LA was a steaming pot of gangs forming, splitting apart, re-forming, ground taken, and territory marked out. Every kid had to prove himself to be in a gang, and the violence exploded on every street.

I grew up in that violence. It was all I ever knew. At home with my daddy, at school with the teachers, on the streets with my buddies. Violence was a way of life, a natural instinct brought out by the necessity of survival.

Some escaped through education, but they were rare.

Most lived their lives by what the gangs said they could and couldn't do.

I was lucky. I got into weight training to get big so my daddy wouldn't whup me no more. My body was built for it, with strong joints. I ate everything I could get without complaint. The bigger men saw what I was and trained me until I got big. Then one day, my daddy didn't whup me no more. The busted nose and jaw I gave him saw to that.

From that day, I swore no motherfucker would whup me. Not ever. I got big, freaky fucking big, and freaky fucking strong. My life was in the gym–hours every day, every week, every month. Lifting and lifting. Pushing weight and growing like a motherfucker.

My size got me in fights, and I went into the pen when I was just a boy. That's where I learned how to lift like the inmates lift. Heavy weights and a solid regime. Disciplined and strong.

My life went into power lifting. Blasting through local and regional competitions and destroying every motherfucker that stood against me. I was unstoppable, a motherfucking real-life superman. I broke records for bench press and bicep strict curl again and again.

Then I came to this fucking country. This stupid, dumb-ass, mother-fucking backwards country, and some young punk whupped my ass. The flight had fucked me up. The jet lag, the change of air, the different food, the cold and damp all fucked me up, so when I lifted, I knew I wasn't doing well. That punk beat me fair and square, which I could take. But taunting me like I'm some motherfucking bitch ... Well, I swore no motherfucker would do that to me. I snapped and beat the fucker to death with a dumbbell. He wasn't the first motherfucker I killed, but that was the first time I had a room full of fucking witnesses.

Ten fucking years I spent in that prison. That old, dirty, stinking fucking hole. Surrounded by dumb motherfuckers and missing my own people every fucking day. Because I was American, because I was black, because I was big, everyone wanted a piece of me. So I had to fight, and I did fight. I whupped more ass in that hellhole than I ever did on the streets.

Those memories flood through my head as I lay dying on the dirty street. That young punk's head exploding from the dumbbell bursting his skull apart. The people I'd fucked up and hurt. The looks on their faces when they knew they were done. Those things came into my mind.

The pain was more than I ever felt before. I been stabbed, shanked, beaten, and shot, but nothing comes close to what went through my gut. Thousands of nails digging into my insides. Broken glass moving through my veins. I fought against it. I refused to submit and gave it every mother-fucking thing I could.

But it took me. The darkness came down, and I knew I was done for. This was the end. My heart slowed. My breathing got harder. Everything shut down, eyes gone, hearing gone, all feeling gone.

So be it. Fuck it. Fuck all of ya.

But I ain't dead, or at least I ain't dead now. If I was dead, I wouldn't be aware of still lying in this motherfucking street. Except there ain't no pain now, no pain at all. There ain't nothing. Just a feeling of peace like I ain't never known before, like I want to lie here forever.

It changes. The peace goes. Hunger is there now. I am mother-fucking hungry, more hungry than I ever was. Dead people don't get hungry. Dead people don't feel a motherfucking empty feeling in their stomachs.

I'm alive, motherfucker. I sit up, feeling the strength in

the abdominal muscles as they flex. My arms feel bigger and stronger than ever before. I open my eyes and see the death around me. A strong smell that I know is blood, but it's mixed with shit and piss too. I never smelt nothing so strong before.

Bodies everywhere. A thick fucking trail of them going back to the back door of that store we busted through. My arms are fucking huge. The muscles are standing proud, pushing the veins out. Holy shit, I feel strong. Stronger than fucking Samson with his mother-fucking hair. Like fucking Schwarzenegger from the first Predator movie.

Motherfucker, this is the best I ever felt. I am fucking superhuman. My legs push me up so I'm standing. Clenching my fists to tense my forearms; knots of muscle bulging under my skin.

The power in me is fucking awesome. My shoulders are buzzing. I roll them round, feeling the muscles flex and relax. I move my head side to side as popping noises sound out. I truly ain't never felt this good.

Thought I was dead. Thought I was fucking gone and shit, but I ain't gone nowhere. I'm right here, standing proud. Those things are still here. The dumb-ass fucking things that took me down. Fucking red eyes all staring at me and shit.

'Which one of you fuckers tried to kill me? I ain't never gonna get whupped, not ever ...' I walk over at 'em. The things don't try and attack me now. I'm too fucking strong now. Something else, something different. I don't wanna hurt them no more. But they whupped me down, so I gotta fuck 'em up, but I don't want to. They staring at me, looking all sorry and shit. They didn't mean no harm. They just hungry is all. Dumb motherfuckers just wanted some food. Be wrong to beat on them now.

Guess I must be one of them. Must be. They ain't trying to attack me, and I know I got bit. I still got the marks on my arms and neck. I got bit and went down. Now I'm up, and they ain't doing shit but staring at me. I must be one of them. Only I ain't one of them. I'm me.

Movement. Colin sitting up, looking all weird. His eyes are red like the things'. For the first time, I don't wanna whup his ass anymore. The other prisoners sit up too. All of them with red eyes and staring at me.

We all been bit. We all like these motherfuckers now. But I can speak and think same as I used to. Fuck, better than I used to. My mind is clear. No pain anywhere. Just feel like a strong motherfucker.

'Get up,' Colin looks at me. Dumb fucker just stares, so I tell him again, 'Get up.' He listens that time and stands up. 'You speak too?'

'Yes,' his dumb ass replies, with his stupid head bobbing up and down like some puppy dog. Only he ain't no stupid puppy dog. He's one of my kind now.

'You all speak?' Couple say yes, Some just stand there, saying fuck all. They all staring at me like I did something special. Not just the prisoners, but all the things too.

My mind fills with thoughts I ain't never had before. No, that's wrong. They ain't thoughts, but a feeling, like a sense of something.

Control.

That's it. I feel control. All up on these motherfuckers. I ain't no telepathic freaky fucker, but I can sense them, in my mind.

These motherfuckers looking at me like they in love or some shit. Fucking motherfuckers. But it ain't love like they wanna blow me or shit but love like they wanna worship me. Like I'm a god.

Yeah, bitches, like a god. That's how I feel, like a mother-fucking god. All powerful and shit, like those Viking gods with the big arms and big beards, only I ain't no white Viking motherfucker.

I'm nodding my head, grinning at them. They looking back at me all full of love. Holy shit, my arms ain't never felt this big before. My legs too. They feel all pumped and massive, like I just did a fucking dose of roids.

Fuck that hunger is strong. So mother-fucking strong it makes my mouth get all filled with spit. I need to eat, only I don't wanna eat no chicken or steak. I got something else on my mind. Something I ain't never wanted to do before.

'Goddam, I feel good. You feel this good?'

'Yeah, Randy,' Colin grins back at me. He's a good man, Colin. He's my buddy. We go way back, me and Colin. Damn, I love that dumb-ass bitch. I love all these bitches.

Where the fuck were we going? Fuck yeah, we going to that fort where all the fine bitches at. Man, I could do with some fine bitch now with some big juicy titties. I'd fucking eat those juicy titties. I wanna feast on them juicy titties. I wanna fuck 'em and feast on 'em at the same mother-fucking time. Fine bitches and men too. I wanna eat them fellas just as much as them bitches. Hell, right now I'd bite their fucking cocks if I could. I'd suck on them hairy balls and bite the shit out of 'em.

That big house is just back aways. We could go there and get us some eating, but fuck, they just a few there, and I heard that fort got thousands inside. That's what we want– thousands of people to bite and suck on.

'We need a mother-fucking boat. Holy shit, Harry, you look like some scary motherfucker with that big-ass beard and them eyes all red and shit.' He don't say nothing back but just stares like he always did.

'Which way the coast?' I ask the question, and Harry just points behind me. I turn round but don't see shit, just the end of the road and some big, white building.

'What the fuck am I looking at?' Then it hits me. The big, white building ain't no building at all. It's a motherfucking big-ass boat is what it is. 'Holy fuck, that's the god damn strangest fucking thing.' The boat is moored to the end of the road, just right there, at the end of the street.

I start off in that direction; my eyes fixed on the boat. Big and white, with a black chimney thing sticking out the top. I didn't see the chimney on account of the black sky an' all. A big parking lot is next to the road. That must be where the cars wait before they get on. The lot's empty now. Ain't no fucker here but us.

There being a boat there an' all, then that must be the water edge, so figures there'll be more boats round here. As much as I like big things, like my mother-fucking arms, I don't fancy takin' no boat that size. Hell, we'll probably sink the thing, and it gotta be complicated as fuck to make it move.

My boys follow me down to the edge, walking past the big boat and moving further down. It looks like a big fucking river mouth going in towards the land. The open, dark sea on one side, and shit loads of boats tied up on the other side.

We can't walk along the water edge all the way on account on some dumb-fuck putting buildings in the way, so we gotta detour round as we work down the river. My fellas and them things that killed us following behind all meek as you please.

All of us smell it at the same time. That smell of blood, only this is different. It's human blood. Now I know I only just got bit and shit, but that's what it is–human blood. There's fear in that smell too, strong fear. We all stop and sniff the air, turning our heads this way and that. Ain't no breeze, no wind or nothing. The air is sticky and hot as fuck.

The smell comes from a big, old warehouse just to the side. No noise or nothing else coming from it, just the smell. We get close until my nose is pressed against the crack in the door, and I'm inhaling deep.

People inside. More than one. The blood is fresh and close. Just the other side of this door. My mouth is full of spit. That hunger is worse now, driving me to get these doors open. I get hold of the door and give it a pull. It rattles some but don't open. Harry and the fellas take a hold, and we pull together, giving it heave after heave. I guess they feel strong too as the door is wrenched open. Splintering the lock as we drag it wide.

The moonlight reflects of the scared faces staring at us. Young and old, male and female. One of them is holding a rag to a wound on some bitch's arm. She must have cut it somehow and stayed quiet for fear of us hearing her, but the smell did it.

'Motherfuckers,' I greet the people with a big grin as we go inside. They scream, but that just gets us going.

There it is, that feeling I said about. My fellas and those things want to bust on in there and start feasting, but they ain't doing it cos I ain't said they could. Only I don't need to say they can, not loud from my voice. I can do it in my head.

But fuck that, I ain't letting them dumb fucks go ahead of me. No, sir If there's feasting to be done, I'm getting me some. I charge in, grinning at the little faces and getting off on the fear they putting out. They scream and thrash, and some even try to fight back, but it don't matter none. They all fucked.

I get a nice bitch. With blonde hair and big juicy titties. She wails and begs, but my hands hold her like a vice, pulling her in close. Those titties looking all juicy, so I take me a nice, big bite, sinking my teeth into one of them and biting through the material of her shirt.

Hot blood fills my mouth, and I swear I ain't never tasted nothing like it. Like metal or something but hot and sticky, and mother-fucking delicious. I swallow it down, and the lump of flesh that I tore away, that gets swallowed down too. Strangest thing, but once I done that, I don't want her no more. I want me another one. So I grab another one. This one a man trying to hide in the deep shadows of the corner. I drag him out by his ankle. He kicks and cries like a bitch, but I lift him up, all the way up by the ankles till he hangs upside down, beating at my legs. I bite into the back of his leg, in the thick muscle. The flesh comes away nice and easy, all tender and succulent. I swallow that down too, moaning with pleasure at the taste; then, I drop him to the floor. His nose busts open from hitting the deck, and he grabs at his leg, being all like a bitch.

Looking round to get me another one, but they all gone. The greedy sons of bitches have taken them all. Every other one of them is bitten and bleeding. Dying on the floor and shittin' their pants.

A feeling of pleasure grips me. Like I done something good, and now I get rewarded. This is what we're meant to do. Eat the humans. No, not eat them but bite them. Make them be like us. I get why those things were chasing us now. Hell, I'd chase now I know what it tastes like.

I stand back and watch as they die. Just like me, they go kicking and screaming, fighting to the last breath. Then they start twitching and shit, like they getting zapped by a live wire. Minute later, and they're standing up, all with red eyes like the rest of us.

Funny thing is, I don't remember no twitching. Just one

minute, I was dying, and the next I wasn't. Full of pain, and then it was gone, like it had never been there, and it was all in my head.

These fuckers must be the same, except they all dumb and stupid and ain't thinking like I do. No, they looking at me like I'm a god again.

Scooby snack done, and we keep going, following the river. The sides here are just high walls, with the water lapping at them with no way of getting out to a boat unless you willing to get wet. I don't mind getting wet. Hell, I can swim, but fuck, only if I have to.

Further down, we find the berthing place, some pontoons with boats tied on. Big, expensive-looking speed boats all sleek with tiny, tinted windshields so the posh folk don't mess up their fluffy hair.

The big metal gate at the end of the pontoon ain't no obstacle. My strong arms pull me up easy. I ain't never felt this powerful. Even jumping down the other side don't send no pain through my knees like it should. My fellas get over, but the other dumb fucks don't seem to grasp the concept of climbing. Colin looks at the gate and pulls the handle back from the inside, swinging it open to let the others walk through.

On the pontoon, I go from boat to boat, looking to see which one we can take. All of these boats need a key to start them up. We have to go back out the gate and down the water edge. We find another gated pontoon, and I climb over to open it from the inside.

Same thing here–all the posh boats need keys. There might be some way of starting 'em up without a key, but I ain't got that kind of knowledge; carjacking was never my style.

Next one down, and I don't need to climb over the big

gate, seeing as there's a rotten corpse holding it open for us. Looks like rats and shit have been eating at it. All the face chewed off and big lumps missing from the arms and legs, white bone sticking out in places.

Another rotten-ass corpse on the pontoon. Some posh boy that had fluffy hair and wearing them stupid, motherfucking brown boat shoes and tight shorts, with some striped jersey. Fucking dumb-ass is all chewed up too, and he covered in bird shit, so I guess the local vultures or whatever the fuck they have here have been pecking the fuck out of him. But he does have a long, coiled, brightly coloured thing attached to his belt loop, with a big, shiny key on the end. I take the key and work down the boats, trying to stick it in the holes.

It fits in a big-ass mother-fucking stream-lined thing with the tiny windshield and the flat front bit where the posh bitches sunbathe. Ain't much room on here, not enough to take all my posse, so I stick with my gang.

Funny thing is–I think it, and they do it. My gang get in the boat, and I don't have to say shit. They just do it. The other motherfuckers just stand there, staring at me. Hell, I almost feel guilty for leaving 'em, but there ain't no room, and thinking about it, I don't wanna take no big group with me. Those fuckers at the fort will see a big group a mile off. I don't wanna leave 'em, but fuck it. Ain't got no choice.

The boat is easy to use. Gotta be for the dumb fucks that own 'em. Press the button, and the engine starts, lever goes forward and back.

'We tied on, Randy,' Colin tells me. I know we fucking tied on. I can see the fucking ropes for myself through the fucking eyes in my fucking head, but I know he don't mean shit by it.

'Take 'em off.' He does as told. Getting back out to pull

the ropes off, then gets back in quick, like in case we go off without him.

Takes me a few minutes to get the hang of it, smashing and bumping into the side of the pontoon and cracking a few other boats. Making it move is easy enough but getting the thing to turn is harder than it looks. Go back and twist the wheel, go forward and turn it the other way, like a car. Only there ain't no brake to hold it still, so it keeps moving and smashing into other stuff.

Fuck, ain't my boat, so it don't matter. I get us out into the river and facing the right way; then, I push the lever forward. The boat pulls away like a mustang. They got signs saying five knots. I don't know what a knot is, but I guess it's pretty slow. Fuck that, ain't no river police gonna come along now.

Few seconds later, and we're going past the big, white boat and into the open sea. Everything is black as fuck, dark, with no lights anywhere. I guess normally there be lights everywhere for the ships to aim at, but now is just darkness. The moon is bright as fuck, and I know the mainland is that way, so I figure we just aim *that way* and see what happens.

Motherfucker, this feels good. The wind blasting into my face. Hot wind, not like in the yard when we get outside time and the cold, damp wind gets under your clothes. This like Miami or some shit. The water is flat as fuck too. Ain't no waves nowhere, so the boat just goes straight on with hardly any bouncing.

'Harry, you know where this mother-fucking fort is?' I have to shout coz of the engine noise. He nods back but don't say nothing.

He puts his left arm up and points across the water. 'Southampton,' he says, then holds his right arm up and points across the water but down aways. 'Portsmouth.'

'Which one we need?' He drops the left arm and holds the right one still. Portsmouth. Everyone in the world has heard of Portsmouth and the English navy, and that famous ship that sank when it came out.

'Is the fort on the water?' He nods again. 'We don't wanna go there. They'll hear us …' He nods. Fuck, I see the thing in us has made him a new man, all chatty and shit.

Man, that juicy titty was good, tasted so damn good. That leg too. Both of 'em tasted good as shit and makes me hungry just thinkin' bout it.

That fort is fucked. We gonna fuck it up and eat every motherfucker in there.

CHAPTER TWENTY-THREE

'Listen ... Can you hear it? Yes? Coming from the water ...'

'I hear it, Marcy,' he cocks his head to one side, opening his mouth to hear better. The dull thud of an engine coming from the river. It ticks over for a few minutes, then roars to a loud scream.

I sprint towards the big vehicle ferry, just in time to see the large cruiser go flying past. Fully loaded with big men.

'Was that them?' I ask one of the inmates stood near me.

He nods back, watching the boat as it melts into the darkness of the water. 'That's them,' he tells me in the same flat tone.

'Are they turned?' Reginald calls out as he jogs up, being too slow to keep up with the sprinting.

'I don't know, too far to tell.'

'None of the bodies are the inmates,' he reports. 'They're all old living challenged. I mean old as in the number of days they've been turned, not old in terms of their physical age. None of them are fresh, and judging by the number of bodies, I would suggest they were opposed by a formidable group, which would fit the profile of the inmates. There is a large pool of blood in the middle of the road but relatively fewer bodies in that area. I determine they got turned, went down bleeding, and then went off.'

'That's an assumption ...'

'No,' he cuts me off, 'more of a calculation based on the evidence. What does it matter? Either way, they are gone, and it does not impact on your ... our plans.'

'If they are turned, then they have clearly retained intelligence by the fact they're using a boat, which means we could have joined forces.'

'Joined forces?' he asks me with surprise. 'I thought your plan was to kill them for what they did.'

'If they were human, yes, but not if they were turned. There'd be no point in holding them accountable for their previous sins.'

'I understand,' he nods in agreement, glancing back at some of the sex offenders in our group. 'Well, that's your vehicle ferry,' he adds, looking up at the ship. 'Can any of our living challenged drive it?'

'I don't know. I can't access what they're capable off. Go and ask them.'

'Right, well, I'll do that then, shall I?'

'Yes, Reggie, you do that.'

'I mean. We couldn't get one of the others to do it ...? Young Jerry here would make a great asker of questions ... And please, my name is Reginald.'

'Reggie, what's wrong?'

'Nothing,' he answers too quickly, his voice just a tone too high.

'What is it?'

'Nothing, Marcy. Really, there is nothing wrong ... Only how many more are we going to get that are capable of speaking? Only it seems we do have rather a lot now.'

'Why is that a bad thing?'

'Oh, I am not suggesting it's a *bad thing,* only if we have so many speakers, then why not use them to speak ... instead of me all the time.'

'Well, why don't you ask them to speak, then? I ask you, and you can delegate to them.'

'I can do that, can I? Delegate, I mean?'

'Yes, Reggie, you can delegate. You have been delegating for most of the day anyway.'

'Only when I've seen you are busy, and I haven't wished to disturb you.'

'Well, feel free to delegate away, delegate to your heart's content.'

'Jerry, go and find out if anyone can drive this boat, please,' he tells the boy. Jerry scoots off quickly, heading towards the massed group standing quietly.

'We're growing, Marcy. Look how many there are now, and I still can't quite believe how those last ones volunteered.'

'After what they'd been through, you can hardly blame them. Reginald, you need to understand this cannot all rest on one person. This is not about me. This is about us, the species. If something happens to me, then you have to be able to take over. If you go, then it has to be another one. The thing inside us wants you to adore me, and it wants you to turn as many as you can. You must fight against that, Reggie. There is another way here. I know it.'

He stares at me, nodding gently.

'That means,' I look at him and then at the others stood with us, 'that if I don't make it, then someone else has to hand themselves over to the fort and make them understand. Tell them about the diabetes. Mildred, you tell them about your arthritis and the others that don't feel pain. Tell them what happened at the house and how this took away all the pain. This thing might cure HIV or Hepatitis, cancer even. The possibilities are too big for us to just let it go. Promise me.'

'I promise, Marcy,' Reggie says earnestly.

'No, Reggie, I mean promise, really promise, not just from the devotion you feel for me. Not that, but from you ... from all of you Swear it.'

'Marcy, I swear it,' Reginald says in a firm voice.

'I will go if you fail,' Mildred replies. 'They may see me as less threatening anyway. Maybe I should go instead of you. Or possibly with you?'

'That's a good idea,' Reggie beams, 'a very good idea.'

'Me too. I swear it,' Sally adds. 'You could have ripped us apart, but you didn't. I feel that hunger now. I know we all have it. I will willingly go in your place.'

'No, I will go, but just be prepared to take my place.'

'Marcy, my dear, may I make a suggestion?' Mildred asks.

'Of course.'

'If you go alone, they may see just one with retained intelligence, and from what you've said, they will know some of us can retain our ... er ... personality for want of a better word, but if several go with you to represent a cross section, it may assist in showing them it's not a trick or some ploy to gain entrance.'

She makes a good point. A very good point. She looks old and dignified, with her greying hair swept up into a tight bun. If I approached with her, maybe Jerry and Sally, Reginald too, there is no way we could look threatening. But that puts more at risk of being killed outright.

'I'll consider it,' I nod back. 'Seriously, it's a very good suggestion, but we have to weigh it up with the risk of us all being killed outright.'

'Which is why you shouldn't go,' Reginald cuts in.

'Reggie, that is the chemical reaction talking. You have to guard against that and understand this is not about me.'

'Sorry … it's very hard,' he mutters.

'We all feel it, Marcy,' Mildred says. 'You don't have that feeling towards yourself, so perhaps you don't understand it. We all feel devoted you, an intense feeling of deep love. Especially Jerry,' she adds with a smile at the boy running back towards us, holding the hand of an adult male communicator. The sight warms all of us. The action is completely unnecessary. The male host would simply follow him as requested, with no need for physical contact. But the boy has retained enough character to *want* to hold his hand and lead him. That very action is why this must be done.

I know for a fact that not one of the hosts in this crowd would ever harm a hair on that boy's head, nor any of the children within our group. Even the sex offenders we turned do not feel any urge towards anyone other than equal and matched love.

'Can you drive it?' Reginald asks the man being led by Jerry.

'I can,' he replies flatly.

'How?' I ask him.

'I was second officer for another ferry company,' he replies.

'What's your name?' Reginald asks.

'Howard,' his reply invokes a sudden silence as Reginald glances at me.

'Howard? Do you know Howie?' Stupid question. How would he know him, but it comes out before I can think.

'No.'

'Do you have any children?' Reginald asks, taking a look at the age of the man.

'No, I was gay.'

'Was gay? Why was?' I ask.

'I'm not anything now.'

'Tell me, Howard, do you fancy anyone?' His reply interests me greatly.

'No.'

'No urges of a sexual nature at all? Do any of you feel attraction to anyone?'

'You,' I get a chorus of replies.

'Other than me ... That's the infection or virus, or whatever it is inside of you talking. Apart from me?'

Shaking heads all round. I fancied Darren, but then that must have been the infection within me, making me feel like that. It went the second he died.

I glance round at some of the men gathered here. I don't feel devotion to anyone, not the same as they do towards me. I feel loyalty and love for them, but not that extreme emotion they're experiencing. Some of them are very attractive. Chiselled features. Some look intelligent and cultured. Some of them are handsome enough to have been models. I can certainly admire their form, their physical attributes, but I don't feel an attraction to any of them.

No, that almost feels incestuous, like we're related. The mere suggestion of sexual activity with any of them repulses me. That could cause a problem. If we are to survive as a species, then procreation would need to take place, but procreation needs urges, and without urges, there will be no procreation. Unless they just do it as an act of breeding without the pleasure.

What the hell am I thinking about this for? I'll be planning the soft furnishings for our houses next. Shaking my head, I look over at Howard, marvelling at how a mere miniscule coincidence could cause a reaction.

'Well, Howard, you're in charge of this bit. Tell us where you want us.' Reginald beams at the man, taking great pride in his new ability to delegate.

'I will check,' he replies before walking off towards the boat. Jerry walks back over to my side, where he's been since he turned in the house.

Waiting in the balmy night air, we could almost be a gaggle of tourists waiting to board a boat for a pleasure cruise. Nearly all of the ones closest look uninjured. The bitten ones are further back in the main crowd. They're even talking to each other. Well, the ones that have retained intelligence are anyway. Having almost normal conversations about what they did in their previous lives, and as with any small place, they soon start mentioning places and people they all know. Moaning about the state of the roads and how busy it gets in the summer season with all the coaches driving about.

The surrealism astounds me to the core. Thousands of people just stood, waiting patiently. No pushing or shoving, no moaning at having to wait or the heat. No one griping about their feet hurting or having a sore back. No one lighting up and annoying everyone else with their cigarette smoke. Children and adults just stood together, with a handful at the front chatting amiably.

'Howard's back,' Reginald nods towards the walkway at the side of the boat and Howard walking back towards us. He approaches quietly, coming to a stop a few feet away and standing motionless, arms hanging at his sides.

'Is it okay?' I ask him.

'Yes, they can get on. Please put them into the vehicle

section at the bottom so the weight is evenly distributed,' he speaks without expression.

'Reginald, would you care to delegate? What else do you need?' I direct the question at Howard.

'Please give me a few minutes to get ready and then you can untie the ropes. The tide is in with very little pull. I can hold the vessel in position.'

'Of course.'

He turns and walks away as Reginald turns to speak with the communicators, delegating his little legs off.

The communicators work quickly, but then, once the instruction is given and they know which way to go, there is little else to worry about. No pushing and shoving, or tickets that need to be collected, and none of them will rush to the little café kiosk to get served before everyone else.

Reginald marches ahead, guiding them onto the big, flat sections at the bottom where the vehicles normally park, using the massed living challenged, as he calls them, as ballast.

It takes just minutes, and I wonder how much longer it would take with humans and all the issues they have. Definitely a lot longer. Jerry stays by my side, smitten with love as he stares up at me. Bless, at least he's not goggling at my cleavage. The lights on the ship flicker on as Howard gets the engines going. The ship looked inert and lifeless before, but now the lights are stark against the darkness everywhere else. A sign of life, and a warming sight at that.

We walk up the ramp, entering through the narrow hatch into the stairwell. The host bodies are all stood evenly spaced throughout the vehicle section. Jerry and I go up the stairs, coming out in the empty passenger lounge. We walk a circuit of the central area, going round the café and small shop until we find the door leading to the bridge.

At the top, we walk in to see Howard directing other hosts, telling them to press this and turn that. His flat voice is the only real sound, none of the others say anything but just do as he tells them. The ropes are untied, and he starts pulling the vessel out from the dock, gliding it backwards, out into the open sea.

The pre-recorded safety message starts blurting out, thanking everyone for travelling today and making them aware where they can and can't smoke and asking them to deactivate their car alarms, finishing off with wishing them a pleasant voyage.

The whole thing is seamless from start to finish. Effortless almost. Reginald and a few others make their way onto the bridge, like a gesture that they're part of the top table, so standing in the vehicle section doesn't apply.

'So dark,' I murmur quietly. The motion is so stable it almost feels like we're still and the land is moving away. No lights anywhere. No streetlights, no buildings, nothing. Just a dark silhouette, with the roof tops glinting from the moonlight.

Howard turns the ship round, which causes a mild vibration as we go against whatever tide there is. The vibrations ease as he settles on course and powers the ship to move forward.

We're away. Heading towards the mainland and the fort while I pray Howie is the decent man I think he is.

CHAPTER TWENTY-FOUR

'Jesus Christ, that's fucking massive,' Cookey exclaims from his position on the GPMG. 'It's just fucking massive, like huge.'

The drive here was uneventful. We stuck to the motorways, purposefully taking a longer route to avoid the city centres.

Coming down towards the site now, we can see the vast, sprawling refinery. Like a city almost. The thing just goes on and on, stretching off into the distance. It looks alien to me. Something that means nothing. A complex network of giant silvery tubes and pipes running between gargantuan, white silos. The whole design of the place is on a grid, straight roads leading between the silos and the concrete buildings.

From our position, we can see the harbour entrance. A wide mouth that goes deep into the land with a myriad of commercial docks, pontoons, harbours, and jetties.

On the seaward side of the refinery, there's a pontoon and something in the water with big, silver-coloured tubes running back onto land. A super tanker, the type they use to ship oil around the world, is moored alongside. More tubes and pipes run from the ship into structures that must be pumps used to move the crude oil through the big pipes into the refinery.

The silos must store the different types of fuel as they go through the various processes to turn it into petrol or diesel, or whatever else they make here.

We're still some distance off, which gives us an opportunity to recce the land, all of us looking out for any sign of vehicle tankers.

I take the junction marked for the refinery and start heading down towards it. Coming down from the hill, we lose sight of the refinery. The road is wider than normal, which, I guess, must be for the constant flow of heavy vehicles using it.

At another signposted junction, we turn and start to see the first real signs of the refinery. A high, metal fence fixed securely into the ground and topped with coils of razor wire runs alongside the road. Big warning notices are fixed to the fence at regular intervals, warning of security patrols, CCTV, and only authorised personnel beyond this point.

The refinery would have been a viable terrorism threat, and what better way to cripple a country than by taking out its ability to make the fuel usable.

Within a few hundred metres, we see another sign fixed to the side of the road. This one is large and hand-painted, only recently erected by the looks of it. THIS AREA IS PROTECTED BY ARMED GUARDS. WE WILL SHOOT ON SIGHT. TURN BACK.

'Shit, looks like someone else got here first,' Clarence says as I bring the speed down to a slow crawl.

'Cookey, you better get down, mate,' I call out just as Dave tells him the same thing. The lad drops down, grabbing a bottle of water and staring out the windscreen at the road ahead.

'Look,' Clarence points down the road to a huddled mass on the verge. As we get closer, the shapes come into distinction. Something we've seen time and time again– bodies piled up and left to rot in the sun.

I stop the vehicle alongside as Clarence peers down. There are more piles further up, stacked at regular intervals like the old signs on the fence.

'They ain't all those things,' Clarence says, still avoiding using the Z word. 'Some people in there too. Been shot by the looks of it.'

'Not good,' I reply. We push on, going at a crawl until we reach the next pile of bodies.

'Same again, mixture of people and those things,' Clarence reports as he looks down from his window.

'Some on your side up there, Mr Howie,' Dave points to another stack on the other side of the road. The piles are set at almost the same distance apart from each other. A clear and visible warning of what will happen if we proceed.

'Maybe not such a good idea after all,' I say quietly.

'Keep going, Mr Howie,' Dave urges.

'You sure? This doesn't look too good, mate.'

'Just a bit further.'

'Fair enough,' I push my foot down gently, easing the vehicle forward and passing more piles of bodies.

'What's that?' I ask, pointing to a much larger mass in the distance. The view becomes clearer as we get closer. Several cars pushed together and burnt out.

'Controlled burning,' Dave says. 'See the even scorch marks on the ground? Someone was with the fire, preventing it from spreading.'

'Shit, are those bodies in there?' I ask at the distinct shapes within the vehicles and more stacked to the sides.

'Yeah,' Clarence replies, 'burnt with the vehicles.'

'Christ, they've killed a lot,' I say. 'Reminds me of when we went into your compound in London, all the bodies hanging up.'

'Chris did that as a warning, but they were all those things and already dead. Some of these look like normal people.'

'We can't tell that from here. They could have bite marks,' I reply, thinking of last night and the people we killed who had yet to turn.

'Maybe,' he says quietly. 'Fuck!' he exclaims. Another large sign has been fixed to the side of the road. Again, this one is hand painted: TURN BACK. YOU WILL BE KILLED IF YOU PROCEED.

The sign is fixed into the ground by two thick posts; bodies have been arranged at the base of the sign. All of them in the sitting position. Men, women, and children all sat upright. Their backs either resting against the posts or each other. A rope tied round the sign holds them in place.

Every single one of them has bullet wounds in their heads. Execution style shots in the front of the head. The backs of their skulls are mostly missing as the rounds took the back of their heads off.

'Are they zombies?' Cookey asks. I understand what he means. It's impossible to tell from here. They just look like normal dead people.

'Dave, you get up top. I'll go and look,' Clarence says.

'On it,' Dave replies. He scrabbles up top onto the GPMG, shouting down when he's ready. Clarence quickly opens the door and drops down, running in a crouch to the bodies.

He stops in front of them, kneeling down to examine the face. His arm reaches out to open an eyelid, then another. He checks several of them before running back.

'Just people,' he says after slamming the door. 'Not one of them had red eyes.'

'Fucking hell,' Blowers mutters.

'Couldn't see any bite marks from what I could see either.'

'They just been killed, then,' I reply.

'Looks like it. This place would have been a magnet for anyone living locally. Big fences, loads of buildings, and the sea on one side.'

'Like our fort,' I say.

'Exactly, just much bigger,' he replies.

The sight of the bodies jars me. Normal people just looking for somewhere safe. I bet they didn't care about the fuel inside and just wanted to be behind the big fences.

'We going back?' Cookey asks.

'We should,' I reply, my gaze still fixed on the bodies. A little girl with golden, curly hair and wearing a blue dress. Her feet look tiny in matching blue shoes. The people with her must be her parents.

Executed.

Murdered.

I ease the vehicle forward, pushing further down the road. Clarence glances over at me, then turns to fix his head facing forward.

We had to kill last night, but we killed those that had been bitten. Not innocent people like Debbie said we did.

More bodies have been positioned sat up, leaning against the fence. Gruesome and morbid. Some with open eyes staring out. Birds and carrion have clearly been attacking some of the corpses. Still, we drive on. The inside of the Saxon in silence now. No banter or conversation.

'SHOTS,' Dave calls down.

'Where from?' Clarence shouts, grabbing his assault rifle.

'AHEAD.'

We peer forward, scanning the road, the trees, and the fence. I hear the lads in the back making ready, checking magazines, and pulling their rucksacks on.

We follow the curvature of the road, a long, sweeping bend that obstructs our view of ahead. The road straightens out to reveal a white pickup truck stationary in the middle of the road, maybe two hundred metres away. Armed men stand to the rear of it, pointing their weapons down at a cluster of people kneeling on the road, with their hands behind their heads.

On sight of us, several of the men lift their weapons to aim in our direction. A couple keep their guns pointing at the people on the floor. The kneeling people are all in a line, stretched across the road. Two of them are lying down, already shot by the looks of it.

From the size of the people kneeling, it's easy to see two of them are children. Distinctly smaller than the others, but still with their hands on their heads.

One of the armed men runs to the truck and pulls a radio out, speaking into it.

'They've got to be human,' Clarence says. 'Those things don't kneel down.'

'Dave, if they start shooting those people ...'

'I will,' he cuts me off, his voice calm and deadly as always.

I push on, going slowly towards the truck. The men look

worried, looking at each other, then at the man holding the radio.

'They'll be calling for reinforcements,' Clarence says. One of the men walks to the line of kneeling people and grabs a woman by her hair, dragging her towards the vehicle. He uses the butt of his rifle to hit the back of her head, forcing her into the rear passenger seats. The noise of her screams carries clearly to us.

A man moves forward, shuffling on his knees; his arms outstretched as thought begging. An armed guard slams the butt of his gun into the man's face, driving him to the floor.

'Shit,' Clarence curses. The armed men seem worried, shouting at each other and pointing at the people on the floor.

'We've got to do something,' Lani says.

'They've already killed two of 'em,' Nick adds.

'Mr Howie? I can take them …' Dave calls down.

More of the kneeling people scream in terror. Some of them dropping down, and others stretching their arms out. One of them shuffles to get in front of a child and gets two guards slamming their rifle butts into her head, forcing her to the floor.

One of the kneeling men drops to the floor, rolling away to rise quickly to his feet. He starts running towards us, screaming for help with his arms in the air.

A guard lifts his rifle, firing several shots at the running man. The rounds hit him, sending him spinning to the floor.

'DAVE–' I shout, the last of the word is cut off as Dave opens up, taking down the guard who shot the man first. The GPMG gives short bursts as Dave moves from one guard to the other.

The guards react quickly, start bursting away and returning fire. Two of them open up on the line of people, firing at the far end and strafing their weapons across the line before being blown apart by the heavy calibre bullets of our GPMG.

I grab my rifle and jump down, the weapon up and aiming as my feet start striding out to the right, keeping clear of Dave's arc of fire.

Clarence follows suit, out the vehicle and aiming at the truck. The rear doors burst open as the lads jump down, jogging round the sides and out from the vehicle.

The man on the radio throws it on the floor, lifting his gun toward us. I fire several shots at him, sending him crashing into the pickup truck. Clarence fires at the pickup's tyres, blowing them out. More shots ring out from them, but they're panicked and aimed at the vehicle. Loud pinging noises ring out as the bullets ricochet off the armour plating. Our rifles fire single shots, picking out targets. The GPMG doing the same, small bursts firing until the guards are all shot down.

'CLEAR,' Dave shouts.

'MOVING IN,' Clarence responds. 'COVER.'

'COVERING,' Dave shouts back.

We stride in, the rifles still up and aimed towards the truck. The silence doesn't bode well. I speed up, jogging towards the line of bodies.

Clarence and Blowers move past the rest of us, both of them checking the guards and kicking weapons away.

We check the bodies of the people who were kneeling. All of them cut to pieces by the close-range shots fired into them. Heads blown apart, skulls and brains blown everywhere. Blood pissing out to pool on the hot road surface.

All of them dead.

'Fuck it, fuck it,' Cookey mutters with a hard edge to his voice. 'Too fucking slow. We were too fucking slow.'

'They all dead?' Clarence calls out.

'Yeah,' I reply.

'Cunts, utter fucking cunts,' Nick shouts, 'fucking wankers ...'

Dave jogs over, assault rifle at the ready. He glances along the line of bodies before looking up and away, scanning the sides.

'CUNTS,' Nick shouts even louder, his voice cracking with emotion.

'Be quiet,' Dave says bluntly. 'It's done.' Nick bites his tongue, his face quickly becoming set as he glares down at the murdered people.

'Get the weapons into the vehicle,' I call out.

'The girl's in the truck,' Lani says, heading towards the rear doors. She opens the door as the rest of us stare over. 'She's here ... Hey, it's okay. Come on, it's okay,' she starts speaking in a soft tone. Gently pulling the girl from the vehicle.

The woman climbs out, shaking and trembling all over. She screams at the sight of the bodies, breaking free from Lani to run over. She drops down, screaming and sobbing, pawing at the bodies. She moves to one of the children, lifting the torn body up to cradle it.

'She needs to get in the Saxon before they come,' Dave says.

'Lani, you and Cookey get her inside,' I add. Blowers and Nick move between the guards, collecting the weapons and checking pockets for magazines.

A groaning noise comes from a guard as Nick rolls the body over to check the pockets. 'This one's alive,' Nick shouts.

I'm there instantly, looking down as the guard comes to,

opening his eyes and groaning in agony from the bullet wounds in his stomach.

'He was the one that shot the people,' Clarence growls.

'Can you hear me?' I ask the guard. He stares back, groggily at first, coming more to his senses as he looks up at us. He nods; his face pale and drawn.

'Why did you kill them?' I ask him, my voice hoarse and flat.

'Had to ... We're told to,' he replies, barely above a whisper.

'Who by?'

'The bosses. They said no one can come near the place. There's signs up ...'

'How many people you got in there?'

'I don't know,' he whispers, clutching at his stomach. He groans, but I notice his eyes look around sharp enough. I step forward, bringing my foot down onto his stomach, applying a small amount of pressure, which causes him to scream in agony.

'How many?'

'Hundred ... about hundred,' he gasps.

'One hundred ... You got one hundred people in a site that big?'

'Yeah ...' he nods, desperate to please me and stop the agony.

'Are they all armed?' He nods back.

'What about women?' Clarence asks. The guard pauses, then shakes his head, staring wide-eyed.

'I just did as I was told. They'd kill us otherwise.'

'He's lying,' Clarence growls. 'One hundred is too easy, and no women? For a hundred armed men ...?'

'Your choice,' I step back and look at Nick glaring down at him. Pure fury etched on his face. Blowers looks the same. Dave stares out, scanning the perimeter. I draw my pistol and aim it at the man's head. He whimpers, tears coming from his eyes as he begs me not to shoot.

'Tell me the truth. How many have you got in there?'

'But ...' he stammers, so I shoot him in the leg, sending a round through his thigh. He screams and grabs at the wound, curling into a ball as he sobs.

'Just under two hundred men, loads of guns we got from the police and barracks. We got women for cooking and ... other things,' he spits the words out quick enough now. Gasping between words as he writhes in agony.

'Where did the men come from?' I ask him.

'Most worked here, night duty when ... when it happened. Some ex-army ... went out and got the guns ...'

'Why are you sealing it off? This place is huge. You could have thousands in here.'

'They said we'd get attacked for the fuel ... said we had to defend it until help comes ... We took a few in ... families and shit but ...'

'We need fuel. Where do we get it from?' Clarence asks.

'You won't get it ... all the trucks are well inside ...'

I shoot him in the other leg, just to sharpen his senses a little. 'Okay,' he screams, 'please ... stop shooting me.'

'We need fuel. Where do we get it from?' I speak slowly, enunciating each word.

'You can't ... you fucking can't get it ...' he groans with the pain, clutching at both his legs, his stomach still bleeding heavily. 'Everything is inside. You can't get to it.'

'Liar,' Clarence roars, he reaches down with one hand and pulls the man to his feet, ragging him about while screaming in his face, 'tell me, or I swear to god I'll rip you limb from limb.'

'You can't ...' he sobs, '... can't.' Clarence throws him down to the floor. The man promptly passes out, bleeding heavily from the several bullet holes in his body.

'He was still fucking lying,' Clarence spits. 'Two hundred would get lost in there. Got to be loads more than that.'

'We should go,' I say quietly.

'Go? I ain't going nowhere,' Clarence replies. 'These fuckers are killing innocent people ...'

'We came for fuel.'

'Boss, we can't just leave them here. They'll kill anyone that comes near it. That isn't right.'

'Clarence, we can't go round the fucking country saving everyone. We got our own problems to deal with, and don't forget why we're here ... for Meredith.'

'I can get in,' Dave cuts in. 'I can get in and take them out, then open the gates for you.'

'Two hundred armed men? Maybe more if Clarence is right.' I ask him.

He shrugs nonchalantly. 'Yes.'

'No, no, we're going back. We've got to get fuel for Meredith. That's our top priority.'

'Mr Howie, they just shot children in front of us ... We can't just go,' Nick cuts in.

'And we killed them. They're all dead. This isn't our fight. We can't risk our lives like that when we've got to get fuel so they can test–'

'Dave can go in here. We wait, then hit the front hard. We've got the Saxon which is armour plated,' Clarence continues with a determined look on his face.

I look at them, Clarence, Nick, and Blowers. All three staring at me with hard looks and desperate to do something. I've got the same feeling in me, that this isn't right, and we should take action, but if we get killed …

'Mr Howie,' Lani calls out as she walks from the Saxon, 'she's already been raped. The other women too. They did that, then lined them up to shoot them.'

'Cunts,' Nick growls again.

'Give me a smoke, mate,' I say to Nick. He takes one out and hands it over, passing one to Blowers. 'Dave?'

'Yes, Mr Howie?' he replies, still scanning the perimeter.

'We'll go for the front and draw their fire. I don't want you going in, but you can take the sniper rifle and pick them off if that's any good.'

'Okay, we need to see the ground by the entrance. We should go now if we're going.'

'We're going,' I say. The lads nod at me with grim faces.

We load back into the Saxon. The girl sitting in the corner of the bench seat, with her knees drawn up to her chest, sobbing quietly.

Dave takes the canvas bag holding the sniper rifle and takes it out. Nick moves to the GPMG but gets told to sit down by Clarence who squeezes himself up.

'Go in hard, Boss,' he shouts down.

'Ready?'

'Yes, Mr Howie,' Dave replies. I push my foot down, easing the vehicle forward and round the pickup truck. Gathering speed, we steam down the road. The high fence on one side, and the tree line on the other.

The entrance is surprisingly close, with a long, straight road heading towards a high fence topped with coiled razor wire. A concrete, flat-roofed building separates the two lanes–one for going in and one for going out. Vehicles have been put in nose to tail across the front of the fence, making a solid defensive wall.

Figures move about by the concrete building, and I can see more running about behind the fence. Clarence opens up immediately, strafing the concrete building with short bursts and aiming along the fence line. Shots get fired back at us, striking the metal outside with loud pings.

The image of those people kneeling and begging for their lives just to be shot like animals is strong in my mind. Children with heads blown apart. The worst threat humanity has ever known, with a real and present danger of our species being wiped out, and we still do shit like that.

They could have secured this place with the armed men and allowed entrance to thousands. Rationed the supply of fuel and used it as a starting place for humanity to fight back.

Greed and power. Murdering people to keep what they've got. Not even people that pose a threat but innocent families just trying to find a safe place. Clarence is right. We can't walk away from this. It's got fuck all to do with us, but at the same time, it has everything to do with us. No police are going to come to the rescue, no armies or diplomats anymore. If we turn away, it makes us as guilty as them. We've got firepower, equipment, and experience now. This is our fight. We've made it our fight.

'HERE,' Dave shouts. I slow the vehicle down, keeping face-on to give Clarence the best position to fire. 'COVER ME,' Dave adds as he gets to the rear doors.

'THE DOORS ARE AMOURED, USE THEM,' Clarence shouts between a brief pause of firing. I grab my assault rifle, making it ready before opening my door. Angling myself on the step, I aim over the door, firing at the figures running about. Blowers climbs to the front, opening the passenger door and doing the same.

Noise everywhere, a huge deafening roar of small arms fire and the solid bass drumming of the machine gun thudding out over our heads. Dave slips off to the side. Running low, he disappears into the tree line.

Small bits of earth exploding show where the shots were aimed at his route. A round hits my door, slamming it into my body and causing me to slip from the vehicle and land on the floor.

'COOKEY, COVER MR HOWIE,' Blowers screams as he opens up. Cookey throws himself over the seats, leaning out of the door as I scrabble backwards. Tarmac and concrete exploding round me as the rounds strike closer. I run back to the rear of the vehicle, taking cover as the lads return fire.

A different sound comes from the tree line, a sharp crack different to the GMPG and the assault rifles. Another one, then another. I climb into the vehicle, making my way past the girl to the front. Looking through the windscreen, I see men dropping down as each distinct crack sounds out.

'I FUCKING LOVE DAVE,' Cookey bellows. Another crack followed a split second later by a body falling down. Dave picks them off, one by one, as Clarence strafes back and forth. The heavy calibre rounds taking big chunks from the concrete guard building.

'THEY'RE TAKING COVER,' Clarence shouts. The tree line comes alive as the guards inside the compound concentrate their fire on the sniper. Leaves, branches, and tree bark splintering.

'Nick, get the loudspeaker going,' I call down to him.
'MAGAZINE,' Clarence bellows. 'NEED COVER.'

'IT'S READY,' Nick shouts, handing me the handset.

'COVER CLARENCE,' I shout out. Nick, Lani, and I get out the rear, leaning round the back of the Saxon and firing into the fence and guard building. The men inside don't show themselves now, taking cover to take pot shots back at us.

We fire steadily, aiming across the width until Clarence shouts he's finished. Back inside the vehicle, I get to the front and grab the handset for the loudspeaker.

'Ceasefire,' I call out. Clarence drops down as Blowers and Cookey pull themselves back into the vehicle.

'GIVE IT UP,' my amplified voice booms into the air. 'WE'LL TEAR YOU APART. GIVE IT UP NOW. WE'VE GOT HEAVY WEAPONS AND TRAINED MEN. GIVE UP NOW, AND YOU WON'T BE HARMED.'

They cease firing from their end. A silence falls as we wait for a reaction. The lads making use of the time to check their weapons, change magazines, and get water.

'WHO ARE YOU?' an amplified voice comes back to us. Someone using a handheld megaphone.

'WE CAME FOR FUEL. WE SAW YOUR MEN KILLING INNOCENT PEOPLE ON THE ROAD.'

'I SAID WHO ARE YOU?' the voice comes back with an angry tone that cuts off with a gargled yell as a sharp crack sounds out from Dave shooting the speaker.

'I SUGGEST YOU GIVE UP. WE'VE GOT ALL FUCKING DAY. Lads, get ready to fire again if they fuck about.' Cookey and Blowers position themselves to lean out. Clarence holds ready to go up on the GPMG. Lani and Nick wait at the rear doors.

'DON'T SHOOT,' another voice comes over.

'PLEASE DON'T SHOOT,' this voice sounds less aggressive, with a pleading tone.

'OKAY, CEASE FIRE …' I add for Dave's benefit. 'GIVE UP NOW. WEAPONS DOWN AND ARMS UP. OPEN THE GATES.'

'YOU'LL KILL US,' the voice shouts back.

'WE SHOULD FUCKING KILL YOU, BUT WE WON'T IF YOU DO AS YOU'RE TOLD. WEAPONS DOWN, ARMS UP, AND COME OUT SLOWLY.'

'WE CAN GIVE YOU FUEL.'

'WE'LL TAKE THE FUEL AND KILL EVERYONE IF YOU DON'T GIVE UP NOW.'

'LISTEN, WE'LL GIVE YOU FUEL. YOU WANT FUEL. WE CAN SEND A TANKER OUT FOR YOU.'

'I SAID GIVE UP …'

'WE'RE NEGOTIATING …' the voice almost pleads. 'YOU CAME FOR FUEL SO WE CAN GIVE YOU FUEL. AS MUCH AS YOU WANT.'

'DAVE,' I say the single word. A sharp crack, then silence. I imagine the speaker's head being taken off and the megaphone falling to the floor.

'WE'RE NOT HERE TO NEGOTIATE. ANYONE ELSE TRIES IT, AND WE OPEN UP AGAIN. I'LL SAY IT ONE LAST TIME … WEAPONS DOWN, ARMS UP, AND COME OUT SLOWLY. YOU HAVE THIRTY SECONDS.'

Shit. I just ordered the execution of a person. The ease of it shocks me. Just saying one word, and a man dies, shot by a sniper rifle. He could have been a decent person, a normal man caught up in this mess and trying to survive like everyone else. Then I think of the real survivors that were kneeling down on the hot road, thirsty and frightened after watching their women being raped.

A shot rings out, instantly followed by a pinging noise, and Clarence cursing as the shot just misses him. He opens up, thudding the GPMG across the front of the entrance. Firing into the rows of vehicles and then at the concrete building.

'GET CLOSER,' Clarence bellows.

Cookey climbs back into the rear, giving me space to get into the driver's seat and move the Saxon closer to the entrance. The line of fire from Clarence becomes concentrated as he aims at certain parts, getting a better view as I drive slowly forward. The sharp crack of the sniper rifle, and men inside falling down or going off spinning as they're taken down.

The GPMG ceases for a second as Clarence yells for me to stop. He pauses, then fires again at movement beyond the fence.

'Ram the gate, Boss,' he calls down.

'Everyone in and close the doors,' I yell out. Blowers ducks inside and slams the passenger door closed. Twisting round, I see the rear doors being pulled shut by Nick and Lani.

'Ready?' I yell out.

'Go,' Clarence shouts. I push my foot down, aiming at the left side, guessing that would be the lane in.

The powerful engine roars to life as the vehicle surges forward. Gaining speed, we brace as the solid metal front of the vehicle impacts with the high fence panel. The vehicle just takes the impact and keeps going, ripping the gate off its fittings as we power through. The GPMG starts up again, firing across the inside of the compound.

Bodies already litter the ground. Loads of them with guns and rifles lying next to their outstretched hands. The sheer fire power of the general-purpose machine gun has obliterated the inside, peppering walls and ripping men apart.

More men are running about, frantically trying to find cover. Clarence fires for a few more seconds while we watch from the inside of the vehicle as the guards get shot to bits.

'Ceasefire,' I yell out as the men in the compound start throwing their guns down and holding their hands in the air. The machine gun stops abruptly, and we hear the sniper rifle fire at men still holding weapons. Heads explode as skulls are blown apart by the high velocity rounds sent by Dave.

'CEASEFIRE. PUT YOUR WEAPONS DOWN,' I shout through the loudspeaker. More of the men throw guns down and stand with their arms stretched up. Dave, thankfully, stops shooting them and lets them surrender, and for one awful minute, I did think he might just carry on.

From the inside, I see a wide road leading off into the refinery. A large, open area on one side, marked on the road as Tanker Parking. No tankers here, just empty space with a few vehicles parked up.

The men stand clustered together, glancing between us and the downed bodies scattered about.

'Clarence, give me cover,' I call up.

'Got it. Just don't get in the line of fire,' he shouts back. I open the door and jump down, pushing the door closed behind me. Moving towards the men, I keep my assault rifle up and aimed. They all look clean and well-fed.

'Where are the tankers?' I call out, still thinking of the main objective to get the fuel.

Shots sound out from further down the road, followed by the sound of a vehicle accelerating towards us. Clarence swivels the gun and opens up, firing at whatever's coming our way.

The men take the opportunity to burst apart, running for the guns lying scattered about. I open up, firing into the men. The doors of the Saxon open up as the others jump down, firing into the men as they run to grab weapons. Dave takes several out, getting head shots as skulls explode with a spray of pink mist.

We cut the men down, leaving just two, who drop to their knees, begging not to be shot. Dave takes one of them out, his head exploding in a puff.

The GPMG still firing down the road. I turn round to see another pickup truck being shot to bits, the rounds of the machine gun shredding the thing apart. Bodies lay scattered about it as the men must have jumped off to start shooting and were cut down. Clarence stops shooting, holding his aim down the service road.

Aiming my rifle at the single man left alive, I walk towards him. 'Where are the tankers?'

'Down there,' he wails, nodding his head towards the road.

'How far?'

'About half a mile.'

'How many people you got here?'

'I don't know,' he stammers, tears running down his face.

'Yes, you do. You do fucking know. Lie again, and I'll fucking kill you ...'

'Hundreds ...We got hundreds.'

'Where did they come from?'

'Most work here; some came in from the estate when it happened. Please ... I got a wife and kids.'

'Shut up. What estate?'

'The housing estate south of the refinery. It's where most of the workers lived. I live there with my wife and children. I got two daughters, please ...'

'Who killed all the people on road? Who put the bodies so they're sat up?'

'We got some ex-army guys here. They said everyone will come and try and take the site. They said we had enough here now, like, and we couldn't take no more in. They said it was like the most important fuel depot in the country, and we had to defend it ....' He gabbles on, speaking quickly between ragged breaths. 'They said we had to keep the bodies there to put them off coming here. They come every day, loads of them, like ...'

'So you keep killing them?'

'We had to, didn't have no choice, like. Some said they wouldn't do it and got beat up, like. They said we're in it together, and we had to do it, or they'd be kicked out,' he calms down slightly, just enough for his northern accent to become more apparent.

'That included raping them as well, did it?'

'I didn't know nothing about no rape, like ... I didn't ... I'm married, with two kids. I ain't raped no one.'

'Where did all the guns come from?'

'The ex-army guys. Couple of 'em were in the territorials and went to their base. They got police guns too from the stations.'

'They got more guns inside, then?'

He nods. His face deathly white with fear.

'How many?'

'Loads,' he replies.

'Get these weapons into the Saxon,' I say to the others. They move quickly, running between the bodies, scooping them up, and running them to the back doors of the Saxon.

'We need fuel,' I say to the man, 'and you are going to help us get some.'

'Me? I can't ... They'll kill me–'

'We'll kill you if you don't,' I cut him off. 'Your choice, and try anything, I'll shoot your fucking cock off and leave you to bleed out. Someone call for Dave to come down.'

Cookey grabs the loudspeaker, relaying the order. The weapons get collected and put into the vehicle. The lads finishing just as Dave jogs easily through the destroyed gate with the sniper held ready.

'You alright, mate?'

'Yes, Mr Howie.'

'Good shooting, mate.'

'Thanks, Mr Howie.'

'And the one who surrendered ...'

'Oh him ... I thought he had a gun.'

'Did you bollocks,' I smile at him. He walks over to the body and rolls it over so it's face down. He bends over and pulls a pistol from the dead man's waistband.

'How the fuck did you see that?' I ask him in shock.

'Through the scope,' he replies seriously, nodding at the scope on the sniper rifle.

'Yeah, I know that ... I meant how did you see it from that distance?'

'Er ... through the scope,' he replies again.

'Yeah ... forget it. This bloke said they got loads of guns in there. Some of them are ex-army or in the territorials and went to their local base.'

'Oh,' Dave says.

'Yeah, oh ... but he's going to help us get to the tankers.'

'How far away are they?'

'He says about half a mile.'

'Oh ... Okay. Do you want me to go and get one?'

He would too. He'd walk there with a bread knife and kill the hundreds of people without breaking a sweat.

'How you going to bring it back?' I ask him.

'Bring what back?'

'The tanker? How you going to bring it back? You don't drive.'

'I'll get one of them to drive it,' he shrugs. 'No big deal.' He looks at the man kneeling down. 'Have you got heavy weapons in there?'

'I don't know,' he stutters. 'What are heavy weapons?'

'Like that one up there,' Dave points to the GPMG on top of the Saxon.

'Yeah,' the man nods, 'just the one, like.'

'Can you drive the tankers?' I ask him.

'No,' he shakes his head, 'not me. I just worked in the maintenance department, like.'

'Fuck it, we need the fuel. Let's go now. You're leading the way,' I point at him. 'Get up.'

I push the man towards the Saxon. Dave makes him wait while he gets a small length of rope from the vehicle and binds the man's hands behind his back. Once tied, he gets pushed inside and made to stand behind the seats, Blowers and Nick flanking him.

'Cunt,' Nick growls at him. 'You're a nasty fucking cunt.'

'Rapist fucking wanker,' Blowers adds. They both glare at him with hard faces.

'I didn't do no raping,' the man whimpers.

'Straight down there?' I ask after getting into the driver's seat.

'Aye, straight down that road.'

'If you tell the truth and help us, I promise we'll let you

go. If you lie or do anything stupid, you will die. Do you understand?'

'He's nodding, Mr Howie,' Nick says.

'Right, here we go.' The Saxon starts towards the road. I push it quite quickly, intent on making ground before they get time to organise themselves.

'Keep going,' the man calls out.

Clarence and Dave quickly swap over. Clarence squeezes his big frame over the seats to get into the passenger side, getting his assault rifle and staring out the front.

'Next right,' the man shouts. The road we're on is marked as C Avenue, with the side streets having numbers like the American grid layout. We pass 12th Street, then 11th.

'What street do we need?'

'Eh?' the man replies.

'He's fucking lying,' I shout. 'He should know the layout exactly.'

'You cunt,' Blowers punches him in the back of the head, knocking him forward. 'What fucking road?'

'Stop. It's on D Avenue.'

'Why are we going down C Avenue, then?'

'You fucker,' Nick shouts as both he and Blowers reign blows down on the man.

'CONTACT,' Dave roars. A barricade across the road blocks out progress. A row of vehicles parked end on end, with men stood the other side, pointing guns at us. They open up first, the muzzle flashes distinct with the sounds of assault rifles. Dave is a split second behind them, firing the GPMG with deadly accuracy. Several men get instantly blown backwards, not realising our aim from this distance would be so good.

'Where are the tankers?' Blowers shouts at the man.

'D Avenue ... I swear it, like ... I swear,' his voice sounds hoarse and gargled as he spits blood out from his bleeding mouth. 'Fuck ... oh fuck ...' the change in his tone makes me turn round. Lani is stood behind him, holding one of her knives against his throat while pulling his hair back.

'D Avenue ...' he whispers, his voice almost drowned out by the GPMG.

'Which way?' Lani shouts.

'Take a left, go left.'

I twist the wheel, coming off the power and letting the weight of the vehicle slow it enough to take the corner. Dave must turn with the vehicle as the fire continues to be directed straight into the hastily formed barricade.

We enter into 10th Street, the last left turn before the barricade. Only a short street with big, high chimney stacks soaring into the sky and a complex network of tubes and pipes running everywhere.

'Which way now?' I shout.

'Right! You gotta go right.'

I bring the Saxon to a halt, craning my head down to the right and seeing the vehicles being pushed into position as more men run into the area.

'The tanker yard is past them. You gotta get past them,' he yelps as Lani digs the knife into his neck.

'Dave! We're going through ...'

'Roger that, Mr Howie,' Dave shouts back. I turn the wheel and push my foot down hard as the engine builds to a huge roar.

Shots ring off the outside of the vehicle as we draw closer to the vehicles. Dave opens up, firing into them and killing men as they run about.

'Brace,' I shout a warning, which unfortunately is too

late. The vehicle jolts as it impacts the first vehicle, shunting it out the way. From behind me, I hear muted curses and a funny gargling sound.

'What's that?' I call out.

'Lani just cut his head off,' Nick shouts.

'You shouted too late. I had the knife at his throat.'

'Is he dead?' I ask, which I realise is a stupid question.

'He has no head, Mr Howie,' Cookey says with as much tact as a house brick.

'Oh fuck ... Any ideas?' I shout to Clarence.

'Nope, just keep going,' he says, twisting back round to face front. 'She actually cut his head off,' he adds.

'Really? His actual head?'

'Yeah ... Clean off ... Don't ever cheat on her, for fuck's sake.'

'Jesus ... What a woman.... Is it too early to propose?'

'What did he say?' Lani shouts as Clarence bursts out laughing.

'The boss asked if you'll marry him,' he shouts.

'If he gets us out of this bloody mess, I'll have his babies,' she shouts to hoots of laughter from the other lads. I shake my head–the visual image of that bloke's head rolling about the floor while we talk about marriage and babies. I should be on happy pills.

'Er, can anyone see a tanker?' I shout as we trundle down D Avenue, the outside of the Saxon ringing like a giant xylophone from the shots being taken at us.

'Why's Dave firing like that?' Cookey shouts. His voice gets cut off by the girl at the back screaming in blind panic. 'Oh shit. Sorry, love,' Cookey says.

'She alright?' Clarence asks, twisting round.

'What happened?' I ask.

'Oh, that head just rolled into her foot,' he says, losing interest and turning back.

'Dave, why are you firing like that?' Nick shouts up.

'So I don't blow the place up,' he shouts down.

'Oh, fuck,' I exclaim, suddenly realising we're in the middle of a giant fuel refinery.

'Shit, oh shit, he's gonna blow it up ... I know he will,' Cookey yells.

'He won't,' I yell back, turning into another side street.

'He did one before, didn't he?' Cookey asks.

'It was seen from space, Cookey,' Clarence grins at him evilly.

'Oh shit,' the lad replies with a whimper.

'We're being chased,' Dave shouts.

'Where's the fucking wing mirrors?' Clarence shouts.

'We fucking lost them ages ago, mate,' I reply.

'Fire out the back doors. We've got contact to the front too,' Dave shouts down.

The lads get to the back doors, pushing them open and firing their assault rifles almost instantly.

'What is it?' I ask Clarence as he twists round.

'Another pickup with blokes on the back,' he replies.

'How many fucking pickup trucks have they got?'

'I don't know ... but one less now,' Clarence adds as the lads and Lani cheer. A loud crash sounds out behind us, which I guess must be from the pickup truck smashing into something. Hopefully the something isn't a flammable something.

'There,' Clarence points down the road to a wide, open space with a row of white fuel tankers parked up, all of them marked with the refinery logo.

More shots ping off the Saxon. The shooters hidden

from sight. Dave returns fire, taking care not to hit anything that looks like it could blow up.

'How the fuck we gonna do this? You'll get cut to bits if you go–'

'We'll have to go round again,' Clarence cuts me off.

We drive quickly past the fleet of tankers, both of us looking at them longingly and hoping no one tries to shoot them. I take the next right, powering up the short side street. More people go running off, diving behind cover as we go flying past them.

I keep going up the long, straight avenue, ignoring the first right turn to buy us time.

'Get on the loudspeaker ... tell them we'll the blow it up if they keep firing at us.'

'I don't think it'll work,' Clarence replies. He takes the mouthpiece and shouts into it, 'CEASEFIRE NOW, OR WE'LL BLOW THE REFINERY ... CEASEFIRE NOW, OR WE'LL BLOW THE REFINERY ...'

'Dave, stop shooting for a minute,' I shout out. He instantly stops, dropping down to get cover while we keep taking right turns and driving in a big circle.

Clarence keeps repeating the same message, his deep tones amplified as I take the numbered side streets and cross the avenues.

'Clarence, wait,' Dave says. He leans towards the hole of the GPMG, listening intently. 'They're shouting to each other,' he relays.

'LEAVE NOW, OR WE'LL KILL YOU ALL,' an amplified voice booms out from several points. Must be a safety Tannoy system.

'STOP SHOOTING US, OR WE'LL BLOW YOUR REFINERY UP,' Clarence replies with his own amplified voice.

'YOU CAN'T BLOW IT UP ...'

'WE CAN BLOODY TRY ... DO YOU WANNA SEE IT? Dave, give something a blast,' he adds quietly.

Dave scrabbles back up and starts firing indiscriminately as Cookey drops down to cover his head, whimpering loudly.

Dave finishes and quickly drops back down as I realise I'm holding my breath and waiting for the boom.

'WE CAN DO THAT AGAIN,' Clarence says.

'DON'T BE SO STUPID. YOU'LL GET BLOWN UP TOO.'

'THEN LET US HAVE TWO TANKERS OF FUEL.'

'IS THAT ALL YOU WANT?' the voice comes back with an incredulous tone.

'YES,' Clarence replies.

'YOU BUST IN HERE AND KILL EVERYONE FOR TWO FUCKING TANKERS?'

'PRETTY MUCH. OH, AND THE BODIES YOU LEFT OUTSIDE TOO. YOU KNOW, THE BODIES OF THE WOMEN AND CHILDREN.'

Silence comes back for a second as I imagine frantic conversation taking place between whoever is holding the microphone and the people around him.

'OKAY. CEASEFIRE ALL ROUND. TAKE TWO TANKERS AND LEAVE.'

'ARE THEY ALL FULL?'

'YES.'

'WHAT ABOUT KEYS?'

'WE'LL BRING THEM TO YOU.'

'DON'T FUCK ABOUT, OR WE'LL BLOW EVERYONE UP. OH, AND WE GOT ONE OF YOUR

BLOKES HEADS IN HERE. DO YOU WANT IT BACK?'

The lads snigger as Clarence grins. 'Nice touch,' I add quietly.

'YOU CAN KEEP THE HEAD,' the voice comes back.

'Nice of him,' Nick says.

We drive in silence. Not one shot exchanged from the people holding assault rifles and police issue black coloured guns.

'Fuck, I can't remember which way it is now,' I say at the end of a numbered side street.

'Right,' Clarence says at the same time as Blowers says 'left'.

'Bollocks.' I take the right, heading down an avenue surrounded by big, dirty, while silos built into the square segments of land, with raised banks of earth round each one. Chimneys, pipes, tubes, weird looking machines are everywhere, giving the place a surreal, futuristic industrial look.

'YOU'RE GOING THE WRONG WAY,' the voice booms out.

'Sorry, Boss,' Clarence grimaces.

'Now we just look bloody stupid,' I retort.

'What like we don't already? Charging several hundred armed men for a tanker of fuel that we could have got at the docks. Not to mention Lani cutting all their heads off,' he replies.

'One head ... I cut one head off,' Lani says pointedly.

'I said we should go for the docks,' I say with a shake of my head. I turn the vehicle round in the entrance to another side street, having to shunt forward and back several times while being stared at by several grim-faced, armed guards.

'No pressure then,' I mutter under my breath, then

swear loudly as the front of the Saxon scrapes along a wall, with a screech of metal and a round of 'ooohhhs' coming from the back. Some of the armed men outside shake their heads which just makes me go red in the face.

'Fuckers … fucking fuckers … fucking fuck fuckers …' I mutter angrily to myself as I get the Saxon back onto the avenue and facing the right way.

'WELL DONE,' the voice says with a distinctively sarcastic tone.

'Cheeky fucker,' I shake my head again and become aware of the silence in the vehicle. 'Don't you lot bloody start.'

'Soooo, it's, er … very warm again today,' Cookey says innocently.

'Yeah, definitely another hot one,' Nick replies in the same slow tone.

'Better than rain, though,' Lani adds.

'I think we could do with a drop of rain,' Blowers joins in.

'Yeah, alright, you lot can piss off,' I call out with a grin.

'There, just down there,' Clarence points ahead as we come into view of the row of tankers.

I look over at the big man and realise what he asked for. 'You said we wanted two tankers … Who is going to drive the other one?'

'You can drive it,' he replies.

'Me? Haven't they got loads of gears or something?'

'It's easy enough. One of the lads can drive this back.'

'I'll have a go,' Nick offers. 'I always wanted to drive a big lorry.'

'Nick driving a mobile bomb … Is that wise?' Cookey asks.

'You ever driven one before?' Clarence turns to look at him.

'No, but I'll have a go.'

'You fancy it then, mate?' I ask.

'Yeah, definitely,' he excitedly replies.

'Fair enough,' Clarence says.

We slow down, crawling the last few metres to scan the area. Coming to a stop, we wait as armed guards walk into the area, standing at a distance but making their presence known.

'I don't like it,' Clarence mutters.

'Me too,' Dave adds. 'They shouldn't be stood there.'

'PULL YOUR MEN BACK,' Clarence speaks through the loudspeaker.

'THEY WON'T DO ANYTHING,' the voice replies after a pause of a few seconds.

'THEN PULL THEM BACK,' Clarence repeats.

Another pause, and the men all drop their heads as though listening to something, then start pulling back.

'They must have radios,' Blowers says.

'Fucking hell, Blowers … You're quick,' Cookey mutters.

'A MAN WILL APPROACH NOW. HE'S GOT THE KEYS.'

We watch as a man dressed in black combat trousers and a khaki top walks into view. He makes a point of bending down to place his assault rifle on the ground, then standing up, and turning round to show he's unarmed. He walks towards us with his hands away from his body.

'Right, come on, then,' I start opening the driver's door.

'I thought Nick was driving the other one,' Clarence asks.

'He is, but we got to get the keys first. Nick, you hang on here a minute.'

'I'll come,' Dave starts towards the rear doors.

'No, mate, stay here and get ready to use the GPMG if it goes bent.'

Clarence and I clamber down, wincing from the heat and bright sun beaming down. The area feels hot and arid, with no natural plants or foliage but just industrial equipment, tarmac, and hard, baked earth. The sun glints blindingly from the metal tubes and pipes, and I have to use my hand to shield my eyes, putting us at an instant disadvantage.

'Can't see a fucking thing,' Clarence growls. I stare down at the ground, trying to let my eyes adjust to the glare.

'Quick, move in,' someone shouts. I glance up to see silhouettes of figures running towards us.

'TRAP,' Dave roars from inside the Saxon.

A heavy weight crashes into me as shots are fired. I recognise the sound of rounds pinging off the metal armour of our vehicle. Huge hands grab and pull me along as Clarence shouts for me to move. Getting to my feet, I follow after him, both of us staring at the ground and half squinting as we duck down a narrow alley running between a mass of pipes.

'Get down,' he mutters. We pause in the shade, blinking and rubbing our eyes as we draw our pistols, both of us having left our rifles in the vehicle.

Shots fire from all around. The metal ricochets coming from all directions as they focus their fire onto the Saxon. The GPMG opens up with a thudding boom as Dave returns fire.

'We can't get back to the Saxon,' I say hoarsely. 'We'll be cut to bits. Shit.' I fire my pistol at the figure appearing at the end of the alley. The figure spins back from the rounds striking his chest, his assault rifle clattering to the floor.

'Nice shot,' Clarence says as he crabs along to grab the fallen man's gun. He checks the magazine and takes spare ones from the man's pockets, shoving them into his own before easing his way towards the end of the alley.

I watch my end. The pistol raised and held with two hands like Dave showed me. Rounds strike all around, bouncing off the pipes and the ground at the alley entrance.

'DON'T SHOOT THE FUCKING PIPES,' the amplified voice booms out. The shots coming our way instantly ease up as the order is obeyed, buying us some time. The firing at the Saxon just intensifies as they direct their aim that way instead. The GPMG keeps firing in bursts. Loud screams and shouts of agony sound out as Dave hits target after target.

'THE TWO BETWEEN THE PIPES, YOU ARE TRAPPED. PUT DOWN YOUR WEAPONS NOW.'

'You think he means us?' I ask sarcastically.

'Reckon he does, Boss,' Clarence replies. He fires quickly, yelling in triumph, 'Got one!'

'They won't shoot us in here,' I call out.

'Yeah, but we can't get out either,' he replies.

'Stalemate ...' I cock my head, listening to the Saxon engine grow louder. I try to peer out the end but have to quickly duck back in from the rounds hitting the ground inches away.

'STAY THERE, MR HOWIE,' Nick's voice comes over our loudspeaker.

'Incoming,' Clarence calls out. He fires the assault rifle he took from the man, using short, controlled bursts.

'MR HOWIE ... THEY'RE RUNNING TOWARDS YOU,' Nick shouts a warning. I keep the pistol aimed at the end of the alley, waiting to press the trigger at anything that appears.

'THEY'RE JUST AT THE END. TWO OF THEM ...' Nick relays.

'Fucking cunt needs to shut up,' one of the men shouts from round the corner of the alley.

'You coming in or what?' I shout out.

'You impatient, then?'

'Yeah ...' I lie down on the floor, lifting my aim to where I think their chest height will be.

'NOW,' Nick shouts as one of the men jumps out and opens fire into the alley. I fire the pistol, striking him in the legs first, then readjusting to get him in the chest. He staggers back from the force of the bullets, dropping down to sprawl out on the ground.

'ONE LEFT,' Nick shouts.

'Come on then, fuckwit,' I shout.

'Fuck this,' I hear him mutter.

'HE'S RUN OFF ...' Nick relays.

I twist round to see Clarence still taking single put shots at his end. Crabbing down, I head towards the body, hoping to get the assault rifle he was holding, but the body is lying out of reach.

'GET READY,' Nick shouts. I stare out, wondering what they're doing. The Saxon reverses to the alley, leaving enough room for the rear doors to swing open. Cookey, Lani, and Blowers kneeling inside and waving me towards them.

'Clarence,' I shout. He turns round, grinning like a maniac.

'Cover me,' he shouts as he starts running bent over. Blowers stands up, aiming over Clarence, towards the end of the alley. I run and dive into the back as Blowers fires.

Clarence dives in, landing on top of me as the three of them pull us in and close the doors.

'They're in,' Lani shouts. Nick pulls away as Dave drops back down.

'You okay, Mr Howie?' he asks with concern.

'Fine, mate,' I reply with a gasp from having Clarence's bulk land on top of me.

'Yeah, I'm fine too, Dave,' Clarence mutters.

'Er ... what's the plan?' Nick shouts.

'Well, it appears they don't want us to have a tanker of fuel,' I reply, getting to my feet. 'Give me that microphone,' I climb over the seat and grab the handset. 'WHAT'S THE MOST EXPLOSIVE THING IN HERE? THE PIPES? THE SILOS? OR SHALL WE JUST GO FOR THE TANKERS ...?'

'CEASEFIRE,' the voice orders. 'CEASEFIRE NOW ...'

'Mr Howie, is that a GPMG?' Nick points ahead to a small group of men running into view with what looks like a heavy calibre machine gun on a tripod.

'Yep ... Dave ...' I shout in alarm. He's already getting up the hole and grabbing our own heavy weapon.

'Get down,' I pull Nick down as the other weapon opens up, the front of the vehicle being hit by sustained firing.

Dave opens up, slamming rounds at the other group and shredding them to pieces within seconds. He keeps firing, aiming at the gun as it skittles and bounces across the ground.

'Who's up for the docks?' I shout as Dave drops back down.

'Sounds good to me, Boss,' Clarence replies. 'I bloody said we should try there first.'

'Nick ... time for us to go, mate,' he pushes his foot down, moving the Saxon along as we go past the coveted fuel tanker trucks. Dave goes back up again, resuming his short burst firing as Nick navigates his way back onto the main avenue. Bodies lie everywhere, torn to pieces from our firing.

It seems every gun they possess is trained on us as the Saxon takes a battering from the small arms fire.

'Why haven't our tyres blown out yet?' Cookey asks.

'Run flat. They're not normal tyres,' Clarence shouts over the symphony of bangs and dings that come from all around us.

Dave fires ahead of us, cutting the armed guards down as they lean out to fire at us. Time and again, he gets direct hits, and we keep seeing the mini explosions of blood and pink matter puffing into the air as the rounds strike home.

Nick takes us straight down the avenue, heading back towards the entrance we came in from as another pickup truck powers out from one of the side streets aiming straight at us. Nick floors the Saxon, the engine screaming out as the pickup rams into the driver's side with an almighty shunt that swings the back end of the Saxon round, causing Dave to miss his target with the GPMG, striking a thick pipe, which causes high pressure liquid to start spraying out.

Nick brakes hard and controls the Saxon well, bringing the speed down while avoiding hitting anything. We come to a stop, all of us staring out the window at the liquid spraying from the pipe. The hole it comes from seems to get bigger, forced wider from the pressure of the liquid inside. It sprays high into the air, a thick, black liquid that coats everything in sight.

'Nick ... get going, mate ... Quick! Get fucking going,' I mutter quietly. The guards haven't seen the damaged pipe and keep firing at us. Some of the bullets creating little sparks as they impact on the armoured panels. Nick eases the vehicle round to face the correct way, the action seeming to be so incredibly slow.

Everything slows as we all twist our necks to stare out at the liquid spurting into the air. Nick floors the accelerator. The engine roaring as we start moving away.

'CEASEFIRE. STOP FIRING NOW!' the amplified voice screams with urgency, repeating the words over and over.

I'm not exactly sure what happened next. It could have been a spark from a bullet hitting the side of our vehicle that ignited the fumes from the liquid or it could have been a badly aimed shot fired directly at it, or it could have simply been the super-charged heat of the air creating the exact right mix of heat and gasses that caused the liquid to combust.

What I am sure of is that the liquid did start to combust. It flared slowly–a thin, blue flame that danced clearly along the floor. For a couple of seconds, I thought it might go out. But it didn't. The thin, blue flame spread and made other thin, blue flames. Those few flames caused more flames, and within a couple more seconds, the ground around the split pipe was on fire.

Then the spray caught alight, which was an amazing thing to see. One second, a dark distinct spray of viscous liquid; then, within an instant, it was alive with scorching, hot flames licking at the air.

We power away, gaining distance with every passing second. The flame holds at the pipe, seemingly content to just ignite the liquid as it comes out. A huge battle taking place at the opening of the pipe between the pressure of the liquid coming out and the hunger of the fire trying to get in.

'GO,' Dave roars as he drops down from the GPMG.

His voice the loudest I have ever heard, but then he knows what's coming.

The Saxon steams down the avenue, racing towards the entrance. I open the passenger door and lean out, staring back at the flames spewing from the pipe. The amplified voice still booming out, but the words lost from the roar of our engine.

Clarence cracks one of the rear doors open, the lads and Lani peering out of the gap at the flames that seem to grow larger and more fierce with every second. The sky above the flames shimmers from the heat; dirty, oily smoke pouring up into the still air.

We reach the entrance we came in from. Nick driving straight over the bodies of the men we shot down. He aims well, scooting straight through the ruined gate and onto the access road.

The flames grow larger—a dull roar that reaches us despite the increasing distance and the sound of the engine. Then they stop. Gone.

'Close the door,' Dave orders calmly.

'Why it's stopped?' Cookey asks.

'It hasn't,' his words are flat and lifeless but strike a chord in all of us. Cookey stares in horror for a second, unable to tear his eyes away from the patch of sky where the flames were.

That same patch of sky erupts as a huge fireball detonates into the air, followed a split second later by a deafening, bass-filled roar. Both Cookey and I stay watching out the open doors, completely unaware of how fast Nick is driving.

The fireball grows larger and larger, reaching high into the sky. A solid wall of flame that seems contained and almost spherical, like a twisting tornado. The sight is awesome, mesmerising even. Then another one goes. I say another one as I have no idea what it is, but whatever is next to the fireball goes up, adding another massive explosion that rocks the ground. We all feel the vibration that shudders the vehicle. The heat wave from the first one hits us as dry, charged air blasts against the vehicle.

The second fireball just melts into the first one, creating a wider, twisting wall of flame that dances hundreds of feet into the air.

I twist round, seeing the determination on Nick's face as he concentrates on the road ahead. I think of what Dave said about the people in the international space station seeing the refinery explode before, and I can't imagine it was anywhere near as big as this one.

Smaller explosions reach us, dull thuds like fireworks popping off in the distance. The pipes and tubes must be melting with the heat, spilling their explosive contents to be ignited and join the fireball.

The Saxon is going flat out now, which isn't that fast in comparison to most modern cars, but the size and weight of the thing makes you feel the speed more acutely. The chassis vibrates noisily, causing us to tremble and judder. Cookey hangs on tight as he and the others stare out the still open rear door. I'm hanging on for dear life too, still unable to stop watching the flames scorching the sky.

They grow larger every second as more dull thuds and smaller explosions reach us. Dark, solid fragments fly high into the air to go spinning off deeper into the refinery. Those fragments will be super-hot, and judging from the height they reach, they'll plummet down with incredible force and cause even more damage as they land.

One of the silos goes up next, and it dwarfs the previous explosion. Making it look like a match head in comparison.

A huge, thick broiling plume of deep red and yellow flames soar up and up. The sound reaches us a second later. A sound so deep it resonates through our bones.

The road starts the incline, heading further away from the refinery. Just one silo as far as I can tell. Just one and already it fills the sky.

Another one goes, followed an instant later by another. It must be the ones closest to the first, being set off in a chain-like reaction. The people in the refinery must be dead already. Nothing could survive what we're seeing. The heat would melt them in their boots; the lack of oxygen would suffocate them.

Still, we climb the hill, getting higher and higher, and with every metre we climb, the view of the refinery opens up. The sight sickens me for the few fires underway are tiny in relation to the whole of the site. What we saw, the teaming huge flames reaching into the sky, were just a fragment, just a taster of what's to come.

The others realise it too. Lani turns to me with an intense look on her face. Cookey and Blowers stare at each other quietly. Clarence stands with his back to me, staring through the gap. Only Dave seems unbothered as he watches out the front window.

'Are we far enough?' Lani asks. 'Dave, are we far enough?'

He turns slowly, staring first out the back door, then at her. He shakes his head. 'Not yet ...'

Another silo goes, and this time we see the detonation from the ground upwards. A spontaneous combustion that shoots another fireball up. Another goes; then, a whole row is set off one by one. Big, white silos that look perfectly clean and round from here just go up, spewing their contents as though to destroy the sky.

Smaller fires break out, distinctly bright against the dark ground. Smoke billows as the fires spread. A tube must ignite as a long spume of flame goes off, zipping from left to right within seconds, like a fuse from a stick of dynamite.

It detonates something, which sets something else off. More tubes ignite. Flames zipping left to right, right to left, up and down. A whole cross-section of shooting fires that light the ground up like a laser display.

I try to calculate our distance. We're topped out at just over sixty miles an hour. That's roughly a mile a minute. Three, maybe four minutes since we left, so maybe three or four miles distance. That sounds good, but right now, staring back ... it doesn't feel anywhere near enough.

The refinery goes up. The whole thing detonates into a supernova. A burning sun grows from the ground–devils, demons, and monsters of hell rise from the earth to screech into the sky.

A mushroom-shape of flame that grows and increases in height, girth, depth, width, and every other dimension known. It must be alive, for a thing such as this cannot be anything else.

It rises higher and higher. So bright that the sky around it seems to darken. So bright that it almost burns my retinas from looking at it. So huge that I have to crane my neck to see the top, and still, it grows higher.

The shockwave spreads out in a wide circle, simply making the ground flat. Everything that was there is removed. Houses, buildings, cars, trees. Nothing can withstand the blast. The seaward side of the refinery is gone from view, and I can only imagine the devastation such a blast must be causing.

Then the sound comes. A furious roar of rushing wind and dragon's breath that just hits in one full-on symphony of noise. The shockwave comes with the noise. A deafening, evil, dry, and scorching wind. I slam the door closed and see the others get buffeted deep into the Saxon as the pressure slams the rear door closed. Everywhere is noise. Just solid noise that seems to lift the Saxon into the air, rocking and jolting us.

I'm screaming. Nick is screaming as he grips the steering wheel. Debris flies in front of us. Smaller items cascade down onto the road in front of the vehicle or go flying past the windows. A hurricane of wind that sends missiles off vertically and high into the sky to come whizzing and spinning back to earth.

Dirty air buffets us all around. The blue sky is gone from view as a sea of brown and scorched greys sail all around us. Everyone is screaming, but they do it silently for nothing can penetrate the wall of noise that is suddenly and forever more our existence. This must be hell. We died in the explosion, and this is it. An eternity of pressure, of noise, of screeching and knowing with every ounce of your being that you cannot survive. My ears pop repeatedly from the pressure changes in the air. My throat becomes sore from the screaming and the heat. My eyes blur from the sights I cannot stand to see.

I blink and blink, desperately trying to clear my vision. What fills my view is Dave, stood there, holding onto something above his head with both hands. His face looks serene and without fear. He looks at me and smiles, a slow grin that lights his face up. His eyes tell me not to be scared for this cannot be hell, because if it was, the devil would be on his knees in front of Dave, praying for forgiveness.

I smile back. A slow reaction that I do not, now and perhaps never will, understand. I reach out and touch

Nick's shoulder. He screams with panic and fear. I grip him harder, squeezing and shaking.

He slowly turns his head to look at me and sees me smiling. His scream drops off as tears roll down his face. He nods, slowly, then faster, and grins back. It changes his face. His eyes sparkle as he eases his foot from the accelerator and turns back to face the road.

Outside the window is awful–just a black sky with faint hints of blue in the distance. Debris is still being buffeted past us, but thankfully, the weight of the vehicle and the distance we made seems to have kept us safe.

Cookey and Blowers are both hanging on for dear life. Clarence has wedged himself in front of the girl we saved. I'd forgot all about her with everything going on. Lani is sat next to her, with the girl clinging on to her for dear life.

I climb over the seats, still unable to hear anything properly. A rushing sound comes from outside, and my ears are ringing from the noise. Dave looks at me questioningly. I point to the GPMG, and he nods. Climbing up, I ease my head out of the hole and stare in wonder at the sky above.

Then I twist round and see the truest wonder I have ever seen. The mushroom fireball is still raging away but diminishing and growing smaller. The sheer power of the pressured fuel has been exhausted, and it's just the flammable liquids left to burn out. I still can't see past the site to the river, but I can just make out the outskirts of the refinery. Already the surrounding area is a blackened wasteland of smouldering fires and twisted, unidentifiable lumps.

The folly of man hits home harder than ever. The one place left that could have kept us going for many years with fuel and equipment, and now it's gone. Blown to bits by a stray bullet and all the people inside incinerated. Shit. What have we done? Even now, on the very brink of our species being wiped out, we still fight and kill each other out of greed and jealousy.

Looking up into the blackened sky, I see our future mapped out. Dark, boiling clouds gathering that will be visible for many miles. The tremor alone would have been felt like an earthquake. The fallout from this will be catastrophic for years. But then no one will be here to see it. Fifty years from now, the sea would have reclaimed some of the land. Plants and vegetation will grow back. Animals and birds will nest and continue to live, and it'll repair.

Right now, looking at the sheer destruction we caused, it almost seems a good thing that we're being culled. We'd fuck this planet up completely if we stayed.

CHAPTER TWENTY-FIVE

'Harry, you dumb-ass motherfucker, which way we going now?' Randall demands of the big ex-biker. His red, bloodshot eyes looking even more awful above the long, shaggy beard. He looks about as though contemplating, then points away to one side, away from Portsmouth.

'You sure now? Don't be fucking sending us on no long walk,' Randall looks about the area. They crossed the sea easy enough in the boat, taking it steady for risk of hitting something unseen in the water.

With the bright moonlight, they were able to make out the distinct skyline of Portsmouth city and use it as a guide, heading east along the coast, away from anywhere that might be populated.

By the early hours, they were beaching the boat on a deserted shore and wading through the shallows to wait on the sand. Randall watched his men closely. The stupid chat between them was gone. Colin was the only one that made any form of observation or dumb comments. The others had become quiet and business like, doing exactly as bid.

They all looked to Harry, waiting while he got his bearings and decided the direction. Then they set off, a group of hardened and experienced criminals marching along the shoreline in near silence.

'Tell me about this fort? And don't be giving me no one word answers ... I need to know how we get in, which direction we come, so don't be just saying it's big or shit like that,' Randall glares at Harry. Harry glares ahead.

'Back is on the sea. Don't know if there is a door. Front has flat land for maybe a mile. Got two walls, both big and made of concrete. Big gate in the middle.'

'Holy fuck, we can't cross that flat land; they'll see us coming ... You know of any tunnels or shit?'

Harry shakes his head, rubbing the bottom of his beard against his chest.

'Any other doors round the side?' Randall asks. Harry thinks for a minute, then shrugs.

'This is a mother-fucking perplexing issue right here ... How the fuck we gonna get in?'

'Why not just knock on the door and ask,' Colin says with an innocent grin.

'Are you really that stupid?'

'We can talk. We just knock and–'

'Hey, yeah, that's a real good idea, Colin. Say, you people with your guns, can you open up and let us mother-fucking brain eaters in, please? Holy shit, man, that's got to the dumbest fucking thing you've said so far. How the fuck are you still alive? You should've have been terminated at birth, you dumb fucking ass ...'

'Well, it was only an idea,' Colin replies huffily.

'And a stupid mother-fucking idea at that ... Don't speak. No, don't say a mother-fucking word, or Harry will start using your fucking teeth to comb his beard.'

They walk on in silence. Randall brooding as he

thinks of how to get inside the fort. The hunger inside him is immense–a strong urge to rip and tear, to destroy, and dominate. The going is hard, and as the sun rises into the sky, they all feel the intense heat bearing down on them.

They walk around sweeping bays of golden sand. The clear, blue waters lapping gently at the shore. Green fields and meadows border the beach. A perfect summer's day in an idyllic setting. Birds swoop amongst the sand dunes that roll gently away into the distance. Gulls cry and float serenely on the warm currents of air. Rabbits, already feeling braver from the lack of human contact, run and bounce through the grassy dunes.

Twelve days of no people, and the sand looks virginal, with no signs of footsteps or sandcastles. No screaming children covered in suncream, being chased by harassed parents with bright red, sweaty faces.

All of the beauty of the area is lost on the men. The urge to feast and to please Randall is the driving factor. Nothing else matters now. They could be walking through a barren wasteland of scorched earth, and their reaction would be no different.

Hours pass as they march on, hugging the shore and keenly watching the distance for signs of the fort.

They see it easily. A large edifice stark against the surrounding organic nature of the area. Sturdy walls built high on a spit of land that juts out into the sea.

Randall pauses his group, knowing they will be spotted if he continues straight along the shore. He leads the men away from the sea and into a beachside residential area of large houses, cafés, and restaurants. All of them looking empty and dark.

Hidden from view, they make their way through the

roads and lanes, catching glimpses of the fort in the distance.

As they get closer, Randall realises the spit of land the fort is built on forms a bay that separates them with a wide expanse of water. The spit stretching much further into the sea than the rest of the shoreline.

They can either work their way round the bay and come in from the north or go across the water, and enter into the flatlands. A boat would be no good, too easily seen by any lookouts. Coming in from the north is just the same. A group of large built men walking through that flat ground would be instantly visible. The south is an option, coming up to the fort from the seaward side.

'I surely hope you dumb fucks can swim,' Randall mutters without taking his eyes off the glittering surface of the water.

'I can't,' one man replies in a flat tone.

'Then you best be good at drowning quietly,' Randall stares at him intensely. The man nods without showing a flicker of emotion.

Randall takes them through gardens and grounds to the shoreline, holding the men in the cover of the trees before sending them down one at a time to ease themselves into the sea, with strict instructions to only keep their heads out of the water.

He watches as the first one goes down, running bent over until he reaches the edge and wading through the shallows to the deeper water. The man keeps going, not flinching once as he walks until only his head is showing, then turns to wait.

Randall hangs back, waiting with the one who said he couldn't swim. As the last one runs out, he draws his knife and stares at the man. They lock eyes. The man shows no fear or concern at being confronted by Randall holding a blade.

'Can't risk you making noise,' Randall says quietly.

'Okay,' the man replies. Watching as Randall jabs the point of his knife forward, thrusting it deep into his stomach. The man looks down at the handle sticking out and Randall's hand gripping it. Still, he shows no reaction as Randall starts turning the knife slowly. Twisting the blade deep within the man's gut.

'Holy fuck,' Randall whispers, his eyes locked on the man he's stabbing. He pulls the knife out and watches as a thick stream of blood soaks the front of the man's top, a bright crimson stain spreading quickly across his stomach. The man just stares down at it. The knife is plunged in again, a deep thrusting motion that drives it up to the hilt. Randall draws it out and stabs again, then again. Aiming all round the stomach and then the sides.

The man drops down as his internal organs are pierced. The infection unable to contain the damage being sustained to the host body.

Randall goes with him, a wild look in his bulging eyes as he stabs and stabs, sinking the knife into the soft flesh and relishing in the violence of killing someone who shows no reaction.

Eventually he stands back, chest heaving and dripping blood from his soaked arm. The man lies still, his eyes staring up at Randall as his blood drains away.

'Motherfucker,' Randall shakes his head, 'you do die quietly, don't you? If I'd known that, you could have come with us ... Sorry, buddy.'

'I understand,' the man replies. His eyes close slowly as he slips away, dying for the second time.

Shrugging and shaking his head, Randall turns round

and heads down to the water. He crouches like the others and quickly wades in. Taking care to sweep his legs along rather than bringing them up and down.

Within a couple of seconds, he's out into the deeper water, feeling the relief of the water cooling his sun-baked body. He drops down to soak his face, coming back up as the water drains down from his head, dripping from his beard.

With the knife pushed into his waistband, he kicks out, lifting his feet from the sea floor and gently kicking his way towards the opposite shore.

He glances about, seeing the inmates doing the same thing. They go slowly, all of them using some form of breaststroke to avoid lifting their arms over the surface of the water. This close, the heads look distinct against the smooth, natural colour of the sea. But from a distance, he knows they'll be very hard to spot, especially with the bright sun reflecting off the sea.

They reach the other side without issue, stopping when they feel the bottom of the seabed coming back into reach of their feet.

'Wait here,' Randall whispers, telling the men to pass it on quietly. He swims forward, keeping his body low in the water until the very last second, then quickly rising up to run crouched into the long grass of the verge.

He drops down onto his belly, then starts crawling away from the shore. The high grass ends within a few metres of the shore, forcing him to hold still and watch.

To his left is the ruined housing estate, the twisted, blackened stumps of houses and buildings. The flatlands look vast from his position, with no form of concealment. To go across here would be stupid.

Looking across to the fort, the raised earth banks

obscure his view of the main gates, but he can see the high walls, sheer in design, with no way of getting over them without a rope and making a lot of noise.

He edges backwards, snaking his way through the grass and back into the water, swimming south, heading away from the land, and following the contour of the spit of land as it stretches out into the sea.

Several of them hated the water and detested swimming, with memories of cold municipal community swimming pools from their school days and being forced to dive down to grab a brick while wearing pyjamas. But now they swim without complaint. Content to follow Randall.

The small beach disappears as the spit of land goes into deeper water. The side of the fort lunging straight into the sea. This means they can get closer, swimming just feet from the wall and reducing their chances of being seen. They follow the long wall as it curves round to reveal the long back section. A large collection of boats is moored up away from the fort, all held in place by anchor chains plunging down into the depths.

Keeping close to the wall, they make their way along, going as slow as possible to avoid making any noise. Randall in the lead, with the others strung out in a long line.

The rear door comes into view. A solid wooden thing built flush into the wall, and without tools they would have no way of getting it open. A narrow shore has been created around the door, just enough land for the people inside to walk out and move a few feet to the sides.

Randall pauses a few metres from the door, treading water and examining the wooden structure. He works out which side the door is hinged on and that it opens outwards. Perfect.

He moves gently to the land, using his powerful arms to

pull himself out of the water. Without speaking, he motions for the men to come closer, pulling them up easily and then waiting while they flatten themselves against the wall. Their wet bodies smearing the concrete and dripping water onto the sun-baked ground.

The last one is pulled out. Randall gets against the wall, having to stand closely cramped with the other men so there's enough room. He gets to the side of the door and grins.

All he needs now is some dumb-ass motherfucker to stroll out and take a piss.

CHAPTER TWENTY-SIX

'We'll have to dock in the Portsmouth ferry terminal.'

'And why is that a problem?' Marcy asks.

'This boat has different dimensions to the fleet used for the Portsmouth route. The dock is purpose built to the sizes of the vessels.'

'Oh, so are we too big or too small?'

'Too wide. The length is not an issue, but we may have a gap at the front. The other consideration is that there may already be a vessel in the dock.'

'What do we do then?' She stares ahead, out of the bridge window, at the inky black sea and the first signs of dawn showing against the horizon.

'Find another dock,' he replies. She looks at him quickly, unsure if he was being sarcastic. So hard to tell with the flat, monotone voices. She shakes her head, convincing herself he was just answering honestly.

She turns round as the bridge door opens, blinking at the sight of Reginald walking through with April.

'What on earth have you got on?' she asks with a puzzled smile.

'Life jackets,' Reginald replies stiffly. 'I took the precaution in case of a disaster at sea. Here, I've got one for you.' He holds up a bright orange flotation jacket.

More communicators walk onto the bridge, all of them wearing the same orange life vests. Marcy stares from one to the other, amazed at the sight.

'Reggie ... it's a perfectly calm sea in the middle of the summer, and we're moving between the Isle of Wight and Portsmouth ... with absolutely no other ships moving anywhere ... at all ...'

'Be that as it may, there are still precedents where accidents can occur, and I thought it wise to take this simple step to prevent any loss of life. Yes, I can see you find this highly amusing, but really, you should be setting an example to the others.'

'I'm not wearing a life jacket, Reggie.'

'This is fundamental personal protective equipment when on board a vessel at sea ...'

'We're not *at sea,* Reggie. We're crossing the tiny bit of water between the Isle–'

'I think you will find that regardless of the voyage or the intended destination, we are technically at sea. Captain, is this not the case?'

'Yes,' the captain replies, 'I mean no. That is most definitely not the case.'

'You willed him to say that!'

'Reggie, I didn't,' Marcy laughs.

'He said yes, then he paused, and said the opposite, and you had that look on your face.'

'What look?'

'That look, the I'm-willing-someone look.'

'I don't have a face for that.'

'You do. She does, doesn't she, April?'

April pauses, staring first at Marcy, then at Reginald. 'No, she doesn't.'

'You did it again! This is really most unfair, and I have to ask you to stop willing people at will. It is a special thing that should be used properly and not for mocking me.'

Marcy bursts out laughing; tears rolling down her cheeks. 'I didn't that time ... Honestly, I really didn't.'

'Oh, stop it now.'

'I really didn't. April said that herself.'

'Great,' Reginald huffs with a sulky tone, 'two of you mocking me. I suppose everyone will start doing it now.'

'Oh, Reggie, come here ... I'll put it on if it makes you feel better,' she laughs, taking the life vest from him.

'It's not a matter of making me feel better. It's a matter of safety.'

'We're zombies, Reggie. Safety doesn't really factor into what we do.'

'First of all, the term is living challenged and not that Z word ... Second, my name is Reginald, and there is no reason why we should not be incorporating basic health and safety measures into our actions.'

'Good god, Reggie ... This is the apocalypse ... the end of times ... I don't think health and safety matters one bit anymore ... Ah, look, it doesn't fit,' Marcy says. Having shrugged her arms through the holes, she attempts to pull the zip up, her breasts refusing to be squashed flat enough. She breathes out and tries again, yanking the zip which just makes her boobs wobble in the low-cut top she's still wearing.

'Marcy ... yes, I can see it doesn't fit. Please stop wobbling them like that. I don't know where to put my eyes.'

She looks at him with a mischievous glint in her eyes, yanking on the zip again and making her boobs wobble even more. 'But Reggie ...' she purrs, 'I'm just trying to do what you said ...'

'Stop it ... Stop it now. Oh, good lord.' He turns away, blushing furiously and shielding his eyes with his hand. 'April, please go and get Marcy a larger size life jacket.'

'Yes, Reggie,' April replies. Marcy's mouth drops open as April smiles and walks off.

'Did she ...?' Reginald looks up in shock.

'She did,' Marcy laughs, pulling the life jacket off.

'Did you will her to say that?' he asks with narrowed eyes, staring at her suspiciously.

'I don't think I've ever willed April. No need to ...'

'Well, can you will her not to call me that?' he pleads.

'Nope, you just said I shouldn't be willing at will all willy nilly.'

'Yes, I did. Well, I shall be having words with that young lady. I think she fails to realise there is a hierarchy to this organisation, and I for one find it immensely disrespectful to be called by an abbreviated form of my correct title.'

'Name, not title,' Mildred corrects him. 'Title is used before name to show position, rank, or standing in life.'

'This is ganging up ...' Reginald wails. 'You're all ganging up on me.'

Marcy laughs again. Shaking her head, she turns back to look out the window. The horizon is distinctly lighter now, pushing deep shades of blue into the receding night.

'Is there another way instead of docking at Portsmouth?' Marcy asks with a serious tone. 'I'm not comfortable with moving such a large horde through a city centre, especially not one like Portsmouth.'

'There are harbours all along the coast, but they are tidal and will not have the clearance we need.'

'What do you suggest? We really cannot dock in a city. It's too much risk.'

'I concur,' Reginald adds in a serious voice, 'and a good idea if I may say so. I should have thought of that before. My apologies.'

'No need. I only just thought of it myself. So what other options do we have?' she asks the man piloting the ship.

'We can beach the vessel and simply walk off but that would render the ship useless, or we can anchor away from the shore and use the life vessels to shuttle our people inland.'

Marcy pauses at the phrase he used, *our people,* a collective ownership and to her, an important step in the right direction. He could have said *your people* or many other forms of address, but he didn't–he said *our people*.

'How long would it take to do the second option? Do all the emergency life vessels have engines?'

'No, two of them do and very powerful engines too. The idea is for the passengers to get aboard the flotation devices and attach them in a line to the two boats with engines. They simply pull them into the shore.'

'And that way we leave this ship safe in the sea, without causing any damage to it?'

'In a manner of speaking, yes. Of course, in this mild weather, the vessel should suffer no harm, but if the weather were to change and the vessel's anchor was not secured properly, it could drift and cause damage.'

'It's the best option we've got. I don't want to ruin this ship unless we have to. There's no need for that ... Reggie? What do you think?'

'I agree. The second option would be the best. I understand your concerns at not damaging the vessel, and it also means we choose our landing ground, which, of course, is the most important thing.'

'Agreed. Captain, change the heading to one zero four six. Full steam ahead.'

'I don't know what that means,' the captain replies.

'Nor do I, but I always wanted to say it. Er ... can you take us somewhere safe so we can get off?'

'Yes.'

The boat gently swerves out from the intended destination of Portsmouth harbour, instead pointing out to sea to cruise past the coast.

Once safely past the harbour mouth, the naval supply ship clearly in view, they watch the shore, looking for the perfect place to land.

'There,' Reginald lowers the binoculars, handing them to Marcy and guiding her view, 'that's got to be the boat the inmates took last night.'

Marcy brings the powerboat into view, focussing on the beach area where it lies. Nothing obvious from this distance. She lowers the binoculars, looking up into the deep blue morning sky.

'Why have they come here?' she muses, more to herself than an outright question.

'They had to land somewhere, and it does look a safe spot,' Reginald replies.

'But they could have gone straight over. They've taken a longer route like we are, and we're only doing it so we get closer to the fort.'

'A perplexing conundrum indeed,' Reginald sighs, 'and one which we may never know the answer to, but it does look a good, clear spot ... Those dunes will be good to move them into straight away. Keep them out of sight until we've undertaken a full reconnaissance.'

'I don't like it. I don't want to land in the same place as they did. They could be in those dunes now, watching us.'

'It's a perfect spot, and besides, I think they have more to fear from our several thousand than the ten or so of them,' Reginald says.

'We'll be too close to the fort if we go much further,' the captain adds.

Marcy stops to think for a minute, weighing the options up. The spot is perfect, which is why the others must have used it. Discrete and isolated, with no buildings in sight. 'Go for it. How close can we get?'

'The seabed shelves quite quickly here. We cannot go that close,' the captain responds.

'Close as you can. What do you need from us?'

The former second officer and now newly promoted captain (a promotion he had been working towards for the previous ten years and knew it would be at least another five or six years before he reached the top) explains the processes to Marcy, Reginald, and the few other communicators on the bridge.

Once the position was found, he anchored the vessel and moved out onto the upper decks, releasing the explosive charge in the lifebuoys, which sent them popping out of the metal canister, down onto the surface of the water already inflated. The large, round, rubberised flotation devices were held in place by ropes while the host bodies moved from the car decks, jumping the gap to land safely on them.

Several missed the mark and plopped into the water with a splash. Of those, a few were recovered and dragged onto the rafts.

While the mass exodus of the infected hosts was underway from the boat to the buoys, the captain moved to the two powered vessels and rapidly winched them down to the water.

Marcy, following the captain, once again marvelled at how quickly the whole process was done. No one stopping to ask questions. No one screaming in panic or pushing. Just silent work undertaken with a slightest of input from the communicators.

The powered vessels manoeuvred between the round buoys, scooping up the trailing ropes to fasten them together.

Within half an hour, the process was complete, with every host moved from the vessel to the rafts. An incredible feat, considering the sheer numbers of those aboard the ship.

The rafts were jammed full and heavily overladen, but with a perfectly flat sea and no wind, the only danger was some small splashes coming as they were dragged towards the shore.

Once in the shallows, the hosts slip down and wade onto the hot beach to stand patiently and wait for instruction from their beloved leader.

'Truly remarkable,' Reginald remarks. Standing in the shallow water, with his trouser legs rolled neatly up, holding his shoes and socks up high and still wearing the orange life jacket, he looks to the horde steadily massing on the beach. 'The whole thing done with no fuss.' He turns to look back at the ship and the second powered boat dragging the rafts in. 'Remarkable,' he repeats. Walking out of the water, he winces as the sand clings to his wet feet and ankles and moves further up the beach.

Easing himself down, he starts dusting the sand from his toes, using his socks to wipe them dry, then carefully pulls his socks back on. The shoes follow, which are diligently laced up, after which he rolls his trouser legs down and tuts at the new creases formed.

Finished, he stands up, plucking his shirt sleeves straight and making sure he's tucked in properly.

'Right, that's that. What's next in our grand adventure?' He beams at Marcy stood watching him, with the bottom of her jeans sodden up to the knees. Even Mildred, the genteel, old woman simply hoisted her skirt up to wade through the water and enjoyed the cooling water on her feet.

'Captain,' Marcy calls the former second officer, sticking to the new title given by Reginald, 'you know this area better than us. Which way is the fort?'

The captain points east. 'Few miles that way.'

With the inflatable rafts pulled up onto the beach, they set off. Three distinct groups form as they walk. Marcy, Reginald, and a few at the very front. These being the ones that possess more of their natural faculties. The second group consists of the communicators–those that can talk but lack the general independent intelligence of the first group. Then the main horde–the slobbering, drooling, red-eyed, head-wobbling, massed zombies.

Reginald looks back, noticing the three groups and the natural way they formed. Glancing round, he takes in Marcy, watching her distant look and sensing the turmoil she feels.

What Marcy feels is conflict. A deep conflict that threatens to pull her every which way possible. The urge to feast is strong, so strong that it constantly nags at her will. Find more hosts, do it now, we must find more hosts and take them. But the same inner argument remains–to keep taking hosts will lead to an end with no more hosts. Then what? This is the way. This has to be the way.

The interaction between April and Reggie, as innocuous as it appeared, left a strong impact on her. April made a joke, a feeble, weak comment that wouldn't raise an eyebrow in any other circumstances, but April was a communicator. One of the hosts that could speak and do as requested without appearing to have any individuality. April was evolving. She understood the social dynamics and adapted her behaviour accordingly.

Two species that will fight to the death for dominance over the other. The damage already inflicted may well be beyond recovery, so many billions of lives destroyed in just twelve days. If this carries on at the same rate of progress, there might not be anything left in another twelve days.

There is another option, one that forces itself into her mind. Don't go to the fort but turn as many as possible, and lead them in the new way. But that new way would be the same, existing to turn more hosts, and the same inevitable conclusion will be there.

No, this is the only option. This has to be done. If they have doctors and medical equipment that can test and isolate the infection, it could be the one thing that saves mankind. Not the mankind of old, but the new mankind. This must be done.

Determination settles within her. The inner turmoil once again suppressed and held in check. Once again, she speaks with the hosts around her, those able to communicate. She tells them again that no matter what happens to her, they must see this through. They must present themselves to the fort and tell the people inside the truth.

So close now. So close to the fort and seeing it through. She takes a deep breath and walks on, resolute and determined.

CHAPTER TWENTY-SEVEN

'Listen, I was never a firearms officer, but I've been a police officer long enough to know that you do not discharge a weapon into a crowded environment. What Howie and his group did last night was unforgivable,' Sergeant Hopewell pauses, looking at the crowd gathered round her. Deep within the tented city of the inner fort, she stands in full uniform, holding a mug of coffee with her hands and holding court to the eager crowd with her voice. 'It really is that simple. How many people died? Forty ... forty people gunned down by untrained people reacting in panic,' she shakes her head sadly, taking a sip of the coffee. 'This has to be a stable society with rules and laws. The same rules and laws that governed us before this event must apply here. We have properly trained and experienced people here who can protect and guard us, and I know for damn sure they won't just fire into a crowd of people blindly, hoping for the best.'

'They were shooting babies ... just shooting them dead, and cutting their throats open,' one woman says tearfully.

'Did you see that?' another man asks shocked.

'No, but I got told by someone who did see it. They said they was just shooting babies in the head. Babies that ...'

'But if they were bitten, they had to be shot. We've all seen what happens when they come back,' another voice joins in.

'Babies ain't got no teeth,' someone else adds. 'They can't bite people, and I heard the babies were asleep in their beds.'

'Don't be stupid. They weren't running into tents and shooting sleeping babies. That's just ridiculous.'

'They were punching innocent people in the face, though. I heard an old woman got her jaw broke just for looking.'

'It wasn't an old woman. It was–'

'Listen,' Sergeant Hopewell draws their attention back, 'whatever they did ... however they did it ... it wasn't the right thing to do, given the circumstances. The fact that so many witnesses have said they saw them shooting innocent people and cutting throats is enough to tell us we shouldn't be trusting them anymore ...'

'So what we gonna do now?' a woman asks, her face drawn and pale.

'I've spoken very strongly to the guards and told them in no uncertain terms what we expect from them and that under no circumstances are they to discharge a weapon into the main living area ...'

'But what if one of 'em gets in here? It's only gotta bite a couple, and we're all fucked,' a voice calls out.

'And how are they going to get in?' Sergeant Hopewell replies quickly. 'Our gates are locked and bolted. The walls are too high to climb, and we've got lookouts everywhere. That's my point. Howie and his lot didn't know if we had one inside here. They just guessed and decided to deal with it their way.'

'So that lad wasn't one of them things, then?'

'All I can say is that it was never proven that he was one of them. He walked back in with the others right as rain, and then a couple of minutes later, he's being stabbed to death.'

'What about his body? Someone could have a look and see his eyes ...'

'The bodies were removed,' Sergeant Hopewell cuts in. 'They were taken to the estate with the others before anyone had a chance to check. My point is that Howie didn't know, none of them knew ... They just charged in here, firing their guns like a bloody video game.'

'What do we do if it happens again?'

'I've just said,' Sergeant Hopewell smiles, 'it can't happen again. I personally don't think it happened like that in the first place. If something happens, shouting and screaming, then we get the guards to get in and see what's going on. We've got thousands of people here, all living on top of each other. There could be fights and disagreements just the same as before. That doesn't mean we just assume they're infected and start shooting everyone.'

'Well said,' a strong voice calls out. Murmurs of agreement ripple through the crowd. The uniformed police sergeant looks the part, an older woman of sound mind and common sense, and here she is, taking the time to drink coffee with the normal folk. Howie never did that. None of his group ever stood about, chatting and drinking coffee like the average people.

Throughout the morning, she works her way through the tents, stopping to speak to groups of survivors, talking about the night's events and how she thinks it was all done wrong. Like a politician canvassing for voters, she expresses her beliefs in how the fort should be run and plants the seed of dissent amongst the many.

Chris, glad of the respite from having to argue with her every five minutes, doesn't notice her actions. Absorbed by the multitude of tents and structures, she is lost from view while he goes about, trying to get everything done.

Sergeant Hopewell, on seeing a group of the engineers carrying the GPMG up to the top of the inner wall, makes her way towards them. Approaching carefully and with an interested look.

'We're getting it fixed into position,' one of the engineers replies after being asked what they're doing.

'Oh,' she replies pleasantly, 'and who instructed you to do this?'

'Er … Kelly did, but I think it was Chris that said it should go here,' the same man replies, standing up to wipe sweat from his face.

'Did he now? It's not a problem, and of course, I can see you chaps are only doing what you've been told … It's just that it wasn't agreed through the proper channels, and I'd hate for you to have to do all that work in getting a frame and tripod or whatever made up and then having to take it down or move it …'

'Oh, right,' the man sighs, 'we figured it had been agreed …'

'No,' she shakes her head, smiling again, 'unfortunately not. We've got some highly experienced ex-military personnel within the fort that have yet to be asked their opinion, and I can foresee some conflict. Of course, I don't know anything about the placing of a weapon such as this, but then neither does Howie, and unfortunately, it was his idea to put it here.'

'Howie? But he knows what he's doing,' the man says with a puzzled expression.

'Well, that's the problem, you see. He worked in a supermarket before all this, so no, he doesn't really know what he's doing … but you carry on. We can always get it moved after.'

'Oh … but it's gonna take some work to get it fixed in here. We gotta do it all by hand. No power tools, you see, so er … Do you think it might end up being moved?'

'I think it's highly possible, once we've got the opinions of the experts …' she sighs, taking her hat off to use a tissue to dab at her flushed face. 'That's the other problem … Howie doesn't like taking the opinions of the experts, thinks he can do it all himself.'

'Really? He seemed alright to me,' the man says with a slightly shocked expression.

'Yeah, that's how he comes across, doesn't he?' she stares at him earnestly. 'I honestly thought he knew exactly what he was doing. We all did, but you know … after last night and all those innocent people being shot and stabbed to death, especially the babies … Well, I'm not so sure now.'

'Babies?'

'Sadly so, between you and me,' she lowers her voice, stepping in closer, 'there were quite a few children gunned down last night. No sign of blood or bites on any of them.'

'Shit,' the man gasps, 'we all thought there were biters in here.'

'Well,' she steps back with a shrug, 'that's what Howie said but no one actually saw a biter,' she says, using the same terminology of the man to form a sense of allegiance.

'Fuck, oh god … sorry, I didn't mean to swear.'

'Don't be silly. I'm on your side, I'm all for you chaps getting the right recognition. This fort wouldn't be anything without the hard work you guys are doing, which is why I thought I'd best mention the placing of the gun now, before you put all that effort in ... That's the other problem with Howie–he expects everyone to be working flat out all the time ... and where is he?' She stands back with her arms slightly raised, making a point of looking about.

'Gone for fuel, ain't they?'

'So they say,' she replies. 'How long does that take? What's he doing out there all this time? Just him and his group ... Just seems strange to me, but then,' she shakes her head, 'what do I know? I've only been a police sergeant for twenty years.'

'No, yeah, course,' the man nods at her, 'so maybe we should hang on then ... before we get the gun fixed in.'

'I would,' she says kindly, 'you all look hot. Get yourself a drink in the shade. You need a break, you know, especially in this awful heat.'

'Yeah ... yeah, we are hot. We'll get a drink then and wait for someone to let us know where to put it.'

'Good idea, a nice cup of tea sounds good. I bet there must be some biscuits knocking about somewhere. I'll see if I can get some sent over to you.'

'Really? Biscuits? Bloody hell, that'd be lovely.'

'Just between us, though,' she winks with a smile. 'We don't want everyone wanting biscuits, do we? Got to keep them safe for the real hard workers.'

She walks off with another wink, smiling as she looks out over the top at the flatlands. At the slope, she pauses mid stride, staring across the fort at Chris stood talking to someone, with that bloody dog at his side.

The dog that gives Howie all the power, just because he went out and got it. Him and that bloody Chris. Neanderthal men running around like brutes. She spent years fighting male dominance in the police, and now it's all gone back to how it was, with violent bullies running the show.

She heard the noise last night when it first started. The shots being fired, the shouts, and screams, but she waited, too terrified of moving closer. In the police, there were always brave men to do that kind of thing. Pub fights, violent domestics, armed assailants, and drunken public disorder. She'd done her two years frontline and then spent the rest of her time working office departments and specialist units before moving into the relatively safe custody department with the high desk she could sit behind. Organisation and administration–those were her strong points. So when the fighting started within the fort, she was only too willing to hang back and wait for the worst to be over. Later claiming she was at the far side of the fort and within the rooms, out of earshot.

She hated the way everyone looked up to Howie. He was young, not even thirty years old, and he had everyone in his pocket, and he wasn't even a police officer, just a stupid supermarket manager. And that group of his, the way they called him *Mr Howie* and *Boss.* More and more people were calling her by her first name while more and more were calling him bloody *Mister*.

Resentment and jealousy course through her soul, not that she'd ever admit to having those feelings, not even to herself, instead they're manipulated and translated as righteous anger. A sense that *it's being done wrong,* and she is the one to fix it. That and the grief she feels at losing not only her own friends and associates but now Steven and Tom make for a dangerous set of views that are quickly spread around the fort.

Chris pauses after speaking to the survivor, sharing a few words of comfort and listening to the other man's problems for a minute before promising he'll do the best he can, the same promise he repeats time and time again. Not just words either but meaningful promises. As the man walks off, he glances across the fort, spotting Debbie stood at the top of the slope, easily recognisable with her police hat perched on her head.

He sighs deeply, shaking his head with a deep sense of sadness as he understands why he hadn't seen her for several hours and with a deeper sense of sadness at what damage she would have caused talking to people.

He needed to take action. He knew that, but she was still a police sergeant, and that meant something to Chris. She held rank and had proven herself highly capable at getting things organised and done, but the cost now was too high.

Looking round the fort, at the vast sea of tents crammed into the centre, at the many people walking or stood round chatting, he suddenly felt the weight of the burden making his broad shoulders involuntarily sag from the pressure. Right now, he wished he was out with Howie and Clarence, sat in the Saxon and doing the dangerous job instead of trying to placate so many different characters.

Still, at least they're safe in here.

That's something.

CHAPTER TWENTY-EIGHT

'Pull over,' Clarence splutters.

'Here?' Nick asks.

'Yeah, here,' I add. My voice comes out hoarse, and my throat feels rough, like it's been burnt.

Nick slows the Saxon, automatically edging to the side of the road, a habit long ingrained to save blocking the carriageway.

Once stopped, we burst out of the vehicle, coughing and wheezing from the fumes trapped inside. The air is hot and uncomfortable, but at least it's not tainted with burnt oil fumes like the inside of the vehicle.

Lani carries out a case of water bottles and dumps them on the ground, ripping the plastic cover away to start handing the bottles round. Clarence drags the headless corpse out and throws it into the bushes like it's a rolled up carpet being dumped.

'Heads up,' Blowers tries to joke as he pulls the head out but starts coughing instead, dropping the head and toeing it away to join the rest of its body.

'Fuck,' Cookey gasps, a long, drawn-out noise full of

awe as he stares back up the hill. We're on the reverse side of the hill we went up to get away from the burning refinery. The descent has thankfully given us some fresher air and taken us further from the fire.

We stand in near silence, breathing heavily and coughing to clear the stench from our airways. The outside of the Saxon is filthy, covered in a thick, greasy layer of grime that clings to every surface. Like dirty oil watered down and filled with grit.

Beyond the crest of the hill, the thick, broiling, mushroom-shaped cloud still blooms skywards, highly visible not only to us but to everyone within a fifty-mile radius probably. The explosion must have been felt everywhere. It was like an earthquake, and I've no doubt the fort would have at least felt it and been able to see the smoke.

'How long will it last?' a strange voice breaks my thoughts. I snap my head round to see the girl stood with us, staring up at the cloud. She looks different. Drained and pale, but composed.

She looks at me with a level gaze; pale, blue eyes within a porcelain white face and framed by light blonde hair. Small build, but there's a strength in those eyes, a look the same as Lani has.

'How long will it burn for?' she repeats. I break eye contact and look at Dave.

'Few days,' he replies with a shrug.

'My mouth tastes like a gorilla's taken a dump in it,' Nick moans. He takes a pull of water, swilling it round his mouth before spitting it out onto the hot road. It soaks away within seconds, leaving just a dark stain.

'Me too,' Cookey says, chomping his mouth as though eating something distasteful.

'You okay?' Lani asks the girl.

'Yeah,' she nods, staring at the cloud. 'They're all dead, aren't they?'

'Who?' Lani asks.

She shrugs, 'Everyone ... everyone that was in that place.'

'Yeah,' Lani says quietly, looking away at the cloud.

'Good,' she whispers. 'I should feel bad, but I don't ... I feel glad, and I hope they fucking suffered.'

'Can't argue with that,' Blowers says after a pause.

'I'm Howie, by the way,' I hold my hand out and then feel a pang of shame, knowing what she just went through. She looks at my hand and takes it with a quick shake.

'Lillian ...' She drops my hand.

'Nice to meet you.'

'You're Lani. Is that right?'

'Milani, but yeah ... Lani.'

'Thanks for helping me,' her voice trails off. 'I ... er ...'

'Forget it,' Lani says, 'it's done.'

'Okay, but thanks, though ... Were the others all killed?'

Lani nods slowly but holds eye contact with the girl. 'Sorry.'

Lillian sighs and nods back. 'Yeah, I thought so ...'

'Were they your relatives?' Cookey asks.

'Don't fucking ask the poor girl that!' Blowers says.

'Shit, sorry, Lillian, I ... I didn't think ...'

'He never bloody does,' Blowers adds.

'It's okay,' Lillian says. 'No, they weren't ... My family live in the north. I was at university here. I did know them all but ...'

'I'm really sorry,' Cookey says again. 'I'm Cookey,' he holds his hand out respectfully. She takes it the same way she did mine, a short, quick shake and release. The others introduce themselves one by one, offering a quick handshake, apart from Dave who just stands staring at the cloud.

'Dave,' he nods at her after a pause. 'I don't like shaking hands, but Mr Howie keeps making me do it,' He then offers his hand out with a quick glance at me.

'Oh ... you don't have to,' she says with a glance at me.

'Thanks,' he drops his hand quickly and still wipes it on the back of his trousers, despite having not made contact. A habitual reflex, I guess.

'Lillian, we've got a safe place along the coast, an old fort ...' Lani explains. Having already made the connection with the girl, she takes it on herself to say who we are and why we came here. The girl listens, nodding intently. Visually they are the opposite. Lani is dark, with tanned skin, whereas Lillian is very pale, with light hair. Their build is similar. Lillian perhaps being slightly heavier. The eyes, though, they are the same. The same level gaze of someone who has been through hell and realised it didn't break them. The same eyes as the rest of us have.

'You're welcome to come with us,' I add when Lani finishes.

'Thank you,' she says simply.

'But we've still got to get a fuel tanker yet, so there'll be a delay before we get back. Is that okay?' It wouldn't make a difference what she says now, but politeness counts.

She nods and looks at Lani, at the pistol on her belt and the assault rifle held in one hand. 'The guns you took off the men ... Can I have one?'

She looks at me with that same level gaze. I stare back for a second before glancing at Clarence who shrugs '*up to you*'.

'If we run into those things ... or something else happens ... I want to defend myself.'

'Okay, yeah, that's fair enough,' I nod. 'Dave will show you how to use one.'

'Can't Lani do it?' she asks.

'No,' I shake my head firmly. 'Dave does it. Lillian, you are not at risk from any of us. I'll make that clear now … I get what you just went through, and in normal times, there would a period of recovery and grief, but these aren't normal times—'

'I understand,' she cuts me off. 'Sorry, I shouldn't have asked. I didn't mean any offence to Dave.'

'It's not really possible to offend Dave,' Cookey quips, then quickly backs away with a grin as Dave glares at him. 'Sorry, sorry, I was only joking …'

'You must have a death wish, Cookey,' Clarence mutters with a grin.

'Good film. I love Charles Bronson,' Blowers adds.

'I bet you do,' Cookey says.

'Oh, fuck off,' Blowers sighs as Lillian looks at them with a puzzled expression.

'You get used to it,' Lani says. 'It's non-stop. Really, I mean non-bloody-stop.'

'Oh, you love us really, Lani,' Cookey laughs.

'Careful,' Nick laughs, 'she'll cut your head off.'

'See what I mean,' Lani says. 'They'll be mentioning that for the rest of the day now.'

'What? You cutting that blokes head off?' Cookey laughs.

'You mean the head you cut off?' Blowers joins in.

'Okay, okay,' I cut in. 'Dave, would you show Lillian how to use a gun, please, mate.'

'Pistol and rifle or just rifle?' He asks.

'Rifle will do for no. You can do the pistol dry fire when we get going.'

'Okay, Mr Howie. Lillian, come with me, please,' he slips smoothly into his sergeants role, leading the girl to the rear of the Saxon.

'Got a smoke, Nick?'

'Do you want a packet, Boss?' Nick replies.

'Nah, I'll just keep asking you.'

'Okay,' he taps one out and hands it over as I fish about for a lighter.

'Here, Mr Howie,' Cookey holds his out.

'Cheers, mate,' I light the smoke, coughing from the harsh pull of smoke after the thick smoke we just went through.

The three lads stand in silence, smoking away and staring at each other.

'Lads!' They all look at me. 'I know exactly what you're thinking, but take it easy ... After what she's just been through ... Yes, she's very pretty, but take it easy ... Understand?'

'Yes, Boss,' Nick nods.

'Got it,' Cookey says seriously.

'Me too,' Blowers adds.

'You think she's pretty?' Lani cuts in with a glare and a sharp intake of breath from Clarence.

'Careful, Boss, she's got a knife,' he says as the other three burst out laughing.

'Well, no, I don't think she's pretty, but er ... well, the lads here obviously think she's pretty, so you know, I was just saying, you know, from their perspective ...'

'Definitely,' Blowers takes it up with a serious nod.

'I was just saying how pretty she was, and the Boss said he didn't think she was pretty at all,' Nick says with an air of pure innocence.

'Men,' Lani shakes her head.

A shot rings out from the back of the Saxon. We all flinch, reaching for our weapons before relaxing with wry grins. Then we wait at the side as Dave quickly puts Lillian through the basics. Four of us remembering back in Salisbury when Dave did the same with us.

'All done, Mr Howie,' Dave calls over, walking round to the side, with the now armed Lillian with him. 'I've given her the same weapon as us so there's no issue with ammunition.'

'Makes sense. We ready to go?'

'I don't know if it helps, but you said you're looking for fuel?' Lillian says, holding the rifle across her chest self-consciously, but already I can see the simple act of holding a weapon makes her feel better.

We all stop to stare at her. She looks round at each face, sensing the sudden change from easy-going banter to serious faces.

'Er ... there's a depot opposite the place I stayed in. There was always tankers parked up there at weekends. I don't know if there'll be any there or not ...'

'Worth a go,' I reply with a smile. 'Do you know the way?'

She nods. 'Maybe ten minutes from here. Not far, but the place was crawling with those zombie things.'

'Aahh,' Clarence grimaces, 'I hate that word.'

'Ignore him,' I say. 'So there were loads of zombies, yeah?' I ask placing emphasis on the zombie word.

'Was that zombies?' Cookey joins in with a grin.

'Someone say ZOMBIES?' Nick laughs.

'Little shits,' Clarence mutters, climbing into the passenger seat.

'Loads,' Lillian says after another puzzled glance at the lads.

'Loads as in how many?' I ask.

'I don't know. Hundreds, I think … They were everywhere.'

'What was that? Hundreds of ZOMBIES?' Cookey shouts.

'Cookey,' Clarence shouts, with a warning tone firmly edged into his voice.

We load up and pull out, following the main road until we're directed by Lillian to pull off and head into the built-up area of the main towns that border Southampton.

The lads ask her questions, friendly and non-invasive and done with their usual light-hearted banter. We find out her family was from the south but moved up north for her father's work. She stayed down here to finish college and then go for university, studying business and finance and living in student accommodation. One older brother who was in the army and posted to Germany when the outbreak started.

As with Lani, she explained it in a blunt fashion, with no emotion, which is something we've become used to. The feelings those conversations spark are just too painful to deal with. So why bother.

The inner towns are the same as before, only the decay is starting to show more. The burnt-out houses and cars look old and charred instead of freshly burnt. The cadavers in the road are decomposing in the high heat, literally melting into the surface of the pavement and roads.

Large pools of dark stains writhe with thick, white maggots, and flying insects buzz everywhere, rising from the corpses they feast upon.

We see the odd infected here and there but don't stop to engage them. Instead we push on, driving the big vehicle through the grimy, shitty streets as directed by Lillian.

Nick takes the GPMG, glad of the chance to have a discrete smoke up top, thinking that Dave won't notice, as if anything gets past him, but he lets it go without comment.

'Just up there,' she points to a wide road–a row of large, terraced houses on one side and commercial properties on the other. The houses look distinctly student accommodation, cheap and large, with overgrown front lawns full of mismatching garden furniture; the windows that are intact have old, faded posters in them.

Only a handful of infected are gathered in the street, just stood there, swaying back and forth, with drool hanging from their mouths. They look awful, really haggard and drawn and barely recognisable as human, other than their basic form. Days spent in the hot sun have withered them down. Skin drawn tight across bone, deep, recessed eyes, and matted, filthy hair.

'Halfway up, there's another road on the right that goes down to the depot I was saying about,' Lillian points, leaning through the gap between the seats. 'There were more than this,' she adds, looking at the small horde.

'Must have gone somewhere else,' I reply, turning the vehicle into the road and moving slowly towards the horde.

'What are we doing with them?' Nick shouts down.

'Cut them down,' I shout back, imagining the big grin on Nick's face. The gun explodes to life, firing a short burst into the horde. Lillian watches with interest as the bodies are ripped apart. Rounds slamming into their chests and stomachs. The bodies flying backwards from the impact of the bullets.

The small horde is cut down within seconds; just a pile of bodies left to rot on the ground with everything else.

'We might get more contact now,' Clarence explains to Lillian. 'The noise will draw them out.'

'Why didn't we just go past and leave them here?'

'We could, but then come night, they'll turn into the nasty fuckers and be a risk to any other survivors,' I reply.

'So you kill all of them?'

'Groups like that—we will if it doesn't get in the way of what we're doing.'

'How many have you killed?'

'Thousands, maybe tens of thousands.'

'Seriously?' she asks with surprise. 'Turn right here ... See that big gate down there? The tankers are parked behind that.'

We drive down to the big metal gates she indicates. High sided with big signs warning of security patrols and CCTV and no naked flames beyond this point.

'Nick, can you see over the top of those gates?'

'No, you want me to climb up?'

'Yeah, is that alright?'

'Okay,' he scrabbles up to stand on the roof of the Saxon. 'They're too high,' he shouts down.

'How did you see them?' Clarence asks.

'My room was on the top floor. I saw them driving down here and could just see the tops of them through a gap in the wall,' Lillian says.

'The gate's locked with a big chain,' Nick shouts.

'Yeah, we can see that. We'll have to pull the gates off ... Can't risk smashing them open if we don't know what's on the other side.' I wait for Nick to drop back down, then manoeuvre the vehicle so the back against the gates.

'I'll cover with Cookey, Lani, and Dave if you and Blowers get a chain rigged up,' I say to Clarence. 'Lillian, you stay with Dave.'

We clamber out, once again feeling the impact of the heat. Within seconds, we're sweating freely as we move out to cover both sides of the street. Clarence and Blowers work quickly, getting a thick chain from inside the Saxon and attaching it to the gates.

Glancing round, I see Dave stood next to Lillian, moving his gaze between the street and her. He makes a quiet comment, and she adjusts the way she holds the rifle, pushing the butt of the gun more into her shoulder.

'Ready. You want me to drive it?' Clarence calls out.

'Carry on, mate,' we move out, away from the gates as Clarence gets into the driver's seat. He pulls away gently until Blowers shouts the chain is taut; then, he powers on, pushing the vehicle onwards. The chain pings tighter and pulls the gates open. The padlock and chain snapping from the pressure.

'Whoa,' Blowers shouts, waving his arm. Clarence jumps down, holding his assault rifle at the ready.

'Nick, you stay here and cover the street. No one is to fire inside that compound. We are not blowing any more tankers up,' I call out as we move towards the gates, with Dave taking the lead.

We pull the gates open and stand smiling at the sight of the solitary tanker parked up at the far end of the large parking area. The rest looks clear, and the gate being locked is a good sign of nothing being in here.

'Hope it's full,' Cookey says quietly.

'It'll be locked. The keys must be in that building,' Blowers nods his head towards the single-story, squat building at the back of the compound.

We head over and wait while Clarence sizes the door up and starts giving it big, hefty kicks, being watched by a grinning Cookey. The solid door takes some battering before finally relenting and busting open. By which point, Clarence is bright red in the face and getting angry.

'Nice and cool in here,' Blowers shouts from inside. The rest of us slip in through the ruined doorway. The windows have blinds covering them, and the thick walls have prevented the heat from building up. The air is stale and musty but decidedly cooler than outside.

We all breathe a sigh of relief and wait while the two lads toss the office, searching for the keys.

'Yes!' Cookey exclaims as he opens a desk drawer. He pulls out a packet of Hobnob biscuits and grins. 'Bloody love Hobnobs.'

'You love knobs,' Blowers mutters. 'Got 'em,' he adds, picking a set of keys up.

'Dirty bastard,' Cookey chuckles. He pulls a glossy magazine out of the drawer and holds it up. A picture of a busty woman on the front with two big, yellow stars covering her nipples. 'Who has a wank in their office?' he laughs.

'Here, you need these?' Blowers throws a box of tissues at Cookey.

'Yeah. Is there a toilet?' Cookey quips.

'Come on,' I laugh. Blowers throws the keys over. Outside, we cross the hot parking area towards the tanker. I unlock the door and climb up, gasping at the heat inside the cab.

'Fingers crossed,' Clarence starts checking the dials inside, waiting for me to turn the ignition on so they give a correct reading. 'With any luck, it would have been loaded up before coming back so it was ready for deliveries on Saturday morning ... YES!' he shouts, making us all jump.

'Is it full?' Lani shouts from outside.

'To the top,' Clarence replies. The mood lifts instantly as we break out in big grins, giving cheers.

'Well done, Lilly,' I shout to the girl. 'Brilliant, mate. Great idea.'

'Cracking,' Clarence grins at the girl, 'well done.'

She smiles back as the others all say the same thing. She doesn't know the importance of the fuel to us. We've explained about Meredith, but the full impact can't be the same to her as it is to us.

'You driving this back?' I ask Clarence.

He nods, still grinning as sweat runs down his bald head.

'Take one of the lads with you.'

'I'll go,' Cookey shouts.

'No,' Clarence groans. 'Only joking. Get in, then,' he adds at seeing the lad looking crestfallen, 'but no silly bloody jokes.'

'Yeah ... you love my jokes,' Cookey beams.

The rest of us cross over the yard and load up, switching the air con on for a few minutes to bring the heat down. I pull the Saxon out once Clarence has the tanker moving, going back up the road as we navigate our way through the town, back onto the motorway.

'That went well in the end,' I say to Dave sat in the front with me.

'It did, Mr Howie.'

'So that's two refineries you've blown up now.'

'Yes.'

'Was this one bigger?'

'Sort of. The other one was more modern and produced more oil but was smaller in size ...'

'Was it in the Middle East?'

'Yes.'

'Why did you have to blow it up?'

'I was told to.'

'Why did they ask you?'

'Because I'm good at blowing things up.'

'No, I mean why did they want it blown up.'

'Oh … I don't know.'

'You don't know?'

'No, they never said.'

'So they just asked you to blow it up, and you did, without asking why?'

'Yes.'

'Dave, did you ever … like … assassinate anyone?'

'Yes.'

'Oh, yeah, you blew that cow up to kill the cow herder.'

'Yes.'

'Anyone else?'

'Yes.'

'Who?' I expect him to say he can't really say. He pauses for a second as though in thought.

'Five politicians, four generals, two colonels, one doctor, three engineers, then another doctor, then two more politicians …'

'Hang on … You said five politicians … Did you forget about the other two?'

'No, I was going in order.'

'Oh … Were they all at once? The five, I mean?'

'Yes.'

'How did you do it.'

'Car bomb.'

'Shit … Then four generals. Were they together?'

'No, one at a time in a set order.'

'Fucking hell, mate … You killed doctors? You can't kill doctors.'

'You can … I did.'

'Why doctors? What did they do?'

'They were informants, leaking information about our covert operations.'

'How the fuck did they know about your covert operations?'

'They worked for us. They were army doctors.'

'Shit, no way ... How did you kill them?'

'I drowned one in his shower, and the other ...'

'In his shower?'

'Yes.'

'How do you drown someone in a shower?'

'I put the shower head in his mouth.'

'Oh, yeah, course ...'

'And the other I blew up.'

'How did you blow him up? Another car bomb?'

'No, I sellotaped a grenade to the head and pulled the pin.'

'Fucking hell, Dave, you can't do shit like that ... Isn't that like torture or something.'

'The information that was leaked caused a covert team to get compromised. They were tortured and put to death.'

'Hmmm, fair enough then, I guess.'

'Were they all men? Did you have rules like no women and no children?'

'No.'

'Which one no? No, they weren't all men or no, you didn't have rules?'

'Both, they weren't all men and no, I didn't have rules. Children are never targeted, though.'

'But you killed women?'

'Yes.'

'How did you kill them?'

'I just told you. I sellotaped a grenade to her head.'

'Her? Oh, she was a female doctor?'

'Yes.'

'Did you ever refuse to do one?'

'No, I didn't refuse, but a few I couldn't complete. One of them had children with him all the time, and I couldn't get to him without hurting the children.'

'So you left it?'

'Yes, I was told to.'

'Would you have done it if you hadn't been told to?'

'I would have found a way.'

'Have you ever been shot?'

'No, shot at but never shot.'

'Captured?'

'Once.'

'What happened then?'

'I got away.'

'How did you get away?'

'I walked.'

'No …' this can be hard work sometimes, 'like how did you do the getting away?'

'Oh … I killed them.'

'How many?'

'Eight.'

'Fuck! You are shitting me.'

'No.'

'In one go? You killed eight in one go?'

'Yes.'

'Mate, you're like Liam Neeson in that film when his daughter gets taken …'

'Taken.'

'Yeah, that's what I said … She gets taken.'

'The film, it's called Taken.'

'Oh, right. Yeah, it is.'

'You mentioned it before.'

'I hope you never become a zombie. We'd be fucked.' I look at him in awe. The fact that he's so normal about it, well, as normal as Dave can be, is the striking thing. Poker faced and devoid of expression.

'I'd shoot myself in the brain if I got bit,' he replies.

'No offence, but I'd shoot you in the brain if you get bit, and I'd keep on shooting ... and then still leg it at as fast as I could while throwing grenades at you. You'd be like some super cyborg zombie like the terminator ... just refusing to die.'

I twist round to check the others, forgetting for a second that Clarence and Cookey are in the tanker and wondering why it's so quiet. Blowers is stretched out on one bench with his eyes closed while Lani and Lillian sit talking quietly on the other one.

'How did she take to the shooting?' I ask Dave.

'Good,' he nods. 'She's very angry. It's in her eyes and the way she holds the rifle.'

'Can't blame her.'

He doesn't reply but stares out of the window. On the motorway now, with the green fields on either side and the tanker behind us.

'I wonder if Clarence has punched Cookey yet.'

'He likes Alex. We all do.'

'Bloody hell, mate, did you just admit to liking someone?'

'Yes. I like all of them.'

'Christ, you're becoming more human every day. I don't know what's happened to you, Dave! You're just not the man I met ...'

'Sorry,' he replies with a wry grin, which shocks me even more.

'Maybe we'll finally get some rest now they've got the

fuel,' I sigh deeply, settling back into the seat with a feeling of accomplishment.

'Maybe, Mr Howie.'

'Hope so, mate. We deserve it. That's if Sergeant Hopewell hasn't had us banned from going back in.'

We drive on in silence, gradually making our way back to the fort. Blowers snoozing from the warmth. Nick humming to himself up top while smoking. Lani and Lillian chatting quietly, and the other two driving the full tanker of fuel behind us. Funny how things work out. If we hadn't of gone to the refinery, we'd never have met Lillian and then not found the tanker. Now here we are, driving back with the mission complete, and other than blowing up the country's biggest refinery and causing a massive supernova mushroom cloud and destroying miles of surrounding countryside and which also probably caused a tidal wave that flooded down the river ... other than that, it's not been that bad.

Not too bad at all.

CHAPTER TWENTY-NINE

'You understand, Debbie,' Graham whines, 'we really should have a multi-faith area where people can worship. After everything we've all been through, a quiet place to reflect will be good for the soul.'

'I know, Graham, I agree, but apparently Lord High-and-Mighty Howie said we can't have one, and everyone has to do what Lord Howie says.'

'He's wrong,' Graham says quietly. He watches the sergeant closely, seeing the stress on her face. 'You should be in charge here. You're a sergeant *and* with the police ...'

'I know he's bloody wrong,' Sergeant Hopewell snaps, 'and thank you for the vote of confidence. Things would be run a great deal better if I was in charge. I can tell you that.'

'You've got our support. The whole congregation is behind you, and not just the Christians either, but all of us.'

'Thank you, Graham. You know ... really, we should be looking at a place of worship, but getting them to *give any ground up*,' she makes finger quote marks, 'is impossible.'

'What about outside?' Graham persists.

'We can't go out the front. It's too risky until we've got an alarm system in place.'

'The back then?' he asks.

'The back? What, out that door? There's only a bit of ground there.'

'That's all we need, a quiet place to reflect and say our prayers, a non-denominational area for persons of faith to offer their prayers, and the ground is surrounded by water, so there is really very little risk.'

Sergeant Hopewell stares across the fort to the back wall, remembering the small patch of ground they used when the women and children fled from the battle.

'I don't know, Graham,' she hesitates. The fort has to be kept secure–that's the whole point. But then he did just say his group pledge their support to her, and if she can get enough supporters, then asking Howie and his group to leave will be easy. Get rid of them and get back to things being run how they should, with committees and meetings. The right people in the right roles, and everything being overseen by her. 'Let me have a think about it.'

'There's a lot of us,' Graham offers discretely, 'and we all have families and the people living near to us ... We can muster a lot of support should you need it when you decide to take leadership.' Graham lets the words sink in. For days Graham had been promising a place of worship and is aware that some of the religions are starting to question his ability to lead them and make arrangements. Not being of any set religion himself, Graham found himself in a central position and able to walk amongst the different sects with ease. Now, they were waiting for the place of worship, and he was under pressure to deliver it.

'Okay,' she nods, 'leave it with me. I'll try and get something worked out today.'

'That's great, Debbie,' he smiles and nods. 'I know you're busy, but if you need any help, just ask. There's plenty of us willing to roll our sleeves up and muck in, you know.'

'I will, and thank you again for your support. It'll be nice to know I can count on you when the time comes.'

'Of course,' he smiles once more and steps away, heading back towards the tents. Finding a place of worship will secure his position amongst the religions. Being in a central organisational role was important to Graham; it gave him a sense of responsibility. Going back now and saying he's secured a place would be great, but going back and saying that he not only may have secured a place but he's already scouted it out, that would be better, far better.

He deviates his route, heading towards the back door, lost in thought of having all the religious people staring at him as he delivers the good news. *Of course this has taken me some very careful negotiations and putting pressure on the right people at the top, but you all know me ... ready to sacrifice myself for your good causes and never one to back down, so I've got us a special place where only the people of faith can go. Of course, I will be administrating the area to ensure fair play and smooth running ...* He smiles to himself, knowing how good he'll look.

And even better was that it was right at the water's edge. He should introduce some kind of water cleansing ritual. Something that would get those religious girls into the water wearing flimsy t-shirts with their breasts poking through. Yeah, like those girls from the internet at the wet t-shirt competitions. He licks his lips at the thought of holding them steady while they dunk down under the purifying water. Staring down at the long thighs, he might even be able to touch one, you know, if the girl slipped or something…

He wasn't a pervert. He knew he wasn't a pervert. He never looked at actual pornography, just the wet t-shirt competitions. He loved them. More than any other faith, he loved girls in wet t-shirts. Damn, he missed the internet and could feel himself start to grow.

Graham wasn't an ugly man and knew that several of the women liked him. But they were the frumpy, fanatical types, shapeless and boring. No, he wanted the slim girls with the big boobs and the tattoos on their lower backs. And those hip-hop girls that made their bottoms bounce, they were good too, but getting the girls to bounce their backsides might be quite hard, where-as getting them into the water shouldn't be too difficult.

He could do one-on-one spiritual cleansing sessions. That would do it. He'd have to do the men too, but they would be done quickly, in and out. In fact, the men could be done in groups, and the women in private, you know, to give them some privacy and decency. That back area with the high wall and the single gate would be perfect.

Buoyed up and excited, he made his way to the back wall, smiling and grinning at the people as he passed them. Especially the girls. This hot weather was making them strip down to the barest of clothes, and some … some were even walking around in just bras and shorts. They look hot. Maybe he should drag a hose out and start showering himself off in view, encourage them to do the same.

The back first. Check the back and get the news to the others, then maybe look at getting a hose out. His own hose was starting to bulge, so he quickened his pace, marching to the back gate.

In dismay, he spots the guard stood there, holding a

shotgun, leaning against the wall while smoking a cigarette. He snorts in frustration. He needs to be somewhere private. The growing strain in his pants is starting to hurt.

'Hi,' he smiles at the guard, holding his hand out, 'I'm Graham. I'm on the main committee for the fort, you know, trying to get everything organised.' He rolls his eyes and smiles.

'Er ... hello,' the guard replies, an older man with thinning hair and a paunch.

'How's it going here?'

'S'alright,' the man replies, 'bleedin' hot, though ... and my feet are killin' me.'

'Poor chap,' Graham makes a sad face. 'Well, I've come to check the back area. We're thinking of putting it to use. I just spoke to Sergeant Hopewell and agreed I'd come check it out ...'

'Ted said no one was to go in or out without him or Chris saying anything.'

'Ah, Ted, great chap, really good chap, and a good friend of mine. Yeah, he does have those instructions, but I think something got lost in translation. He means unless told by anyone from the main committee.'

'He definitely said just 'im and Chris.'

Damn this man. Graham smiles knowingly. 'Also gives you a chance to take a break, get something to drink. Hey, you should get one of the hoses out and wash your hot feet off. I'll be here, keeping watch until you get back.'

The man shuffles, looking down at his feet. The thought of running cold water over them is too tempting to resist. 'Yeah ... well, you sure, like? You know I don't wanna get in trouble or nuffin.'

'Don't be silly. Fine man like you needs a break. I just spoke with Sergeant Hopewell, and she's in overall charge here anyway. Go on, get yourself a sit down in the shade for fifteen minutes.'

'Alright, 'ere, you want this?' The man holds the shotgun out.

'Er ... yeah, okay.' Graham has never fired a gun in his life but now realises that if the guard thinks the gate is protected, he will relax better and give him time to relieve himself. He takes the shotgun, surprised at the weight.

'Right, be fifteen, then,' the man starts to walk off.

'No need to be exact. Take longer if you want,' Graham calls after him. He waits for a second before turning to pull the bolts back on the gate. Dirty, big, solid bolts that he struggles to pull back. Then a big key left in the lock.

With the shotgun resting against the wall, he finally gets all the bolts and locks undone, pushing the thick, solid wooden gate open and stepping through. The sight of the water finishes him off, just the image of the wet water, the same wet water that will soak those tops and make the material see-through.

Groaning with anticipation, he steps out and pushes the gate closed with his foot, taking a step back to prevent anyone from pushing it open. With his eyes fixed on the water, he dreamily unzips his trousers and pulls his engorged penis out. The sudden release of the confinement excites him even more, as does the feeling of the open air on his member. His hand starts working the shaft as he stares out at the sea. His mind full of images of gorgeous girls all wearing white t-shirts and rising slowly up from the water to reveal their nipples straining against the sodden material. He groans audibly as his hand works faster, putting himself in the middle of the image of all those girls draping over him and pressing those wet t-shirts against his bare chest.

His eyes flutter closed as he nears climax, the first

climax he's had in days. Other than the quick one he had in the toilets of the visitor centre the other night, and that was ruined by some rude man banging on the door and telling him to hurry up.

Ah, there it is, the climax building up. The sensation at the back of his balls that start to tingle just before ejaculation. The image builds to a crescendo, the girls slowly peeling those tops off to reveal their pink and brown nipples ... No. No good. They have to be wearing the tops.

'Put them back on,' he whispers to himself. The girls do as told, pulling the tops back down to show the sodden look. The orgasm builds slowly, threatening to make his legs go weak. This is going to be a good one. Several days of being trapped inside, waiting to be released.

'You dirty motherfucker,' a deep voice growls in his ear, the hot breath tickling the back of his neck. Graham freezes mid stroke, right at the point of orgasm, with the semen dripping from the tip of his penis.

'You are one fucked-up motherfucker,' the voice growls again, an immensely deep voice with a strong accent. Graham's life flashes before his eyes. Not for one second thinking he is in danger, but that someone has caught him wanking and will tell everyone.

He screws his eyes shut. His dick now limp in his hand as the goo drips from his still clenched fist.

'I'm gonna bite the fuck out of you, but don't be thinking for one goddam second I'm gonna enjoy it.' Strong hands grip Graham, pulling him back. He goes to scream but finds a very large, rough hand clamped firmly over his mouth.

He squirms desperately as he feels teeth brushing against his neck. The pressure gets harder as they start to bite. His flesh tearing as the mouth bites down. Pain sears through his neck, burning as he struggles in vain. The mouth releases, but the pain continues. Spreading through his whole body.

Within seconds, another pain is flaring deep in his stomach, a wrenching, churning feeling that causes his legs to give out. The strong arms hold him in place, the hand still firmly over his mouth.

Graham squirms and bucks, his penis flopping about as his body writhes. He feels his heart beating slower and slower. The sensation of sickness through every part of his body. His vision starts to go, darkness creeping in from the edges. Dark, everything black. Just his mind is left. A mind only too aware of what's happening.

His heart stops, and Graham dies. Going limp in the arms of a disgusted-looking Randall, who looks down over his shoulder at the flaccid member dangling away.

'Put that thing back in his pants,' he whispers to Colin.

'Me?' Colin blanches, blinking his red, bloodshot eyes.

'Yeah, you. Put that fucking thing away. Man ain't got no decency, dying with his dick hanging out.'

'I ain't touching his wotsit, Randy. It's still dribblin'.'

'Put that mother-fucking thing away now, you dumbass,' Randall snaps. Colin flinches from the ferocity of the larger man, bending over to wince as he gently grips the thing and pushes it back into the dead man's pants.

'Don't fucking play with it, you motherfucker,' Randall adds with an evil smile.

Graham starts to return, his body twitching slowly and building to the convulsions. Still gripped by Randall, his body shudders until it goes still. The eyes opening to reveal the red, bloodshot gaze.

'He's one of us,' Colin nods as he leans round to look at Graham's face. Randall lets him go, physically turning the man round to stare into the red eyes, taking in the slack-jawed appearance.

'Close your fucking mouth, you look like a dumb motherfucker.' Graham does as told, closing his mouth with a smacking noise.

Randall steps to the door and cracks it open enough to peer through quickly. Nodding, he pushes it to and moves back to Graham.

'You go back in, go deep, right in the middle of those motherfuckers, keep your fucking head down, and when we go in, you start biting every motherfucker you can get. You understand?'

Graham nods back dumbly, his eyes staring at Randall with a look of love and awe. Randall turns to another of his men. 'You go after him and go left. Ain't no motherfucker there right now. Head down and walk natural, make it look like you lost something, and get as far as you can.'

The two men slip inside. Those looking in that direction simply see the familiar form of Graham walking with another man, both of them looking for something on the ground. The men separate and walk opposite directions, Graham heading into the densely populated tent city while the inmate skirts the inside of the wall.

Randall watches through the crack in the door as they disappear from sight. His intelligent eyes ablaze with the thought of what's to come. Spying the shotgun leaning against the wall, he quickly reaches in and grabs it, thrusting it into the arms of another inmate.

'You gonna be one of their guards, hold it across your body and go down the middle, keep your fucking eyes down like you checking the gun or somethin'.' The man holds the weapon across the crook of his arms, like any normal guard strolling about. After checking the area is clear, Randall gets the man inside, watching through the gap as the man assumes the role of camp guard and steadily walks down the middle of the camp, one of his hands fiddling with the breech of his gun that he stares down at.

Three inside, and every second they get deeper amongst the dumb motherfuckers. Randall darts back at seeing a woman looking at the gate, a puzzled frown on her face at seeing it slightly open. She walks towards it, peering intently and looking round for the guard that should be there.

Randall grabs Colin, turning him so his back is to the gate and making him stand like he's having a piss. The gate pushes open, the woman tutting at seeing the back of the man stood urinating into the sea.

'That's gross,' she chuckles. 'Couldn't you wait?'

'Sorry,' Colin says without looking round, 'I was bursting… Don't tell anyone, will you?'

'Nah, you're alright. Looks nice out there.'

'Have a look,' Colin turns round, keeping his head down as he pretends to be fiddling with the zipper on his trousers.

She steps out, her eyes staring at the shimmering stillness of the water, the openness of the sea captivating her after days of being locked inside. Hands grab and pull her to the side. Harry holding her tight as Randall moves back to the gate.

With her mouth covered and the bear-like man holding her, there is nothing she can do to stop from being lifted bodily off the ground like a rag doll. Another inmate moves in, pulling her skirt up to reveal an expanse of thigh. He bites quickly, tearing at the flesh and holding his mouth over the wound. She bucks and squirms, but like Graham, her resistance is futile and the inevitable happens.

Two minutes later, and she's stood on the ground as

Colin washes the blood from her leg and marvels at how quickly the wound clots.

Randall sends her back inside with the same instruction to keep her fucking head down. She does as told, slipping into the fort and walking straight into the living quarters of the many refugees.

Looking at the outline of the guards on the wall at the far end and the distinct shape of the long-barrelled weapons they hold, Randall senses they could still be in danger. There could be guards on all sides, ready to fire down into the crowds if anything happens.

What he needs is a distraction. A big mother-fucking distraction that will buy them a few seconds to run in and get deep within the crowds.

They say the devil takes care of his own. The old adage comes true as the distraction is freely given.

To the west, far in the distance, a huge explosion takes place. A deep, rumbling sound that rolls over the open water with a sound like thunder from a summer storm. All activity in the fort ceases as the strange sound fills the air. Every guard on the walls, at a height advantage from those on ground level, stares across at the plume of flame and smoke scorching up into the air. The distance is great, but even from here, they can tell the explosion must be huge.

Those with local knowledge know it must be the refinery. That site being the only thing in that direction and area that could cause such a detonation.

Randall grins with disbelief and gets ready to run inside. The disbelief grows as the survivors closest to the gate, seeing it open, head towards it, running out the back to stare across the sea at the fireball in the distant sky.

The first couple give only a brief glance at the men already stood there, the spectacle in the distance too wondrous to look away from. Thick crowds pour out of the gate, standing packed on the little shore.

Randall and his inmates stand quietly, all of them shielding their eyes as though to protect against the glare of the sun. They shuffle into the crowd, gently jostling to get within the ranks.

'Get back inside and lock that gate,' someone shouts from inside the fort. Ted appears at the gate, wearing his police uniform, with his flat cap tucked on. 'Come on, we can't have this gate open …' he urges the people back inside, swapping comments about how it must be the refinery going up from the heat and the safety procedures failing.

Randall keeps his head down, knowing how distinctive he looks. He sinks his shoulders and rubs at his face. Flanked by some of the larger inmates, he slips inside with the crowd. All of the inmates moving with the mass as they stroll back towards the tents, chatting excitedly to the others about what they'd seen outside.

Ted, shaking his head with annoyance at where the bloody guard has gone and intending to rip him a new arsehole, slams the gate closed, rams the bolts home, and turns the key.

Randall glances back; his men are spread out. Deep within the confines of the fort. Locked in. Sealed.

And so it begins.

CHAPTER THIRTY

Marcy stands in the street with her small, carefully chosen group clustered round her. Reginald, April, Mildred, and Jerry. A small, non-threatening group of infected chosen exactly for the way they look and their gentle manner.

'They're all inside the houses,' April reports.

Marcy looks back down the street, at the large, detached beachside houses with their pastel-coloured, wooden fronts. The horde all out of sight inside, sheltering from the sun and taking it in turns to drink from the cold water taps.

The decision to leave them here was contested, as usual, by Reginald, with him arguing that it wasn't safe for Marcy to be so exposed and unprotected. Marcy countered that they couldn't approach the fort with such a large number of zombies. To which Reginald countered that they were not zombies but living challenged, and surely there must be somewhere closer they could be hidden.

'And what if we fail? What then? What will they do without their leader?' Reginald had protested, knowing it was his final attempt to dissuade her.

'Another leader will surely present themselves and do

things how they see fit,' she replied. 'It won't matter for us … We'll be dead.' She knew the comment would upset him and watched with a mischievous grin as he shuddered.

'Maybe I should stay here and keep watch, then,' he feebly attempted to get himself out of any potential danger.

'Reggie, I will not order you to come with me, nor will I make you, but I want you to come of your own choosing.'

He squirmed for a minute, already knowing what his answer would be but just delaying the inevitable. Finally he sagged, sighing dramatically. 'You know full well I'll come with you.'

'Thank you, Reggie,' she said with genuine sincerity.

They set off, walking round the large bay to head towards the spit of land. Nervous excitement builds in her stomach, the same conflicting internal arguments grow as both sides forcefully put their points across.

This is suicide. We'll be shot on sight, slaughtered before we get anywhere near the place. They'll torture us and burn the bodies. We should get more hosts, turn more, and increase the numbers. March with a massed army and then try the negotiations. If it fails, we can attack and turn them. Sneak inside and turn them with stealth and cunning. Find another way. This is wrong. Wrong. Wrong.

No, this is the right thing to do. The infection must evolve to survive, and that means our species has to evolve. We cannot survive on our own. We need to harness the good of our kind, the resistance to disease and pain, and couple it with the intelligence and ability to learn what the humans have. Only by combining our strengths can we survive. We take away their thirst for violence and control. We remove the greed and jealousy. A perfect blend creating a perfect being. No war, no starvation or famine, no suffering.

But we are the better species. They do not deserve what we have. Don't share what we are, make them us. They will use it to further their twisted aims.

Neither is the better species. We must combine and integrate. The better species will be created from both of us. If we carry on, then we run a real risk of both species dying out.

And so it continues. She walks in silence, feeling the scorching heat from the sun on her bare arms. Her skin continues to tan. The infection having drawn back as much as possible, it leaves her body still functioning in much the normal manner. Her long, raven hair sways as she walks; her slender, tanned arms swing gently with the rhythm of her movement. Full, pink lips part to lick the beads of sweat forming on her upper lip. Her hand moves without conscious thought to her backside, fingers gently brushing the bite mark that Darren left.

Sweat runs down her face, gently sliding over her jawline and down her slender neck. She shivers from the sensation and feels as the sweat follows the natural contours of her body.

They skirt the bay, keeping back from the shoreline and sticking to the inner roads. All the time heading closer and closer to the fort. The big bastion that stands proud and defiant at the end of the spit of land. Sheer walls of grey concrete.

As she gains glimpses of the land, she looks at the sweeping flatlands and imagines Darren there with his mighty army, getting destroyed by the few good men that opposed them.

The bravery of Howie is clear. That he chose to fight back instead of running and hiding. She saw glimpses of him on the Isle of Wight. Always one step ahead, and she felt the power coming from him when he fought single-handed in the stairwell of the church tower. She felt the fear of the hosts as they charged at him.

Still, he spoke with kindness and respect; still, he was polite and offered her a way out. Inviting her to come with them. But she was under Darren's spell then and without the ability to think like she does now. If only she had taken that offer and simply walked up those steps. Would it have changed the outcome, or did all those things need to happen?

And at the end when he looked down on the dying form of Darren. Stood there so proud and true. He could have tortured Darren and made him suffer, but he didn't. He acted with grace and decency.

Everything hinges on him. If she can just make contact with Howie and make him see through her eyes. Make him realise there is another way.

They reach the edge of the ruined estate, looking aghast at the blackened surroundings with stumps of scorched brick walls. Vehicles melted into the twisted surface of the ground. The stench of death invades the air. High piles of bodies stacked deep and wide and left to fester in the sun. Swathes of insects rise and fall from the corpses, generating a loud and sustained buzzing sound.

The small group pick their way through the mess, gaining the central road now cleared of debris, with fresh tyre tracks running through it.

As one they stop and look to the sky, reacting to the deep roll of thunder that rolls across the sea. Puzzled faces stare up at the cloudless heavens. A slight tremor beneath their feet coming from the ground itself. They glance around in alarm, fearing an earthquake.

'There,' Reginald points to the west, at the thick plume

of bright orange flames that sear high into the air. Dirty, black clouds spume from the flames, creating a distinctive mushroom shape like the television footage of nuclear bombs being detonated.

'Must be Fawley,' Reginald adds in a quiet voice.

'Fawley?' Marcy asks.

'Oil refinery, just outside Southampton.'

'Oh,' she replies, staring in wonder at the sight. Even from this vast distance, the fireball looks huge. Up close it must be dreadful, terrifying even.

'Ominous,' Reginald remarks.

Marcy smiles at his clear nerves, looking down as he nervously taps his hand against his leg.

'It's miles away, nothing to do with this,' she replies.

They set off, working down the central, rutted road and out into the flatlands. The fort in the distance but getting closer with every step they take.

CHAPTER THIRTY-ONE

She stands by his side, watching the hundreds of interactions that take place all around. People everywhere, and the smells they produce are fascinating. Far stronger than when she lived in the den with the pack. The scent of cooking, unwashed bodies, faeces, urine, blood, and vomit. The loss of her little one still weighs on her soul. She felt stronger when she was with the new pack. Fighting with them and being with them seemed right and natural. Now they are gone too, and she has this man.

He has strong energy and is a leader. She senses this and accepts that she is to stay with him, moving where he moves, going where he goes, standing when he stands. She doesn't mind this as plenty of people rub her ears and head, which she likes, and the man keeps offering her water to drink and food to eat.

She stares down at the ground, sensing the rumble before hearing it. Her head cocks to one side as she feels a change in air pressure. The rumble comes, like the noise that is made when the water falls from the sky and the sharp lights spark everywhere. The people around her all stop and listen, feeling the tremor from the ground.

She senses the fear increase in the people as they rush to the far side, trying to see over the wall. They run to the front and back, climbing the slopes to get higher.

The man runs through them, heading towards the hill that goes to the top. She runs easily by his side, her long legs striding gracefully as her pink tongue hangs down, bouncing out the side of her mouth.

The man makes noise, and the people move out of his way. His status of pack leader is strong here. All the people stop and stare across the sky. She can smell burning, but it's from far away and not a threat to them.

The people make noise to each other. The noise gets louder and faster as their excitement grows. A sense of unease comes over the man. She feels his hand stroke the tops of her ears, something she's become accustomed to just in this day.

Chris stares at the fireball, knowing in the pit of his stomach that Howie and his team will be involved. The deep worry lines increase as he scans the horizon as though seeking some sign that they're alive. Dave and Clarence will keep them alive. Both of those men would sacrifice themselves for Howie, but then so would he.

Howie has a rare ability, something so seldom seen that it beggars belief. The way he captivates people and gets them on side. That funny, self-deprecating manner that erupts into passionate fury, but done in a way that doesn't scare people. It doesn't *intimidate*, it brings his words home with a deep poignancy. All of those that stood close to

Howie on the field that day felt it. All of them felt the power pour from the man. The way the things wilted from him. At that point, he was undefeatable, and the pure energy of the man was like something never seen before.

More than anything, Howie and the dog have to survive. Chris feels it deep within his soul. Knowing that Clarence and Dave both feel the same gives some comfort at the sight of the fireball. The whole area must have gone, and he shakes his head at the power and destruction being wrought in that place.

With a sigh, he turns away, spotting Ted at the far side of the fort ushering a group of survivors back through the gate. Silly buggers must have gone out for a better view. At least the rear should be safe with that small beach and the deep water.

He looks out over the wall, to the estate in the distance and thinks of the bodies stacking up, then down at the dog stood patiently next to him.

'Let's hope they got that fuel, eh?' She looks up at him with a big doggy grin, blinking her big, brown eyes. Chris watches as her head snaps to look back inside the fort. Ears pricked and eyes set. She sniffs the air, smelling them. Scenting them amongst the people.

She makes noise.

'You've fractured your elbow,' Doctor Roberts looks down at the man sat on the chair in the examining room. 'Normally, we'd put it in plaster, but we do not have plaster. Normally, we'd give you strong painkillers, but we cannot spare them either, so a good, old-fashioned sling it will be, and we'll get you some paracetamol and ibuprofen.'

'Is that it?' the man winces as Doctor James starts to apply the sling round his neck, drawing it tight to lift and hold the arm into the body.

'Afraid so,' Doctor Roberts replies, his bushy eyebrows dropping to a deep frown. 'We've got far worse cases that need the strong stuff.'

'But it's bloody killing me.'

'Oh, don't whine. I hate whiners ... Would you rather we amputate it?'

'What?' The man looks up with shock.

'Amputate it?' Doctor Roberts barks. 'Cut it off, man! We can do that if it makes you feel better!?'

'No,' the man gasps, 'I don't ... You said it was only a fracture ...'

'Well, then stop your bloody moaning and bugger off. We've got other patients to see.'

The man stands up, looking in horror at the fierce doctor. He turns to look at the other doctor, who just shrugs and smiles.

'Nice work, Doctor James,' Doctor Roberts says as the man scurries out.

'Thank you, Doctor Roberts,' he smiles. 'You know he'll be in agony with that elbow.'

'Yes, I know,' Doctor Roberts says with a deep sigh. 'Poor blighter ... Still, there's always someone worse off, wouldn't you say?'

'Yes, Doctor Roberts,' Doctor James smiles. Having worked with Doctor Roberts for long enough, he knows the man is one of the most skilled doctors he's ever worked with, and although his bedside manner leaves a lot to be desired, his compassion knows no bounds.

He follows the older doctor through to the ad hoc

hospital room crammed with an assortment of beds and mattresses, all of them filled with the worst cases.

They ignore the first few and head straight towards a bed on the right. Both doctors nod respectfully at the worried looking man sat next to the bed holding the hand of the young, pale-looking boy.

'How are you feeling?' Doctor Roberts asks in a deep, soft voice. He bends closer to the boy and rests a hand on his head, smiling at the young face.

'It hurts a bit,' the boy says quietly.

'I bet it does,' Doctor Roberts replies. 'But you are being so very brave, and I would say,' he leans in closer to whisper, 'you're the bravest patient we've got in here ... Wouldn't you agree, Doctor James?'

'Definitely, without doubt,' Doctor James says with a wink. The man in the next bed looks over and smiles, nodding his head.

'Now I'm just going to check, so you stay still and carry on being the bravest boy I have ever met,' Doctor Roberts pulls the thin sheet back to reveal the boy's pale body. He gently eases the dressing away and examines the stitches from the incision made to remove the boy's burst appendix. The wound looks clean and healthy, resulting in a warm smile at the boy. 'Very good, very good indeed. You'll be up on your feet in no time at all, out there playing in the sun and causing more mischief, no doubt.'

'I like it here,' the boy says. 'It's quieter than outside ...'

'I'm sure you do,' Doctor Roberts tussles the boy's hair, giving him another big grin. 'I'll come back and check on you in a little while.'

'Thanks, Doctor,' the man says with real meaning. He stands up respectfully as the doctors leave the bed.

'Any news on the fuel?' Doctor Roberts asks.

'Not yet. Howie's still out, I think,' Doctor James replies.

'That bloody Sergeant was in here again earlier, talking nonsense to the patients. I gave her what for and sent her packing,' Doctor Roberts speaks quietly as he strides down the room.

'Very worrying. We may have to step in if it gets much worse,' Doctor James says, hurrying after him again.

'Yes … yes … keep an eye on her. Chris has already been in, asking if we'd speak with her.'

'I think we should,' Doctor James says with a hard tone.

'Well, we can't section her, and we don't have any sedatives to spare … Hmmm, but then it's a clear-cut case of mental incapacity, so we'll have to do something.'

'Maybe we should just talk to her quietly first, the two of us. We can have Chris nearby if … well, in case he's needed,' Doctor James suggests.

'Agreed, get that Ted chap too. She listens to him. Find somewhere private and quiet. We don't want to humiliate the poor woman.'

'Okay, Doctor, leave it with me. I'll send someone for you when we're ready.' Doctor James walks off, his own white lab coat flapping at his knees. Doctor Roberts stands quiet for a second, thinking of the best way to approach the subject. It's been a long time since he had anything to do with this kind of thing.

He glances up at the sound of the deep rumble of thunder before walking out the front of the examination tent to stare up at the clear sky.

'What was that?' he asks Doctor James stood a few metres away and also staring up at the sky.

'No idea,' he replies.

'Bugger it. I hope they aren't blowing something else up,' Doctor Roberts tuts and walks back inside.

'More work for us if they do,' Doctor James mutters as he walks on.

'What the bloody hell are you lot doing down here?' Kelly snaps as she walks into the workshop to find the small group of engineers sat round drinking tea.

'What?' One of the engineers jumps up, looking guilty.

'You should be up the top, fixing that gun in place,' she walks towards them with a scowl.

'They said not to. That sergeant lady came up and said they were moving it.'

'They? Who are they?' Kelly asks with a confused look.

'I dunno. She just said there was some experts that were deciding where to put it,' the man says defensively.

'The experts did decide where to put it, which is on that bloody wall where I showed you. How long have you been in here?' She moves to the carrier bag used as the makeshift bin. 'Quite a while by the looks of all these teabags in here, and where did you get biscuits from?' She fishes the empty pack out, holding it up while staring with an accusing look.

'The sergeant gave 'em to us,' the man mutters weakly, knowing they've been caught red-handed.

'Did she now?' Kelly asks slowly. 'And that was at the same time as she suggested not fixing the gun in place, was it? Was it?' she asks louder.

'Yes,' the men nod, looking at their feet with a sense of shame.

'Right, well, from now on, you do not take any orders or

instructions from Sergeant Hopewell. If you are in doubt, you ask me or Chris. Got it?'

'Yes, Kelly,' the men murmur.

'Good. Now, did you eat all the biscuits, or did you leave any for me?' she softens her tone, knowing when to ease back. After all, they were just following instruction from Debbie.

The men grin, holding up a chipped plate with a small stack of digestives piled up.

'Well, get the kettle on, then. I'm gasping for a brew,' she smiles, taking a seat and groaning from taking the weight off her feet for the first time in hours.

'How's the alarm?' one of the men asks, more relaxed now their fearsome boss was sitting down and doing something mortal like eating a biscuit.

'Okay,' she nods, holding her hand over her mouth to prevent biscuit crumbs from flying out, 'should be done in an hour or so.'

'Bloody hell! What's that?' The men all stare towards the open door, then back at Kelly as though expecting her to know.

She shrugs, shaking her head as they all move quickly outside. The deep rumble fills the air, and a slight tremble in the ground vibrates through their feet.

'Ain't thunder,' one of them remarks.

'Earthquake?' another asks.

They stay near the door. Their expert eyes watching for any signs of movement from the structures. Scanning the walls, tents, and the visitors' centre.

'What was it?' one of them shouts to someone up on the top of the inner wall.

'Fawley by the looks of it ... Must have gone up,' the man shouts down.

'Fawley? Bloody hell. I used to work there,' one of the men mutters.

'Didn't you do a stint there, Kelly?'

'Only for a few months, contracted in for a job,' she replies. 'Big site, though. I wouldn't want to be near it right now.'

'Luckily we ain't,' another engineer adds.

Sarah sits quietly at the desk, reading through yesterday's admissions to the fort and checking the job skills. The engineers have enough people for now, the cooks are doing well. Cleaners are what they need. People to move amongst the tents and remove the litter and debris building up. Oh, and more guards, always more guards, and of course, medically trained people.

She admires the detail entered on the sheets by Terri and Jane. The clear, handwritten notes of any skills or training the refugees have, with comments added to the top of the sheet for people with vital skills.

'Hi, Sarah!' She looks up as Roger Hastings strolls into the room. 'Oooh, it's cooler in here,' he says, fanning his face with a hard-backed notebook.

'Doesn't feel like it. It's stifling.'

'Better than being in that sun, dear,' he replies. 'The tan is nice, but it makes me wrinkly, and I dread the day we run out of anti-wrinkle cream.' Sarah laughs at his camp manner. 'I think we should do our own raiding party, you know. We could get a pink vehicle and dress in pink fatigues and go on a beauty products raiding mission ... The Glam Raiders,' he says with his hands out front and fingers splayed wide.

'I like it,' Sarah laughs.

'We could take Dave to protect us.'

'I don't think he'll leave Howie's side.'

'Well, they'll all have to come with us. Those big, nasty brutes in their tough clothes looking all … all brutish.' She laughs again as he increases the camp manner for her benefit. 'Anyway … Now, what did I come in here for, other than to moan about the lack of moisturiser …? Oh yes, stores, my dear, they're getting somewhat large, and we may have to consider moving them to another set of rooms.'

'The stores? Are they running out of space already?'

'Afraid so, that blasted lorry your brother brought back from the cash-and-carry has got it jammed to the rafters, plus all the little odds and sods the newbies are bringing in with them.'

'Right,' she sighs, 'where can we put them?'

'The visitors' centre. It's in the middle and easily accessible for everyone. There's plenty of space in there that's not being used, and it might help us ration our supply of toilet roll. They can get a supply before they go and do their dirty business.'

'Good idea,' she nods in agreement. 'We could ask Kelly to get a big countertop made up to prevent people just walking in.'

'And some shelving to keep everything off the floor.'

'Okay, check with Chris. He's about somewhere. If he's happy with it, then carry on and get it done.'

'What about Sergeant Hopewell?' Roger asks in a serious tone, the camp act dropped instantly.

'Forget her. She's getting worse, and we can't afford the delays.'

'What was that?' Terri asks, walking into the room. She removes her hat and wipes the sweat from her forehead.

'Roger suggested we use the visitor centre for stores. They're running out of space where they are …'

'They've ran out of space,' Roger corrects her.

'Yeah, well anyway, so we can use the visitor centre. I said check with Chris, and if he's happy, then go ahead and get it sorted.'

'And I asked about Sergeant Hopewell,' Roger adds.

Terri looks back at Sarah, the conflict clear on her face. Her loyalty to Debbie is obvious, but even she can see the decline in her sergeant's behaviour. 'Oh, this is bloody awkward,' she sits down heavily and stretches her legs out. 'Debbie has always been a role model for me. Seeing her like this is just horrible. It's like she's having a nervous breakdown or something, honestly … I really don't know what to do.'

'I think Chris has spoken with the doctors. They're going to be speaking to her very soon,' Sarah says quietly.

'Ooohhh,' Roger winces, 'that won't go down well.'

'No, it won't,' Terri agrees. 'What a mess,' she shakes her head sadly.

'Have you tried talking to her?' Roger asks in a gentle tone.

'Didn't work,' Terri replies. 'She just snapped and started on about loyalty and it being time to pick sides.'

'Oh, no, really? That's awful,' Sarah grimaces. 'Poor woman. I know she's causing damage, but I feel for her. I really do.'

'We all do,' Roger adds. 'Right, well, I'll go check with Chris and get it underway, er … what do I say if she asks me what I'm doing?'

'Tell the truth,' Terri replies. 'I can't see how she'd get upset about something like that.'

'Okay,' Rogers says without confidence, 'if you hear me scream, please come and rescue me.'

The two women laugh. 'Fancy a coffee?' Terri asks.

'Sounds lovely,' Sarah smiles.

'Ooh, why not, always got time for a coffee with the girls,' Roger adds.

'Any more newbies?' Sarah asks, using the term coined by Roger for the new arrivals at the fort.

'Couple this morning,' Terri replies as she switches the little gas burner on and fills a battered saucepan with water from a bottle, 'but nothing since … Glad of the break if I'm honest. It's bloody hot out there.'

'Where's Jane?' Sarah asks.

'She's having a coffee with the guards. I think she fancies one of them … No. I know she fancies one of them,' Terri laughs.

'Oh really?' Sarah smiles. 'Which one?'

'That tall guy with the dark hair.'

'Oh, him. Yeah, he's nice,' Sarah nods.

'Nice! He's bloody lovely, tall, dark, handsome, and he's got a six pack, and …' Roger pauses for effect, '… and no hairy back.'

'Hairy back!' Sarah bursts out laughing.

'Trust me, my dear, you get to my age and finding a man without a hairy back is very difficult,' Roger says.

'Well, I think he likes her too. They keep chatting, and I've noticed he keeps appearing on duty when she's out there.'

'Good for her,' Sarah adds.

'Lucky bitch,' Roger snipes with a well-meaning smile. 'Oh, that's what I need, a big, strong man to come and whisk me away from this awful place.'

'Like Clarence?' Terri asks with a raised eyebrow and a smirk at Sarah.

'Ooh no, dearie, he's certainly got muscles on top of muscles but far too much of a brute for me.'

'Well, I don't think someone here agrees with you,' Terri smiles again.

'Oh, give it a rest. I think he's lovely ... He looks like a bear, but he's soft as a kitten, really,' Sarah laughs easily.

'So?' Terri asks expectantly. Roger matching the gaze as they both look at Sarah.

'So,' Sarah grins, 'what?'

'You know full well what!' Roger laughs. 'So what's he like, you know,' he gives a theatrical wink. 'What's he *like?*'

'And when exactly would that happen? He's off with Howie killing zombies every five minutes.'

'Ah, that's sweet, a stolen romance in the midst of all the destruction, a snatched kiss under the moonlight, holding hands under the desk at the meetings,' Terri says dramatically.

'I wish,' Sarah mutters with a roll of her eyes. 'I think I'm competing with my own brother.'

'Urgh, that's gross,' Terri laughs.

'Oh, I don't know,' Roger gives a wry smile.

'I didn't mean it like that. I meant they all bloody adore him. How can a girl compete with that?'

'Well, far be it for me to say anything,' Roger raises his eyebrows, 'but I can see why they adore him. That smouldering intensity, dark eyes, brooding and dark ... Does it for me!'

'Do you mind?' Sarah laughs. 'That's my brother.'

'He might be your brother, dearie, but he's certainly not mine,' Roger laughs.

'I tell you how you compete with that,' Terri grins,

'Make-up and a low-cut top. Works every time … and a push-up bra for good measure,' she adds with a laugh.

'I'll try it. Next time he comes in, I'll get all glammed up and lean against the door frame in a sexy pose,' Sarah replies.

'Sexy pose?' Terri laughs. She lifts the pan and pours the hot water into the three mugs. 'Mind you, there is something special about Howie …'

'You're telling me,' Roger adds. 'Imagine being in that vehicle with them on a hot day. Those hard bodies stripping off to the waist, narrow waists, defined chests, all covered in sweat and glistening …'

'Roger!' Sarah exclaims, still laughing.

'Oh, I don't know,' Terri stares away dreamily. 'I think I could manage a few hours out with them. Those lads of his are very cute,' she adds slowly, emphasising the last word.

'Just give me one of them,' Roger says softly. 'I'd even take Dave.'

'Dave!?' both the girls say with shocked grins.

'He might be little, but you know what they say …' Roger smiles. 'It's not the size of the tool but the man holding it!'

'Oh, not Dave,' Terri laughs, shaking her head. 'He's lovely but no … Nick, yes. Blowers, quite likely. Cookey I could manage …'

'Manage?' Sarah carries on laughing.

'Yes, manage,' Terri nods, 'but not Dave. He wouldn't know when to stop.'

'Suits me fine,' Roger adds with a grin.

'Howie's changed,' Sarah says in a soft voice as she takes the offered mug. 'He was always so softly spoken, funny, you know, always messing about and making me laugh, but the way he is now … different,' she tails off with a distant look.

'He frightens me sometimes,' Terri says quietly. 'Not like I'm scared of him, but like … you know … the way he is, so intense, and that look he does …'

'I know,' Sarah nods. 'He was never like that before … the way everyone looks to him, and the energy he gives off. I look at him and think that's not my brother … and the way he fights, like he's possessed.'

'Well, you heard what happened during that big fight outside,' Roger says.

'I think everyone has by now,' Sarah replies. 'That's got to be exaggerated …'

'I don't know,' Terri shakes her head, 'enough people are saying it. They all heard him, and they keep saying it was like the things were too scared to attack him.'

'Yeah,' Sarah says sadly.

'I fancied him like mad,' Terri adds, 'you know, I did. I still like him but not like that now. No offence, I know he's your brother and all that …'

'Oh, none taken, don't worry,' Sarah says. 'I know what you mean.'

'Besides, I've heard he likes that Lani girl?'

'He does, but he's useless around women,' Sarah chuckles. 'He turns into Hugh Grant if he likes someone, stuttering and stammering. Quite sweet really …'

'Just adds to the charm,' Roger adds.

They all freeze as the rumble rolls across the fort, looking down at the ground and the vibration coming through their feet.

Ditching the coffee mugs, they run outside, watching everyone running to the far side and staring up. They look up at the clear sky and move further away from the wall.

The rumble ends and they watch as Chris runs up the slope with Meredith. Word soon spreads as those with a view tell others. A big explosion in the distance; then, someone says it's Fawley refinery.

Terri watches the look of fear cross Sarah's face, knowing Howie and his group have gone for fuel and then hearing the fuel depot has just exploded.

'They're probably nowhere near it,' Terri offers softly.

'Yeah ... yeah, you're right. That's miles away ...'

'They'll be in Portsmouth somewhere, attacking some giant horde of zombies and having the time of their lives,' Terri smiles. 'Come on, let's get that coffee.'

CHAPTER THIRTY-TWO

'What was it?' The woman asks her husband as he walks back into the tent.

'I didn't see anything, but they all saying Fawley refinery has gone up. 'Ere, mate, I think you got the wrong tent.' The man turns at the hulking form of Randall slipping inside the large canvass structure.

'Sorry,' Randall murmurs.

'No worries,' the man says with grin. 'What the–' his voice gets cut off by the large hand gripping his windpipe. Lifted off the ground and propelled across the ground as Randall grips the woman by her throat and drives them both down to the floor. He squeezes hard, preventing them from screaming out. They both thrash and buck, flailing useless fists against the hard muscle of the big American.

On his knees, with a throat gripped in each hand, he drops down and rips a chunk of flesh from the woman's face before twisting his head and going for the man's ear. Ripping it clean off and spitting it aside. He holds the throats until they start blacking out, easing the pressure to prevent killing them before the infection can course through. As they slip under, he releases and watches for a minute, listening to the normality of the sound coming from outside.

They start to twitch, two bodies lying prone on their backs, convulsing until they both sit up and open their eyes. Randall nods with an evil grin before darting outside.

Back in the sunshine, he walks into the middle of the compound, surrounded by tents and thick crowds of people.

A scream sounds behind him, an ear-piercing wail as a woman falls to the floor, with the husband-and-wife team tearing the flesh out from her neck.

'NOW,' Randall roars at the top of his voice. The signal is heard by his men. Strong hands grabbing bodies, and mouths biting into necks, faces, hands, arms, legs, anything they can get they bite.

Randall grabs a man running past, pulling him in and tearing a hole out of his cheek before throwing him away. He grabs another, biting into the top of the man's shoulder, and then pushes him hard.

Two steps, and he grabs a woman, physically picking her up and biting into her neck. The hot blood spurting over his face, soaking his beard. He throws the woman aside. The blood coursing down his throat, driving him to feast and kill.

A child screams as he lunges at her, sweeping her up in his arms as he strides further into the living area of the survivors. He bites into her thigh before casually casting the screaming child aside. A man runs at him with a hammer, swinging the tool wildly. Randall catches the man's arm mid-swing and drags him in, sinking his teeth into the man's nose and wrenching his head aside. He kicks the man away and keeps hold of the hammer.

He runs ahead and slams the heavy metal head onto

another man, stunning him. He bites down into his neck and shoves him deep into the crowd.

All around screams rip through the air. Shouts sound out as everyone runs in different directions.

Harry, his long, grey beard already covered in wet, sticky blood, surges into the crowds. His big frame forcing a lane through. He grabs body after body, biting into the flesh, saliva flooding into his mouth as he passes the deadly infection again and again.

Colin rampages from tent to tent, running in to grab at people trying to hide. He laughs with unrestrained glee as he grabs an old woman and bites one of her fingers off. He chews the solid digit for a second before spitting it back into her face. A teenage boy strikes him across his back with a heavy stick, driving him forward. The boy comes in for another strike and gets kicked in the stomach. Bent double, he finds Colin grabbing him roughly and biting into the top of his skull.

The inmates work quickly, a frenzied feast as they lash out, biting anything they can grab.

Ted draws his pistol and runs into the fray, his arm raised as he tries to identify who is biting. He spots a large man with a long, grey beard covered in blood. The man grabs a woman and bites her. Ted fires into the man's back. H staggers forward but stays on his feet. Turning to grin, he starts coming at Ted.

The old policeman backs up. Aiming again, he fires into the man's chest, watching with horror as the man takes the bullets and keeps coming.

Something heavy slams into him, taking him to the ground. He lands on his back and catches a glance of a big black man with a thick beard on top of him. Ted scrabbles to bring the pistol up, but a solid fist slams into the side of his head, stunning him. He drops the pistol but fights out, slamming his fists into the sides of the man's head. He feels the pain as teeth bite into his knuckles. Screaming in rage, he yanks his fist away, blood pumping freely from the skin torn away to reveal the white knuckle bone.

The pressure is released as the man disappears, jumping up to run off. Ted grabs the pistol and raises it to fire, hesitating at the utter bedlam erupting all around him. People everywhere and no clear targets. He looks down at his hand, at the ruined skin on his knuckles. The red eyes of the man that bit him.

He tries to stand, his legs buckling as pain grips his stomach. He gets to his knees, thick tears welling in his eyes. He roars with frustration, knowing what will happen.

An inmate drops down in front of him, punched away by another man. Ted quickly raises the pistol and fires into the inmate's head. The skull explodes as the grey matter is spewed out onto the dirty grass.

The pain wrenches at his inside. Gasping for breath, he lifts the pistol and pushes the end into his mouth. *At least I got one.* He offers a prayer and pulls the trigger. Instant blackness as the top of his skull is taken off.

Kelly and the engineers rush out of their rooms, stopping to stand in shock at the scenes of violence in front of them.

'Get in and lock the door ...' Kelly turns to the men. Her words are cut off as she is taken off her feet by an inmate charging her down.

The engineers react quickly, lunging in to attack the man, kicking and punching him away. Kelly screams in agony, clutching a ragged laceration in her neck. Thick, red blood pumping out between her fingers. The inmate grabs one of the feet launched at his head. Gripping the ankle, he bites into the calf muscle. The man screams at the pain shooting through his lower leg. He wrenches free and drops down. The inmate springs up and takes another engineer, driving him backwards as his teeth gnash and bite at the man's face. The man twists and turns his face, the ferocity of the attack rendering him unable to do anything. Teeth bite at his lips, tearing the bottom lip off. The inmate pushes him down before running back into the crowd.

Doctor James, halfway across the fort towards the police office, freezes at the first scream. He spins round to see the interior of the living area erupt into an instant riot.

'GUARDS! GUARDS!' he bellows back to the gate. Several men appear, carrying long-barrelled weapons–rifles and shotguns. They start running towards the affray, already aiming.

Not one shot is taken. The guards, too terrified of firing into the crowd after what Sergeant Hopewell said to them, hesitate and pause, trying to identify targets. They go too deep, too worried about firing into the densely packed crowds. Graham, the preacher, turned by Randall just a few minutes ago, runs towards the guards with his head down. They pause even longer, recognising the man. Graham gets to the first one and lifts his head at the last second. He barrels into the guard, sending him sprawling onto the ground. The man screams in panic as Graham lashes down, sinking his teeth into his forearm brought up to protect his face.

The guards spin round and fire at the two men. The distraction proves to be their undoing as another inmate breaks from the crowd and takes another guard down. The confusion and fear grip the guards as they start backing away. Unable to react and too terrified to run.

Doctor James runs for the gun dropped by the first

guard. He dives at the last second, grabbing the weapon by the stock and dragging it into him. He lifts it up and aims at the crowd. An infected, bright red blood dripping from his mouth, runs from the middle, towards the doctor. He pulls the trigger, cursing when nothing happens. His fingers feel for the safety switch, fumbling in panic. Too late. He swings the gun out to batter the thing away. The blow goes unnoticed as Doctor James is grabbed and taken to the ground. He fights with fierce determination, kicking, bucking, and punching as hard as he can. He screams as he feels the teeth sinking into his neck, feeling the rip of flesh as the mouth savages at him.

The thing jumps off and runs, aiming for another victim. Doctor James, clutching his neck, gets quickly to his feet and runs back towards the hospital. 'LOCK IT DOWN!' he screams. He repeats the words several times before the pain in his stomach pulls him down to the rough surface of the ground.

Roger Hastings yelps in panic at the immediate explosion all around him. Halfway to the visitors' centre and in the thick of the crowds, he freezes, rooted to the spot in blind terror. He starts to move, walking quickly, jogging, then all-out sprinting. Aiming for the visitors' centre with a flash of an idea to get inside and lock the doors. A huge man steps in front of him. A big black man with a thick, black beard. Roger runs straight into him, unable to swerve or stop. Randall absorbs the impact without a flinch. He wraps his arm round the former curator and holds him tight. Roger wails in terror as he feels his cheek being gouged by teeth. Randall turns and sends Roger spinning off to sprawl on the ground.

He gets quickly to his feet and starts running again. His hand pressed against the burning pain in his face and feeling the hot, sticky blood pumping out. He almost makes it, getting just a few feet away from the entrance before, as with many others around him, the pain rips through his stomach and drops him to the ground.

The epicentre of the action spills out as the inmates grab anyone they can. Bite after bite is taken. Flesh ripped and torn, small wounds, big lacerations, arteries opened, faces torn away. The savagery of the attack grows as the inmates, led by Randall, become frenzied and insatiable.

Randall moves with a swiftness that belies his size. Powering over short distance to barrel into small clusters of terrified refugees. Using the strength in his enormous arms to grip and hold them still. He casts the bodies aside after each bite. Forcefully pushing them away so they have time to get up and run before the infection takes hold, running further into the crowds of desperate, trapped survivors.

Sarah and Terri, drinking their hot coffee, both run outside on hearing the fracas. Their faces drain of blood at the horror of the fort, at the violence discharging and spilling out.

'Meredith,' Sarah yells. She scans the area, frantically searching for the dog. She can hear it barking, the deep sound distinctive over the noise of the fighting.

'We've got to get Meredith,' Sarah starts running, heading for the slope as the last place she saw Chris and the dog.

Terri hesitates, frozen in fear at the sight. She sees the guards running into the centre and turns to head back inside the police office. She slams the door and rams the bolt home, backing away as the sounds from outside just get worse. A small, grimy window to the outside is all she has to peer out, an ancient thing covered in filth and dust. She presses her face close to the small, lead lined panes and watches with increasing panic as the guards fail to stop the mass fighting. People she knows, people she'd spoken to get taken down yards from the office. Bitten savagely and left to bleed. Those same bodies start twitching within minutes as the infection takes hold. Soon there are infected running freely within the fort; desperate battles and fights take place.

A child runs past the window screaming, being chased by an inmate. Terri feels the vomit rise as the girl is yanked back by her hair and quickly covered by the inmate as he descends to feast. She screams at the sight, an instinctive reaction that she snaps off as quickly as it comes out. The inmate looks up, fixing his red eyes on the window, fresh blood dripping from his mouth.

He slowly looks along the wall to the door and springs up, slamming his body against it. Terri cries out in fear and looks for an escape. The rooms are sealed–no other way in or out.

She backs away, going further into the room. The door bursts open with a splintering sound as the infected staggers inside, breathing hard, with growling noises emanating from its throat.

Terri yells in fear and starts throwing anything she can get her hands on. Mugs, the gas hob, the saucepan. She grabs the hole punch and stapler and launches them at the thing. It advances without a flinch, the objects bouncing harmlessly of its body.

She turns to run into the back rooms. The thing chases, howling as it dives forward and grabs her ankle. She goes to the floor, frantically cycling her free leg to land blow after blow on the creature's face. It starts dragging her in, drawing her closer to the open mouth, lips pulled back, and teeth already chomping.

Screaming, she sits up and starts beating at it with everything she has. The grip loosens, and she breaks free, the action causing her to jolt backwards. Scrabbling to her feet, she turns to run, but the thing is on her. Landing heavily on her back. She staggers forward, holding both of their weight on her strong legs. Twisting and turning her head, she runs backwards, slamming the thing into the wall.

Teeth bite down into the back of her neck. She roars with defiance and keeps ramming her body against the wall. She head-butts backwards, feeling the crunch of bone as the back of her skull breaks the nose of the man on her back. She does it again, harder and faster. The thing lets go and slides down. She spins, full of rage, and kicks at his face. Forced over to the floor from the barrage of blows, the thing's head rests against the wall as Terri aims kick after kick into the face. She pulverises it, driving the bones inwards to penetrate the brain. The thing dies long before she stops kicking.

'Terri,' she spins at the sound of her name being called to see Sergeant Hopewell running in.

'I'm bit,' Terri gasps. She reaches round to touch the back of her neck. She pulls her hand away and curses at the sight of the blood.

'Oh, Terri,' Sergeant Hopewell stares at her young friend. She walks forward as Terri begins to sob, loud wracking sobs that send hot tears coursing from her eyes.

'You're going to be fine,' Sergeant Hopewell reaches out and draws the girl in, holding her close.

'Sarge ... I'm bit ... bit,' Terri sobs harder. She wraps her arms round Debbie.

'Come on now. You're going to be fine. It's just a scratch not a bite.'

'I felt him bite me ... He fucking bit me ...'

'Oh, Terri,' Sergeant Hopewell holds the girl close, shaking her head as her heart breaks. Outside, the noise grows worse, a multitude of screams, shouts, anger, hurt, pain, and fury.

Terri's legs give out, causing Sergeant Hopewell to grab the girl and help lower her to the floor. The papers from the desks scattered all over the floor.

'Urgh,' Terri clutches at her stomach as the pain takes hold. 'I don't want to die. Not like this. Please … save me … save me …' She grabs at Debbie's arms, squeezing hard as the pain increases.

'Terri, oh my … Oh, Terri,' Sergeant Hopewell strokes the girl's head, brushing the hair from her face. Tears fall from her eyes to land on Terri's head.

'Don't! Kill me … Don't let me come back …' Terri gasps.

'I will,' Sergeant Hopewell says softly.

'Promise me …'

'I promise. Oh, Terri … listen, you're going to a better place ,okay? A much better place. Just close your eyes and breathe, Terri. There'll be light and warmth, and all your friends will be there, all your family too. That's it, breathe, Terri, just breathe and relax … It's going to be so much better there. I'm so proud of you, Terri, so very proud … Close your eyes and know we all love you very much, so very much.'

She holds the girl, murmuring soft words and stroking her face with a soft hand as Terri slips away. As she feels the life leave her body, Debbie breaks down into hard sobs. She holds Terri close, willing this to be a nightmare, willing it to end. Steven, Tom, and now Terri … all gone.

'That's touching as fuck,' a deep American voice says quietly behind her. She stiffens at the sound, the sobs ending instantly.

'Do it, then,' she snarls with fury.

'Oh, I will,' Randall replies.

She braces, holding Terri tight as she waits for the pain. It comes quickly as Randall drops down and shoves his mouth against the back of her neck. She refuses to cry out from the pain, refuses to show that reaction but instead clenches her teeth, and stares at the floor.

'All done. You'll be one of my motherfuckers very shortly,' the American chuckles. He gets up and walks out. Leaving her alone with Terri. She feels the blood coursing round the side of her neck and dripping down her chest.

Gently, she lowers Terri to the floor and gets up. Knowing she has but a minute or two. She looks round, searching for anything she can find to fulfil the promise she made.

Checking drawers and desks, she finds nothing that would help or do the job quickly. She checks the side of the office, where the gas boiler was and the small collection of tea things. One old, thin-bladed bread knife with a serrated edge. She grips the handle and stares at the thing. A promise is a promise.

'Forgive me,' she whispers as she drops down to Terri's side. She holds the knife in both hands and rests the edge against Terri's exposed neck. Breathing harder and harder, she forces the courage into her arms. Squeezing her eyes closed, she takes a breath. Pain explodes in her stomach as the first convulsion fires through Terri. Debbie keels to one side, gasping and clutching her stomach. Gritting her teeth, she picks the knife up and, with shaking hands, presses the blade to Terri's throat.

An electric current courses through Terri, bucking her upper body and knocking the knife aside. Debbie fights the pain and flounders for the knife, crying hot tears as she desperately tries to pick it up.

Sobbing and in agony, she starts to lose her vision. Crying out loud, she begs for another minute to fulfil the promise. She collapses forward, landing on Terri. The knife clasped weakly in her hand. As she starts to slip under, she feels Terri's body moving. The oxygen supply to Debbie's brain starts to slow. Feeling Terri move underneath her, she believes Terri to be recovering. She smiles in happiness. She was wrong. Terri wasn't dying. She was just passed out.

As one pair of red, bloodshot eyes open, another pair of human eyes close for the last time. One dies and one comes back.

Sarah races through the fort. The knife that Clarence gave her already drawn and held in one hand. She swerves and twists through the fighting bodies. Someone lunges at her. She slashes out with the blade, scoring across the face and not waiting to see the result, and runs on.

All around her, the survivors are being taken down. Faces with horrific injuries everywhere, just like the start of the event. She purses her lips and runs faster.

Something slams into from the side. She goes down in a tangle of arms and legs, the wind knocked out of her. Without conscious thought, she drives the end of the knife into the body of whatever is on top of her. Plunging the point in again and again. Stabbing with ruthless determination as she writhes and lashes out.

She twists violently and clambers on top of the body. An adult woman with wild, red eyes and blood stains on her teeth. Sarah stabs down, sticking the blade deep into the neck. She gets up and staggers back, the knife held out in front of her.

The melee is pressing in closer, shutting down her view of the far sides. Just bodies fighting and dying. She starts off towards the front of the fort, pushing and kicking at people to move out of the way.

A hand grabs her ponytail and pulls her backwards, lifting her off her feet. Screaming, she crashes down and looks up to see the face bearing down at her. She stabs upwards, driving the point of the knife deep into an eye socket. Blood and gore burst out, coating her face. She rolls away, holding her breath and keeping her mouth closed until she's wiped the filth away.

Up again, and she charges through the crowd. Hands reach out to grab her. She ducks and twists, lashing out with the knife and slowly getting through.

'Sarah!' a voice screams her name. She turns to see the young lad from the gate. The one Terri uses as a runner. He stands there, looking terrified and flinching as two burly men fall down in front of him, fighting viciously.

She runs and grabs his wrist, pulling him along behind her. 'Where's Chris?' she shouts.

'I don't know,' the boy wails. Sarah feels the tug as an infected grabs at the boy and tries to pull him back. She spins round and lunges in, sticking the knife through the throat and hacking away to ruin the flesh. Arterial blood sprays out as the body falls. She pulls the boy behind her, once more fighting her way through the erupting crowds.

'There,' the boy shouts. She turns to see him pointing at Chris on top of the wall, with the dog at his side.

Sarah sizes the distance up, the thick crowds of people fighting and attacking each other. With a yell, she yanks the boy and charges in. Forcing her way through, stabbing and slashing everything that gets in her way. She stumbles and trips. The boy helps her up. They press on, slashing through until they break free on the other side.

A sharp pain flares in her left leg. She glances down to see an infected savaging her calf. Stabbing down, she ends the thing and pulls the boy into her.

'Go to Chris, go now,' she pushes him away. He falters, unsure of why she's staying.

'GO NOW,' she screams, the veins in her neck bulging from the force of her voice. He backs away, turning to run.

An infected lunges for the boy. Sarah darts forward and takes the thing down. Stabbing again and again into the chest. She jumps up and turns her back to the slope. Staring the crowd down. Daring any of them to try and stop the boy. Howie's blood courses through her veins, that same blood that turns her into a warrior for the two minutes of life she has left.

She ignores the pain in her leg as she attacks again and again. She holds the base of the slope with her life. Stabbing and cutting anything that comes near it.

The pain grips her stomach. She growls harder and ignores it. Charging at another infected as it lurches towards her. She stabs forward, the pain exploding inside her and sending her bodily into the infected. They both go down. Sarah on top and hacking away. Crying in agony as she refuses to yield to the pain. Another set of legs stride past her. She twists and grabs an ankle, bringing the body to the floor. She pulls herself over and stabs the knife down.

As blackness descends, she stabs again and again and roars with utter defiance. She screams her brother's name. She screams 'Howie' again and again, as though her voice will carry to wherever he is.

The thrusts of the knife grow weaker, her body shaking

with pain. The agony simply too much to take, and she sags down, breathing short and shallow gulps of air.

'Howie,' she whispers. Her heart beats one final time. Sarah, sister of Howie, dies at the foot of the slope, her life given to save the boy.

Chris stares down at the dog as she barks. Her hackles up and ears pricked. She tenses, every muscle in her body straining as she stares into the fort. He follows her gaze, trying to see what she's barking at.

There, in the middle, a big black man with a thick beard stands tall and screams 'NOW'. Carnage erupts as screams sound out from all directions. Chris watches as all over the tent area, people are taken down and bitten. The big man in the middle grabbing at body after body, biting and throwing them aside like litter.

His professional eye takes it in. Several of them have got inside and are now launching an attack from deep within the living area. Everywhere he looks, people are being savaged and taken down.

It'll spread. That's it. The fort is lost. He watches as the guards run in, feeling a tremor of hope as he wills them to start firing. They don't. They hesitate and ruin the only chance they had.

The GPMG, it's been fixed to the top of the wall. He turns and drags the dog away, heading back up the slope with her. She pulls and yanks at her lead for a few seconds, desperate to be released to charge in and kill the things.

He shouts at her and pulls her roughly back. She concedes and goes with him, sensing his fear. He runs up the slope and onto the top. With a heightened view, he can see how much the violence has spread already.

'What do we do?' one of the guards posted as a lookout on the wall shouts as Chris runs past him.

'Fucking pray,' Chris shouts back. He runs on, skirting the edge as he aims for the position of the machine gun. Just turn it around and fire into the crowd. No matter what happens, the dog must survive. If that means killing every living thing within here, then so be it.

He stops aghast at the sight of metal fixings stacked at the agreed position. None of it assembled, and no sign of the machine gun. He casts around, thinking it surely must be here. He runs on, thinking they've put it somewhere else and not told him. No, it's not here. Instinct tells him exactly what's happened, and he vows that if he gets through this, he will personally put a bullet through Debbie Hopewell's head.

He turns quickly, his eyes sweeping the vista of the flatlands and spotting a small group of people coming down the central road.

Meredith. He has to get her out of here. She's all that matters. He grips her lead and starts back along the wall, staring down at the devastation being wrought below. It's already spread far and taking in all parts of the living quarters. He watches as a man batters his way through the door of the police office and disappears from view.

Pausing for a second, he plots a route–go down the slope and round the inside edge of the front wall. Get to the gates and get the dog outside. The route is already blocked by people fighting, but there's no other way.

He aims for the slope and starts running. Getting to the top, he spots Sarah forcing her way through the crowd, dragging one of the runners with her. He shouts a warning as an infected lunges at her leg. She falters as he bites, and she stabs down. She pushes the boy away and shouts at him before turning back to fight the attackers off.

The boy runs at Chris, tears falling from his face. They meet halfway along the slope as the boy runs straight into his arms.

Chris drops down and grabs the boy's shoulders. 'Listen to me. I need you to do something, something very important, the most important thing you will ever do in your life. You can run fast, can't you?'

The boy nods, a quick movement that causes the tears to fly from his face.

'I need you to take the dog and run. You run out this fort, and you keep running. You hear me? You don't look back ... You don't stop for anything. You get out and run ...'

'But ...'

'No buts. LISTEN TO ME,' Chris shouts at the boy. 'Go straight up that road and keep going until you find Howie. You tell him what's happened here, tell him the fort is gone, everything is gone, and you tell him to stay away,' Chris glances over the boy's shoulder as Sarah goes down, adding more urgency to his voice. 'Can you do it? You will do it!'

'What about you?' the boy asks.

'I'm going to make sure you get out. Take the lead now, hold it tight, and do not let her leave your side ... Do not let her go . No matter what happens to me, you get out with the dog and run, got it?'

'Okay.'

'I said GOT IT?'

'Okay,' the boy nods, his voice firmer. Chris presses the lead into the boy's hand and makes him wrap it round his wrist.

'Stay behind me, but you see a chance to run, then you take it, run fast, run faster than you've ever run before, and don't stop.' He grabs the boy and hugs him. He doesn't know the boy but can see the terror in his eyes, and knows his own life is about to end. That last human comfort, from a man to a child.

'I'm scared,' the boy whispers.

'I'll protect you. I won't let anyone hurt you, but you've got to run, find Howie. Promise me.'

'I promise.'

'Swear it.'

'I swear,' the boy sobs.

Chris pushes the boy gently away and nods at him. A single tear rolls down his face and soaks into his beard.

'You're a good lad,' Chris smiles and stands. He draws the pistol from his belt and starts down the slope, urging the boy to stay close.

With Sarah down, the infected fight closer to the base of the slope. Chris walks steadily towards them. One breaks free and starts up. Chris fires once. A clean headshot that drops the body instantly. He holds the gun up as they reach the base. Another lunges, a single shot, and the body drops. Chris uses his free hand to keep the boy behind him. Meredith barks and growls, but she senses the fear in the little one holding her lead. She knows the man wants her to protect the little one. She makes more noise. She tells them to stay away for she has no fear of them. She has killed them before, and she'll kill them again.

'Stay close,' Chris shouts. He fires again, dropping another body that comes at them.

The progress is slow, painfully slow. Too many bodies falling and moving to risk going faster, but every step is one closer to the front.

He fires again, another body slumps to the ground. Meredith roars at the things, her lips pulled back to show her teeth. The boy struggles to hold the powerful beast. She could break free with ease. She could pull him behind her without noticing it, but she doesn't. She knows she is to defend him, so she holds her position. This pack rely on her to hold her position.

Chris fires twice, cursing as the first one clips a shoulder. He counts the bullets and calculates there must be two left. With long-practised movements, he ejects the magazine and rams his last one home, sliding the top back to engage the first bullet.

They keep going, Chris tracking any potential target and only firing at those that come their way. The rounds quickly diminish as the fighting intensifies. Chris moves faster, using his spare hand to keep checking the boy is behind him.

Yards from the gate, and he can sense they've almost made it. One last group of survivors fighting with desperation at a horde of infected. They block the path, to go round them takes them further into the melee.

'OPEN THE GATE,' Chris bellows at the survivors. One of them, a tall guard with dark hair sees Chris shouting and focusses his attention.

'OPEN THE GATE! WE'VE GOT TO GET THE DOG OUT.' The man looks at the boy holding the dog and nods his understanding. He says something to the rest of his group. One by one, they glance over, and Chris can see the understanding in their faces. All the guards know of the importance of the dog. It must survive no matter what.

The guard with the dark hair turns and pulls the bolts back. He twists round to lash out at an infected lunging into him before going back and pulling the last one free.

'This is it,' Chris shouts to the boy. 'We'll drive them back, and you get out. Remember what I said ... you run ...'

'Okay,' the boy shouts back and swallows his fear down. He fixes his eyes on the gate, the view partially blocked by the number of bodies fighting in the way.

'Tell Clarence I said he was a fat wanker,' Chris shouts.

'WE'RE GONNA DRIVE THEM BACK. READY?' Chris roars at the men pressed against the gate. They nod back, still lashing out with whatever weapons they could grab, knives, bats, sticks, shotguns, and rifles reversed and swung out.

Chris aims the pistol and fires into the crowd of infected. The bullets slam home, ripping skulls apart. The pistol clicks empty. He ditches it.

'NOW,' he bellows. He draws a large knife from his belt and charges. The guards rally. They roar in defiance and fight out. Driving the infected back from the gate.

Chris slams into the first few. The sheer momentum of his weight and speed forcing them further away.

The guards fight with everything they've got. To the last man, they force the infected back and create space behind them.

'GO!' Chris shouts to the boy. He squeezes the lead and runs for it. An infected breaks free and runs behind Chris, charging at the boy.

Meredith lunges forward, rising onto her back legs and tearing at the thing's face with her huge teeth. She tears the man apart while the boy dangles on the end of the lead. As the thing falls, the boy pulls the lead and runs down the tight space created by the guards fighting forward.

He gets to the gate and pushes it open, pausing for the briefest of seconds to glance back at Chris. The big man grins, white teeth gleaming against his black beard. Chris nods at the boy and watches as he slips out of view.

More infected charge at the small group. The ferocity of the attack increases with every passing second.

Chris fights out with savage intent. His knife cutting, thrusting, and stabbing. More come at him and more die. The guards start to fall, the press of bodies overwhelming them. One by one, they falter and die. The small group whittles down as the fighting becomes harder and harder.

The thick stack of bodies builds ever higher as Chris refused to be defeated. He roars with anger, using his strength and experience to kill and kill, and keep killing.

The guard with the dark hair drops from a sudden lunge of several infected taking him off his feet. He screams as the teeth tear into his body. The last thought on his mind as he dies is that of Jane, the quiet but beautiful girl that kept him company these last few days.

'What the fuck are you motherfuckers doing?' a deep voice booms out. Chris back away, half in a crouch position with the knife held ready. His hands and arms slick with blood. The infected hold back, waiting as the huge American strides into their midst.

'He just one mother-fucking man,' Randall shouts. 'Look at all these dead bodies ... Did you do this?' he directs the question at Chris.

Chris stares back, eyeing the size of the man and taking in the red, bloodshot eyes.

'I mother-fucking asked you a question!' Randall demands.

'Get fucked,' Chris spits.

'Me get fucked?' Randall blanches. 'I ain't the one surrounded by fucking zombies now, am I?'

'You can still get fucked,' Chris mutters.

'See, I don't think you know how this works. I tell you to get fucked, and you literally ... get fucked. You understand now?'

Chris backs away as the man walks slowly towards him.

'Harry, take this motherfucker out,' Randall clicks his fingers. Chris watches another big man emerge from the crowd. This one with a long, grey beard.

Harry walks towards Chris, no emotion displayed in his dead eyes. Chris pauses, waiting until the last second. He feints as though to run back but twists and lunges in. Harry is quick but not quick enough to stop the long knife blade being driven to the hilt in his gut. Chris jerks the handle left and right, twisting and gouging before pulling the blade free. He steps back as Harry looks down at the wound. He looks up at Chris and comes on again, not showing any reaction to the stab he just received.

He lashes out, sending a fist towards Chris's head. Chris just leans back and lets the knuckles gently touch his nose. He sends one of his own in, a hard punch that smashes Harry's nose. Chris follows it through by driving the knife deep into Harry's side. He pulls the blade out and stabs again, the motion getting faster as his other hand reigns blow after blow to the ex-biker's face.

Harry staggers backwards, overwhelmed by the ferocity of the attack. Blood pumps from the wounds in his stomach and sides. Chris rams the knife through his chest, puncturing a lung. He rips the blade out and side swipes at Harry's neck. The sharp pointing driving deep inside. Chris jerks the blade free and watches as the main artery is opened. Blood arcs out from Harry. He staggers for a second before falling to his knees, then topples over to lie face down and inert.

'Like I said,' Chris pants, 'get fucked.'

'Oh, you think you a bad motherfucker,' Randall grins down at Harry's bleeding corpse, 'a real bad motherfucker … Let's see if you can do that again.' Randall runs forward, the speed of the man surprising Chris. He tries to swipe out with the knife but finds a big, gnarly hand wrapped around his wrist.

He looks in shock as Randall holds him steady. Chris pulls and pushes, but the bigger man refuses to budge.

'Ain't so strong now, are ya? You dumb-ass motherfucker,' Randall goads him.

Chris punches out with his free hand, sending a fast, hard, straight punch to the Americans face. Randall swats it away like an insect. Chris twists and drives his back into the other man, trying to throw him over one shoulder and break the grip he has. Randall steps backwards and pulls Chris with him. Assuming a mock bored expression, he watches as Chris tries to break the grip on his wrist.

Then he lashes out. Randall punches Chris in the face. An almighty blow that breaks Chris's nose. Blood spurts out of his nostrils, pouring down into his mouth. Randall hits again and again. He keeps hitting as Chris's face is slowly destroyed. The cheek bones are broken, the eye sockets are fractured. But he refuses to go down and stays wobbling on his feet.

Randall stops punching and watches Chris with interest. A puzzled expression forming as Chris starts laughing. Gently at first, then harder and harder.

'What the fuck?' Randall looks round at the sea of infected faces staring at him.

'You find this funny? You find me mother-fucking funny?' Randall demands.

'Not you,' Chris guffaws. 'I'm laughing …' he spits a thick glob of blood out of his mouth, a tooth flying out with it. I'm laughing at what … .what'll happen when you meet …' he spits again, clearing his throat. 'Clarence,' he adds with a laugh.

'Clarence? Who the fuck is he?' Randall asks.

Chris laughs harder, tears mixed with blood pour down his ruined face and soak into his beard.

'I said who the fuck is Clarence?' Randall draws the man in closer.

'Give me my knife, and I'll tell you,' Chris whispers hoarsely.

'You dumb-fuck …' Randall retorts. He pushes Chris away. Releasing the grip on his wrist. 'Take it, then … You dying anyway.' Randall toes the big knife towards Chris and readies himself for the anticipated attack.

Chris bends over slowly and grips the handle. He rights himself and sways on the spot. One eye already closed from the beating. He stares round and takes in the sight of the infected.

'You,' he points the knife at them, sweeping it round, 'are all fucked. Howie and Dave and Clarence will end you…. All of you …' He laughs again, a bitter, humourless sound.

'Howie?' Randall asks. 'I keep hearing that motherfucker's fucking name. Where the fuck is this Howie …?' he looks round to exaggerate the point.

'Oh, you'll meet him,' Chris spits. 'You'll meet all of them.'

'This is fucked up,' Randall shakes his head. 'Come on now. You got ya knife. Let's get this done,' he beckons Chris on, goading him to attack.

'Like I said the first time …' Chris pauses as he lifts the knife, 'you can get fucked.' He roars with anger as he drives the point of the knife deep into his own throat. Coughing and spluttering as he hacks away. He sinks down from the pain and blood loss, suffocating and drowning at the same time.

He sticks one finger up at Randall as a final insulting salute and topples forward, bleeding out and dying. Images flood through his mind, images of his wife, of his fallen comrade Malcolm. He thinks of Clarence and Howie, then of the dog. The dog that holds the cure and is now running far from the fort. As his eyes close, a warm feeling floods through his system. He heard Howie say that prayer that day. He heard it inside his head. If he heard that prayer in his head, then it can only mean one thing. God does exist.

He dies smiling.

CHAPTER THIRTY-THREE

'Howie to Clarence.'
'Go ahead, Boss.'
'Just checking to see if you've punched Cookey yet?'
'Not yet. We're discussing the finer merits of bikinis versus swimsuits.'
'Oh right ... sounds interesting.'
'I said I prefer swimsuits as it leaves more to the imagination and is classy, whereas young Cookey said he preferred skimpy bikinis, preferably with the lady holding her bikini top in her hand as she walks down the beach.'
'Ah, now I have to agree with Cookey, definitely bikinis, but not the holding of the top bit though, I hasten to add before my head gets cut off.'
'I bet she's stood behind you now holding that meat cleaver.'
'Definitely bikinis.'
'Lani just shouted that she prefers bikinis.'
'But only if you have the figure for it.'
'She just said only if they're fitties, though.'
'I never said that.'

'Cookey said the same thing. I won't repeat his words exactly …'

'Swimsuits. I think they're sexy as anything.'

'Blowers just said he's with you and prefers swimsuits.'

'Cookey said to tell him he prefers tight speedos.'

'Urgh, not dick-stickers. They're gross. Got to be shorts.'

'Lani said she hates dick-stickers and prefers shorts.'

'Dick-stickers? What are dick-stickers?'

'Speedos, Clarence. They mean speedos or tight trunks.'

'I got an echo then from you and Cookey saying the same thing. You'd better get rid of your trunks then if she prefers shorts.'

'I like my trunks.'

'He better not wear dick-stickers.'

'Hello, Lani!'

'Hello, Clarence. Tell Cookey that Blowers is missing him. He's sat all alone on the bench.'

'I'm not missing him. It's bloody peaceful in here.'

'Blowers wears dick-stickers all the time. He wears them instead of underpants.'

'Piss off, Cookey.'

'That's better than the spider-man pants you wear, Cookey.'

'Get bent, Nick, go and wash your y-fronts.'

'Does Nick wear y-fronts?'

'Yes, Lani, he does … brown and yellow ones.'

'Cookey, I don't fucking wear y-fronts.'

'And his other pair are paisley.'

'I hate pants as much as dick-stickers. Got to be tight boxer shorts.'

'You hear that, Boss? She prefers tighty-whities …'

'I heard, Clarence … We need to stop at an underwear shop.'

'I never said tighty-whities. I said boxer shorts. Lillian is nodding. She agrees with me.'

'How about a bloke wearing a G-string?'

'No, Cookey, that's gross, and Lillian agrees with that too.'

'Blowers, you got to ditch that G-string, mate. I said it was gross.'

'Okay, Cookey. I'll do it when we get back. How about a mankini?'

'What, like Borat?'

'Yes, Lani. Cookey wears a mankini like Borat.'

'Fuck off, Blowers, you said it turned you on.'

'Do you two ever agree on anything?'

'No, Lani, they bloody don't.'

'Is Nick having a crafty smoke up top?'

'Piss off, Cookey, you fucking snitch. Dave will hear that.'

'I heard it.'

'I've put it out.'

'Thank you, Nicholas, and Alex?'

'Yes, Dave?'

'You're making the first brews for being a snitch.'

'What? Okay ... Sorry, Dave.'

'Ha, that fucked you up.'

'Fuck off, Blowers. I'm gonna rim your coffee mug.'

'I've been doing yours every day. Didn't you notice?'

'I thought it tasted familiar!'

'Dirty bastard. Do you want cheese with your tea?'

'Urgh, no! That's disgusting. Pack it in, you two.'

'Sorry, Lani.'

'Sorry, Lani.'

'Blowers, why are you saying sorry over the radio? She's sat opposite you.'

'Er, good point. I don't know why I did that.'

'Ha. I know what we can do. I spy with my little eye something beginning with ... R.'

'Cookey, we're not playing eye spy.'

'You have to play eye spy on a road trip, Blowers. It's the rules.'

'Road.'

'No, Dave, not road.'

'River.'

'No, Dave.'

'Rivets.'

'No, Dave.'

'Rectangle.'

'No, Dave.'

'Riding.'

'No, Dave.'

'Radio.'

'Yay! Dave wins. Your turn, Dave.'

'K.'

'You have to say the words.'

'I don't want to say the words, Mr Howie.'

'It's the rules. You have to say the words.'

'The boss is right, Dave. You've got to say the words.'

'Okay, Clarence. I spy with my little eye something beginning with K.'

'Knife!'

'No, Mr Howie.'

'Bugger, I would have put money on that.'

'Knee.'

'No, Lani.'

'Key.'

'No, Simon.'

'Kissing?'

'No, Alex.'
'Kite?'
'Where can you see a kite or kissing, Cookey?'
'Fuck off, Blowers. Catapult.'
'That's with a C.'
'Oh ... Sorry, Dave.'
'Thick fucker ...'
'Piss off, Blowers. You have a try, then.'
'Er ... knapsack?'
'No, Simon.'
'Lillian said knot.'
'No, Lani, but a good guess.'
'Not begins with N.'
'Knot, you thick wanker ... like tie a knot.'
'Oh, yeah ... You're still a dick, Blowers.'
'Knuckle.'
'No, Clarence.'
'Oh ... knives!'
'Yes, Lani. Well done.'
'I said knives.'
'You didn't, Mr Howie. You said knife.'
'You did say knife, Boss.'
'Bloody tight if you ask me.'
'I spy with my little eye something beginning with B.'
'Boobs.'
'No, Cookey.'
'Breasts.'
'No, Cookey.'
'Bazoingas.'
'No, Cookey.'
'Baps?'
'Alex!'
'Sorry, Dave ...'

'Blowers?'
'No, Dave.'
'Bright.'
'No, Dave.'
'Brown?'
'No, Dave.'
'Black.'
'No, Dave.'
'Beige.'
'It's not a colour, Dave.'
'Burgundy ... Oh, it's not a colour.'
'No ,Clarence.'
'Blackbirds?'
'No, Cookey.'
'Bums?'
'No, Cookey.'
'Bottoms?'
'No, Cookey.'
'Butts?'
'No, Cookey.'
'Bumholes.'
'Ha! No, Cookey.'
'Alex ...'
'Sorry, Dave.'
'Boots.'
'Dave wins!'

'Almost home. Shit! Is that Meredith? What's she doing outside? Clarence, it looks like Meredith is on the road.'

'Roger that, Boss. Who she with?'

'Too far to see. Just a small group. They're running at us.'

'Pull over. We'll make ready.'

'Roger. Switch on and make ready. This ain't right ...'

CHAPTER THIRTY-FOUR

She lets the boy pull her through the gate. She wants to be released to kill the things, but she knows her place is with the little one. She must stay with the little one.

They cross the inner alley to the outer gate, and she waits as the boy pulls the bolts back with shaky hands. She can hear him crying, and the fear in him is great.

Passing through, she stays at his side as he starts to run. The words from Chris strong in his mind as he breaks into a sprint.

She keeps pace with him. Running faster and faster. The boy pumps his arms, loosening his grip to let the lead play out longer. Eyes blurred from the tears, but he keeps his head up, stretching his stride out as his running coach told him at school. He tries to breathe properly like he was taught, but the crying has upset his rhythm, and he gets knocked out of sync.

Run and keep running. Don't look back. Find Howie.

The boy fulfils the order. He runs like the wind, with fear driving him on. The heat starts to work at him. He gasps for breath but keeps going. Chris told him to run and keep running. No matter what happens, keep running.

His legs pump as his feet fly over the rough road. His slim frame powering along as the tears continue to fall. Past the embankments and into the flatlands. His stride is open and easy.

She glances up at him, seeing the wetness round his eyes. Something she's seen many times recently. She looks ahead at the figures in the distance. They don't concern her. Just a few of them that she can kill with ease if they pose a threat.

The running feels good. Her legs opening up and stretching. She breathes easily, enjoying the rush of air over her face.

A scent wafts to her nose, a faint smell caught on the warm currents of air gently rolling over the flatlands. That smell. But the things are behind them. Not in front.

The smell grows stronger. She fixes her eyes on the figures now getting closer. It's them. The smell is coming from them.

She slows down. The boy yanks at the lead to drive her on. He doesn't know what they are. She can't let him run into them. She braces her feet and slows more.

'Come on,' the boy yells with a sob.

She makes noise. Warning him of the danger.

'Please, come on,' the boy sobs and yanks at the lead.

She stops dead and refuses to budge, showing her teeth and growling at the things coming closer.

'We've got to keep running,' the boy cries harder, frustrated at being stopped by the dog. He wipes the tears from his eyes and looks up to see a group of people walking towards them. Three women and a man. They look kind.

Two beautiful, young women, an old woman, and a small man wearing glasses and a tucked-in shirt.

Meredith cocks her head. The energy from them is different. They smell of the things. They are the things. But not the same things. She growls deeply and watches closely. The hunger in them is different. They don't want to eat the little one.

Unsure, she keeps her eyes fixed on them and stands her ground. She shows teeth so they know who she is. She makes herself big so they don't attack. Look at me. Look at my size. I am strong, and I will destroy you.

Marcy watched closely as the boy came out of the fort and started running down the central road. She could see just from his manner that something wasn't right. He was fleeing from something.

He left the gate open behind him too–surely not something done with such an important place.

'Maybe he's a messenger? Come to ask what we want,' Reginald suggested as they watched the boy.

'Why the dog, though?'

'I don't know, Marcy. Maybe it's his pet.'

Marcy watches as the boy runs closer; then, the dog starts to pull back. Her eyes flick between the dog and the boy. Looking at the size of the animal now growling and showing her teeth.

'He's crying,' Reginald observes.

'Hey,' Marcy calls out, 'what's wrong?' She looks with concern at the boy. He's clearly running from something and sobbing heavily as he pulls the dog to keep moving. He sobs harder, tears running freely down his face. His narrow chest rising and falling as he gasps for air.

'Are you okay?' she softens her tone. Her words seem to

spark a reaction in him, the soft tone or the non-threatening appearance of the group.

He pulls the dog harder, coaxing her to keep going. She does so reluctantly, taking small steps but keeping her eyes fixed on the group.

The boy cries out with fear and frustration and simply drops the lead to run at Marcy. She drops down into a crouch and catches him as he runs in and wraps his arms round her neck. His tears wetting her cheeks as he sobs and sobs.

She rubs his back soothingly, feeling him shaking from head to toe. The dog moves slowly forward, getting ready to leap at the first sign of aggression. She keeps her eyes fixed on Marcy. Lips pulled back, showing her huge canine teeth with that deep, bass growl coming from her throat.

'It's okay, it's okay,' Marcy repeats softly.

Meredith watches. They stink of the things, but the energy is completely different. There is no sense of the predator in them. The man in the group even emits a sense of fear as he backs away from the dog, nervously rubbing his hands.

The female holding the little one makes soft noises, the same soft noises her pack leaders used to make to their little one.

'They're … they …' the boy sobs harder. 'Howie … got to …'

'Ssshh, take your time,' Marcy says, 'calm down and get your breath, take your time … Everything will be okay.'

'Howie … got … gone … all gone …'

'Who's gone? What about Howie? Take your time and try to breath normally,' Marcy keeps on with the soft words, gently bringing the boy down into a state of calm. His breathing eases from near hyper-ventilation to mere gasps. He clings to Marcy's neck, too afraid to let go.

'That's better,' Marcy smiles. 'Now try again.'

The boy takes a deep breath and eases himself from the crook of Marcy's neck. 'Sorry ... I made you wet,' he says weakly.

'It's okay.'

'Here,' Reginald holds out his cotton handkerchief. She takes it and wipes her neck before telling the boy to close his eyes. She starts cleaning his face, gently wiping the tears away.

'What's happened?' she asks as she dabs at his cheeks.

'The things got inside ... the zombies ... They were killing everyone and ... and ... Chris said I had to take the dog and get out. He said I had to find Howie and tell him not to go back ... He said run and don't look back and keep running until I find Howie. He said to tell Clarence ...'

'Slow down,' Marcy says, forcing her tone to be calm, her hand frozen above his face, 'say that again.'

'The zombies are inside,' the boy repeats. 'They're killing everyone. Chris told me to get the dog out and run and find Howie. Howie is like our leader ... He kills all the ...'

'I know Howie,' Marcy cuts him off, 'and Dave, yes? And Cookey and Blowers ...' She repeats the names Darren had told her.

Naming them seems to revive the boy. He takes the handkerchief and uses it to blow his nose.

The boy wipes his eyes again and looks up at Marcy. His mouth drops open as he looks into her eyes. The blood visibly drains from his face. He looks to the others and sees the same red, bloodshot eyes staring back at him.

'Take it easy,' Marcy says softly. 'We're not going to hurt you, okay? We're not the same as the others ...'

'But ...' he takes a step away, his eyes flicking to each of them.

'Young man,' Mildred says kindly, 'if we wanted to hurt you, we would have done it by now. This lady is called Marcy. My name is Mildred, and this is Reginald and April.' The others nod in greeting, keeping their faces neutral.

'You're zombies,' he says dumbly.

'Kind of, but not the same as the others,' Marcy replies. 'Why have you got to get the dog out?'

The boy hesitates, suddenly unsure if to tell them of her importance. The woman seems so calm and kind. They all do. And the old lady was right, they could have taken him several times by now.

'Okay, you don't have to answer if you don't want to,' Marcy adds after a pause. 'You said the things are inside? How many of them?'

'I don't know,' the boy answers. 'They were everywhere ... The whole place was going mad ...'

'What's your name?'

'Joe.'

'How many people were inside the fort, Joe?'

He shrugs, full of fear at what to say or do.

'You said you've got to find Howie. Where is he?'

'He went out for fuel. I've got to wait for him.'

'Okay ... Joe, do you think everyone in the fort is infected now?'

He nods, fresh tears spilling down his cheeks, his bottom lip quavering. 'Chris got me out. The whole place was fighting. Everyone had bite marks. Sarah saved me, but she got killed ...'

'Sarah? Is that Howie's sister?'

He nods again, his chest starting to heave as the sobs bubble up from deep inside.

'You poor thing, come here,' she opens her arms for him again. He hesitates, but the sobs burst out again. 'I promise I won't hurt you, Joe.' Something propels him into her arms again. The feeling of safety at being enveloped by maternal, loving arms. The warm softness of the female form providing comfort.

'See, no one is going to hurt you, Joe,' she rubs his back again as she looks up at the look of worry etched on Reginald's face.

'What do you want to do?' Reginald asks.

'They shouldn't attack us,' Marcy replies. 'We should be safe to go inside.'

'I'm not going back,' Joe cries out.

'I know, you don't have to go back. We're just talking, Joe. Just talking, that's all …'

'Or we wait here for Howie to come back,' Reginald suggests.

'That might be sooner rather than later,' Mildred remarks. They turn to see the front of the Saxon coming through the estate. A large fuel tanker driving slowly behind it.

'Is that Howie's vehicle?' Marcy asks Joe. He nods back, stepping away from Marcy to watch as the Saxon slows to a stop.

Marcy stands up, subconsciously adjusting her top and smoothing her hair down. Her heart beating faster as she realises the time has come. She glances back at the fort, wondering who's taken it and why now.

'This could ruin everything,' she says quietly.

'Too late now,' Mildred replies.

'We could still try and run,' Reginald suggests.

'Don't be silly, Reggie. We're here now. We'll just have to see it through,' Marcy replies.

'But you heard what Joe said ... The fort's gone, which is what we should be doing.'

'No,' she says firmly, 'we're here, and we're doing this.'

Reginald nods and looks back at the big army vehicle. Swallowing nervously, he takes a step closer to Marcy. Closer for his own peace of mind.

Closer so she can protect him if it all goes wrong.

CHAPTER THIRTY-FIVE

I recognise the woman, something about her seems familiar, but I can't place it. Must be the heat of the day and the fumes we've inhaled.

I bring the Saxon to a halt a good distance away, and we climb down. All eyes fixed on the group stood with the dog. We pause as the lads grab assault rifles, and we wait for Clarence and Cookey to jog over and join us.

'That's one of the runners,' Blowers protects his eyes from the bright sun and stares at the young lad stood with the group. Then to the others. A small, smart-looking man with glasses and a shirt that's tucked in. An older, refined looking woman with grey hair held tight in a bun and two beautiful adult women.

One with the low-cut top and black hair. She's tanned and stunning and very familiar.

My eyes are fixed on her as my brain frantically tries to work out where I've seen her before. Something in context. Not from the fort … No, that doesn't feel right. A few quick glimpses are all I've had.

She smiles, and although I can't see them, I can tell her

eyes are as fixed on me as mine are on her. That smile. I've seen it. My heart is beating faster, and my stupid brain is trying to tell me something.

Where do I know her from?

I glance at the others. They all look normal. The lad from the fort looks upset, and the dog is snarling. Her lips are pulled back, but she's not attacking. Meredith is staring fixed at the woman with black hair too.

'Hello, Howie,' she says. I recognise her voice too.

'Do I know you? I recognise you but …' The air around me feels charged, making the hairs on the back of my neck prickle. Then she looks at me, and I stop dead as our eyes meet, and it feels like time stops.

The whole universe ceases to expand. The world doesn't spin. The whole of creation ceases to be in that one second. Eternity passes. The seasons change as summer drifts to autumn, with a chill wind blowing at my face. Snow falls all around me, then melts away as the spring sun once more comes to shine. It happens again. And again. Faster. Wind. Snow. Sun. The hours of the day blur into one never ending cycle of stars, moonlight, and sunshine. I'm spinning round and round, but I'm still, everything around me is spinning. I'm falling, but I know I will never reach the bottom for there is no bottom. Just the fall. I'm lost. Lost in the wilderness, surrounded by an impenetrable forest that stretches for infinity in every direction. I am the first man to walk the earth. I am the first being that used fire, and I gave creation to all things around me. Then I destroyed it. I destroyed everything, and I did it again. I made life just so I can destroy it. I made suffering and pain just so mankind can feel the beauty of life. I am the father of every child born. I am the son of every mother.

'MR HOWIE,' Dave's voice booms through my skull,

snapping me back to reality. I glance round to see every gun is held and aimed straight at her, even Lillian. Mine is still at my side.

'Marcy,' she says, her eyes still locked on mine.

'MOVE AWAY FROM THE BOY,' Dave roars. None of them move. Not one of them willing to take an order from anyone apart from this woman that stands in front of me.

'Howie, you need to listen to me …' her tone is soft and pleading. Her face, despite the awful, red eyes, betrays concern and deep worry.

I stay silent, unable to speak. Nothing seems real. This isn't real. This is all a fucking dream.

'Howie … look at me,' she commands. I didn't even realise my gaze had dropped. I look back up at her and feel my senses returning; the reality of the now coming back, and I know exactly who she is.

'What the fuck are you doing here?' I snarl, the anger building in my gut. 'Dave, get that boy and the dog away from them. If they so much as move, fucking shoot them.'

'On it. Clarence, cover me,' Dave replies.

'Covering. You're clear,' Clarence calls out.

'Mr Howie …' the boy stammers.

'His name is Joe,' Marcy says softly. 'He has to tell you something, something awful, and you need to listen to him, Howie. You all need to listen to Joe and stay calm.'

'What? Joe … what's going on?'

Dave swoops past, his pistol held in a two-handed grip. He darts between the group and gets in front of Joe, then leads him round the outside and back to our side.

'Howie, please listen to Joe. You don't have much time,' she turns to stare at the fort, then looks back at me with that same worried expression.

'Joe, what's happened? You stay the fuck there, don't fucking move ... Any of you.'

'We will not move an inch, Mr Howie. You have our solemn promise,' the small man with the glasses says in a quiet, serious voice, 'but I would also urge you to listen to young Joe and do so quickly.'

I turn to see Dave leading Joe towards me. The dog still staring fixed at Marcy. Joe's face looks terrified, tear-streaked, and his eyes swollen from crying.

Crouching down, I wait for him to come in front of me. He looks terrified, shaking with fear.

'What's happened, mate? Why are you here with these ... er ...?'

'They didn't hurt me. They're zombies, but they didn't hurt me, Mr Howie ...'

'I can see that, Joe. Why are you out here with Meredith?'

'The fort ...' he bursts into tears, loud, heaving sobs.

'What about the fort?' I ask him gently. 'Joe, what's happened?'

He sobs harder. His legs give out as he sinks to the ground, covering his head. His thin body heaving.

I look up at Marcy to see her biting her bottom lip in concern at the lad. 'Get him away. I can tell you,' she says softly.

'Lani, take Joe to the vehicle,' she rushes over with Lillian. Together they get him to his feet and walk him away, heading towards the Saxon.

'Well?' I demand as he walks off. I glare at Marcy. She looks back, seemingly unsure of how to start.

'The fort's been taken. Joe was running up the road when we got here. He said the things were inside and were killing everyone. Listen to me,' she says firmly as I step towards her. 'This is not from us. We did not do this ...' she motions her group. 'Joe said everyone was being bitten. He said it was all over the place ...' She takes a deep breath and continues, 'He said Chris told him to run and keep running and to find Howie ... to find you and tell you what happened and to tell you not to go back.'

'What?' I say with a shake of my head.

'What the fuck?' Blowers exclaims. He takes a step closer. They all do. Lani leaves Joe with Lillian and moves back towards us.

Marcy swallows and looks to each face in turn. 'You have to listen. I came here ... we came here,' she corrects herself, 'to hand ourselves into you. You said you had doctors and medical equipment ...'

'Marcy, what the fuck is this? What ... the fort has gone?'

'Howie ... please hear me out. We came here to hand ourselves in so you could test us and find a vaccine or ... or I don't know ... work out what this thing is. Someone got here before us, Howie. The things got here and took the fort.'

'That's not possible. It's too well defended. They can't get in.'

'They have, and they are,' she says firmly.

'We have to get in there. Make ready!' I snap the order.

'What about them?' Dave nods at the small group.

'Howie, you're not listening ... The fort is gone. Joe said everyone had bite marks. Just a few turned in there would wipe the place out,' she adds.

'This is a fucking trick. What the fuck are you doing?' I raise my rifle and aim it at her.

'No,' she shakes her head, 'no tricks ...'

'We saw what you were fucking capable of on the island. I fucking spoke to you ...'

'You did! And you said you had doctors and medical equipment. Remember that? You offered to take me in.'

'Someone get Joe up here. This is some kind of dirty scheme. Get down on your fucking knees now! All of you.'

'Do as he says,' Marcy says to the other three. They lower themselves down and stare back at me.

'He's here,' Lani calls out.

'Joe? I know you're upset, but you have to tell me what happened. Exactly what happened.'

'The things were inside. They were already in there. They must have been cos they just started biting everyone. They was biting people and pushing 'em away and biting more ...'

'Where, Joe? Where in the fort was this happening?'

'Everywhere,' he says weakly. I turn round to watch him. He stands just a few feet from me, shaking from head to toe, with Lani holding an arm round his shoulders. 'Everyone had bite marks. Sarah got me. She got me to Chris, and he said I had to get the dog out. He said I was a fast runner, and I had to run away with Meredith cos she's immune, and he said to keep running and find you ...'

'You saw Sarah?'

He nods as fresh tears fall from his eyes. 'She went down, Mr Howie ... She was bit.'

I look down at the ground and take a deep breath. My heart hammering in my chest as my stomach drops.

'She saved me. Chris was on the slope, and she fought them away so I could get to him.'

'Fuck,' Cookey says softly.

'Did ...' I fight to keep control, 'did Chris say anything else?'

'He said to tell Clarence he was a fat wanker,' the boy realises what he's said and suddenly looks frightened.

Clarence rocks on his feet. He drops down to a crouch and bows his head.

'They was fighting at the gate. Chris had a gun and shot them, and then he ran at them and beat them away and shouted and told me to get out ...'

'Oh, my god,' Nick shakes his head, staring at me in shock.

'This is fucked up. It's got to be a fucking trap,' Blowers stammers.

'You did this?' I draw my pistol and ram the end into Marcy's forehead.

'She didn't do nothing, Mr Howie,' Joe yells out. 'She was here when I came out. They was walking down. She weren't inside.'

'You did this. You did this.' I press the gun firmer into her head. She looks up at me, bracing so she doesn't fall back. Pure fury is surging up inside me.

'No,' she shakes her head and stares up, 'not us ... I swear it. This isn't anything to do with us. We came here to give ourselves up to you.'

'Why?' I scream at her.

'Because you said,' she flinches from me, 'you said you had doctors and equipment, Howie. We're not the same as the others. We can talk and think and do normal things ...'

'Darren could fucking speak. Look what he did, the dirty fucking bastard. You did this ...'

'Darren was twisted and corrupt. The infection made him like that. We're normal. We think and speak for ourselves with normal intelligence ...'

'Boss, what we doing?' I twist round to see Clarence back on his feet, his face set and determined.

'We're going in there.'

'You can't,' Marcy cuts me off. 'Eight of you ... against

what? Several thousand? Think, Howie. You'll be slaughtered.'

'What do you fucking care. You're one of them.'

'No,' she shouts with feeling, 'I am not one of them … We are not *them*.'

'Then what are you?'

'We're … different …' she says slowly.

'Fuck off, we're going in there, and we'll fucking kill every one of them. That's what we do …'

'Go ahead,' she yells at me, 'shoot me, shoot all of us. Go inside and see everyone you knew is now turned, then shoot them too, Howie … Shoot your sister and your friends.'

My hand is at her throat, driving her down into the floor as I press the gun into her face. Dave and the others stride forward, aiming their rifles at the Marcy's three associates who start to rise as the sight of me pushing her down.

'You lying fucking bitch!' I squeeze my grip harder, feeling the softness of her neck. Rage burns through me as I stare down into those awful, red eyes. Something about her terrifies me, utterly terrifies me and makes me want to kill her, but at the same time, there's sadness in her eyes, an expression of regret and sorrow.

'Do it,' she gasps. 'I won't fight you.'

'You took Sarah …'

'Not me.'

'She was all I had left …'

'I didn't do it,' she fights for air, saliva dribbles from her mouth. 'It wasn't us. We don't take anymore.'

'You're lying,' I scream at the top of my voice, my face inches from hers.

'She's not,' the old woman shouts. 'I gave myself willingly to her. She wouldn't take us. We all gave ourselves to her.'

'Shut the fuck up,' Blowers shouts at the woman.

'Young man,' the woman stares at him with an icy glare, 'you may tell me to shut up but do not swear at me.'

'I'm not lying, Howie, neither is she. We've got thousands of us hidden away. We came here to find you, Howie ... to surrender.'

'BITCH,' I scream, spittle flies from my mouth, landing on her cheeks.

She tries to swallow. I feel it beneath my hand, her face going red from the tightness of my grip.

'So you don't take, then?' I growl at her. She shakes her head, a small movement restricted by my hand and the pistol jammed into her forehead.

'You don't want to feast and bite,' I say the words slowly, savouring them, drawing them out. 'Why not? Don't you have the hunger they do? Don't you want to bite and take my blood?'

She shakes her head again. Staring at me with terrified eyes.

'Liar,' I whisper at her. Sarah is gone. She's dead. One of them. The whole fort has been lost. Chris, Terri, Ted ... all of them.

'I'm not lying,' she whispers.

I release my hand from her throat. She gasps for air, drawing in huge gulps. 'Yeah? Don't wanna bite me?'

'Mr Howie,' Dave shouts in alarm as I push my hand to Marcy's mouth.

'Bite me, come on, fucking bite me!' She tries to squirm, pulling her head away. I push the gun harder into her forehead, grinding the back of her head into the earth. 'Come on, you lying bitch, bite me, fucking bite me!'

She clamps her mouth shut and stares at me with defiance, an angry stare that she holds for several seconds. Then she opens her mouth. I push my thumb into her mouth and feel the warm wetness inside. I can feel her teeth gently brushing against the sides of the digit.

'Bite it, make me one of you!'

Her head moves side to side, refusing to yield. She savours my thumb. I can tell she does. I can tell she wants to bite. Her tongue runs over the end, licking and caressing it, but she doesn't bite.

'ENOUGH,' Dave roars.

I pull my hand away and gently lower the pistol from her head. A perfect, round hole left marked on her skin from the barrel. I stagger away from her, taking steps to the side.

'Give me your hand,' Dave follows me. He pulls a small plastic bottle of anti-bacterial gel from his pocket and grabs my wrist. He squeezes the gel out and rubs it onto my thumb, coating my hand and wrist with the disinfectant. I stare back at the fort, the pistol hanging limp from my hand.

'Where's my rifle?' I suddenly realise I don't have it.

'I've got it, Boss,' Nick says. He walks up and hands it over as Dave let's go. 'Here,' Nick passes me a cigarette.

I take it and light the end while I stare at the fort. Disgusted at myself for what I just did. A deep sense of shame flooding through me. I can't take this in. Everyone in the fort is gone. This must be a trap, something to lure us away. But then she could have bitten me. She could have simply clamped down with her teeth, and I'd be infected. The shame of hurting her like that conflicts with what she is. Confusion clouds my mind. She killed Stephen and Tom. She killed my parents and everyone I ever loved, but she didn't bite me. I feel sickened. Sickened from the thrill I felt when I felt her tongue licking my thumb. A flutter inside my gut that excited me.

'Are you okay, Marcy?' the man with the glasses asks from somewhere behind me.

'Don't move,' Blowers warns.

'I want to check on her,' he demands.

'I'm fine, Reggie.'

'Let me check.'

'Don't fucking move,' Blowers shouts again.

'Let them move,' I snap without looking round. My eyes fixed on the fort. I can still feel her tongue on my thumb, the warmth of her mouth, the wetness of being inside her.

I shake my head and focus. Too many things spinning in my mind. My sister ... Sarah. She's inside there.

'We need to check inside. Stay here with this lot. I'll take the Saxon down and look.'

'No way,' Clarence rumbles. 'I'm coming with you.'

'No,' Dave adds firmly. 'You stay here. I'll go with him.'

'Okay,' Clarence agrees.

'Take April with you. She can go inside. You'll be taken if they see you,' Marcy adds.

I turn back to stare at her as the other young woman gets slowly to her feet. I stare at April. She looks at Marcy, then at me without expression.

'No,' Clarence shakes his head. 'We'll all go ...'

'What?' I ask him.

'You'll go for them. I can see by your face, Boss. We all go.'

'No, mate,' I shake my head, 'stay here and wait.'

'Dave, don't let him go inside, bring him back,' Clarence says.

'Okay,' Dave answers.

I start walking to the Saxon. Dave follows me. 'What about the girl?' Blowers asks as April starts walking towards the vehicle.

'I don't care. She can come if she wants.' I climb into the driver's seat, feeling numb. The thoughts still spinning so fast that I feel sick. Like my head will explode if it carries on.

'Nick, get on the GPMG,' Dave shouts. The lad runs ahead, clambering in the back and up the hole.

Dave gets into the back and motions for the girl to sit in the front. She gets in and sits in the passenger seat. Dave draws his pistol and presses it to the back of her head, letting her know it's there.

'I won't do anything,' April speaks for the first time, her voice low and soft.

'No, you won't,' Dave replies bluntly. I start the engine and pull away, veering the vehicle round the group. Marcy watches me closely as I go by. I stare back at her before pulling my gaze away and looking to the fort.

I drive straight down the middle, the speed increasing as I push my foot down harder. The big wheels absorb the ruts and holes of the rough surface. Sweat drips down my neck and from my chin.

The outer door is open. Wide open. No sign of any guards. A figure steps into the doorway, silhouetted in the shadows. It stands there, watching for a few seconds.

Leaning forward, I try to see who it is, straining my eyes but not making any details out. As we get closer, the figure steps out. I brake hard, slamming my foot onto the pedal and bringing the vehicle to a rapid stop. April jolts forward, just managing to put her hands out to prevent her head slamming on the front.

'Mr Howie!' Dave shouts as I open the door and jump down. I stride towards the figure, my heart beating faster than ever before. My breath feels stifled like I can't breathe quick enough.

Dave runs ahead of me and stops my progress. 'Go back,' he says flatly.

I barge through him and keep walking, my eyes fixed on the figure that stands there, watching me.

'Mr Howie,' he grabs my wrist and pulls me back. I try to wrench free, but he grips me too hard. April runs to stand in front of me and faces the figure, like presenting herself as a guard.

'Nick, if she moves, you fire,' Dave calls out.

'I will.'

'Don't, Nick, don't shoot,' I try to say, but my voice catches in my throat.

'Sarah?' I call out. My sister stands there, watching me. She looks uninjured; then, I see the blood on her leg. She looks at the vehicle, then up at Nick, and then finally her gaze settles on April.

'OUT HERE,' Sarah yells out. 'HOWIE'S OUT HERE,' her voice is flat but loud.

'Mr Howie,' Dave grunts as he starts dragging me backwards. I try to fight him off. April turns and grabs my other side, both of them dragging me back to the Saxon.

'SARAH,' I scream.

She starts moving forward as Nick fires a few rounds into the ground in front of her.

'NICK, DON'T YOU FUCKING FIRE.'

'Get him in the vehicle!' Dave pulls me with vicious strength. April digs in, gripping me hard as they manhandle me.

Others start running out of the gate. Nick opens up, firing straight into it and shredding them before they take more than a couple of steps.

I get pushed into the back of the vehicle by Dave and April as Nick continues to fire.

'Can you drive?' Dave shouts at April.

She doesn't reply but climbs over into the driver's seat and takes control of the vehicle. She pulls away, driving forward and then sweeping round in a wide circle before facing back down the road.

'I'm okay.' I get to my feet as Dave stares at me with sharp eyes.

'They're pouring out the gates,' Nick yells down.

'Mr Howie, you need to switch on and deal with this. Everyone is looking to you. Do you understand?' Dave whispers fiercely.

I nod back, gulping as I look at him.

'You can't lose it. Not you ...'

'I'm okay.'

'Are you?'

'I'm fine ... fine, Dave.' He stares hard at me before nodding and looking out the window as April brings the vehicle to a stop beside the group.

I push the rear doors open and jump down, taking a quick glance at the mass of bodies charging out the now open gates.

'Form a line here and make ready,' I shout and point at the ground just behind the Saxon. The lads respond quickly, running over to kneel on the dirt road. They start grabbing magazines and putting them on the floor in front of them. 'Nick, get down here. Dave, on the GPMG. Lillian, stay close to Blowers and follow his instructions. Joe, get inside the vehicle with the dog and stay there. I run back to the front of the vehicle and grab my assault rifle from the side of the driver's seat.

'What about us?' Marcy shouts as I run past her.

I stop dead and stare at her, then at the other three, April now stood back with them.

'We need to leave here. Don't do this. Don't kill them,' Marcy says.

'Why not?' I ask her with a humourless smile as I eject my magazine and check it.

'Because you know them. They're your people. Joe said the dog is immune,' she speaks quickly with nervous glances at the thick crowds in the distance. 'What if we can find a cure? You kill them, and that's it … no going back.'

'How do we find a cure, Marcy?' I ram the magazine back into the assault rifle. 'The doctors are now your lot and all the equipment is in there.' I yank the bolt back.

'There'll be somewhere else we can try. Just go … Get in the vehicle and go … Let me try and speak with them.'

'What?'

'Let me try. I'm one of them Howie. Get in your vehicle and get ready to go. Let me try, please, let me try.'

'Marcy, they're not us,' April cuts in. 'There was no connection, nothing … The one I saw was like a stranger.'

'I'm not you, April,' Marcy says without hostility.

'They are not our kind, Marcy. She saw me, looked at me, knew what I was, but showed no reaction.' The long speech makes me realise how flat her voice is, like monotone and without expression.

'Aren't you all connected?' I ask.

'No, it doesn't work like that,' Marcy replies with a frown.

'Your fucking boyfriend had thousands,' Nick shouts. Closer to us, he hears the conversation.

'I don't know how it works,' Marcy exclaims, 'and we don't really have the time to discuss it right now.' She looks to the crowd marching towards us.

It looks like every member of the fort has come out. All marching at the same pace directly towards us.

'Well, there it is,' I say. 'Your woman,' I spit the word out, 'said they're not part of your perfect, little clan, so you can't control them. They're fucking infected, so we kill 'em ... That's what we do.'

'Why haven't you killed us, then? We're infected. We're zombies.'

'Marcy, I think now is not the time to goad this rather angry young man,' Reginald says quietly with a nervous glance at me.

'Are you really going to do this?' she demands.

'Yep ... You know why? Because we get people turning up here every day, survivors that have heard about the safe fort. They'll die if we don't stop these things now.'

'But your sister is in there.'

'No,' I snarl with venomous fury, 'my sister is dead. Everyone in that fort is dead ... Those things are not the people we left this morning.'

'For god's sake, Howie. I'm the same person I was before I turned. Can you not see this?'

'Are you? This big group you said you had ... Where did they come from, Marcy? Because we killed every fucking one of them that Darren had.'

'Listen ...'

'Answer the fucking question,' I roar at her. 'Where did they come from?'

'I turned them, but that was before ...'

'Before what? Before you suddenly decided to hand yourself in? Get fucked.'

'Before I realised what we are,' she yells at me, 'before I understood the potential of this thing inside us. We don't feel pain, we don't suffer ...'

'Save it and fuck off.' I turn away from her. She grabs

my arm and spins me round, her face contorted with a look of pure determination.

'If you kill them, there is no going back. Darren said you were good. He said Howie was righteous and always doing the right thing. If you do this, you're no better than him. He was sick. Do you understand?' She speaks loud and fast, pronouncing every word clearly. 'He was demented from the infection. He thought it was his to use as he wanted.'

'And what? What do we do? Find another doctor and more equipment and somehow find a fucking cure and then come back and give it to them while they all line up and wait patiently? Don't be so fucking stupid ...'

'We can ...'

'What about the survivors that turn up later or tomorrow? What about them? They'll walk down this road and get fucking killed because we're pissing around, trying to find a fucking needle in a haystack. Do you know how lucky we were to find those doctors and get that equipment? We've got the fucking fuel to run the generators right there,' I point back at the tanker. 'We had everything we needed ...'

'So what's your plan?' she asks, folding her arms with a stubborn expression.

'Plan? Nick, do you want to tell her the plan?'

'Kill 'em all,' he says bluntly.

'Every one of them,' Blowers adds.

'With eight of you? How the hell–'

'With a big fucking machine gun and a truly nasty bastard holding it. That's how.'

'Mr Howie,' Dave calls down.

'I didn't mean that, Dave. I was making a point.'

'We don't have enough ammunition for all of them.'

'What!?'

'We used a lot today at the refinery and then getting the tanker ... We won't have enough.'

'We've got the assault rifles ... and all the guns we collected.'

'Okay, just thought I would mention it.'

'Noted.'

'Roger.'

'You lot are mad,' Marcy shakes her head. 'We're not the sick ones ...'

'Marcy, we should go. This isn't our fight,' Reginald says.

'Yeah, Marcy,' I sneer, 'this isn't your fight. Go and fucking pretend not to be a rancid, diseased whore somewhere else.' She slaps my face hard. An instinctive reaction that stings my cheek and turns my head to one side.

'You were meant to be good,' she whispers. I look back at her to see a tear falling from one red, bloodshot eye.

Silence as she stares at me. That single tear rolls down her cheek to be absorbed by the soft skin of her upper lip. It leaves a wet trail, distinct against her tanned skin.

'We're going,' she turns to Reginald, then looks at the advancing horde. Without another word, she walks off, the other three following in her wake. Mildred gives me a withering look as she passes.

'We just letting them walk off?' Clarence asks.

I shrug and stare at the retreating forms as they move up the road towards the estate. 'Shoot them if you want.'

I can't take my eyes off Marcy. The feeling of shame burns through me. Shame at pinning her down and hurting her, shame at calling her a diseased, rancid whore. Shame at feeling the electrifying tingle of pleasure as her tongue licked my thumb. Shame for not killing all four of them. Shame at everything I have ever done, for who I am, and what I've become. Shame for that tear that fell from her eye and the look of hurt she gave me.

None of the lads fire at the four walking away. None of us having the stomach for cold-blooded murder like that, for that's what it would be–murder. They didn't threaten us. They didn't try and hurt us. And that girl April, she put herself between me and Sarah as though defending me. Why? Why do that?

Maybe she was protecting Sarah, but then she'd be facing me if that was the case. No, she was protecting me from Sarah. From my own sister who was one of her kind.

This is fucked up. Everything is fucked up beyond recognition, and I don't know what to do. The horde are coming at us, and every bone in my body is demanding for them to be killed. They should be killed. But they were our people. Chris is in there, Terri, Debbie, Ted, and Sarah. Kelly the engineer and the doctors. All the guards from the gates.

Indecision and shock cripple my mind. Too much, this is all too much. We should just load up and go, find somewhere safe, and hide away. Take the Saxon and the fuel tanker and leave all of this shit. Let them fight to the death and wipe each other out.

But that fort. That fort is our place. We fought for it, killed, and lost our own so we could have that place, and now it's taken from us. Is it worth it? If we killed this horde now, what would be the reason? To take the fort back or revenge? Or simply because they are infected and that's what we do? We kill. We take life and kill.

Where's the limit? At what point do we withdraw and say enough is enough. Those things coming at us now are our own people, women and children we saved, rescued, and brought back to safety. Men who fought alongside us.

Debbie was right. I'm just a supermarket manager, and I'm in way over my head now.

These people are all looking to me for a decision, stay or go. Kill or flee. Murder or live our lives and try to forget this place ever existed.

You were meant to be good.

Who the fuck is she to judge me? She's infected. A dirty, filthy, diseased infected. Rancid and fetid with unclean blood.

You were meant to be good.

Good? Who said I had to be good? This was never about being good. This was about survival and doing the right thing.

Oh.

Shit.

There it is. Doing the right thing. Fuck it. Our way *was* the good way. Doing what was needed for the protection of others. We killed, but we did it to protect our species. I look back at the fuel tanker and feel a sudden pang of guilt for the lives that were lost when the refinery went up. Now there is no more fuel in that place, just a dirty, black cloud scorching the heavens.

Dave grips the machine gun on the top of the Saxon. Joe stands in the back, holding the dog at his side. Clarence stands at the far end of the line. The others all kneeling and waiting. They're all waiting.

We lost the fort, but it's still there. The high walls are still there. The equipment is still inside it with the food and the armoury. The people have changed, but the fort remains.

There are other survivors. Scared people that need somewhere safe and decent. Not like the refinery where evil, twisted men take the power and become corrupt and greedy.

Maddox and his kids and more groups everywhere. Word will spread, and this place will be a beacon for hope.

I see it now. I see what we have to do.

The grip of indecision eases off as my mind settles.

'We have to take it back,' I speak clearly and look along at them all, 'but that is just my instinct. If any of you feel different, then say so now …'

'I agree,' Clarence replies in his deep voice.

'It's ours … We gave too much to lose it,' Nick says.

'I'm in,' Blowers adds quietly.

'Lani?'

'I agree. You know those people, but no more than I knew some of the people on the Isle of Wight. They aren't people now. They're things.'

'Dave?'

'Yes, Mr Howie.'

'What do you think?'

'We should take it back.'

'Cookey, you're unusually quiet.'

He scratches his head with a puzzled frown. 'Er … I kinda thought that's what we were doing anyway … but yeah, I agree, we know them and stuff, and like it's gonna be hard, but er … it's our fort, and we don't really have anywhere else to go … and like … if we don't kill them, then they will do others in and … and … well, that ain't right, and you always said we had to do the right thing …' He takes a breath, 'that er … that chick with the big tits …'

'Alex.'

'Sorry, Dave … That Marcy with the big tits,' he carries on missing the point of Dave's interjection. 'She said you were meant to be good, but like, she meant us, didn't she?

She meant we're the good guys cos like we do what you say … and she said that we shouldn't kill 'em cos they were our people, but she missed the point and … and well, we have to kill 'em cos they'll kill more if we don't, and even if we do get a cure or somethin', then it'll be too late for this lot, and they … well, they ain't the only ones left, are they?'

Everyone stares at the young man as he finishes off and looks awkwardly at the ground. 'Fuck it. I know what I mean, but like … it didn't come out right.'

'It did, mate,' I reply to him.

'Came out perfectly, Cookey,' Clarence adds.

'It did,' Blowers nods at his mate.

'Cheers,' Cookey grins sheepishly.

'Bloody hell. The lad's got a brain buried somewhere in there,' Clarence smiles.

'He hasn't,' Blowers says. 'He wrote that speech ages ago and had it ready.'

'Fuck off, Blowers, I didn't.'

'Big tits?' Lani asks with a shake of her head.

'What? She has got big tits. They were bloody amazing,' Cookey protests.

'Was a great rack,' Nick nods ruefully.

'Rack?' Lani continues to shake her head. 'Is that all you think about? A zombie woman turns up talking and not biting us … and generally being the opposite to every other zombie we've met, and all you see is the big pair of tits?'

'Er … yes?' Cookey grins.

'Is that bad?' Blowers laughs.

'The other one was fit too,' Cookey sighs.

'What was her name? April?' Nick asks.

'Yeah, April, she was fit as …' Blowers says.

'True,' Nick nods, 'lovely arse.'

'Oh, did you see it? It was like ... perfect ... just perfect,' Blowers replies.

'Man ... if I get turned, I hope it's by her,' Cookey sighs again, 'and I know just where she can bite me too.'

'ALEX!' Dave and Lani shout together.

'What?' he says innocently. 'Just saying ... If she put sunglasses on, you'd never know she was a zombie.'

'Can you stop saying that bloody word, please,' Clarence moans.

'Which word?' Cookey seizes on it quick as a flash as Clarence groans.

'You mean zombie?' Nick asks.

'Which one? The zombie word?' Blowers grins.

'Can we focus on the giant fucking horde charging at us?' Clarence snaps.

'They are getting closer,' Lani observes.

'Er, is it always like this?' Lillian asks, speaking for the first time since we stopped.

'Yep,' Lani replies dully, 'always ... always, always, always. They never bloody stop. You'd think this would shut them up, wouldn't you? Oh no!' She shakes her head. 'A nuclear bomb wouldn't stop them.'

The three lads chuckle proudly while grinning at Lillian.

'Boss, we need to start shooting before they get any closer. They'll flank and swarm us otherwise,' Clarence says seriously.

'Okay. Lads, you ready?' I get a chorus of replies in the affirmative.

'Dave, you ready?'

'Yes, Mr Howie.'

I raise my rifle and aim down the sights. 'Fuck 'em!

We'll win.' I pull the trigger and listen to the explosion of sound coming from the assault rifles to my side and the GPMG firing above.

CHAPTER THIRTY-SIX

'You've done the right thing,' Reginald offers. He struggles to keep up as Marcy stalks through the ruined estate. Her face a picture of fury as she strides faster and faster.

'You did everything you could, Marcy. It was just bad luck that someone got to the fort ahead of us.'

She doesn't reply but just stares fixed at the road ahead of her.

'He wasn't a nice man ...' Reginald continues. 'He was rude and very aggressive, not at all what I had expected. You'd think he would at least show basic manners given the effort we've taken to get here, and we did look after that boy until he arrived too.'

She presses on, showing no reaction.

'And pushing that gun in your face was just barbaric ... utterly barbaric. You've still got the mark on your head now. It'll bruise, you know.'

No reaction. A dark look on her face.

'I mean. I know he just found out his sister has been turned, and yes, granted, seeing her stood in front of him like that must have been very alarming, especially, as April said, she called out to alert those inside that her brother was there ... practically giving him up, but be that as it may, and as shocking and distressing as that is, Mr Howie needs to understand that he isn't the only one to suffer loss.'

She doesn't say anything but walks on, the dark look on her face starting to ease.

'Indeed, I am glad to be away from there. As I said, Mr Howie was not what I was expecting in any degree. The power of the man is apparent. His ability to lead appears unquestionable, and I know I certainly felt a level of ... well, I don't know how to say it but ... intrinsic. Yes, I felt an intrinsic fear of him. No, not fear, wariness or, well, just an awareness of who he is.'

Marcy walks on, maintaining the same pace but now looking down at the ground instead of fixed on the distance ahead.

'But good heavens, what does he expect calling you a diseased, rancid whore like that. Unforgivable, truly it was. Again, yes, you did run with Darren, who we know caused the death of some of his closest people and obviously that lad who died that night in the stairwell, so under normal circumstances, one could feel a degree of sympathy for the anger and hurt he feels towards you. But to call you such an insulting term in front of others was abhorrent.'

She begins to slow the frantic pace.

'And that act of defilement. Good god, that was ... well, it was humiliating, is what it was. Thrusting his thumb into your mouth like that. What was the man thinking of?! How on earth you held back and didn't bite down is beyond me. What an utterly stupid act of ... of ... well, of stupidity, yes, a stupid act of stupidity. He was actually looking you in the eye and telling you to bite him! I saw it ... We all saw it ... *telling you to bite him!* Now, that was either the single most bravest act I have ever witnessed or the single most stupidest, and I know full well which way I am veering in my opinion, let me tell you that.'

She stops suddenly, spinning round to stare back and breathing hard.

'What? What's wrong?' Reginald asks in alarm.

Marcy lifts a hand to her mouth and touches her lips gently. She looks at Reginald, who stares back blinking. She looks at April, who stares back blankly. She looks at Mildred, who nods. A slight movement, just a dip of the head. But it's enough.

Marcy starts running.

CHAPTER THIRTY-SEVEN

'MAGAZINE,' someone from the line bellows. Hard habits ingrained from Dave's instruction. The first magazines are ejected and thrown into the back of the vehicle, new ones rammed in, bolts yanked back, rifles raised, triggers depressed.

As soon as we start firing, they start running. Charging across the flatlands towards us. A solid, unbroken, dark mass of infected, thousands of them. They're some distance off, but every step brings them closer.

Whoever is running them has more experience than Darren as the sides of the horde start to overtake the middle. The shape of the ranks bending to a horseshoe.

'They're gonna flank us,' Clarence shouts as he changes magazine.

'AIM FOR THE SIDES,' Dave roars down. As one, the assault rifles adjust position and fire into the moving sides of the mass. Bodies go down as the rounds hit home, but they keep coming. Charging with increasing speed and holding that pattern as the two flanks stretch further out.

The GPMG holds on the middle section, cutting the

numbers down in droves, but even Dave has to focus the fire and give steady, short bursts to control the rapid loss of the large calibre ammunition.

The infected stretch further out to the sides, moving very rapidly to increase the flanking position. I suddenly think back to all the movies and documentaries where they talk about pincer movements, flanking, and buffalo horn formations.

With such a long line, we find it hard to focus our fire, and suddenly, the small amount of guns we have becomes apparent against such a large number of infected.

I fire at the left flank, focussing my fire and aiming for the upper bodies. I down body after body, but I also miss some shots because of their rapid movement out to the sides. The GPMG bursts become shorter and shorter as Dave aims for the central mass.

Changing magazine, I glance round and see the thickness of the ranks still coming at us. Now much closer and gaining with every second. I can see the individual people now, make out male and female. I turn away before I recognise any of them. A quick glance shows me the others doing the same, averting their eyes while they change magazines.

'DAVE. GO HEADSHOTS,' I shout.

'I HAVE BEEN.' He opens up with the last, final burst. A whole line of skulls exploding like melons. Pink mists puffing into the air as he strafes across the central section.

Taking aim, I keep on taking single shots, feeling the recoil of the rifle with each press of the trigger. Watching as they drop and spin off from the power of the bullets.

'I'M OUT,' Dave roars as the GPMG clicks empty.

'GO TO THE FORT AND GET SOME MORE,' Clarence shouts.

'SERIOUSLY?' I shout.

'NO, I WAS JOKING. I THINK WE'RE FUCKED.'

'AIM FOR THE MIDDLE. FULL AUTO,' I shout and turn to aim into the middle. I flick the switch and hold steady as I unload the magazine into the dense central ranks. The assault rifles burst to life as we fire unrestrained into them.

A dull roar sweeps as they give voice, encouraged and charged up from the GPMG running empty. They speed up, coming at us faster than ever.

Changing magazine, I glance round and see Dave quickly showing Joe how to push and load a fresh magazine into a rifle. The lad nods and starts ramming them into the spare assault rifles.

'CLARENCE, TO ME,' Dave shouts. Clarence spins round to see Dave stood there with two assault rifles held at waist height. He aims for the oncoming central rank and pulls both triggers at the same time. His small body judders with the recoil of the two assault rifles.

Once empty, he casts them down and scoops two more up, Joe quickly grabbing the two discarded weapons to change the magazines.

Clarence moves to the back and grabs another one. Copying Dave, he stands with two rifles and empties both at the charging mass.

We fire and fire. The air splitting apart from the noise. The stench of cordite hitting our already scorched throats. Grimy sweat pours down our faces as the sun burns down on us.

With a final almighty roar, they give a final charge, finding more speed and power as they sprint. Faces twisted in utter hatred, teeth pulled back, arms pumping wildly.

'GET IN. GET IN NOW,' I scream out, shocked at the burst of speed they give. They were holding back to keep us static. Waiting until the last second before showing that conserved energy. These are freshly turned and healthy. Full of strength and power.

Clarence dumps his rifles inside and grabs Lillian, launching her into the back. He twists and grabs Lani, doing the same. Dave stands central, holding two rifles and firing into their legs, bringing them to down to trip the ones following, buying us seconds.

I move back towards the Saxon. They're so close now. Just metres away and coming in from three sides. Feeling the back of the Saxon, I give a final burst from my rifle and dive in. Strong hands pull me away from the doors as they get slammed shut. Loud thuds follow within a second as the horde reaches the vehicle.

I'm up and scrabbling for the front, cursing as I see the thick crowds in front of the vehicle. I start the engine as the vehicle rocks from the solid press of thuds and bangs coming from the outside. Bodies clamber over the front and lie over the windscreen, blocking my view. I push the pedal down and feel the vehicle start to move. I press harder and feel as the vehicle struggles to make ground.

I slam the gear into reverse and push my foot down again. The vehicle backs just inches before coming to a halt. Forward and the same thing happens. Reverse, and I ram my foot down, we hardly move. No view of outside from the bodies across the windscreen.

'They're jamming the wheels,' Clarence shouts over the sound of Meredith barking like crazy.

Fuck it, we've been caught out by fucking zombies doing something clever instead of full-on charging. Wankers. Fucking wankers.

I keep trying, turning the wheel hard over and trying to force the movement at an angle. The engine screams with a mighty roar, bellowing its own frustration and anger at being blocked in.

'CAN'T SEE A FUCKING THING,' I scream out and keep trying to jolt forward and back. The things outside roar and slam against the vehicle. Loud bangs that echo dully inside.

With a curse, I give up and grip the steering wheel. My knuckles turning white from the pressure. My breathing gets faster. My heart rate increases. Oxygen floods my system, pumping into my muscles as my heart understands what's about to happen.

An image of Sarah floods my mind. The red eyes, the expressionless face. My sister. My family. Taken by those things.

I climb out of the seat and into the back. Meredith ceases barking and stares at the back of the vehicle, knowing that's where the doors are and what's on the other side. A deep bass growl comes from her throat.

'Here,' Dave holds my axe out, knowing full well what we're about to do. I nod back at him as Clarence picks his up. Dave draws his knives and starts rolling his shoulders. The lads ditch their rifles and heft their axes. Lani pulls her meat cleaver. Not a word spoken.

'Can you drive?' I look at Lillian. She nods, then stares at us all.

'What are you doing?'

'We'll clear the road. Get behind the wheel.'

'What?' She stares at us in shock. 'They'll tear you to pieces.'

'The dog is immune to the infection. She has to survive. Stay in here with Joe. As soon as you see the road is clear, you drive and don't stop for anything.'

'You can't do this,' she shakes her head. 'You can't ...'

'What else we gonna do?' Nick asks with a smile. 'Stay in here and wait for help?'

'Have you called the police?' Cookey asks.

'Yeah, they're sending a patrol car to check it out,' Nick replies with a grin.

'That's good, then,' Cookey grins back. 'Or we could call the AA. Hi there … We seem to be blocked in by a giant horde of zombies. I don't know if you can send anyone but …'

We all chuckle, apart from Lillian and Joe who just stare at us like they've seen a ghost.

'Right then, out the back doors, clear some space. Joe will close the doors behind us, and Lillian will be ready to drive out of here … Any questions?'

Nick lights a smoke and inhales quickly. Dave glares at him then shrugs. The others get quick gulps of water and warm, flat Lucozade. Nick passes the smoke over to me. Cookey lights one and shares it with Blowers. Dave coughs pointedly.

'I'm going first,' I say as I blow a plume of smoke out.

'It's my turn,' Dave replies.

'I said it first.'

'But it's my turn.'

'You two always go first. Give someone else a chance,' Lani states.

'I'll go,' Cookey offers.

'Nope …' I shake my head as I pass the smoke back to Nick.

'I'm the biggest. I should go,' Clarence growls.

'I'm the smallest …' Dave points out.

'I'm the only girl, so I should go,' Lani joins in.

'Nope,' I shake my head again.

'Want the last bit?' Nick holds the smoke out. I nod and take it, savouring the harsh bite.

'But ... where ...? I don't ...' Lillian looks terrified.

'Just drive out of here, okay? Head for a big housing estate down that way,' I point to the side of the Saxon. 'Er, towards Portsmouth ... Find a lad called Maddox and tell him what happened.'

She nods but looks scared to death.

'Get ready, then,' I say softly and nod at her. She hesitates, then moves off, climbing awkwardly over the seat. 'It's just like a car, but much bigger ... As soon as you see the road clearing, you go. Got it?'

She looks up at me over her shoulder and nods again.

'Lani, I don't suppose I could persuade you to stay?'

'Don't even ask,' she snaps with a glare.

'Didn't think so.' I move to the back and stand in front of the doors. Dave pushes into my side and budges me over so we're stood shoulder to shoulder.

'How the fuck we gonna open the doors? They'll be pressed against them ...' Cookey suddenly asks.

Dave and I both turn round and shuffle away as Clarence steps forward and stands front centre.

'Knew I'd go first,' he mutters.

'Only cos you're the biggest,' I mutter back.

We pause for a second until he turns his head and looks at me. 'Well? Say it then!'

'Eh? Oh, sorry ...' I clear my throat. 'Ready, lads?' A chorus of replies. Clarence smiles and looks back to the doors.

'Ready, Dave?' my voice comes out low and hoarse as the adrenalin starts to flood my system.

'Yes, Mr Howie.'

CHAPTER THIRTY-EIGHT

'Marcy, I can't keep up. This ... this is too much ... We're safe and away. Why are we still running,' Reginald gasps for breath, his face flushed and gleaming from the sweat pouring down.

Marcy looks back at Reginald and Mildred, both of them trying earnestly to keep up but clearly struggling.

'Sorry,' she mutters and starts running faster. April picks her pace up, easily staying beside Marcy. The two young women stride well ahead of the other two.

'What ... what's going on? This is too much, really too much. We come all the way over here and get abused by Mr Howie, and then the next thing we're running ... and in this heat! I say this is all too much.'

'Reggie, my dear,' Mildred says, relieved at being able to slow down but feeling a state of happiness at being able to run for the first time in years, 'you do moan rather a lot.'

Marcy and April open their stride, legs working furiously. They ignore the heat and glaring sun, powering on back towards their horde.

CHAPTER THIRTY-NINE

She stands quivering with anticipation. Feeling stronger than ever from being with this pack. The energy between them is unlike anything she has ever known or felt before.

The leader, the man with the dark, curly hair exudes power. The small one is dangerously violent and has no fear, none whatsoever. Nothing. He is void.

She hears and smells them outside the den. Many of them. All around. The pack starts to gather at the doors and waits. She knows they will open the doors. She knows this pack wants to fight. She accepts this as fact and without hesitation. It is organic and natural. The pack fights, she fights. The pack fights together. Strength in unity. She will stand her ground and fight with them.

The little one is to remain here. That is clear. They fight to protect the little one.

She ceases to bark because the fight is imminent. There is no point telling them she is here now. She has already told them who she is. She told she has killed many and will kill them all. She told them to stay away from the little one, but they did not heed the warning. So now they die.

She knows she will fight because no one is holding her. No hands grip her collar or hold the thick skin on her neck. No one has told her to sit or stay.

She understands this means she is to fight with them. The woman is to stay here with the little one. She will protect him in here while the pack goes out to meet the enemy.

Soft, brown eyes fix on the doors. Soft, brown eyes pick out a route between the legs. Soft, brown eyes that have already decided who will be first out the doors.

The energy builds. An electrifying sensation that pumps through her heart. The pack bond is overwhelming.

The big one at the front makes noise to the pack leader. The pack leader makes noise. The big one shows teeth.

This is it. This is the time.

The big one explodes with incredible strength and bursts the doors open. The pack roars.

At the very first twitch of his leg, she is moving, snaking between the legs, barging through those that refuse to move. As daylight flooded the inside of the den, her front legs were already leaving the ground.

As the doors fly open to reveal the things, she is mid-flight, sailing past the big one and out into the open.

The things have their lips pulled back. They show their teeth.

You want to see teeth? She pulls her lips back. Look at mine! They're much bigger!

CHAPTER FORTY

Clarence gently releases the clasp and then explodes, booting the doors open. His enormous strength drives the things back, giving us just enough space to charge.

As the doors go, we give voice. All of us roaring with fury.

Then Meredith sails past my head. Launching herself past Clarence and straight into them. Too late now.

We charge. Clarence leaps with his axe held high. He aims straight for the hole created by Meredith. The strength of the dog is stunning. In the couple of seconds it takes for Dave and I to leap out, she's already killed two and going for the third.

Clarence goes full-Viking, swinging the double-headed axe round and round, creating space, driving them back and slaughtering anything unfortunate enough to be in the way.

Dave launches high, landing several ranks deep. His arms already spinning as he drops down. The rest of us, the mere mortals that we are, just plough in and start killing things.

We fight out, pushing them back from the doors. Axes

swinging and cutting, slicing the things apart. The bloodlust is high as pure rage drives us on. No thought given to who these things were. The thought that someone we know might step in front doesn't factor now. Just death. Kill and kill.

So we do. We kill. It's what we do.

And we're good at it.

'JOE, SHUT THE DOORS,' I scream back. I glance just enough to see Joe already pulling them closed. Not much bloody point now, seeing as no one thought to tie the bloody dog up.

Oh, well. We're here now. Might as well enjoy it. We set to work, destroying anything that comes near us. Lani's speed is amazing, becoming more like Dave with every fight. Clarence uses his strength to slaughter them. The lads use pure brutality. She and Dave, smaller builds and slight in frame, use fluid grace. Dancing, weaving, dropping, spinning. The blades flash and glitter to start with but quickly become bloodstained.

I fight, with my axe becoming an extension of my body. A part of me. The power builds as I go. My wild hacking and slashing become focussed and aimed. Heads split apart. Brains burst. Limbs are taken off. Where I need the axe to be, so it is. I've learnt not to think. Just to let it be.

Whereas before there was rage and fury driving me, now there is calm and a state of being. My mind clears, apart from one image. It should be my sister. It should be my family. It should be plenty of people. But it isn't.

Marcy fills my mind. Not Lani. Not anyone else. I don't fight it but let it come. I push on, the axe swinging gently in front of me. Every step I take finds me closer to the front. There is no opposition now. These things cannot hurt me.

'ON HOWIE,' I hear Clarence roar. I pause, holding

ground and wondering calmly what he means. I glance back at the swathe of broken bodies behind me. Something lunges from the side. The speed of the thing is so slow. I can see the freckles on his nose, the way his hair swishes to one side as he comes in. A dirty, brown stain on one front tooth. I remove his head and watch it tumble slowly to the ground.

The others fight towards me. I turn back to face forward and see several infected coming at me. I wait for them to come. Then I kill them.

'GO,' Dave bellows. I turn back and see we've formed our circle with me at the head. The dog bounds over and loops round us as I start off. Dave is at my side, and we fight forward. Nick lunges out and grabs the dog by her collar, dragging her into the middle. She goes with him but darts back out as soon as he lets go. Not one of them gets near her. She is too fast, too strong, too aggressive. She rips throats out, takes hands off. She leaps and drives them back with the power of her body.

Another roar, and they come in. Driven at us. The sudden press of bodies becomes stifling. My axe whips out and back, out and back. Dave darts forward, spins, and comes back. I lose the feeling and realise where I am and what we're doing. The aggression in them is awful, charging at us with the fresh energy they have.

We start to stagnate, getting bogged down and unable to make ground. Dave takes the lead and charges out. His arms spin as he takes throat after throat out. Bright sprays of blood arcing into the air. Bodies drop and fall as he generates space. We take advantage and fight into it. Axes, knives, and meat cleaver lashing out. The dog senses the direction we move and goes to the front. Holding place beside Dave, she becomes a furious wolf of the wild. Something from folklore as she destroys and destroys. Dave holds to one side, letting her keep hers. The two of them become one.

Animals that fight without fear. Animals that kill simply because they can. Between them, they take the infected apart. Knives and teeth killing time and again. Nothing can stand before them. Nothing can survive that deadly scourge.

The infected press into the sides, charging at us. We fight out, holding our formation and slowly working to the front of the vehicle. We cross the front wing and start moving across. Clarence simply reaches out and grabs the body pressing against the windscreen and throws it away.

Lillian and Joe stare out with mouths hanging open. I grin at them quickly and turn back to the job at hand.

'DAVE, TAKE THE REAR,' I shout as infected start launching themselves off the top of the vehicle into our circle. It gets messy for a few minutes until we gain control of our ground.

Blowers and Cookey holding the back and fighting up until Dave makes his way to them. He shouts for them to move and steps in as they slink away. The things die mid-air as Dave takes them down.

Meredith leaps high onto the front of the vehicle and spins round, her deadly teeth now at head height. She jumps up onto the roof and removes the ones already up there. Taking hold of them in her teeth, shaking and twisting, ragging them with ease. They fall off, squashing more of their own kind.

She comes back to the front and holds ground there, darting left and right at faces and hands. The sight of her is simply beautiful. Her silky, black coat shining in the sun. Her ability to be where she needs to be. Spinning, dropping, lunging, and backing up.

If Dave ever comes back as an animal, it'll be Meredith.

A yell snatches my head round. I turn to see Cookey screaming as Doctor James charges at him. The well-spoken and cultured young doctor now a fetid infected with bloodstains round his mouth and lips pulled back. Cookey wilts, hesitating. Blowers doesn't. He steps in and drives the blade of his axe deep into doctor's neck, almost severing the head. Cookey rallies and charges back in. The vehicle starts to roll forward slowly, but it's enough for the infected to see it.

The roar that goes up is deafening. They come in harder than I've ever known and pour to the front, clogging the road and preventing the vehicle from being able to pull away.

'FUCK. LOOK,' Nick points down the side. I glance down to see a huge black man with massive arms scooping an infected up and driving the body into the arch of the wheels. He grabs another and does it again. Sacrificing his own to prevent the wheels from turning. He keeps going with amazing speed. Slamming body after body down in front of the big rear wheels. The Saxon grinds to a halt. Unable to keep going as he clogs the wheels with bodies.

We're fucked. We can feel it. We can kill and kill, but they outnumber us so heavily that even Dave and Meredith will finally tire before they run out of cannon fodder.

It becomes a battle of survival. Buying time to breathe a few more gulps of air before the inevitable happens. Our circle retracts. We fight shoulder to shoulder as they press in. I need that feeling back. I need that thing that comes over me.

I try to clear my mind, but it won't come. Images of Sarah flood though my head. My parents. Stephen, Tom, Jamie ... all of them. Twisted remains of their gruesome bodies lying rotting in the sun. I see Blowers, Cookey, and

Nick the same, lying in a heap of ruined bodies. Clarence falling like a mighty oak. Lani being ripped limb from limb. I see Dave finally going down under a press of infected.

I had it just a couple of minutes ago. I had that feeling of calm. I need it now. How did I do it?

Marcy.

She dances in front of me, smiling and laughing. The long, black hair swaying in the sun. That feeling as her tongue touched my thumb. Her skin was so soft beneath my hand. Her neck so slender and warm. I could feel her breath on my face.

I hold that image close for it drives me. It fills me with calm. I don't know why, and right now, I don't care. I seize that feeling and let it wash over me.

I'm grinning at them. Smiling as they come. The axe has no weight in my hands. I slip out of the circle and head down the side. Nothing can stop me.

Marcy.

They wilt and drop. They fear me. They all fear me. I swing out faster and faster. Each kill is delivered swiftly for I have no wish to torture or cause them pain. Just to end them.

You were meant to be good.

We are the good, Marcy. We are the righteous. I reach the big rear wheel and hear Clarence behind me. Yelling at me to keep going as he starts pulling them out.

There's no point. They'll just do the other side. But then we only need one rear wheel to be free. I fight out and keep them back from Clarence. The others follow down and form a circle round him as he tugs the bodies free and throws them down.

No sooner than we clear the wheel, they once again attack the front, preventing the vehicle from moving by the sheer press of body weight. Lillian copies what I did and tries to reverse, but with only one rear wheel free, it isn't enough.

'TAKE THE FRONT,' Clarence shouts. I nod back at him as he stands at the rear wheel and fends the infected off.

We split forces as Dave and I fight back to the front. The feeling of calm is still there. It threatens to slip away, but then she comes back into my mind and keeps me focussed. Like nothing can hurt me.

I don't even see the infected now. Just a path in front of me that needs to be taken. My body and the axe become separate to my mind. This must be how Dave feels. Detached and safe. With a confidence that just terrifies them.

But despite how good we might be. Despite how confident we are. The several thousand survivors that we kept safe in the fort will prove to be our undoing. There's simply too many of them.

Dave and I slaughter them in droves, but for every one we fell, more press forward. A never-ending sea of infected faces lunging in with mouths wide open.

They get faster. We fight harder. Separating was another mistake, and we've no hope of clearing the front. The press of them is just too much. They come in harder still, and we do what we can just to stay alive. Back to back, we fight. Spinning round to keep all sides clear. As much as they fear me, they keep charging. Something driving them to untold levels of violence.

This is it. The day we got the fuel and saw a light at the end of the tunnel. But it's also the day we blew up a refinery, killing many people, lost the fort, and then made a monumental mistake as they used a basic pincer movement against us. We didn't even tie the fucking dog up.

It's lost. It's just now a matter of taking as many of them with us as we can. I cry out in horror as we spin round, at the sight of Lillian and Joe staring at me through the windscreen. Behind them stand two infected. The huge black man I saw pushing the bodies under the wheels and another man. He didn't lock the back doors. Joe didn't lock them. The infected simply opened the doors and climbed in.

I roar out a warning, but it's too late. Joe and Lillian scream in terror as strong hands reach round to grab them. Open mouths descend and bite down onto their heads. Blood pumps up, covering the infected and spraying onto the inside of the windscreen.

'DAVE, SEE THOSE MEN?' I roar as loud as I can, my voice cracking from the heat, the dust, the exertion, and from a raging thirst.

'YES.'

'KILL THEM. NO MATTER WHAT HAPPENS, YOU KILL THEM. GO.'

'I WON'T LEAVE YOU,' he bellows as his arms spin out.

'KILL THEM,' I scream. 'CLARENCE!'

'I HEAR YOU,' his deep voice booms out. He and the others out of sight somewhere down the side.

'TWO MEN IN THE SAXON. THEY TOOK JOE AND LILLIAN.'

'WE'RE BOGGED IN. CAN'T MOVE.'

I roar in frustration and lash out, left, right, left, right. It doesn't matter. We're done.

'BOSS!'

'WHAT?'

'I THINK THIS MIGHT BE IT ...'

'NO SHIT ...'

'IT'S BEEN AN HONOUR.'

'THE HONOUR IS MINE, FOR ALL OF YOU ... I'M SORRY.'

'DON'T BE ...'

'MR HOWIE,' Cookey screams.

'WHAT?'

'BLOWERS JUST TOUCHED ME.'

'BLOWERS, DON'T TOUCH COOKEY!'

'SORRY. BYE, BOSS.'

'BYE ,MATE ...' my voice cracks as I hear Clarence give a huge roar, and the lads roar with him. I wish I was with them. By their side so we could fall together.

'Dave.'

'Yes, Mr Howie.'

'There ain't much to say, mate.'

'No, Mr Howie.'

'If you survive this, make sure I don't come back.'

'I won't survive, Mr Howie, not without you.'

'Fight your way out ...'

Meredith appears, pushing through the legs. Hearing me shout, she must have fought her way to us. She's bleeding from several spots but joins us quickly. Still leaping and taking them down.

'Take the dog, Dave, take her and get out.'

'No.'

'Dave, take the fucking dog and get out. You can make it. You know you can.'

'No, and don't ask me again.'

'You're a stubborn bloody man, Dave.'

'I won't leave you, not ever, Mr Howie ...'

'Fine.'

'Fine.'

'Glad that's sorted, then.'

'Me too.'

'FIGHT, YOU MOTHERFUCKERS,' a voice almost as loud as Dave's but with a deep American accent booms from somewhere. The infected surge with a palpable change in energy.

'Dave, with me,' I gasp. He joins at my side as we fight our way back to the Saxon. We clear the ground and climb onto the bonnet and then onto the roof. A couple of quick steps, and I look down the side to see Clarence and the others still fighting out.

Dave runs to the side. 'INCOMING,' he yells and leaps from the roof, landing deep within the ranks of infected.

Fuck that. I'd break and ankle if I tried it. 'Move over,' I shout down. They glance up and budge so I can slide down the side.

I land heavily amongst them, almost tripping on a dead body.

'You're still alive, then?' Clarence yells, his voice as hoarse as mine.

'Only just.'

'FIGHT, YOU DUMB-ASS MOTHERFUCKERS. KILL THEM SONS OF BITCHES.'

'Who is that?' Blowers yells.

'Dunno, but I can guess,' I yell back. The American shouting again spurs them on. They attack and press in, but we stand our ground and fight. Swinging axes and cleaving them apart one by one.

'FIGHT, YOU FUCKERS,' the American screams, closer now. They press in even harder, driving us back against the side of the vehicle.

'FIGHT,' he bellows again. 'GET YOUR FUCKING BACKS INTO IT.'

'Dear god,' Cookey yelps as we struggle to fend them off. 'I wish he'd stop that.'

'Lillian and Joe?' Lani asks between ragged breaths.

'Gone,' I spit the words out with hardly enough breath to speak.

'HOWIE! WHICH ONE OF YOU MOTHER-FUCKERS IS HOWIE?' the American voice booms out.

I don't have the energy, the breath, or the time to say anything.

'COS I'M GONNA FUCK YOU UP …' the voice is close now, very close.

'QUIT,' he roars. The infected suddenly back away. An instant reaction that causes me to almost topple with the weight of the axe after I sent an almighty swing at an infected who stepped back. They stagger back, the hatred and hunger still evident in their eyes. He emerges from the dense horde as they slowly stagger back. Well over six foot in height, broad, and extremely muscular, with the biggest arms I've ever seen, bulging with thick veins protruding from the skin.

More of his kind are standing near him, gathered round like a pack of hyenas circling the alpha male. All of them look tough. Big men with scars, bruises, cuts, bloodied knuckles, and dark, intense looks. Tattoos show underneath the blood and grime. A whole variance of racial backgrounds–black, white, Asian, Indian, and all of them looking extremely capable. They must be the ones that took the fort. I would have seen them in there as they stand out by a mile.

Instant silence settles over the horde. We stand with our backs to the Saxon, chests heaving, gripping weapons that are slick with blood, hands and arms coated in gore and dripping onto the already blood-sodden ground.

For the first time since this fight began, I take a proper look at the infected and start to see faces I recognise. Men and women from the fort. People I had spoken to and passed the time of day with.

The big American looks over us, his evil, red eyes taking each of us in. He finally rests on me and slowly his mouth splits into a broad grin. He doesn't say a word but turns and nods. The infected behind him step away as some figures make their way forward. Stepping out of the line to stand behind the American and stare at him.

Sergeant Hopewell, Terri, and Sarah all stand there, looking at him. Staring with devotion. My stomach drops from the sight, and I hear low groans coming from the lads.

'I'll do it,' Dave says flatly. He takes a step forward and stands ready.

'Who the fuck are you, little man?' the American sneers.

'Dave.'

'So you're Dave,' he grins. 'You're a little fucker ... like a fucking midget. Which one of you is Clarence? I guess that'd be you,' he stares at Clarence who just stares back.

'How you like my bitches?' He motions his head to the three women stood behind him. 'I already fucked 'em ... Fucked 'em good too ...So did all my boys.'

'You fucking cunt,' I take a step forward.

'NO,' Dave cuts me off.

'You gonna kill your sister, tough guy?' He looks at me, taunting, goading. 'You gonna take your axe and cut your own sister down? That's fucked up, motherfucker. That's some cold shit right there ...' He nods to his men, grinning all the time. 'This ... I gotta see.'

The three women snap their heads round to look at me, staring with baleful expressions. Then they charge. My own sister, the only family I have left in the world charges at me, ready and willing to bite into my flesh and turn me. Terri and Debbie both burst with her. My heart misses a beat. I hear the lads scream out. Clarence bellowing from the side.

Dave moves in front of them. His left arm already spinning as he gently swipes the blade across Terri's throat, cutting her jugular open. By the time the skin peels back and the blood starts to cascade out, he has turned and thrust the knife in his right hand deep into Debbie's neck, twisting it first left and then right before yanking it free. He steps back as both bodies, still moving forward from their own momentum, tumble to the floor. Sarah powers on, relentless in her quest to get me.

Dave spins to stand behind her. He raises both knives out to the side and drives the points towards her neck. I clench my eyes shut and scream, others scream near me. I hear someone gasp in shock and then feel an impact at my feet.

As I open my eyes, I look down to see Sarah lying at my feet, her neck savaged by the two knife blades, blood pumping out from both arteries . Dave has already turned to face back at the crowd. One foot forward, the other one back. One arm forward, holding the knife across his chest, the other behind his back. Poised. Ready. Unflinching. Ruthless.

The whole thing was done within a second or two. Clarence stands looking in shock down at the woman at my feet. My sister.

Seven pairs of eyes settle on the big American stood there with a look of puzzlement on his face.

'HAVE IT,' I roar with everything I have, with every ounce of my being. We burst out. The seven of us taking the fight to them, and every one of us aiming for that big fucker.

Frenetic action explodes as they react with lightning speed. Infected surging forward to meet our charge. Dave slips and spins through them, but the infected charge at him with unrestrained savagery. Clarence hacks and slices in desperation to get at him. All of us find opponent after opponent blocking our path. The American laughs, a deep sound that is eerily similar to the way Clarence laughs, but that just sends our big man berserk. He becomes wild with fury. Pure rage etched onto his red, flushed face. He screams and roars as he swings the axe out.

The American moves towards Clarence, grabbing his own infected and launching them aside. He roars and swats them away. Both of them fighting a path to each other. When the route becomes clear, they stand with eyes locked. Clarence drops the axe as the American tenses his arms, clenching his fists to push the veins out even more. The two biggest men I have ever seen staring each other down. Goliaths of almost mythical size. The same height and width. The American is defined and ripped, with clear muscles that bulge. Clarence is just a solid slab of pure, unbridled rage.

'Randall,' an infected shouts and throws a knife out. The American catches it by the handle. Clarence reaches round to put his hand behind his back.

'You got a knife there, you motherfucker?' Randall growls.

'No,' Clarence shakes his head. 'I got a fucking gun.' He starts firing, aiming the shots into the centre mass as he strides forward. The American takes the hits and charges. Clarence ditches the pistol at the last second and side steps, slamming a huge fist into the side of his head.

Randall roars out but keeps his feet. He spins and lashes a straight punch at Clarence. It connects and drives him back. Clarence takes the punch and pauses as the American comes in swinging. Clarence blocks the blows and goes in close, slamming his forehead into Randall's nose. He follows it up with a left hook, then a right, then more blows. One hand after the other, and each one more powerful than the last. Randall reels back, unable to focus or do anything from the reign of blows being smashed into him.

'CLARENCE. YOUR HANDS,' Dave roars. Clarence pauses mid-swing and looks at the bleeding face of Randall and then at his clenched fists. The pause is enough for Randall to charge with the knife stretched out.

Dave lunges in and brings his own knife down in a mighty swing, cutting through Randall's outstretched arm. Severing the hand from the wrist. Clarence staggers away from the blood pumping furiously out of the stump. Randall howls and stares at his ruined arm as Meredith launches up to grip his other arm between her teeth. She heaves backwards, shaking her massive head as her teeth ravage through his flesh. The American stays on his feet, jerking left and right to free his arm from the dog. I take a step back, creating just enough space to draw my pistol. I start firing into Randall's back. The others do the same, drawing their handguns and firing into him.

He stays on his feet, getting jolted and slammed by the bullets. God knows how he does it, but he does. Staggering and howling as the rounds whip through his body. Pistols click empty, and he still stays up, roaring with desperation as he kicks out at the dog. She sidesteps and pulls him towards her, refusing to let go. The lads dart in with axes, hacking at his legs and body. Lani slicing her meat cleaver deep into thigh. I run in, drawing my axe back and swinging it round with all my strength, driving the blade deep into his back. Still he roars defiantly as Meredith tugs and shakes her head. Clarence swoops for his axe, bringing it up and out in one fluid movement. He swings it out with a ferocious yell and powers the blade into Randall's neck. It goes through with ease, taking the head off in one brutal swipe.

As the head falls, the body stays upright for a second, then topples, and slumps to the ground. Meredith finally releases the arm and goes for the now detached head. Sinking her teeth into the face as she lifts it easily from the ground. The infected scream and charge in, and suddenly, we're back, pressed against the side of the Saxon and slashing out. I'd hoped that the loss of their leader would take the fight out of them. The opposite happens. They charge in with everything they've got. The whole of them pressing against us, and we have nowhere to go.

A dull roar fills the air. A different sound that comes from a distance. It grows louder as we slash and hack.

The roar gets closer, a thundering noise that vibrates through the ground. Then an almighty screech, and something impacts the infected from the far side. The power of the impact drives them off to the side. The whole crowd getting pushed away. Confusion erupts, and we take full advantage of it. As they go past, we lash out. They rally and fight back. The roaring screech comes again, and I feel the crowd ripple as pressure is applied from the outer edges.

A glimpse through their ranks, and I see the lines at the back are facing out, fighting at something else. We get swept along, physically moved by the pressure. The fighting becomes close and brutal, with short, hacking lunges. I scream out and start wrenching my axe from left to right, powering it back and forth. Slowly, body by body, I gain space and find I'm alone. Swept into their midst by the pressure of the wave of whatever hit them.

Separated. we fight alone. The screech comes on again,

louder and determined. The infected push into me but are facing the other way. I slash back and forth, cutting them down and striking into their backs.

More infected pour through the ranks at me, facing me as they charge and shove their way through. I can't understand what's going on. Most are facing out, but then others are charging in. Something grabs me from behind and pulls me down. The infected charging through launch into my body and drive me to the floor. Hands grab at me. I lose the axe and start punching, kicking, slamming my forehead into them. They smother me, and I scream in pure desperation as I wait for the bites to start. I can't move. I can hardly breathe from the pressure of the bodies on me. The sound of the battle becomes dull and far away. I try to scream, but the weight on my chest prevents me from drawing air.

I clench my eyes and wait, knowing this is it and giving thanks that at least we took that nasty fucker down. I pray to the lord to let my team go without pain. I pray to take them into heaven. I pray for Sarah's soul.

I start to suffocate, unable to draw breath. They could be biting me all over my body, and I wouldn't know. My senses are dulling as my body starts to shut down from the lack of oxygen. Blackness creeping in. I fight back, pushing it away, but it just comes on stronger.

Movement. Voices. Something moves on me. My arm comes free, and I try to punch out, but there's nothing left to fight with. The pressure on my chest shifts, and I draw a gulp of air, then another. My head becomes dizzy from the oxygen flooding into my system. My vision blurs, but I feel strength returning. I will energy into my free arm and start punching at the thing on top of me. Driving my fist again and again into the warm body. It shifts again, and I buck, thrusting my hips up and twisting to the side.

'MOVE,' a female voice shouts. It must be Lani. 'GET OFF HIM,' she shouts again, and the pressure on my body is gone. I scrabble backwards, trying to get to my feet, but my head feels woozy. I fall back down and feel hands grabbing to lift me up. An infected face swims in front of my eyes. I punch it hard on the side of the head. It lets go, and I stagger round. More infected in front of me, so I punch out at them and reach for my pistol, but it's gone, dropped somewhere.

'HOWIE, STOP,' she yells, but I can't see her, just infected everywhere. I keep attacking them, fighting to break free of the tight circle they've formed round me.

Arms grab me from behind. I wrestle to break free, but she whispers close to my ear, 'Stop … It's over … It's done …' Her breath is on my ear, 'Howie, stop … It's over …' She holds me closer, wrapping her arms round my chest. I reel at the words but feel myself sinking into her embrace. My legs give out. She goes to the floor with me, still holding me from behind. 'It's over, Howie … It's over.'

Tears sting my eyes and pour down my face. My hands reach up and grab at the arms holding me. I hold them tight while I gasp for air. 'Breathe, Howie, just breathe … You're safe now.'

The words slide into my mind, comforting, soft as the air she exhales. The warmth of her body makes me sink into her. My vision clears enough for me to see the infected stood round, watching. I struggle to break free, ready to fight them off and protect Lani.

She grips me harder and holds me down. 'It's okay. They aren't going to hurt you, Howie … It's over …'

She says it, so it must be true. She wouldn't lie to me, but why aren't they attacking me? I'm turned. I must be turned. I'm one of them, but I'm still me, and I hurt everywhere. Something has gone wrong. I'm turned but not fully. I have to kill myself, end it before I turn fully.

'Kill me ... don't let me turn ...'

'You're alive, Howie ... Your alive and safe. You haven't been bitten.'

'I ... I don't ...' She holds me closer, and I feel her lips against my ear, soft and warm. I reach a hand up and feel her head and the long, soft hair that hangs down. I caress the back of her neck, feeling the warmth and security she gives me. The contact of a woman. The soothing touch and caress that only a woman can offer.

My other hand rubs along her arms, finding her hand. She splays her fingers and lets mine entwine so we're together. Connected. Minutes go by as my heart rate slows and my senses start to return.

I look down at her slender arms, at the tanned skin. I feel the pressure in my back of her breasts pushing against me. Breasts of a full-figured woman, not of a lithe, slim woman.

'Marcy,' I whisper.

'Yes,' she whispers into my ear. I look up at the infected gathered round us, and I realise. These are her infected. Her horde.

She saved us. It was her horde that attacked and drove the others back. That's why they're not attacking me now.

'Now do you believe me?' she whispers. I nod but don't say anything. Her fingers squeeze mine, and she kisses my ear. A soft, fleeting sensation that is gone as quick as it was there.

'Get up,' she helps me to my feet. Our hands slip apart, and I step away to turn slowly and look at her. She stares back and holds her head up high.

'GET THESE FUCKING THINGS OFF ME,'

Clarence's muffled voice booms out. I spin round but see I'm stuck in the middle of a small circle.

They break away, melting back to let me slip through. I see a huge mound of bodies, all of them heavy built men and women, with Clarence's feet poking out the end, wriggling as he yells.

Marcy nods at them, and they start to climb off. He thrashes and bucks the same as I did as the pressure leaves and then throws the last body off his stomach.

He sits up and looks first at me, then at Marcy. He makes the connection far quicker than I did.

'Oh,' he says simply, 'right ... They saved us then.'

'Yeah.'

'Where are the others?'

'I don't know.' The infected peel away, leaving a distinct view of infected bodies piled in heaps, each one of them pressing the lads down. Only Dave stands upright, still holding his knives and staring suspiciously at the massive pile of infected bodies surrounding him.

'Mr Howie,' he nods at seeing me, not a flicker of surprise on his face.

'They didn't get you down, then?'

'No,' he shakes his head, 'they tried.'

'Leave them,' Marcy calls out. I turn to see the piles of bodies disentangling themselves. Slowly sliding off to reveal the bloodstained cargo trouser clad legs of the lads. Nick and Blowers are the first to be released. They both sit up and stare around. Seeing Clarence, Dave, and me stood with Marcy.

'What the fuck?' Blowers asks, shaking his head.

'She saved us,' Clarence says.

'Eh? Your zombies killed the other zombies?' Nicks asks. 'That's fucked up ...'

'Where's Cookey?' Blowers looks round with alarm on his face.

'I'm here,' a muffled voice calls out, 'and I'm staying here.'

'Cookey, get up,' I call out.

'No, Mr Howie. There is a big pair of boobs pressing into my face. I'm in heaven. Just leave me here …'

'Get off him,' Marcy calls.

'No, don't get off him …' Cookey yells from under the bodies. 'I heard what you said. These zombies fucked up the other zombies, so we won … So let me stay here.'

'April,' Marcy calls out.

'I'm here,' she replies from the tangle of bodies.

'Is it April with her boobs in his face?' Nick asks. 'You jammy bastard, Cookey. I had some blokes arse in mine.'

'Blowers will get jealous. Is it really April on top of me?'

'Yes,' April replies.

'Fuck! This is the best day ever! Please, please let me stay here … I'll make the brews for a month …'

'Cookey, I fucking hate you,' Nick shouts with a shake of his head. 'Is she like wearing a top?'

'Yeah, but the boobs are coming out a bit. Like the actual boob is touching me. No nipple yet, though. Is Marcy there?'

'Yeah, right here,' Blowers replies as he massages his neck.

'Marcy?' Cookey calls. She looks somewhat startled at being addressed directly and from someone buried under a mound of bodies.

'Yes?' she replies.

'Would I catch zombie if I licked her boob?'

'Get him out!' I yelp while darting forward. Clarence

and the lads rush towards the pile as Marcy yells for them to get off him.

'No ... No, piss off. I won't actually lick it. I was just asking ... Piss off and leave me here. Oh, for fuck's sake,' he groans as we push and shove the bodies away, who do their best to untangle themselves from him.

'Can I help you up?' Nick smiles as he extends a hand to help April to her feet. She smiles as Blowers rushes in to help too, taking hold of her other arm.

'I was bloody enjoying that,' Cookey grumbles as he sits up with a flushed and glistening face, then gives an enormous and unashamed grin. 'I'm in love,' he flops back down with a groan.

'Are you okay?' Blowers asks with concern.

'Fine, mate,' Cookey sighs.

'I wasn't asking you fuckwit ...'

Cookey glances up sharply to see him staring at April, with Nick on the other side still holding her hand. 'Oi,' he yelps, scrambling to his feet, 'get your filthy paws off her.'

I cast round at the bodies, just a sea of infected stacked deep all around us. Body parts, heads, limbs, and gore everywhere. The axes lying amongst the bodies. Pistols left dropped on the ground. The side of the Saxon is coated in a thick, gunky layer of blood and filth.

More infected stand back in a wide circle around us. I half wish I could have seen them fighting each other. Infected against infected. How did she do it? How could they tell each other apart?

My head still feels weird with a throbbing pain building in my temples. I feel weak and drained, like I'm drunk. Bodies are everywhere. Detached heads staring with open eyes to the sky. Tongues poking out. I glance across at

Marcy, then at Blowers and Nick stood next to April. This is fucked up, completely fucked up.

'Where's Lani?' My senses flood back for a second as I realise she's not with us. 'Lani?' I shout. The lads break from April and cast about, looking for her.

'Lani?' I call again. We start running to the side of the Saxon where the bodies are lying thick on the ground. Our bloodied hands grasp the corpses, pulling them aside, pushing them over. Clarence simply throws them away.

My hands slip into cleaved skulls. Grey matter sticks to my fingers. The lads get more bloodied as they search through the cadavers.

'Lani?' we all shout, calling her name.

'Didn't your lot get her?' Clarence shouts to Marcy.

'I don't think so,' she replies.

'Don't think so? How can you not know?' I yell with frustration.

'It doesn't work like that. I told you ... I can't see her either.'

'HERE!' Cookey shouts. He pushes his hands down into a pile of corpses and starts wrenching them away. The goofy clown gone as he works with serious intent. We scrabble towards him, slipping and tripping on the bodies.

'Lani,' Cookey shouts. 'Hey, Lani!' He pulls a body up with a heave and dumps it to the side before dropping down and reaching into the pile.

Clarence gets there next, kneeling on the corpses to help pull her lifeless body out. We all dive in, knees and feet sinking into the fetid corpses. Many hands grasp and lift her clear of the mess, carrying her as gently as we can. Each of us giving small instructions and telling the others to be careful.

'Wound in the stomach,' Dave says dully.

'See it,' Clarence replies. He carefully pulls the blood-soaked material of her top away from her body. He takes the knife handed to him by Dave and cuts the material to reveal a deep wound in her abdomen.

'The cleaver,' Dave remarks on peering down. 'Straight cut made with a sharp blade, bigger than a knife ...'

'Her hand must have been trapped when the crush started,' Clarence shakes his head. 'Big blade like that and all that pressure.'

I press my fingers into her neck and pause. 'She's got a pulse ... very faint, but it's there.'

'Check her eyes,' Dave says. I gently pull one eyelid back. Her eyes are normal and white.

'The infected blood could have got into the wound,' Dave adds.

'She hasn't turned, though,' I say hopefully.

'Mr Howie,' Dave says, and from his tone, I can tell what he's about to say, 'too much blood loss, Mr Howie. She won't make it.'

'She might,' I croak back at him.

'No,' he replies, 'not from a wound like that ... I'm sorry.'

I brush the blood and sweat-soaked hair away from her face. She looks like she's asleep. Just resting, taking a nap before she gets up and makes coffee. I feel numb. Too numb to cry. Too numb to feel anything. Sarah, now Lani. My mind can't take it and simply refuses to acknowledge what's happening.

Her hand lies across her chest. The same hand I held while we slept. Numb. Blackness. Nothing.

'Go,' Dave says softly after a minute of silence.

'She's still alive,' Nick whispers.

'Nick, she's lost too much blood. The wound, it's too deep, mate. She'd need a blood transfusion, surgery, and anaesthetic to survive ...' Clarence's deep voice explains slowly.

'We can try,' Marcy says from somewhere behind me.

'You're not turning her,' I snap.

'She might pull through. She won't be in pain, and she won't suffer ...'

'Will she be like you?' Cookey asks with wide eyes.

'Like me? You mean her character and intelligence?' She shakes her head. 'I don't know ... I can try but ...'

'Try how?' Blowers asks.

'It's ... I don't know. Very few of us can talk and think but ...'

'But what?' I prompt her, the faint glimmer of hope shining through the darkness.

Her eyes fix on mine with a searching look, those red eyes staring deep into my soul. 'I can try,' she says finally, breaking the eye contact.

'Try how?' my voice comes out with a hard edge.

'I can will her to be as she ... as she was, but she won't be exactly the same, Howie ...'

'But if she speaks and thinks, she will be,' Cookey says.

'She'll be devoted to Marcy, not Mr Howie,' Reginald cuts in. 'She will feel utterly devoted like we all do. She may retain full intelligence, but she will not feel any loyalty to you.'

'Eh? But you just risked your life to save us?' Nick asks with a confused look. 'If you're only devoted to yourselves, then why do that?'

'I'm not them,' Marcy replies softly. 'I am the alpha. That seems to be how it works. You keep what you turn.'

'Smithy didn't turn all those cunts,' Blowers spits. 'He had fucking thousands of 'em.'

Marcy shrugs. 'It changes, evolves ... Like it's constantly trying new things ...'

'What would Lani want?' Cookey asks, staring down at her. 'If she had the choice, what would she do?'

'She'd say no,' I sigh. 'We all would, wouldn't we?' The question hangs in the air. We look at each other, realising that maybe the decision wouldn't be that clear cut.

'We've still got Meredith, haven't we?' I glance round, looking for the dog.

'The dog is shut in the cab of the tanker. She was killing my people too well.'

'Boss?' Clarence looks at me. They all look at me. Waiting for me to decide the fate of yet another life.

'Dave?'

'Yes, Mr Howie?'

'What would you do if it was me, if there was a chance I would come back the same as I was?'

'Marcy said you wouldn't be the same. Lani wouldn't be the same.'

'So what would you do? In this exact situation right now, me lying there ...'

'I'd ...' he hesitates, seemingly lost for words, thinking hard. 'I'd ...'

'He'd bring you back,' Clarence cuts in, 'then kill you if you weren't the same.' He's right. Dave's devotion to me is the same as they are to Marcy. But if I wasn't exactly the same, he'd kill me.

'But then we'd all do the same if it was you,' he adds.

'Then the decision is made,' I reply and look at Marcy. 'Do it.'

She stares back at me like she wants to say something, a searching look that's made all the harder to read with her red eyes. Instead, she comes forward, brushing past me. The scent of her fills my nose. The closeness of her makes me tingle inside. Something electrifying and dangerous. My sister and Lani have just been killed, but all I can think about is Marcy.

She drops down and leans over the wound on Lani's stomach. With one hand holding her hair out of the way, she gets in close. I don't see what she does as her head blocks my view, but she lifts up less than a minute later. 'Done,' she says and gets to her feet.

She walks back past me, her eyes holding on mine as she goes. Her fingers brush against mine, a fleeting touch that makes my heart race, but I glare hard at her and turn away.

We watch in silence, staring at Lani closely. Seconds go by, then a full minute. Nothing happens. Clarence presses his fingers into Lani's neck and concentrates, jerking back when the first jolt passes through her. We've all seen it before, but it's still mesmerising. Lani convulses and twitches, her body spasms, limbs flick out; then, she settles. We all stare at her eyes, waiting for it. When they open, I feel a sudden sense of regret at what we've just done. Like it's unholy or dirty. The red eyes stare out unfocussed. She blinks and sits up. Turning her head to look straight at Marcy.

'Lani?' Cookey speaks first, desperate to know if she's the same. Lani keeps her gaze fixed on Marcy, ignoring the lad.

'Lani,' Clarence's deep voice this time, her name spoken firmly. Still no response. Lani has the look of the massed infected. Expressionless and empty.

'I'm sorry,' Marcy says softly. 'It doesn't work every time.' I look round to see Reginald staring at Marcy with a puzzled expression. He sees me watching and quickly looks away. I spin round and see Marcy moving away.

'Where are you going?' I call after her.

'We need to clear this mess up,' she replies coldly.

'That's it? You just walk off and start cleaning up?'

'What?' She turns to stare at me with a cold expression. She takes a breath and softens her tone, 'It's done. You got the fort back. You need to wash and rest. We can take care of this.'

'But ...' I go after her.

'You need to rest, and those clothes will have infected blood on them,' she adds, turning away.

Lani moves off, not glancing at any one of us. She walks straight past me like I don't exist. Following behind Marcy. I reach out and grab her arm, pulling her round to face me.

'Lani, it's me ...' She stares back at me and just stands there, not a flicker of recognition passes through her eyes. Nothing. I let her arm go, and she walks off.

'Your vehicle is covered in infected blood,' Marcy calls out from the back of the Saxon. 'Walk back to the fort. We'll get it cleaned and bring it to you ...' she speaks softly and goes still. The infected all around us start moving in. They grab at the bodies and start pulling them onto the grass of the flatlands.

Dave walks to the back of the Saxon and climbs in. Blowers goes with him, taking the assault rifles and kit bags before handing them round. We check magazines and make ready before moving out to pick our fallen axes up.

'We'll bring everything to you,' Marcy says, watching us, almost a command.

The lads look to me, waiting to see what I do. I take my axe and start walking, the assault rifle and kit bag strapped to my back. They grab theirs and fall in next to me.

Within a few minutes, we're away from the death and walking on clean ground, staring at the empty fort ahead of us. The death and destruction at our backs. None of us speak. Nothing to be said.

A loud bark stops us in our tracks. We turn to see an infected staggering back from the door of the tanker cab as Meredith bursts out. She savages the thing, ripping its throat out before dumping the body and looking round.

Dave whistles. Her head snaps round, and she starts running. Ears flat against her head, low and sleek. She bounds up to us, tail wagging as she snakes through and round our legs.

We carry on walking, with Meredith running ahead to sniff the ground. After a few minutes, Nick speaks up, breaking the silence, 'Mr Howie, we shouldn't take anyone else into our team.'

'Okay,' I reply. The others nod. The six of us have survived everything that's been thrown at us, and even now, we walk away again with hardly a mark on us. The dog, cut and bitten, still bounds on full of energy. She's survived too.

She's one of us.

CHAPTER FORTY-ONE

'How do you feel?'

'I feel fine.'

'Any pain?'

'No.'

'Do not do anything until the wound has healed.'

'I understand.'

'And remember what I said.'

'I will.'

'What did I say?'

'You said I am not to speak to anyone other than you and only when we are alone.'

'Good Do you have a problem with that?' Marcy stares into her eyes.

'No,' Lani replies, staring back.

'Do you feel any connection to Howie? Any feelings at all?'

'No, Marcy.'

'You can say if you do, be honest and tell me the truth,' Marcy wills her to be truthful, directing the conscious thought at Lani.

'I don't,' Lani replies.

'Good,' Marcy repeats with a satisfied nod. 'Stay close to Reggie.'

He sighs deeply and rolls his eyes. 'It's Reginald,' he says again, 'and why can't she talk to me?'

'Because I do not want them knowing she can speak.'

'Why ever not?' Reginald asks, pushing his glasses up his nose. 'Surely it will make no difference to them.'

'They've been through enough. Knowing Lani can speak will only upset them further.'

'You mean Mr Howie.'

She pauses, mouth opening to speak, to deny the innocently asked question. 'Yes,' she admits, 'and also the rest of them.'

'Why did you kiss Mr Howie?' Reginald asks still with the same innocently probing tone. Marcy glances sharply at Lani, searching for any reaction. None shows, so she shrugs and looks back to Reginald.

'Comfort,' she offers after another pause.

'Comfort?' Reginald nods. 'And may I ask why you brushed your hand against his when you walked past him?'

'You don't miss a trick, do you, Reggie?'

'Forgive me, Marcy,' Reginald says in response to the edge in her voice. 'I did not mean–'

'No, you're right,' Marcy cuts him off. 'I told you to speak freely, and you are. I ... I don't know why I did that ... He has something ... I don't know.' She looks about, trying to give words to her thoughts but failing, not a conscious act, not a planned intentional *thing*. A feeling, a deep feeling that makes her tingle and feel weird.

'I see,' Reginald says slowly. 'Giving consideration to your allowance of me to speak freely, then I must vehemently advise against any course of similar conduct. No good can come of such ... well, of such a liaison. Indeed, in my capacity as observer and taking into account my extremely limited, well, rather non-existent experience of matters of a romantic inclination, I observed the manner in which he looked at you, which gives me great concern for any suggestion that he reciprocates ...'

'What?' Marcy shakes her head. 'I got about half of that. Did you say he was looking at me?' she demands.

'Oh, dear me,' Reginald shakes his head. 'Marcy, you're not a thirteen-year-old girl with a crush. You have great responsibility ...'

'When was he looking at me?'

'Marcy, I never said he was looking at you in terms of a permanent fixation of his eyes. Merely that yes, he did look at you, and that there appeared to be a somewhat perplexing look about him when he did so. Be that as it may, I do not know Mr Howie, so I am unable to ascertain if that is his normal countenance, and I rather regret mentioning it now.'

'Reggie ...'

'And as for those testosterone-fuelled boys of his gooning over young April,' Reginald carries on with a stern look at April, 'I think that is something that should be strongly discouraged.'

'They are just lads,' April replies. 'They mean no harm.' Marcy and Reginald both stare hard at the young woman.

'April, it would appear that you are developing an individual character. Are you aware of this?' Reginald asks.

'I am not aware of it,' April replies.

'Did you hear that?' Reginald turns to Marcy.

'I did. She gave a longer answer than just saying *no*.'

Marcy considers the implication and switches her gaze to Lani. If April develops and evolves, then what is to stop Lani doing the same or any of the others?

'Have I displeased you?' April asks.

'No, April. I encourage you to think freely. Now, please … we have much to do.'

CHAPTER FORTY-TWO

'Switch on and keep your eyes open,' Dave instructs as we get to the big outer double gates, forced open when the fort occupants stormed out. We pause and move left and right to gain a view down the sides.

Entering through, I see one of the medical tents has been trampled down from the mass exodus. The others, set further back, appear fine. We hold in the middle while Dave checks one side and Clarence the other. Both return, reporting all appears the same as before.

We already have a view of the interior, just the first few metres beyond the internal gates. We pass through, Meredith running ahead and being watched closely by all of us in case she shows any reaction.

She doesn't but just runs back and forth, sniffing the ground. Silence greets us. An absolute silence of an empty and lifeless place. Not a soul inside. No noise, not even the rattle or sway of tents as the air is as listless as we feel. Just hot and stagnant, without the slightest of a breeze.

We venture deeper in, staring round, with our rifles raised and ready. A small circle of us moving quietly, each of us sweeping our eyes over what was a teeming city full of life just a few hours ago. Now empty and void.

The tent city looks demolished. So many of them trampled and pulled over during the explosion of violence. Blood and gore everywhere.

We pass by the remains of Chris. His form recognisable from the thick, black beard. A knife stuck in his throat still gripped by his hand. Clarence stares hard, as though seeking solace from the evident fact that Chris took himself rather than got turned. Another big man with a long, grey biker beard lies nearby. His bloodshot, dead eyes staring up at the sky.

'Look at that,' Clarence smiles and nods towards the slope. We all turn round to see a trail of bodies running from the base of the slope to just inside the gates. Then a great many more surrounding Chris. 'The tough fucker took a few with him,' Clarence says.

'He did loads,' I add, 'and that big bastard too by the looks of it.'

'I bet it was him that gave that big yank our names. Probably at the same time as he told him to fuck off, poor bastard ...' He shakes his huge head sadly and sighs. 'Good on ya, Chris. You went out fighting.'

He kneels down and feels for Chris's neck, pulling a thick metal chain out with two old-style dog tags on the end. 'He always insisted on wearing these old things, like he was Vietnam vet or something.' Clarence yanks the chain and stands back, putting them into his pocket before turning round and nodding at me.

'You alright?' I ask him.

'Not really,' he shrugs, 'but what can we do? Fuck all ... Best get on with it.'

'I liked Chris,' Dave adds to our surprise. 'He was a very

good soldier, professional and competent.' Bloody hell. That's about the best compliment you'd ever get from Dave. I smile, imagining Chris stood watching us with a huge grin, his white teeth showing through his beard and calling us all soppy fuckers.

We move on, sticking to the right side and moving down the fort. Checking rooms and seeing more signs of the violence everywhere. The police offices are a mess. The door kicked in and stuff strewn everywhere. Big pools of blood cover the floor.

The stores look normal and untouched. The armoury the same. We move down to our rooms and find them also untouched. We don't linger but press on, moving down the wall to check the outer sides and the many rooms and recesses.

Trepidation steals over me as we enter the hospital section. We view the empty beds all in a row and work our way through to the rooms where the hospital equipment was left. All of it still covered in plastic sheets and, as with everything else, untouched.

We file back outside, no talking amongst us. Just a heavy weight pressing down on our shoulders. Feet feeling heavy and tired. Legs moving slowly. Arms like lead.

'Here,' Dave holds a case of water bottles in his hand brought out from the hospital. He drops it down and rips the plastic outer casing back before throwing the bottles up at us.

Nick walks slowly to the side wall and pulls the end of a hose free. He twists the tap and drags it back. Kneeling on the ground, he holds the end up, the water trickling out softly to pool on the sun-baked earth.

Meredith goes straight to him and starts licking at the water. 'Hang on,' Cookey mutters. He walks back into the hospital and comes back out carrying a stainless steel bed pan.

Nick adjusts the flow of water, filling the pan. Cookey puts it down, and we stand back, watching Meredith drink as quickly as possible. Her tongue darting in and out as she takes the cool liquid in.

The seven of us drink water in silence. Seven parched and dried mouths gulping the life-giving liquid into our systems. Seven minds thinking only of the water and the thirst we had. Seven throats that suddenly feel less sore. Meredith drinks and drinks, her feet planted apart. The end of the hose pouring water into the bowl, refilling it as she goes.

We cast bottles aside and grab more. Nick takes out a pack of smokes and hands them round. We light them up, coughing from the first pull. Still nothing is said. Nothing needs to be said.

None of us want to move into the tents and clear them. The area is big, and it's hot. Hotter than anything I've ever known, and we're exhausted. Completely drained both physically and mentally. Just numb. Filled with a dark emptiness of thoughts. How did we survive again? How are we still walking untouched?

Nick pulls the hose out from the bed pan and directs the steady flow onto Meredith's back. She doesn't flinch but carries on drinking. The water runs pink from her coat, red, bloodied water dripping down.

'Turn it up,' he asks Cookey. The lad nods and walks over to the tap, gently turning the tap until Nick nods. With a firmer spray, he moves the hose up and down her body, sluicing the blood and gore from her.

She licks the bowl dry and looks up at him. A clear request for more water. He fills the bowl to the top and carries on. She simply drops her head and goes back to drinking.

I step in and look at her sides. Just a few bite marks that have already stopped bleeding. The other wounds look okay, and I realise her dressing has come off, revealing the shaved areas of her coat where the wounds must have been inspected by Amy and Doctor Roberts.

'Did anyone see Doc Roberts?' I ask as I think of him.

'Yes,' Dave replies. I nod, knowing what he means by the simple answer. Meredith then decides that we all need a wash too and shakes her coat, a sudden violent action that soaks us quicker than we can jump away.

Nick just stands there with his eyes closed, getting the full brunt of the water. The cigarette hanging from his mouth gets drenched, goes out, and starts to bend in the middle, going limp.

Cookey chuckles at the sight and wipes the dog water from his face. Blowers smiles as he ditches his smoke and goes for another one. Even Clarence gives a small smile, but with two very sad eyes staring out.

'Come on, we'll get it done,' I sigh and pick my rifle up and wait for Cookey to turn the tap off. Then we head to the tents, smoking while holding our rifles one-handed, using our feet to shove downed tents aside. Checking inside ones that are still upright. The odd body here and there, but nothing worse than we've seen many times already.

It takes ages, gradually moving deeper and deeper. Checking every place an infected could be hiding or secreted. I don't think for one second one would be hiding, but it needs to be done, so we do it.

Finally, we end up in front of the visitors' centre and wait while Dave goes in to check, him telling us to relax and wait. None of us argue but let him carry on, knowing full well it would take an army of infected with tanks to get him. Even Marcy's lot couldn't get him down.

He strolls out with a curt nod, 'Clear.'

'Done, then,' I reply and turn to stare back across the fort.

'What now?' Cookey asks.

'Get cleaned up, weapons and kit, and sleep ...'

'I'm starving,' Nick adds.

'And some food, then ... After that? I haven't got a fucking clue.'

'Ah, you always know what to do, Mr Howie,' Cookey gives me a sudden grin. His confidence in me is touching.

We head over to our rooms, none of us knowing what else we should be doing. It does cross my mind to lock the gates and keep the things outside, but Marcy has clearly proven her intent to us, and besides, with just six of us and a dog, we couldn't hope to hold it against them for very long.

Cookey brews up while we start sorting our bags out and cleaning our weapons. Most of us dropped our pistols after we shot that big chap, but at least we've still got the rifles and axes.

Kit and weapons done, we head outside with our coffees and take it in turns to use the hose, peeling our filthy clothes off to be scrubbed. Down to our underwear, we wash and clean our clothes, stopping to sip coffee and smoke cigarettes. The conversation remains stilted and slow, all of us just too bloody exhausted to think of what to say.

We leave our clothes outside in the sun to dry after getting Clarence to wring them out, his strong hands squeezing every last drop of moisture from them.

Teeth brushed. Skin scrubbed. Hair washed, and still I feel grimy and filthy. The sweat already starting to drip down my face. The lads go inside, heading to their rooms for sleep. Too drained to think of food or anything else.

I head into my room and look down at the two mattresses on the floor. Still, I don't feel anything but numb. Just numb. It doesn't feel right to be in here without Lani, so I drag my mattress out and walk it into the day room and push it into a corner.

The dog trots over and lies down next to it. Dave comes out to check the noise, nods, and pulls his own mattress out. I don't bother telling him not to bother. He wouldn't listen anyway.

He closes the door as I crash out, lying back on the soft mattress and feeling a deep, deep tiredness come over me.

A slight hissing noise sounds by my head, followed by an awful stench. I grimace and twist round so my head is at the other end. The dog looks up at me, then rests her head again.

After choking for a few minutes, I feel the pull of sleep sucking me under. My eyes getting heavier and heavier. I should be crying. We all should be. We should be wailing and smashing things up, doing anything we can to get rid of the pressure inside us. We should be drinking hard liquor and getting smashed.

But we don't. We just sleep instead.

CHAPTER FORTY-THREE

'Fuck! That hurt.' I snap awake from Cookey cursing as he walks into something.

'Turn the fucking lamp on,' Blowers whispers, which is more like a shout in the small room.

'I can't see the pissing lamp,' Cookey whispers back.

'Ssshh! You'll wake Dave and Mr Howie,' Nick's voice comes from somewhere.

'Bit late for that,' I groan. Sitting up, I open my eyes and blink. The inside of the room is pitch black, with no discernible difference between my eyes being open or closed.

'Where are your torches?' Dave asks.

'Er ... yeah, Blowers, where's your torch?' Cookey says.

'Where's your fucking torch?' Blowers whispers back.

'Why are you still whispering? They're awake now,' Cookey says.

'Clarence isn't,' Blowers snaps.

'Am now,' a deep rumble comes across the darkness.

'Oh, well done, Cookey!' Nick sighs.

'Fuck off. Shit! What's that? Oh ... oh, it's just Meredith. Shit, that made me jump.'

A bright, piercing light shines out as Dave guides his torch first into Cookey's face, making him yelp, then at Blowers and Nick, both of them yelping as the bright light hits them.

'That's for forgetting your torches,' Dave says flatly. 'The lamp is there.' He shines the beam of light onto the gas lamp on the table.

'I can't see anything,' Cookey whines. 'My retinas are bleeding.'

'Stop being a twat,' Blowers makes his way to the table and starts fumbling for the lamp, his own eyes clearly still dazzled.

'Stop, Simon,' Dave stands up. Well, the torch beam lifts higher, so I assume he stands up. 'You'll burn the room down. I'll do it.'

The torch light bobs to the table and rests on the surface. Dave's hands come into view, then the flare of a match and the hiss of gas. An orange glow then illuminates the room, revealing the three lads stood there in their pants, looking sleepy.

'What time is it?' Clarence calls.

'Er ... almost two,' Nick replies.

'What, in the morning?' I ask, shocked at how long we slept.

'Yep, and I'm bloody starving,' Nick rubs his stomach.

'Didn't they howl, then?' I ask. 'I haven't heard them.'

'They didn't,' Dave replies.

'Can someone open that door. That dog's arse stinks.' I waft the air in front of my nose.

'Yeah, I'm going for a smoke while Cookey brews up,' Nick says.

'Why me?' Cookey asks.

'Cos you got April's boobs in your face,' Blowers replies, walking across the room.

'No, I said *if* you left me there, I'd do the brews for a month, but you didn't … You bastards pulled her off and then started flirting with her. Smooth fuckers …' he tuts.

'I'll bloody do it. You three piss off outside and give me some peace,' Clarence grumbles. He walks through the door, into the dayroom and stretches. Like a bear rearing up onto its back legs.

'Yes!' Cookey takes the victory and heads for the door. Meredith squeezes out as soon as he pulls it open. 'Bloody hell, she needed a piss,' he calls back. 'Fuck. Er, Mr Howie?' he calls.

'What?' But I'm already up and heading for the door at the tone in his voice. We cram through, all of us responding to Cookey's voice.

'Fuck me,' Nick stares out.

The Saxon stands just down from us, facing away, with the rear doors open. We can see it clearly in the darkness from the many flaming torches stuck into the ground. Long sticks with flickering flames dancing into air, embedded into the ground at set intervals.

The glow of the flames casts the interior of the fort in a soft, orange glow. Warm and inviting. We start moving forward, venturing towards the Saxon. Dave shines his torch inside to reveal the gleaming back area. The bench seats scrubbed clean. The rifles we dumped in the back are all stacked on the ground to the side, along with our pistols. All of them wiped clean of blood and gore. Dave climbs in and moves to the front, shining his torch. 'All cleaned,' he calls back. 'Not a drop of blood anywhere.'

'Smells nice too,' Nick leans in, sniffing the inside of the vehicle.

'Pine disinfectant,' a voice says from behind us. We spin round to see Marcy stood there. 'It was actually toilet cleaner, but it did the job. I'm. er, sorry if we woke you. We tried to be quiet.'

She's changed her top, wearing a plain, white t-shirt now instead of the low-cut vest top. The light casts her skin in a golden tone and shimmers from her long hair.

'Er ... it's okay,' I reply, my voice low and hoarse from a combination of sleep and the sight of her. I suddenly become aware of being stood there in my underpants. I think we all do by the awkward fidgets of hands going to the front of groins.

She laughs, a clear, rich sound that fills the air. 'Get dressed. We've got some food for you. Coffee all round?' She smiles and walks off into the darkness.

'Food?' Nick perks up. 'I'm starving. What kind of food is it?'

'You'll see,' her voice drifts back.

'Er ... we getting changed, then?' Clarence asks in a low voice.

We head back over to our room, finding our clothes all neatly folded in piles. All dried and ready to be put on.

'Fuck,' Cookey exclaims again. He goes to his pile and picks his t-shirt up. He stares at it for a second before sniffing it suspiciously. 'They've washed them again. It smells ... well, it smells nice.'

'Really?' I grab my trousers and hold them to my nose. A clean, floral smell comes from them. We get dressed, feeling the comfort of fresh, clean clothes for the first time in days.

'Boots have been done too,' Clarence remarks as he hefts his up to inspect them.

Meredith spins to growl at someone approaching from the shadows. Nick grabs her collar while we squint into the light. The figure comes into view. April, carrying a tray full of steaming mugs.

She looks at the dog, then smiles at us before stretching down to place the tray on the ground. The three lads leaning forward to stare at her bent-over backside. She twists round to stare back at them, smiling as they all quickly look away.

'Food will be ready soon,' she walks off, again with several men staring at her backside.

'What's going on?' Blowers asks suspiciously but without taking his eyes off her retreating form.

'I don't know,' I reply quietly.

'Might be poisoned,' Nick tears his eyes off the woman to look at the coffee. 'Cookey. you should try one first.'

'Why me?'

'Because you're the ugliest.'

'I'm not the ugliest ... Blowers is.'

'No, he's the gayest.'

'You're the stupidest, then,' Blowers retorts. 'Here, I'll take one for the team.' He lifts a mug and sniffs it dramatically before taking a sip. He shrugs and nods, 'Tastes alright.'

'Well, you wouldn't taste the poison, dickhead,' Cookey says. 'That comes later.'

'Oh, right,' Blowers takes another sip. 'Fuck it.'

'Maybe they're laced with the zombie virus just so I turn and April can have her way with me,' Cookey says with a wishful expression.

'You wish,' Nick laughs as he takes a mug. We dive in, grabbing mugs while looking around suspiciously.

'Dave, if I turn and I'm not evil, please don't kill me ...' Cookey says.

'Okay, Alex,' Dave replies in his flat voice.

'Seriously, her boobs were right in my face ... like actually touching me.'

'Okay, Alex.'

'I think she pulled them out a bit for me,' Cookey leans back to rest against the wall and stretch his legs out. 'In fact, the more I think about it, I reckon she saw you two ugly bastards and went round you to get at me.'

'You're such a twat,' Blowers replies.

'You were closest, that's why. You probably saw her coming and dragged her down on top of you,' Nick says as Blowers laughs, spitting his coffee out.

'Yeah,' Cookey grins.

'Seriously, though, is this fucked up or what?' Nick asks, looking round at us.

'Feels that way, mate,' I reply.

'Why they being so nice?' Blowers asks.

'I don't know,' I look round at them. 'Marcy said she wanted to hand herself in for testing, that they were different and not like the others. Maybe this is their way of showing it.'

'You think?' Clarence asks.

I shrug, 'I don't know. What else can it be? They could have killed us several times over by now. Either that or they want something, but fuck knows what.'

'Fancy a walk down?' Clarence asks. We all rise up and head inside to grab our rifles before taking our mugs and walking down, towards the tents.

As we get closer, we see they're back in order. The

ruined ones removed, and all the litter and debris removed. We see figures lying prone within them. Infected looking asleep. No talking, no noise, just hundreds of bodies lying on their backs scattered throughout the various tents. Meredith walks with us, flicking her head side to side to watch.

'Bodies have gone too.' Dave shines his torch towards the slope, at the now clear ground.

'They have been busy,' Clarence remarks. We walk on, quietly scanning the area and marvelling at how orderly everything is, eerily ordered. Too ordered.

'This is creepy as fuck,' Blowers stares round and chucks the last dregs of his coffee on the floor. 'Fucking place is crawling with those things, sleeping in the fucking tents and living here like it's their place ...' his lip curls up with sudden distaste.

'They saved us, though,' Nick replies.

Blowers just carries on staring round, his dark eyes scanning from tent to tent. 'Yeah,' he says after a lengthy pause.

We walk onto the main central aisle and further down, drawing closer to much brighter lights in the centre.

Meredith raises her head, sniffing at the air, followed closely by Nick. 'What's that smell?' He cocks his head to one side just like the dog. 'Cooking ... that's food cooking!'

Walking closer, we all get the scent of hot food being cooked, spices mixed with wood smoke and gas.

Nick sniffs harder as he concentrates, 'Curry ... that's bloody curry, that is.'

'It fucking is,' Cookey joins in with the sniffing, taking long inhalations through his nose. The dog is already wagging her tail, with her head fixed in that direction.

Flaming torches surround a collection of tables and chairs, all of them brought out from offices or rooms and pushed together. Grills and gas burners flame away with pots of steaming food cooking in them. The distinctive scent of curry wets my taste buds, making me realise how completely and utterly famished I am.

We stop and watch as Mildred, the grey-haired, old lady, moves between the pots, stirring and checking them. Reginald and Marcy stand nearby, talking to her. Reginald sees us and stands upright, cutting his sentence of midway. Marcy turns, smiling as she walks over.

'It's ready. Sit down. We'll plate it up.'

'What's going on? What is this?' I ask. Despite the hunger, I'm starting to feel manipulated from this contrived environment.

'Food,' she replies simply. 'We made enough for you too.'

'What does that mean? You too?' I demand.

'We've been clearing up this mess all day. You were sleeping, and we were working, and now we're hungry. Like I said, we made enough for you too.'

'Hungry? For food?'

She pauses and thinks before answering, 'We need to eat just like you. Please, sit down so we can talk.'

'Mr Howie,' Nick asks quietly, 'I can see you're cross, but I'm starving. I can get some food from the stores if you don't want to eat here but ...'

'Howie, it's just food. Let your lads have a decent meal,' Marcy smiles warmly. 'Come on, come and sit down.'

'Boss?' Nick asks. He looks at me, waiting for my answer before moving.

I nod and walk forward, staring at the pots and then the plates stacked up. I move round, as though I'm likely to find something wrong, something I can point at and shout 'ha-ha! We've caught you!'. But there isn't anything.

Just some tables and chairs and the delicious smell of hot food.

'Is that curry?' Nick blunders straight into the kitchen and lifts the lid of a pot, cursing when he burns his fingers.

'Yes, it is. Now, go and sit down,' Mildred shoos him out, waving her hands at him.

'Where did you get curry from?' Nick asks.

'Your stores were very well stocked,' she replies.

I take a seat. The others all sit down too, assault rifles placed by our legs as we self-consciously sit at the table and look around.

April appears carrying a big plastic cool-box. She sets it down and flips the lid before pulling out bottles of beer dripping from the cold water they were resting in. She walks down, placing one in front of each of us, giving a big smile to Cookey, who just stares at her like a puppy.

'It's cold,' Nick touches the bottle. He takes a big swig and sighs deeply, 'Shit ... that's nice.'

Clarence and I look at each other, both of us feeling very unsettled and wary. Plates get loaded with big heaps of boiled rice. Curried food gets spooned on as April and Marcy move back and forth, placing the plates of mouth-watering food in front of us.

Nick goes to dig in but sees Clarence and I both waiting. Reluctantly, he pauses, his fork hovering over the food.

We watch as more plates are put down on the table; then, Marcy, April, Reginald, and Mildred come and join us.

'Tuck in,' Marcy prompts. I lift my fork and load it up, lifting it slowly to my mouth while staring at the four of them. I don't want to eat it. I don't want to take their food, but my stomach is rumbling, and I can't remember ever being this hungry.

I shove the food in and close my eyes as my taste buds explode from the flavour. Succulent meat with sweet, curried sauce. I take another forkful and keep going. The rice is fluffy and perfect with just a hint of salt.

It may be the hunger or twelve days of eating shit snack food, but I cannot remember ever eating anything so nice.

'Boys, you need to slow down, or you'll be sick,' Mildred remarks. I pause with the fork halfway in my mouth and look at the lads attacking the food with gusto. Shrugging, I keep going.

The beer is cool and refreshing. The bottles get drained, and April goes to get more for us. Nick waves her back with a mouthful of food and helps himself, plonking a whole load of them in the middle.

I eat and eat, savouring every bite and feeling the pleasure of chewing real food. My stomach fills quickly, having shrunk from not eating decent meals for so long. Clarence just keeps going, his arm dropping and lifting as he pushes the food into his mouth.

'Can zombies eat, then?' Cookey asks between mouthfuls.

'We prefer the term living challenged,' Reginald replies, 'and yes, we can eat.'

'Living challenged?' Cookey lifts his eyebrows. 'Is that what you call yourselves?'

'That's what Reggie calls us,' Marcy replies.

'I thought you just wanted to eat brains and shit. Well, not shit as in poo, but you know, brains and flesh,' Cookey continues without a care in the world. We all look to Marcy, waiting for the reply.

'We do,' she says bluntly. 'Every one of us feels an incredible urge to eat human flesh. Don't look at me like that. You know exactly what we are, but—'

'Hang on,' I cut in, pushing my empty plate away.

'Let me finish,' she then cuts me off. 'Do you want some more?' she asks, motioning towards my plate.

'No, no, thank you. It was lovely, but I'm full.'

'Is there more?' Nick asks. 'Is it in that pot? Can I get some?'

'Help yourself, take what you want,' Marcy calls out as he heads into the cooking area. The others, apart from Dave and me, head over to refill their plates. Marcy moves down so she's sat closer, pretty much opposite me.

'As I was saying …' she continues. 'Er … will this conversation put you off your food?' she asks the lads.

'No fucking chance,' Nick quips, then looks at Dave with an apologetic expression. 'I meant no, er, no, it won't.'

'Thank you, Nicholas,' Dave nods.

Marcy reaches for a bottle of beer and screws the cap off. 'We all have the urge. It's like the strongest thing you can imagine, and it never stops, but we are still people with bodies the same as you, and we need food and water the same as you.'

'But those things don't eat. They just stand there drooling in the same place for days and days, waiting for someone to come along.'

'And we are not those things,' Marcy replies. 'Well, yes,' she nods. 'The ones in the tents would be if they were left alone, but …' her voice trails off. 'It's hard to explain.'

'Try,' I prompt her.

She tilts her head as though in thought. Her hair falls to one side as her mouth purses. 'Right … well … sorry to bring this up, but Darren turned me. He could speak and think, but he was messed up. You were the only thing he could focus on,' she looks at me. 'He was driven to destroy you. I saw you kill him. I saw all of you stood over him as he died, and I thought you were going to come for me, but you didn't. You left. So I did what I thought was the right thing and set about getting more ...'

She explains her story, and here, in the soft flickering lights, in the sultry, warm air, drinking a cold beer after eating a hearty meal, it seems perfectly normal. I watch her closely, not only taking in what she says but watching her mouth as she speaks. The way her lips move, the way the end of her nose twitches as she talks. Her high cheekbones that show when she smiles, her eyebrows that lift and fall as she expresses herself.

One thing is clear—she's brutally honest. Telling us how she marched with an ever-increasing horde through the towns and villages, establishing a method of clearing street by street. She explains how most of the hosts are the same as normal. Barely functioning host bodies that have a sole purpose of finding more hosts. Then a few, like April, could speak but had no individual character. She told us that Darren could access them like a hive mind with a collective conscious but that she couldn't. She could will them to do things but only basic functions, and the more intricate the function, the harder it was. She called them communicators, the ones that could speak. She said how she felt that having a hive mind would be too complicated, and she didn't want that. That it appeared that when she needed more to communicate with, so more were able to do so.

Then there were the exceptions to the rule like Reginald and Mildred. Both of which were able to think freely, but they held an absolute devotion to her as she had to Darren.

Marcy talked openly about the main town on the Isle of Wight and how she took out the fortified and secure High Street. Weirdly, we all smiled and laughed as she explained about poor Robbie. Such is the setting of the scene we are in that we feel relaxed and comfortable enough to relate to her tale.

Then she felt a change starting. That she wished they didn't have to suffer to become part of the new way. She told us about the prison and some sex offenders and how she wanted to punish them, but once they had turned, they were free from any past sin, and to punish them again would be the same as humans had always done.

'I went back to Reginald and gathered the ones that could speak.' She sips at her beer. 'I asked them a series of test question, you know, who lived in a house, who lived in a flat, who had what job ... That was so I could be sure they were able to answer fully. Then I asked if any suffered from diseases like diabetes. One of them said he did, that he had to take insulin every day, but now he didn't because he was no longer diabetic.'

'What?' I lean forward and stare at her.

'He said,' she stares back, 'he said he was no longer diabetic, he didn't need insulin. We asked some others and found some had been on medication for things but, and this is the issue, they were all freshly turned. Forgive the way I say that.'

'No, carry on,' I prompt her. Nick pushes his plate away with a belch and apologies before pulling his smokes out and handing them around.

'Er ... mind if we smoke?' I ask Marcy.

'We're zombies ... Do you think we mind?' she jokes. The lads all grin at her, clearly entranced.

'Anyway, they were freshly turned, so we couldn't be sure if they were just masking whatever symptoms they may have had, but it seems clear to me that the infection, the disease or virus or whatever this is, that it can heal us quicker. Normal things that hurt you don't bother us so much. We can take more punishment and mend easier. They don't feel pain or suffering ...'

'They?' I cut in.

'I do. So does Reginald but not Mildred. This is why we came here. The infection has ... I don't know ... like retracted to the very least it can be with me and Reggie, like it's testing me or letting me see how far I can get with my own intelligence.'

'So you deal with that how? By not turning anymore people and coming here to hand yourself over for testing?'

'Well, yes,' she nods. 'After that, we didn't turn anyone else. Ah, no, we did with Mildred and her group, but that was different.'

'Different how?' I ask.

'Just different,' Marcy stares back at me.

'Different how?' I ask again, unwilling to let the point go.

'The people that took your fort got into their group. They gang raped the women and killed some too. We got there just after. A boy was hurt and dying, the same as Lani, so with their consent, we turned him. He came back, and then they pretty much stepped forward and asked to be taken.'

'Okay, go on,' I glance down with a sudden feeling of guilt about Lani.

'Howie, all of this,' she waves her hand around her, 'we did this without fuss, without bother. We moved thousands of people onto a ferry within minutes; then, we took them off and put them onto lifeboats. No fuss, no delays. We got them here with ease. Yes, they are infected and terrible and all the things you say they are, but ...' She lowers her head to look straight at me. 'If there is any remote chance that this infection can cure diseases, I don't know, AIDS, HIV, cancer, then surely it is a good thing. If the infection can be harnessed so the good parts are used, the lack of violence and aggression, the ability to work together without greed or jealousy ... imagine what could be achieved.'

'So everyone would become infected and lead this perfect life, then? What about when you die, Marcy? What happens when your will is no longer controlling them?'

'No, you're missing my point,' she leans in. 'Not infect you ... vaccinate you from the worst parts of the disease while curing you from everything else. Not human, not us ... something else. Look, I don't know the answers. I came here to find you to help me look for the answers. If you had doctors, I would now be strapped to a bed with April, being tested ...'

'Whoa,' Cookey grins. 'Oh ... sorry ... nice thought, though.'

Marcy grins at him and leans back. 'Howie, I just know that if humans had been left alone, we'd have wiped ourselves out. Constant war and famine, greed, poverty ... This has happened. I didn't cause it, and neither did you. It was thrust on us, so we've just got to deal with it.'

I light another smoke and lean back, thinking of everything she said.

'So,' Clarence leans in, 'you're saying that you think this ... infection can cure diabetes and cancer, and you want to find a way of isolating the good parts of it and not the bad so that mankind can live happily ever after?'

'Essentially, yes. Don't scoff,' she laughs. 'If I had said to any of you two weeks ago that any of this would happen, would you have believed me?'

'Fair point,' I concede.

'I have proven that we are capable of making something good come of this ... before it's too late.'

'By making everyone be like you?'

'No, Howie, by making them halfway between the both of us–all the good of humanity without the bad. No suffering, no pain, no disease, no greed or war. Everyone working together for the good of everyone else.'

'Communism, then,' Clarence remarks.

'No, because communism is flawed,' Reginald cuts in. 'The idea of communism is perfect, but the second you put a human being in charge of others, you have corruption and greed, with the masses being oppressed and ruled by fear.'

'And your way is different how?' Clarence replies.

'Now, at this time,' Marcy replies, 'yes, I rule all of these with my will. If I withdrew that, they would be coming at you like all the others have been, but what I'm saying is that–'

'I get it,' Clarence lifts a hand. 'I understand what you're saying. Take the good from it but not the bad ...'

'Yes,' she nods.

'How?' I ask her.

'We did this, cleaned the fort and all of these things to show you what we are capable of. I wanted you to see this.'

'Why? And how do we do what you're planning?'

'Why, because we needed you to understand and listen, and forgive me, but there's enough of the woman left in me to know that a clean house, a good meal, and a cold beer does wonders to get a bloke listening ...' she grins mischievously. We all laugh at the way she says it.

'We need you to find a way, find doctors, bring them here, do what it takes,' she adds in earnest. I stare across at her. The red eyes don't seem so bad now. The more I look at them, the more normal they seem. Maybe it's the light and beer.

'I see,' I reply after a while.

'If you want us to leave, we will,' Marcy sighs. 'This is your fort, and you probably think we don't belong here. Say the word, and we'll go, but this will just keep on going, and every day, we both lose so many people. Life after life being wasted and killed when there might be another way. If nothing else,' she leans forwards and stares at me with intensity, 'if nothing else, then do it to find a vaccine for all the survivors, do it to find a cure for us. Whatever your motives are with us, and you have the dog.'

'Meredith!' Nick exclaims. 'Where is she? She hasn't eaten anything yet.'

'She's sat under the table, by my feet,' Dave says.

'Can she eat curry?' Cookey asks

'Don't give her curry. Her farts are bad enough already,' I groan.

'There's dog food in the stores,' April says as she heads off.

'I'll help you,' Cookey calls out, quickly getting up from the table.

'Me too,' Nick is already on his feet, walking after the girl, with Blowers right behind him.

'Piss off, I said I would help,' Cookey hisses at the other two. They walk off, bickering into the darkness.

'I think they rather like April,' Marcy muses with a slight grin.

'Which should be very strongly discouraged,' Reginald says seriously. 'Mr Howie, you should speak with your men …'

'They know what they're doing,' I cut him off. 'They've

been through hell, so letting them piss about flirting with a pretty girl won't hurt.'

'She's not a girl,' Reginald replies. 'She is a living challenged person, and it is not appropriate.'

'April is a beautiful, young woman,' Clarence says, 'and it'll do them good to have something other than killing to think about.'

Marcy and I look at each other, eyes locked.

'Yes, but she is not the same as they are,' Reginald counters.

'Will April hurt them? Will she try and bite or go for them?' Clarence asks. Marcy and I watch each other across the table.

'No,' Reginald blanches, 'not in any capacity. April appears to be developing her own character and greater individuality, which is another reason why we need your help as it appears the individual host has the ability to evolve even when infected.'

'So what's the harm?' Clarence asks. 'They're young lads that should be mixing with people of their own age and having fun. As long as April doesn't mind the attention, then I don't see a problem.'

'Quite the opposite. I think April is enjoying the attention,' Reginald replies, 'but be that as it may, they need to understand she is not the same as them.'

Marcy takes a slow sip from the bottle, her eyes lingering on me. I watch closely, captivated by her.

'Look, Reggie,' Clarence leans forward, stretching a huge, meaty forearm on the table as he takes a big pull from his bottle, 'they're not gonna try and kiss her or … anything else.'

'I should hope not!' Reginald says haughtily. 'That is something that cannot happen unless they want to be turned. Any exchange of bodily fluids will cause the infection to be passed.'

A subtle change as a look of sadness comes into her eyes.

'We have many beautiful girls here,' Reginald continues, 'and granted, yes, they are quite stunning in appearance with full figures, long legs, flawless skin … very beautiful, very beautiful indeed … Er, where was I? Oh, yes, but the danger is that your men will see them as human when they are not.'

'They won't,' Clarence takes another long drink, empties the bottle, and reaches for another. 'They're good lads, very good lads,' he points at Reginald.

Reginald drinks from a bottle. The contrast of the tidy, small man drinking a bottle of beer doesn't quite fit, but he sips away as he and Clarence descend into discussion.

'I am sure they are good lads. They certainly seem very loyal, and you must be very proud of them.'

'Proud isn't the word,' Clarence cuts in with just a hint of slur in his speech. 'They're the best … the best. In fact, you should get all those beautiful girls up here so the lads can let their hair down.'

'Oh, no,' Reginald shakes his head. 'Oh, no, no, no! Young people full of alcohol and soft, flickering lights … Recipe for, er, recipe for … Gosh, I can't find the words I need … Bad things.'

'Here,' Clarence takes another beer and passes one down to Reginald. 'Ah, they won't do anything.' He smiles. 'Just give 'em a nice night for a change.'

'Won't do anything?' Reginald slurs as he drinks from the new bottle. 'I think not! Have you seen the girls? They're beautiful, stunning, gorgeous, splendid! Just, just wonderful creatures!' his voice rises as he goes along.

'Well, where are they, then?' Clarence looks around. 'They should be here, having a drink and relaxing.'

'My thoughts exactly,' Reginald announces. 'We should find them and bring them,' he hiccups, 'bring them here.'

'Yes!' Clarence's voice booms out. 'We need to find these girls and give them some of our beer.'

'What girls?' Nick asks as they walk back. He puts a huge bowl of dog food down on the floor and quickly steps back as Meredith dives in.

'Reggie knows some gorgeous girls that want to come and drink with us,' Clarence exclaims with a huge grin.

'Really?' Blowers asks. 'Seriously?'

'Yep, cos I was telling him how proud of you I am …Me and Dave and Mr Howie are very proud of you, so drink your beers and relax,' Clarence stands up and grabs another bottle, forcing it at Blowers as he wraps a long, heavy arm round his shoulders. Blowers grins and takes a long drink.

'But!' Reginald shouts in triumph as he stands up. He walks closer to the lads, clinking his bottle against theirs. 'But you cannot kiss my beautiful girl. For even though they are quite simply delightful, it would be the kiss of death and a very bad thing,' he shakes his head sadly. 'It's very sad.'

'My lads won't kiss 'em, will you, boys?' Clarence roars. They shake their heads, grinning at the drunken giant.

'And if you do, put a condom on your tongue. Ha!'

'No, no, no,' Reginald shakes his head, 'condoms go on the penis, not on the tongue. I read about it.'

'April!' Clarence grins. 'Here, have a beer but don't go kissing my boys.' He thrusts a bottle at the smiling girl.

'I won't,' she replies softly to three audible, jokey groans.

'You can flirt,' Clarence presses on with a serious face, 'and, and you can flirt … and …'

'And you can dance!' Reginald adds with a shout.

'Yes! You can dance,' Clarence seizes the word. 'You can flirt and dance and … but no kissing and none of the …'

'No sexing,' Reginald points his bottle at April.

'No kissing and no sexing … Okay,' April nods.

'Right, my boys, get ready to move out … We have to find these women,' Clarence roars.

'Yes, and I shall lead you!' Reginald shouts with enthusiasm.

'Mr Reggie shall lead us,' Clarence repeats, 'and we need music, Reggie, and hang on … Girls don't like beer, do they?' His face falls as though a great sadness comes over him. 'And we only have beer …'

'There's wine in the stores!' Reginald shouts. 'Girls love wine. I read that too.'

'Wonderful,' Clarence immediately cheers up. 'We are moving out, but we shall do so stealthily, with stealth and cunning.' He walks off, tripping over the first tent and crashing down with a shout. The lads roar with laughter as they blunder in, trying to help him up. He's so big, he just pulls them down with him until they're all rolling about drunkenly. Eventually, with shouted instructions from a very drunk Reginald, they get to their feet and move off into the darkness.

'April … you coming?' Cookey shouts. April looks at Marcy, who nods while smiling broadly. April moves off to follow the sounds of singing and crashing as they trip and fall through the tents.

'I'll go with them, Mr Howie,' Dave gets up.

'Okay, mate, make sure they don't do anything stupid.'

'On it,' he walks off, holding his assault rifle. I turn back and look at Marcy, both of us grinning broadly.

'They need to let off steam,' I say quietly.

'Sure,' Marcy nods.

'Everything they've been through, and Clarence really liked my sister. He saw Dave kill her. We all did.' She takes a sharp intake of breath and grimaces. 'So ... they need the release.'

'What about you?' she asks with a worried expression.

'Me?'

'You saw it too, plus everything else. You should go with them ,' she leans forward and smiles. 'And those girls are very beautiful.'

'Are they?' I ask.

'Very.'

'Nah, not my thing,' I shake my head. 'Er, Lani won't be with the girls, will she?'

'No, she won't be,' Marcy replies, her expression changing quickly. 'That must be hard for you too, losing Lani?' she asks.

It should be, but I still feel numb. Just numb and void, like none of it has hit home yet. 'Yeah,' I nod and glance away. The only thing I feel is a deep sense of shame at being sat here, drinking beer like this.

'What's wrong?' she asks me.

'Nothing,' I reply.

'All the humour just went from your face. You get a dark look that comes over you. It's ...' she stares at me, searching my face. I hold the gaze for a few seconds and feel myself becoming entranced again. I remember thinking of her when we were fighting, how the image of her got me into that state I needed. I remember the feel of her body when she held me, her warm breath on my ear.

'Howie?' she asks, startled as I quickly stand up.

'I need some air,' I reply without thinking. I start walking off, heading towards the back of the fort, my rifle held in one hand.

I feel angry and wound up at myself. Angry that I'm thinking like this. For fuck's sake, I saw my sister get killed. I saw Terri and Debbie get their throats cut out. Lani turned. And I'm thinking like this. Get a grip.

I still feel a sense of pleasure at hearing her running up behind me, a quickening of my heart. I stare into my soul and hate myself now more than ever.

'Here,' she comes to my side and hands me a fresh bottle of beer. 'You need a release too.'

'Beer isn't the answer,' I take the bottle all the same.

'They don't think that way,' she remarks at the sounds of distant singing and shouts coming from the lads and Reginald.

We walk in silence, side by side. Both of us taking sips from our bottles. I look round at the tents, at the dying torch lights with flames that flicker ever smaller, the shadows growing deeper and longer.

'Do you hate me?' she asks softly after a long silence.

'Yes,' I snarl at her, my voice low and growling. She drops her head but keeps walking. We reach the end of the tents and walk across the rear of the fort, heading towards the rear gate. I fumble for a second with both my hands full.

'Let me,' she steps forward to pull the bolts back while I move out the way, avoiding looking at her and making sure there is distance between us.

She pushes the gate open and steps back, waiting for me to go first. I walk through and move down the narrow beach to stand at the water's edge. The moon is high and bright, casting a silvery reflection on the smooth surface of the sea. Stars twinkle and glitter. No breeze, not even a flutter of wind. Just heat and quiet. Almost perfect quiet apart from the distant, drunken roars of the lads drifting across the fort.

Standing in silence, I feel my pockets for a smoke and curse when I realise they've been left on the table.

She glances over but doesn't say anything. I drop down onto the floor and put my bottle and gun down while I start unlacing my boots. She stands, watching me.

I shrug them off and pull my trousers up, then ease my hot feet down into the cooling water.

'Looks nice,' she comments, her voice low and quiet. 'Mind if I join you?'

'Do what you want.'

She sits down and starts working on her own laces, pulling them out to tug the boots free off her feet. I glance down and see her slip her socks off to reveal long, slender feet.

'My jeans are too tight. I won't be able to pull them up,' she says. She tries anyway, tugging at the bottom of her jeans and trying to force the material up her calves. Grunting with effort, she keeps going, tugging and pulling at them.

'I don't think it'll work,' I laugh at the sight. She glances up at me and smiles.

'Sod it,' she slides her feet over the edge and shuffles forward, plunging the bottom of her legs into the water and soaking the jeans. 'Oh, that's nice,' she sighs.

We slip back into silence, just the tiny ripples of water lapping as she moves her legs slowly back and forth.

'I would have taken them off, but then you'd see the bite mark on my backside.'

'Is that where he bit you?'

'Yep, right on the arse.'

'Must have hurt.'

'It did, lots.'

'What does–'

'I'm sorry,' she speaks over me. We look at each other awkwardly for speaking at the same time.

'What were you saying?' she asks.

'No, you first. What did you say?'

'I said I'm sorry.'

'What for?' I ask her.

She shrugs and stares out at the water. 'For everything, for all of this ... I'm sorry it happened ...'

'Not your fault.'

'Yes, it was,' she faces me. 'I came after you just as much as Darren. You have no idea of the bad things we did, the torture and torment we gave out, the suffering we caused, and just so we could send them after you. So many lives just gone.'

'What do you want, Marcy? Want me to say it's okay and all is forgiven? Because you can fuck off.'

'No. I can never be forgiven for that. The others can be because they don't know anything else. It's not them doing it. It's the infection inside them, but me, I could think, and I still did it.'

'Did you enjoy it?'

'Yes,' she nods, 'I loved it. Sorry if that hurts, but I did. I loved the power and the strength. I could see Darren failing and was learning all the time from him ... but that was before.'

'Yeah, before your grand epiphany.'

'Sarcasm doesn't suit you,' she replies sharply. 'I can lie if it makes it easier for you.'

I shrug back at her. 'It is what it is.'

'I killed men, women, and children. I did it while they screamed and begged. I tore babies from their mothers' arms and laughed while I did it ...'

'Stop,' I growl.

'But I did those things. You've killed. You've probably killed more than me, children too.'

'It's different. They weren't conscious beings that felt pain. They had no awareness of the death or the suffering.'

I glance over and look at the side of her face. Thick tears stream down her cheeks and roll off her jaw, landing softly on her hands. She doesn't sniff or make any show of crying but does so silently.

I feel a stupid urge to comfort her. To put my arm round her shoulders and say nice things.

'Stop it,' I snap instead.

'Sorry,' she whispers so softly. The tears come harder, falling faster. Her chest heaves as she fights to sob without noise. She turns her head away.

'This part of the show?'

She doesn't answer but stays turned away, her body moving with the silent sobbing. Then it gets worse, much worse. She collapses on the ground, heaving as powerful weeping takes over. Still, she stays as quiet as possible, just low murmurs and sniffs, but I can see from the way she moves that she's sobbing her heart out.

The urge comes back stronger. I stare at her form. After what she just said, she deserves the pain. She should be shot for it. But right now, she is also another person and one that has shown kindness and respect to us. She saved us from being killed. She removed our dead and sacrificed her own people so we would live. She fed us and made us feel safe.

For that, for what she's done for the lads, I stretch my hand out and rest it on her leg. She flinches from the contact. I rub softly, feeling the warmth of her body through the material of her jeans.

'Take it easy,' I say softly.

'I can't ever take that away,' her voice is muffled. 'I'll never be able to undo those things.'

'No, you can't,' I reply. 'Nothing you ever do will take that away, and you deserve every minute of pain and agony you get. I hope you suffer for the rest of your life in untold misery, but if what you said in there is true, then you have no choice but to hold it together.'

Long minutes go by. I keep rubbing her leg softly but not speaking. Eventually, her hand reaches out and takes hold of mine. Again, I feel that thrill as she touches me. A pleasurable tingle that flutters my heart. The weeping eases, and slowly, she sits back up. The position she's in means I have to let go of her leg, but I don't want to. It's the last thing I want to do.

But I do. I pull my hand away gently and instantly feel the loss of the contact.

'Thank you,' she sighs and rubs at her face, pulling the bottom of her t-shirt up to dry the tears away. I catch a glimpse of her tanned stomach, and again, my heart starts beating harder. It isn't flat or perfectly toned, but soft and gently undulating from being bent forward. She works for a few seconds, pressing the material of the t-shirt into the corners of her eyes. The top rides up higher, flashing the bottom edge of her bra. I stare for a second and make myself turn away. Fixing my eyes on the water.

'You okay?' I ask hoarsely.

'Yeah, yeah, fine now ... I'm sorry.'

I feel stifled, trapped. I can't be this close to her. The attraction is just too strong. Sweat breaks out on my head and trickles down my neck. The air feels charged and too hot.

'Howie, are you okay?' Her hand touches my back lightly. 'You're breathing really hard.'

'I'm fine,' all I can feel is the touch of her hand on my back. She rubs it for a second and leans in closer.

'Don't ...' I growl.

'What's wrong?' she asks. 'You're shaking.'

I take a deep breath and force myself to exhale slowly. It doesn't help. I try to fix my mind on everything that's happened. On Lani, on Sarah, but that doesn't work either. She's leaning against me now, her body pressed against the side of my arm. The heat from her radiates.

'Howie,' she says softly and drops her head down to look at me. I turn slowly and face her. My heart booms as I see her mouth gently opening. Her soft skin and dark hair that hangs down.

Her breath on my ear when she kissed me. Her arms that were wrapped around me. Her soft voice that took all the anger and rage away.

'Don't,' she whispers.

'What?' I whisper back, staring into her eyes. A deep look of sadness steals over her.

'Don't kiss me,' I realise how close I am, that I'm moving into her without knowing what I'm doing. She closes her eyes but doesn't move.

'Don't, Howie ... please,' she pleads softly, unable to move back, feeling the same urge I do. Her face moves in closer. My arm moves round to her back, feeling the press of her body.

'I can't stop thinking about you ... when you held me ... your voice in my ear.'

I feel her hand glide over my back, to my neck, and into my hair. My own doing the same as it traces along her spine until my fingers brush against her hair, then delve in to feel the nape of her neck. She shudders and exhales slowly.

Our faces meet. Cheek against cheek. We move slowly,

rubbing so very slightly. Our bodies become entwined, arms wrapped round each other.

'Tell me to stop, tell me to leave,' I whisper.

'I can't ...'

'I'm sorry I hurt you. I should never have done that ...'

'It's okay,' she moves against me, our faces lifting and dropping as our skin touches. Mouths moving ever closer to each other.

'When I put my thumb in your mouth ... the feeling was like nothing I've ever known ...'

'I felt it.'

'I wanted you to bite me. I wanted to be with you.'

'I wanted to take you, Howie, not for what I am but for me. I wanted you for me, to be a part of me so I could be a part of you.'

'I want that now ...'

'I do, so much, Howie. I-I don't know what this is ... They fear you. We all fear you. There's a power in you that's so dangerous but so good.'

'You are all I could think about, just you, Marcy ... Every time I held you in my mind, I became unstoppable, untouchable, and that feeling, oh, that feeling of your mouth ...' My hand slides gently over her stomach, slowly higher, over the contours of her breasts. My fingers feel her throat where I gripped her so hard, fingertips gliding up onto her chin. My hand splays out, my thumb finds her mouth, touching the corner of her lips.

'I could never hurt you again, Marcy.'

'I'll never let anything hurt you, Howie. I'd die first ...' My thumb feels the soft movement of her lips and the moist heat of her breath.

'The first second I saw you, Howie, the world was spinning, the ground was heaving. I saw all the seasons flash by me, by us ... Cold winds and deep snow ... Day and night became the same ...'

'I felt that! I saw it ... I saw the snow and felt the wind ... then I was falling.'

'But the bottom was never there. What is this? What is this, Howie?'

'I don't know. I hate you with every part of me. I hate what you are, what you've done, but I want you, I need you ...' My thumb presses harder into her lips.

'I need you. I want to be a part of you. Love isn't strong enough for what I feel, Howie.'

The corners of our lips brush as my thumb presses harder. Her lips part, welcoming my thumb as it slides into the warmth. Her tongue probes the end as I slowly draw it out.

Breathing harder and harder. The pain of denial rising as the temptation increases with every passing second.

Our lips hover, barely touching. My thumb so close to her teeth. Ready to be taken.

To be turned.

To be a part of her.

ALSO BY RR HAYWOOD

Washington Post, Wall Street Journal, Audible & Amazon Allstar bestselling author, RR Haywood. One of the top ten most downloaded indie authors in the UK with over four million books sold and nearly 40 Kindle bestsellers.

GASLIT

The Instant #1 Amazon Bestseller.

A Twisted Tale Of Manipulation & Murder.

Audio Narrated by Gethin Anthony

A dark, noir, psychological thriller with rave reviews across multiple countries.

A new job awaits. **Huntington House** *needs a live-in security guard to prevent access during an inheritance dispute.*

This is exactly what Mike needs: a new start in a new place and a chance to turn things around.

It all seems perfect, especially when he meets Tessa.

But **Huntington House holds dark secrets***. Bumps in the night. Flickering lights. Music playing from somewhere.*

Mike's mind starts to unravel as he questions his sanity in the dark, claustrophobic corridors and rooms.

Something isn't right.

There is someone else in the house.

The pressure grows as the people around Mike get pulled into a web of lies and manipulation, forcing him to take action before it's too late.

-

DELIO. PHASE ONE

WINNER OF "BEST NEW BOOK" DISCOVER SCI-FI 2023

#1 Amazon & Audible bestseller

A single bed in a small room.

The centre of Piccadilly Circus.

A street in New York city outside of a 7-Eleven.

A young woman taken from her country.

A drug dealer who paid his debt.

A suicidal, washed-up cop.

The rest of the world now frozen.

Unmoving.

Unblinking.

"Brilliant."

"A gripping story. Harrowing, and often hysterical."

"This book is very different to anything else out there - and brilliantly so."

"You'll fall so hard for these characters, you'll wish the world would freeze just so you could stay with them forever."

*

FICTION LAND

Nominated for Best Audio Book at the British Book Awards 2023

Narrated by Gethin Anthony
The #1 Most Requested Audio Book in the UK 2023
Now Optioned For A TV Series
#1 Amazon bestseller
#1 Audible bestseller
"Imagine John Wick wakes up in a city full of characters from novels – that's Fiction Land."

Not many men get to start over.

John Croker did and left his old life behind – until crooks stole his delivery van. No van means no pay, which means his niece doesn't get the life-saving operation she needs, and so in desperation, John uses the skills of his former life one last time... That is until he dies and wakes up in Fiction Land. A city occupied by characters from unfinished novels.

But the world around him doesn't feel right, and when he starts asking questions, the authorities soon take extreme measures to stop him finding the truth about Fiction Land.

*

EXTRACTED SERIES

EXTRACTED

EXECUTED

EXTINCT

Blockbuster Time-Travel

#1 Amazon US

#1 Amazon UK

#1 Audible US & UK

Washington Post & Wall Street Journal Bestseller

In 2061, a young scientist invents a time machine to fix a tragedy in his past. But his good intentions turn catastrophic when an early test reveals something unexpected: the end of the world.

A desperate plan is formed. Recruit three heroes, ordinary humans capable of extraordinary things, and change the future.

Safa Patel is an elite police officer, on duty when Downing Street comes under terrorist attack. As armed men storm through the breach, she dispatches them all.

'Mad' Harry Madden is a legend of the Second World War. Not only did he complete an impossible mission—to plant charges on a heavily defended submarine base—but he also escaped with his life.

Ben Ryder is just an insurance investigator. But as a young man he witnessed a gang assaulting a woman and her child. He went to their rescue, and killed all five.

Can these three heroes, extracted from their timelines at the point of death, save the world?

*

THE CODE SERIES

The Worldship Humility

The Elfor Drop

The Elfor One

#1 Audible bestselling smash hit narrated by Colin Morgan

#1 Amazon bestselling Science-Fiction

"A rollicking, action packed space adventure…"

"Best read of the year!"
"An original and exceptionally entertaining book."
"A beautifully written and humorous adventure."

Sam, an airlock operative, is bored. Living in space should be full of adventure, except it isn't, and he fills his time hacking 3-D movie posters.

Petty thief Yasmine Dufont grew up in the lawless lower levels of the ship, surrounded by violence and squalor, and now she wants out. She wants to escape to the luxury of the Ab-Spa, where they eat real food instead of rats and synth cubes.

Meanwhile, the sleek-hulled, unmanned Gagarin has come back from the ever-continuing search for a new home. Nearly all hope is lost that a new planet will ever be found, until the Gagarin returns with a code of information that suggests a habitable planet has been found. This news should be shared with the whole fleet, but a few rogue captains want to colonise it for themselves.

When Yasmine inadvertently steals the code, she and Sam become caught up in a dangerous game of murder, corruption, political wrangling and...porridge, with sex-addicted Detective Zhang Woo hot on their heels, his own life at risk if he fails to get the code back.

*

THE UNDEAD SERIES

THE UK's #1 Horror Series

Available on Amazon & Audible

"The Best Series Ever…"

The Undead. The First Seven Days
The Undead. The Second Week.
The Undead Day Fifteen.
The Undead Day Sixteen.
The Undead Day Seventeen
The Undead Day Eighteen
The Undead Day Nineteen
The Undead Day Twenty
The Undead Day Twenty-One
The Undead Twenty-Two
The Undead Twenty-Three: The Fort
The Undead Twenty-Four: Equilibrium
The Undead Twenty-Five: The Heat
The Undead Twenty-Six: Rye
The Undead Twenty-Seven: The Garden Centre
The Undead Twenty-Eight: Return To The Fort
The Undead Twenty-Nine: Hindhead Part 1
The Undead Thirty: Hindhead Part 2
The Undead Thirty-One: Winchester
The Undead Thirty-Two: The Battle For Winchester
The Undead Thirty-Three: The One True Race

Blood on the Floor
An Undead novel

Blood at the Premiere

An Undead novel

The Camping Shop

An Undead novella

*

A Town Called Discovery

The #1 Amazon & Audible Time Travel Thriller

A man falls from the sky. He has no memory.

What lies ahead are a series of tests. Each more brutal than the last, and if he gets through them all, he might just reach A Town Called Discovery.

*

THE FOUR WORLDS OF BERTIE CAVENDISH

A rip-roaring multiverse time-travel crossover starring:

The Undead

Extracted.

A Town Called Discovery

and featuring

The Worldship Humility

*

www.rrhaywood.com

Find me on Facebook:
https://www.facebook.com/RRHaywood/

Find me on TikTok (The Writing Class for the Working Class)
https://www.tiktok.com/@rr.haywood

Find me on X:
https://twitter.com/RRHaywood

Printed in Great Britain
by Amazon